T4-ALI-582

WITHDRAWN

THE ADVERSARY

THE
ADVERSARY

by *Bart Spicer*

G. P. Putnam's Sons, New York

COPYRIGHT © 1974 BY BART SPICER

All rights reserved. This book, or parts thereof, must not
be reproduced in any form without permission. Published on
the same day in Canada by Longman Canada Limited, Toronto.

SBN: 399-11168-9

Library of Congress Catalog
Card Number: 73-82019

PRINTED IN THE UNITED STATES OF AMERICA

Spicer

ad-ver-sar-y (ad′vər-ser′e)

1. a person or group that opposes or attacks another; opponent; enemy; foe.
Adversary suggests an enemy who fights determinedly, continuously and relentlessly: *a formidable adversary.*

—The Random House Dictionary
of the English Language, 1967

I

THE car drifted quietly through the narrow cobbled streets in the
old section of Rincon and came so smoothly to a stop at the
courthouse steps that the judge did not notice. He was deep in the rear
seat, arms folded, both legs stretched out to a jump seat, chin low on his
chest. He almost jumped when the driver opened the door.

"Looks like bad weather today, sir." The driver held out a coat and an
umbrella, offering the judge a choice.

The judge straightened slowly, arching his back, feeling the tendons
pull with a good tension. He looked up over the low tiled roofline of the
courthouse, beyond the flagpole to the high spalled ridges of the Cobre
Mountains where streaks of dirty dark clouds flew straight out like
pennants from the peaks. It was a rare day for Rincon, humid and sultry,
the air soggy and unmoving down here on the desert floor. The clouds
held rain, no doubt of that, but between the high winds up above and the
thermal updrafts they were being torn to nothing before they could cross
the mountains. Any rain that reached the valley would come gushing
down in flash floods from the steep slopes. The judge shook his head.
"No, thank you, Mario."

The driver shrugged. It was an old argument. He didn't often win.
"The same time, sir?"

The judge stopped, uncertain. "I don't think so," he said slowly. "I
may want you earlier. I'll phone if I do."

He went very deliberately up the short flight to the tall bronze doors,
not hesitant, not reluctant, but savoring the moment and making it last.
Perhaps when a man is about to step off a cliff he allows himself a last
long survey of the familiar sky, draws a deep fortifying breath, and
listens to the stillness inside himself.

He nodded in response to the doorman's salute, turned sharply right and went up to the second floor. He moved past the frosted glass door that bore his name and title and went along the bare echoing hallway to a plain wooden door marked PRIVATE. He let himself directly into his chambers.

It was a good room. When he had first been appointed, Claudia, in a burst of wifely zeal, had insisted on decorating it for him, but over the years he had gradually substituted the bits and pieces that meant something to him, reducing the glossy quality and marking the room with his own style. The light-brown gold-figured Chinese rug had once been in his grandmother's morning room, and he still enjoyed it as much as he had then. The square old mahogany desk, its dark red glow subdued by a hundred years of wax and polishing, had come from a great-uncle who had once been a judge too, and probably a better one, possessed of a great inner certainty and faith in himself and the law.

The high-backed wing chair in dull silk tapestry was nobly English, almost comically noble, like a piece from a Graustarkian fable. And it was the most comfortable reading chair the judge had ever known. The long oak conference table had once been in a Spanish castle, but the deeply sprung modern chairs around it and the elegant one behind the desk were starkly modern, designed by the people who made seats for aircraft, shaped to the human body and its needs.

A very good room. The judge stayed where he was, just inside the door, as sharply aware of what he was seeing as if this were the first time and he wanted to be sure he would remember all the details.

The far door opened silently. His secretary pushed it back against the wall with one shoulder, using both hands to support a deep filing box filled to the brim with opened letters and telegrams. One fluttered to the floor and she made a small exasperated sound as she went toward the desk. Then she saw the judge and smiled cheerfully for him. "I didn't know you were in, sir."

"I sneaked in the back way." He came toward the desk, looked down briefly at the loaded box and then pushed it slightly away. "No, I don't think so, Miss Lyall. Not this morning."

"There are a lot of them today, aren't there?" She picked up the floater and put it in the box, holding it there with her hand, looking at the judge to make sure she understood.

"All those helpful people." The judge shook his head. "No, Miss Lyall. Put them aside somewhere. Make a note of the names and addresses. We will have to acknowledge them, I suppose. But there's no need to read them."

8

"Some of them are—quite nice."

The judge smiled a little and shook his head again.

She took up the box, holding it with a double-arm grip. "Would you like coffee, sir?"

"Later perhaps. Let's wait till Mr. Guthrie gets here and then you might bring some for both of us."

"He's coming this morning? Gordon Guthrie?" Clearly Miss Lyall found the thought exciting.

And why not? Gordie was a celebrity these days, one of those rare few who functioned in an area somewhere between fame and notoriety. In the quiet, rather introverted world of the law he was an explosion. Sometimes, in the judge's estimation, a destructive one. He used publicity with a politician's sureness, always forcing the issue, never retreating. Usually such supremely confident, dominating men moved as a natural course into active politics, and the judge had often wondered why Gordon Guthrie was not tempted. Too much a maverick, probably. And certainly he was far too arrogant and bullheaded for joint enterprises. Gordon Guthrie would never be part of a mob, but given the right circumstances, he might lead one.

"You can get his autograph," he said dryly.

Miss Lyall grinned. She gave a brusque little movement of her chin, expressing independence. "I just might."

"You can have mine, too," he said, smiling as a sort of apology. "You may not believe it but Gordon Guthrie and I once played on the same college football team."

The judge turned toward a side wall and spotted the picture among the solid block of black-framed prints. It was not a good photograph, overexposed and blurred with time, but the faces of the two young men were clear, hugely smiling, shoulders lumpy and grotesque under football pads. The judge stood easily balanced, one foot advanced, poised and slim as a bullfighter. And Gordon Guthrie towered over him by six inches, slouched, massive in a raw-boned way, hair as wild as always, one arm torn off his football jersey.

Miss Lyall inspected the old picture, murmured polite interest, and went back to her work.

Twenty years ago, the judge was thinking. Twenty-two to be exact. His weight was up now and his waistline softened by a sedentary life, but there was no paunch yet and only the slightest thickness around the jaw. Not too bad. He could see his reflection murkily in the glass of the pictures, heavier in the shoulder now, but much the same as the youth of the picture, dark-haired, palely sallow, dressed now as if he were headed for a funeral. Black suit, hard white collar, a small-patterned dark necktie that, from a few feet away, was solidly black. He didn't remember having picked them out purposely, but he must have been anticipating a somber day. He went heavily to his desk and sat straight-backed and precise, hands linked on the leather-edged blotter.

He could hear Gordon Guthrie even through the heavy shielding of the closed door. That deep resonant bellow, clear as steel striking steel, that seemed to set up sympathetic vibrations like a powerful motor running somewhere far underground.

And then he saw him in the doorway and he seemed even larger than the judge had remembered. He carried two overloaded briefcases in enormous freckled hands. He tossed them on a chair, snatched a rumpled rancher's hat from his head and threw it behind him as he came toward the desk in a long-legged shambling swagger, grinning like a shock-headed boy.

"Sorry, Nico," he boomed. "Damn sorry. Hope I haven't held you up. Those headwinds over the Cobres were just too much for us. We couldn't get over. You know we actually came *through* that damn pass? Goddamn monstrous mountains on both sides. It was so hairy I was shaking. I had to let the pilot bring it in. I just didn't feel like flying anymore."

The judge rose, smiling. And there was Gordon Guthrie for you, he was thinking. He just has to let you know he's a big operator who flies his own plane. The man has been in the big money for years. Even by his standards he must be rich by now. But he still makes the flash. Must be a kind of reassurance for him. Lets him know it's really true.

He was a spectacular man, by nature and by intent. He stood six-and-a-half feet tall, a huge bulky man with all of that bulk encased in silky-soft tweeds in the darkest possible shade of gray. Clothes for a constant traveler who might have to dart into a formal courtroom at any moment. The collar was rucked, the wide and colorful necktie hiked around, shirt bulging a bit over the belt. And all of it arranged that way, the judge felt. Gordon was wearing his hair longer these days, he noted. It was still the same coarse sandy tone with some grizzles over the ears, and now it fell low along his neck, feathered out like wings in front of his ears. Give him a flowered waistcoat, the judge thought, and a tooled gunbelt and he'd fit right into any western movie. And he would do equally well wearing the white hat or the black hat. He probably wouldn't care which.

"Very glad to see you again, Gordie," he said in a warmly amiable tone that cost him something. "No, you're not late. I told the county

10

attorney we would send for him sometime before noon. The hearing shouldn't take long."

"Noon. Christ, I hope it doesn't take that long, Nico. I have to be in Los Angeles before court adjourns today. My assistant is holding the fort, but I think the judge is going to want my scalp."

Gordon Guthrie swept a chair away from the conference table, brought it up beside the judge's desk and sat there, rocking the chair back on the rear legs and moving it in an easy rhythm back and forth, always in motion as if he could never let himself come completely to rest. "You're looking fine, Nico. Beginning to look like a Spanish grandee. I was trying to think when it was I saw you last. About five years ago? Up in El Monte? I remember running into Claudia a couple years ago in Philadelphia at the Van Dulken trial. But you weren't there then, were you?"

As you damn well know, the judge thought. "No," he said. He looked across to the open doorway and nodded. "Miss Lyall, you might phone the county attorney and tell him we'll be ready for him in about half an hour. Let me know when he's in the courtroom."

"I was wondering about that," Gordon said. "It will be a courtroom then? Not chambers?"

"Yes, I think the courtroom is appropriate. A *non vult* proceeding does not have to be ratified by a jury, but I think the formal background may give a note of dignity to this exercise." He was speaking stiffly, even pompously, but that, he thought, is what the situation calls for.

Gordon gave him a thin, mocking smile. "You just don't like this deal, do you, Nico?"

"My feelings aren't involved." But they were.

"*Gideon. Escobedo. Miranda.*" Gordon announced the names like an incantation. "They went ahead and changed the rules on you, didn't they?"

"Not only the rules," the judge said sternly. "Those three rulings changed the *substance* of the law. I think you can appreciate the distinction, counselor."

Gordon looked at him with cold flat gambler's eyes, speculatively, weighing him as an opponent. "Bet your ass I do, judge." Then, abruptly, he flashed that swift slanting smile again. He brought one leg up, crossed ankle over knee and held the ankle with both hands, tipping the chair gently up and down, balancing on the tip of one shoe. "I meant to write and thank you for the copy of your book. I just finished it last night. Very good, Nico. I liked it very much. And the title is fine. *Rough Justice.* That has a real ring to it."

11

The judge flushed slightly. "I'm pleased, Gordie. Thank you. I didn't know if anyone would be very much interested in reading about the old days. The law in the early West was a simple business, wasn't it? The issues were always so clear."

"That's what makes the book good, Nico. Clear and simple. A morality play. Like a western movie. Makes a man yearn for the big rock-candy mountains."

The judge could hear the faint mockery in Gordon's deep, challenging voice, but he let it pass. Any man who shows a genuine concern for the ancient virtues must seem comical to a modern realist whose only test is pragmatic.

He sat silently, holding himself very still, contained within that cocoon that all judges learn to hide in. The morning traffic on Coronado Drive outside his high windows made a faint droning sound in the quiet room. From somewhere down the hall a clacking of typewriter keys rose in a brief flurry, then muted as a door was closed.

"We were speaking of Claudia," Gordon said in an abrupt change of subject. "How is she?"

"Well enough, thank you, Gordie." The judge smiled. "At the moment she's off on one of those Greek islands cruises with some friends she met in Cannes." He returned Gordon's courtesy query. "And Ellen?"

"Ellen's with her family in Grosse Pointe for a while," Gordon said with a shrug. Suddenly he grinned. "We both seem to have trouble keeping our wives at home, don't we?"

"It would seem so," Nico said shortly.

There was a pause. The situation had changed now. The initial pleasantries had been exchanged in proper hypocritical form, the empty smiles offered as the real thing. Time for business now, the judge thought.

"Why did you bother coming here today, Gordon? I've been wondering since I got your wire. What's the attraction? There's nothing scheduled that couldn't be handled by one of your assistants. Or do you think that Jonathan Pike is going to need a lawyer of your quality to help him today?"

Gordon chuckled softly, but there was no humor in it. "No, I don't expect Pike will need me today. I just came to watch you write the last chapter. Jonathan Pike has been on my mind, you know. We should have done a lot more for him that first time. Eight years ago. It hangs on me like a shadow. I'd as soon be shut of him. That's why I came. Just to get rid of him."

"Yes, I see. I didn't think this was quite your sort of thing."

"I go where I'm needed, judge," Gordon said in a surprisingly mild tone.

"Which usually seems to be a spectacular murder case." The judge spoke more sharply than he had intended. He flushed when Gordon grinned at him. Watch it, he warned himself.

"It does seem to work out that way, doesn't it? Of course the Pike case has had its spectacular aspects too, hasn't it?" Gordon looked up at the ceiling, blandly amazed at the workings of fate. "I like to think of myself as a sort of shotgun rider, Nico. When the stagecoach people are sending a big payload through hostile country, they want a good man. That's when they send for me."

"Yes, of course," the judge said quickly to hide his distaste. "You have had a remarkable career, Gordie. We've followed it with great interest. You never seem to lose a big case, do you?"

Gordon blew out a noisy breath. "Boy, I wish that was true. I've lost, all right, and will again. But I've never lost anybody to the chair yet. I can take some comfort in that. And I've never lost one because I didn't give my man the very best effort I had in me."

"Yes, I can believe that," the judge said soberly. "The few trial records I've read show that you were always beautifully prepared. And you presented your case with great energy and imagination. Yes, I can believe that you give your clients very good value indeed. But that talent is hardly called for here today, is it?"

"I'm not following you, Nico," Gordon said, genuinely puzzled. "I told you why I was here."

"To lay a ghost."

"If you want to put it that way."

The judge sighed. After a moment he said, "It's going to be different today, without Little David in the courtroom."

Gordon nodded. "It will be different," he agreed. "I think I'm almost sorry. Not quite. Just almost."

"I imagine Pike will be just as pleased as you are," the judge said dryly. "How many of Pike's appeals did David help knock down?"

Gordon looked at him sharply, then shrugged. "David never gave up," he said shortly. "I was sorry to hear about his death."

"Sudden and dramatic," Nico said. "David would have liked it, probably. In court, during summation."

"Sounds like David. Did he win?"

"The defendant was convicted," the judge said stiffly.

"So he won. A good way to go out. David always had an eye for courtroom drama."

13

"And you, Gordon?" The judge waited to make sure Gordon was facing him directly. "You are rather famous for courtroom drama these days. What do you have in mind for today? Do you intend to try any of your explosive circus tricks in my courtroom?"

Gordon Guthrie swung his big foot down flat on the carpet with a thud. He turned an arrogant glare on the judge, and the judge was very much aware of a concentration of nervous vitality that poured from the man as tangibly as heat from a furnace. "Circus stunts?" The voice was quiet but clearly angry.

"In my courtroom, I am in complete control. I had you come here before going to the courtroom because I wanted you to understand that. I don't want to find you in contempt. I would very much dislike sending an old friend to jail, but I will not allow any breach of my rules. I hope you understand me, Gordie."

"I understand you completely, your honor," Gordon said. "Now I want you to understand me. 'Any lawyer who allows a judge or a prosecutor to interfere with his client's rights or even to withhold any of those rights, should be disbarred.' Do you know who said that to me once, long ago, judge? I invite you to guess."

The judge smiled thinly. "I had forgotten that tape-recorder memory of yours. We won't fight about it. The words sound familiar. But I am not speaking of interference. I am merely warning you that I will not permit any grandstand play designed to twist the emphasis of a hearing from its proper focus. Now, let that be an end to it, counselor. I've said all I want to say."

The big man leaned forward, seeming to hover over the judge's desk. Then, with a visible effort, he made himself ease back into the chair. "Well, judge, it's your courtroom. You set the rules. But we aren't going to be battling about anything today. We've just got a routine hearing ahead of us. Almost a formality. Not much likelihood we'll be in contention, is there?"

"None," the judge said flatly. "Not in my courtroom. All right, counselor. Let's be on our way."

He rose quickly and turned toward the stand where his long black silk robe was hanging from its form. He held it in both hands for a quiet moment, staring at himself in the long mirror set in the doorway that led to the courtroom. And drew in a deep fortifying breath. And listened to the stillness inside himself.

II

FROM the north the Greyhound bus had been climbing steadily, almost imperceptibly up the long easy slope to Cobre Pass. Now, in the last cold hour before sunrise, the driver could see his headlights settled gradually in level shafts along the narrow blacktop road. He shifted up to high gear for the first time in half an hour. Another forty minutes and he would be wheeling the big rig into the terminal at Rincon. It had been a good trip. Quiet. No trouble, no surprises.

Jonathan Pike was sitting toward the rear of the bus. He could feel the altered beat of the motor when the bus cleared the pass, hear the heightened tone of the desert wind as they left the protective shield of the mountains. He did not have much more time, he warned himself again. If he wanted to make a move, it would have to be soon. But he didn't dare try it until he was absolutely sure about the tiny bird-boned old dame in the double seat opposite him.

Pike would have sworn she had been sleeping for the past half hour, but then he had thought the same thing an hour earlier and had seen her start awake with no warning, blink her eyes rapidly, and bend again to the magazine in her lap as if she had been reading steadily all the time. She was sitting facing him, braced against the window with two pillows behind her, thin legs sideways on the seat under her light topcoat. Her hair was an improbable bluish purple under the directional beam of her reading light. Her sharp pale eyes were bright and blank as crystal whenever she looked across at him.

His real interest was in the fat-assed five-striper sergeant snoring in the double seat just ahead of him. The window seat of the sergeant's pair was at full recline, the aisle one straight up. Through the angled gap between

15

them Pike had a perfect line on the rich bulge in Fat-Ass' hip pocket. But that wallet might as well be on the moon. He couldn't touch it as long as Lady Bright-Eyes had him in range.

Pike had been waiting a long time now. Since shortly after three o'clock when the bus from Albuquerque had ground to a stop on the graveled turnaround at a military post in the bleak nighttime nowhere. He didn't bother to look. All Army posts are alike, the main gate guarded like the Berlin Wall, and for much the same reason, the extravagantly bright lights, the ritual dance of the MP's, the sullen slouching clumps of bored GI's.

The sergeant had wobbled drunkenly aboard, clawing at seatbacks, and half-fell into the seat ahead of Pike. He squirmed and rolled, trying to find a more comfortable angle. And that brought the bulge of his hip pocket clearly into view. Pike had been viewing it ever since, very much aware of his own flat pocket.

But now time was running out for Pike. Up ahead he could see a faint lightening in the sky. We are running along the first contours of the high desert plateau, he told himself, and hitting a pretty good lick. Those lights ahead mean Rincon is very close now and you are almost too late already, my friend.

He rattled a page of his book, making the paper crackle in the stillness. He was watching Lady Bright-Eyes very closely. No reaction. He put the book down, brought both arms up slowly overhead in a stretching movement. No reaction.

He felt along the side molding of the window, found the switch for the bull's-eye, and flipped it off. He was in deep shadow now and could see her even more closely. Still no reaction. Only her light was still burning, but the row of dim night bulbs along the roof of the bus gave a useful, general sort of light.

Time to move, if you are ever going to. Drop right foot slowly to the floor, straighten a little in the seat. Bend and run a finger around the heel of your shoe. No reaction. Lean forward toward the gap in the seat ahead. No reaction. Ease left hand into the gap. Keep your eyes on her, but don't get clumsy. You don't want Fat-Ass to think you are making a pass.

Pike could feel the thick double flap over the hip pocket. He had to turn away from Bright-Eyes then to watch what he was doing. Two fingers. Pinch fabric lightly up and around the button. Increase tension gradually. Gradually, damn it! That's better. Slowly. Slowly.

The flap swung free. Quick glance across at Bright-Eyes. No change. Still propped against window, legs along the seat, magazine propped on

16

knees. Just keep your goddamn eyes closed. Same two fingers. Not down behind the wallet, stupid! Pinch inside the first fold of leather. That's it. Tighten grip and start to come out. And take your damn time.

He could feel the sweat beading on his forehead. He was breathing shallowly, but he was keeping it quiet. Just another minute now. Take your time. Easy, easy. Damn that blubber-butted son of a bitch. Why in hell didn't he buy a pair of pants that fit him, or get these let out. He fills them like a sausage. Hell with it. The man's drunk. Get the damn thing out. If he feels anything, let the wallet drop and then bluff it out.

It was coming. He had it now. He brought his hand back slowly, steadily. The weight of the wallet was pulling it out of his fingers. He leaned forward into the gap, right hand low and ready, and caught the damn thing just as it slipped free. He sat back with a jerk.

But don't stop now. This is absolutely the worst time to stop. You are dead if anyone catches you with that wallet.

Two fingers again. Flip open. Dig in. Wow. Say it again, softly, gratefully. You were holding pretty heavy there, sarge baby. What are you—a gambling man or a miser? Whatever, you carry a nice piece of change.

Holding the money, he flipped his hand, sending the wallet to the floor. Before it landed he was swinging his foot. He caught the folded leather squarely with his toe and sent it skidding up under the seats.

So now nobody can say the money wasn't yours all the time. He rolled it up and dug his left hand into his pocket for his wallet, turning his head slightly. And looked directly into the bright glassy stare of the tiny woman across the aisle.

He froze. Dead, he told himself. You are dead, friend. You can't possibly get to her before she screams. And when she screams, the driver slows and snaps on the lights. And Fat-Ass wakes up, clawing for his wallet.

But she's scared, too. She's just as frozen as you are. She saw you lift that wallet, and she knows you saw her watching you and still she can't stop staring. But any second now she is going to look up from the money, and then she will be looking straight at you. And then she's going to scream. And then you are dead.

Without thinking, without even any awareness of decision, he ran his left thumb along the thick edge of the bills, riffling them and lifting out the bottom third. He folded the bills over his forefinger and leaned far to the left, sprawling off-balance into the aisle, elbow propped on the armrest. His hand almost touched her seat.

She stared, unmoving. Her eyes swung up, flicked only briefly at his face, then down again, focusing on the money. She moved like a lizard gobbling a fly, swiftly, delicately, precisely. He felt the wad of money slide from his fingers, but he did not see it. Her hands vanished somewhere under her light coat and the money with them. Then she looked at him, and her thin face strained back in a conspiratorial smile.

Jonathan Pike shuddered slightly. He sat up and shaped the remaining money to fit his wallet and turned quickly, hearing a small sharp click.

Lady Bright-Eyes again, still smiling. With her hand out toward him, making the finger-rubbing gesture that is part of the universal language. Gimme.

Pike fought down a wild flare of rage. He could have killed her, would gladly have killed her. But she was out of reach, invulnerable. She could still scream. Her hand was a bird's claw, bony, brightly taloned, rapacious. And her smile was triumphant now.

Pike nodded. She wanted more. She wanted it all. But just maybe she had sense enough to settle for what she could get. He divided the remaining bills in two, by feel. He put his half in the wallet and then rammed the wallet in his pocket. He folded the rest into a small hard pad, over and over tightly, watching her eyes. If she accepted the split, okay. For the moment, okay. If not, he would think of something else and she wouldn't like that. His eyes, the set coldness of his face told her this was all—the end.

She nodded, eager now, and not quite as confident as she had been.

He tossed the wadded money in an easy arc into her lap. He leaned back against the gritty plush of the seat and closed his eyes. His heart was very noisy and he was half sick, choking on a surge of anger he could barely contain.

Pike stood silently and very still in the cool darkness of the terminal's bus ramp, almost hidden behind a square cement pillar. From there he had a clear line on the bus. He could see the door and, dimly through the beaded haze of steam on the windows, had a good angle along the aisle. Sergeant Fat-Ass had not moved. And Lady Bright-Eyes was still in the same seat, same posture.

He had lasted through a bad half hour while the bus was grinding slowly through the nearly deserted streets of Rincon. The driver had snapped on the lights as they came into the city, but few people had stirred until the bus lurched down into a steep underpass below the Southern Pacific tracks and then abruptly climbed back up near the train station. He noted the location of that. Then passengers had begun shaking themselves awake, collecting magazines and handbags, tying shoelaces, squirming to adjust their clothes. Fat-Ass slept like a dreamy baby, making contented little bubbling sounds. And, facing Pike, Lady Bright-Eyes was faking sleep.

He was on his feet, tote bag in hand, by the time the bus began its huge, slow, swinging turn into the terminal. He was first in line when the door flapped open. He was out and walking fast, not bothering then about the duffle bag he had stored in the luggage compartment. Out into the neon dazzle of the waiting room, past two sleepy-eyed porters and through to the dimly lighted street before anyone had time to notice him. He had come quickly, but not running, around the side of the terminal building and back inside by the same route the bus had taken. And now he was in a safe spot where he could see what was happening.

She seemed to sense that he was watching her. She had her coat pulled protectively high under her chin, and he could see only the sharp tip of her nose above the collar. Apparently she was not getting off at Rincon, but just maybe, he told himself, just maybe, she is lying back, waiting for everyone else to clear away and then she'll make a quick run for the streets. With me right behind her. She won't get far if she tries.

Off-loading passengers were still milling around the back of the bus, pointing to their bags as the porters swung them out. There were no travelers getting on at Rincon—too early in the morning to be starting out, probably.

Pike waited patiently as a hunting cat, watching Lady Bright-Eyes hopefully but knowing that he would have to be very careful until he actually saw that bus pulling up the ramp on its way south. Two hours nonstop to Sagrada on the Mexican border. He would have at least two safe hours if no one raised an alarm before the bus left. Probably he would have that much. It was a fairly safe bet.

But he did not give up on Bright-Eyes until a new driver swung up the high steps, counted heads in the passenger area, and pulled the door shut. The engine huffed huge clouds of diesel smoke. Pike did not move as the hot exhaust gases poured over him. The bus nosed cautiously out into the street, paused, and then turned left.

Still he waited. And finally the porters went back inside, leaving his drab canvas duffle bag on the loading platform beside four wired bundles of newspapers. He bent for his tote bag and moved quickly across the ramp. He took out his baggage check, ripped the duplicate tag from his duffle, and put them both on a stack of newspapers.

There were two taxis waiting in the rank in front of the terminal and for a moment he was tempted. But not for long. No one at the terminal had yet had a good look at him and there was no point in pressing his luck. It would be a long walk back to the railroad station, and that duffle was a heavy load. And, he reminded himself, with a small angry grin, he probably had enough money for the cab fare. But he kept walking, slowly, heavily, through the dark streets, backtracking the bus route.

He must be in the old part of town, he thought. Narrow broken sidewalks; low, poorly painted, plaster-coated buildings; small businesses; a lighted all-night garage he carefully detoured; an air of dusty, unprosperous old age. By the time he saw the lights of the train station the sky was noticeably brighter.

He went down the colonnaded length of the white-painted station, smelling the wild sweet reek of geraniums in the shadows. He came from the platform side into an empty waiting room. There was movement behind the ticket windows, but he saw no one. The men's room was sharply right. He turned and shouldered the door open.

He dropped the heavy duffle near the door, took his tote bag with him, and zipped it open on one of the short rank of wash basins. While he was unrolling his shaving kit, he looked at himself long and carefully.

Let's suppose Fat-Ass discovers his wallet's gone and blows the whistle. And if that happens while Lady Bright-Eyes is still on the bus, someone will ask her if she saw anything suspicious, and what will she say? Pike snorted. You know damn well what she'll say.

So pretend you are a Rincon cop, he told himself. Sometime later this morning you will be getting a report from the police at Sagrada about someone who rolled a sergeant on the southbound Greyhound. Got away with a lot of money.

He stopped then. Got away with how much? He dug out his wallet, spread the bills along the glass shelf like a dealer inspecting a new deck. The three bills on top were what he had started with—one five, two singles. The two fifties, three twenties, were Sergeant Fat-Ass' contribution, minus the two-thirds cut that went to Bright-Eyes. He must, he guessed, have peeled his share from the fat end of the wad. He raked the money together and put it away, feeling suddenly very tired and shaky. He held up one hand and, with a sort of bitter amusement, watched it tremble.

That was the most foolish risk you have ever taken in a pretty foolish life, he told himself. You could have managed without that wallet. So you would have had to hit Lee Wallis for a loan first thing, and that would be hard to do, giving any man that kind of edge. Even so, it wasn't worth the risk. If your luck turns bad, the local cops will be looking for you, and that is exactly what you don't want and can't afford.

I wonder how much Bright-Eyes made out of the operation. I hope it was enough to keep her content and close-mouthed.

But he knew it wouldn't be. If anyone got to her, she would talk willingly and at length, probably with complete accuracy. What would she say? He took a step back from the mirror and studied the problem. Six feet, she'll say. Maybe a hundred and sixty pounds. Skinny. Early twenties. There was nothing he could do about any of that. What else? Dark hair worn a little long, with sideboards that came down to the bottom of the ear. Thirty-hour stubble. Dark smudges of tension and fatigue around his eyes. Nothing very distinctive. And some of it could be changed.

He rubbed lotion into his beard and plugged in his electric razor. His beard tended to grow most strongly along his upper lip, and it might just be that Bright-Eyes thought he was wearing a mustache. He smiled slightly as he buzzed it off. A flat cutting device pulled up from the side of the razor, and he used it to trim the hair in front of his ears, chopping it off at the regulation military length. Then he stripped off his shirt and gave himself a quick sponge bath.

Clothes, he thought suddenly, what about clothes? His rumpled black jeans and dusty loafers were almost a uniform these days. But she might remember the shirt, a blue-and-white check in a small bright pattern. He rummaged in his tote bag and found a pale gray sweat shirt. Much better.

He dampened his thick hair with water and gave himself a low left-side part he had never worn before. Hardly recognize myself. Ah, but you are still a handsome devil, you are. Smart, too. And luckier than you have any right to expect. He grinned derisively and turned away.

The waiting room was still deserted when he came out, and he quickly stowed both bags in a coin-operated locker against the far wall. And then he took in a long relaxing breath. All over. And it had gone very well. Nobody saw you make the switch, so nobody can connect you with that guy who got off the Albuquerque bus. As far as anyone can tell by looking, you are just another one of the local Rincon boys, up a little earlier than usual, bone-tired and hungry as hell.

He went in through the swinging doors of the coffee shop, lifted a copy of the morning Rincon *Record* from a stack, and took it with him to the counter, spreading it open as he sat down. A cup appeared magically before him, and a cheerful little butterball waitress filled it without being asked. Pike smiled. He leaned forward to sniff the good hot steam. He ordered a very large breakfast and then flipped to the classified section and went carefully through the listings under ROOMS, APTS FOR RENT.

It took him four tries to find what he wanted. He had almost turned away when the door of the large dingy white house opened and he saw

21

that sloppy old gray-haired bitch glaring out at him. She had given one sharp measuring glance, then turned back into the room behind her and screamed, "Paca! Pacaaah!"

A dark fox-faced girl crept out under her arm and waited for the ugly echoes to die.

"She'll show you," she said. "Fifteen dollars a week, paid in advance. Fresh changes every week. Pay the girl if you want it." And the door slammed, leaving Pike and the girl on the long broken terrace looking at each other. The girl shrugged wearily and tilted her head to tell him to follow her.

And it was just what he had been hoping for. Actually all he really wanted was a place with a separate entrance, but this was perfect. A small wooden hut, almost hidden at the back of a straggly garden thick with untrimmed oleanders and pepper trees, not visible from the main house. It was a strange sort of building, maybe originally a playhouse for a swarm of kids, or even an unusually large garden storage shed. The doorway was low enough to make him stoop, and the room inside was not more than fifteen feet square. There was a narrow against-the-wall kitchenette and the smallest bathroom Pike had ever seen. It was hot inside and smelled stale and dusty. The bed was awful, the kitchenette gear mismated junk, the water rusty, the windows cracked and patched with strips of peeling paper tape. It suited him very well. He brought out his wallet and gave the girl a twenty.

"You can bring me the change with the receipt." He held the door for her and locked it behind them. She was waiting at the edge of the path, looking toward the house. He patted her rump lightly as he came up to her. Nice firm little piece, naked under the thin cloth.

She looked back at him, sullen and unresponsive. "She'll search everything the minute you go out," she said in a thin quiet voice, her lips barely moving.

"Thank you," he said, "but it doesn't matter." He smiled and touched her again. Then she had gone very quickly, leaving him to find his own way.

And now he was back again after collecting his bags from the train station. He had taken a moment to look around outside before opening the door, and he was even more pleased with the place when he discovered that a gate in the back fence led out to a rutted dirt lane that ran through the block of houses. So he would have a certain privacy of maneuver that just might be very useful.

He unpacked quickly, spreading his big bag open on the bed and hanging his good things carefully as he lifted them out. There were only a few left from the big spending days. The dark blue cashmere with the antique silver buttons, that was the real thing. And the smoke-gray doeskin slacks. And the soft black handsewn moccasins, light as dancing slippers. And a few sport shirts worthy of that company. The rest was routine make-do stuff and he stored it fast, closed the empty bag, and slid it under the bed.

He upended his tote bag, distributed his shaving gear in the bathroom cubicle, threw the worn travel clothes in a corner, dumped piles of books and magazines on the rickety bamboo table. Then he sat on the bed and used the point of a nailfile to pry up the flat shiny plastic bottom of the empty bag.

False bottom, officer? Certainly not. This is the way it came from the shop. And the original stiffener had been much like the plastic shield, but it had been cardboard and was apt to bend and buckle under pressure. The plastic was firm enough so that anything stored under it was reasonably safe from snoopers.

He brought out a dull gray-green pliofilm sack and eased the plastic liner tightly back in place. He tossed the tote bag casually on the floor near the bed. He sat bouncing the sack lightly in his hand, wondering. He didn't have time. Not now. Too many things to do, people to see. And he wouldn't want the smell hanging over him. But he could roll a couple and rathole them and know they were there any time he wanted them.

He went into the bathroom, untying the mouth of the sack as he moved. He took out, first, a cardboard block with a dozen thumbtacks stuck in it, a small bundle of rubber bands, and a thick booklet of brown wheat-straw cigarette papers. He laid them all carefully on the glass shelf over the basin and then shook up the compressed stuff in the sack, fluffing it out. Marvelous smell.

He rolled two fat cigarettes, holding the paper over the basin and making sure that all the shreds that dropped went into the bowl and not on the floor. When he was finished, he turned on the tap.

He braced one cigarette behind each ear, packed everything else back in the sack, keeping out one thumbtack and two rubber bands. Then he opened his front door and scouted the neglected garden before going out. He found what he wanted in the farthest back corner near the fence. A dense pepper tree that drooped its branches of feathery leaves almost to the ground. The dull grayish-green sack went high against the bole, as far up as he could reach, pinned there with a thumbtack. He stripped a handful of dusty leaves, rolled them loosely around each cigarette, and tied the thick shapeless bundles with rubber bands. He wedged them

23

tightly along the brittle branches of the tree and stepped back to make sure they were out of sight.

Couldn't be better, he told himself. He didn't like moving around with that stuff stashed in his bag, but he didn't have a source of supply in Rincon and he would want to be very cagy about finding one. That sackful might have to last a long time. But he wasn't going to have it too close. Possession is what you have to worry about. It doesn't matter a damn what they suspect, doesn't even much matter if they get a good whiff of a joint smoking, just as long as they don't actually catch you with the stuff in your hand. And that would never happen to him.

He was feeling better now. A little money, a bright sunny spring morning shining at him, sack of the good golden grass hanging high and safe. And now it was time for him to go inside and stand under a hot shower and figure out just how he was going to handle himself with Lee Wallis.

He walked slowly along the warm noontime streets, keeping to the shadows, moving south along Senate Avenue as Lee had told him on the phone. "Main drag, Jon-boy. Can't miss it. Look for the Frontier Hotel. Big sign hanging up there. You'll find it."

He didn't have the feel of Rincon yet. From what he had heard and read, he had expected it to be more of a resort town. But apparently the winter visitors used Rincon only as a waystop and kept going straight through, heading for the big dude ranches and golf courses far out in the desert valley.

The downtown traffic was largely local, he guessed, judging from the clothes he saw and the sharp speculative glances that were thrown his way as he passed in his blue cashmere and expensive doeskins. Obviously he was overdressed for midday midweek Rincon. There seemed to be two favored uniforms for men—boots, jeans, and big hats for the outdoor types, with something colorful in the way of snap-buttoned tightly fitted rodeo shirts. The office workers wore dark trousers, white short-sleeved shirts, with sober striped neckties pinned halfway down with a decorative slide in Indian silver. The few suits he saw were rumpled summerweights.

The Frontier Hotel was an old one, built before the postwar flood of immigrants brought in the flashy Miami Beach architecture. It was a solid square box half a block long and ten stories high, with a scattering of elaborate stone fretwork along the brick facing. On the wall near the revolving door hung placards announcing weekly meetings of Rotary, Kiwanis, Lions, Optimists. Pike went through the chilled lobby, spotted the neon arrow pointing to the bar, and turned down a narrow corridor past the newsstand to the open double doors.

It was a quiet oblong room facing the side street, done in dark wood and leather and smelling slightly of furniture polish and good whiskey. The only lighting came from a row of half-curtained windows. From the hall Pike could see Lee Wallis at the bar, and he stayed where he was for a long moment, watching him and remembering the sort of man he had been two years ago and wondering how he might have changed in that time.

In the Army he had been erratic, overly enthusiastic, undependable most of the time, but imaginative and very handy in casual barroom fights. I wonder if he has learned how to control that murderous bad black temper. I'm not really sure I want to get into anything tricky with him if he's still as mean a bastard as he used to be.

Lee looked pretty good though, Pike thought. He was riding that barstool like a cowboy, straight-backed, with a certain easy style. He was still a body-builder, obviously, one of the Charles Atlas graduates who had gone on to isometrics and karate. Sizable pads of muscle strained the seams of his shirt. He was wearing a fanciful version of western clothes, tailored sand-colored gabardine with rows of complex stitching and welting, slimline trousers stagged off short to show the tops of his yellow high-heeled boots.

He sat easily, pushing one finger in and out of a puddle of whiskey, watching the pattern he was making and changing it constantly. He still wore a lot of bushy hair, that gritty sort of sandy red that looked like a clump of dried grass. The hair was only slightly darker than his reddish freckled face. He turned on the stool suddenly, sensing someone behind him, his lumpy blunt-nosed face clenched in a scowl, squinting to see better.

"You are one late son of a bitch, buddy," he said in that thin familiar nasal voice. "You ever get any place on time?" Lee put out a big-knuckled hand and levered an extra pressure in his grip. "Looking mighty prosperous anyhow," he said with a quick grin. "Have a drink."

"Beer," Pike said. "You're looking fine yourself, Lee."

"Why not, man. I got it made." He snickered into his glass as he drained it. "Made in the shade, right? Bottle of brew for my guest, Jimmy. And build me another bomb." He was drinking double bourbon on ice, premium bottled in bond, and he watched, tightly suspicious, to make sure he got full measure. "Well, what have you got to say for yourself, man? Where the hell you been? I wrote you three–four weeks ago. What did you do, catch the first covered wagon?"

25

"There was this blonde," Pike began.

"Blonde." Lee snorted. "Story of your fucking life. What happened? You get dry-gulched?"

"I got sidetracked to Malibu," Pike lied. It was nobody's business where he'd been before Rincon or how he'd got to Rincon. Especially how he'd got here. "So what's the big hurry?"

"Hell, I told you I was onto something choice, didn't I? Good as anything you ever had in the Army, I'll tell you that. I figured if you were loose, you'd like to come in on it."

"On what?"

"Riding around. Seeing the sights." Lee winked, screwing up his face tightly. He brought both hands shoulder high and snapped his fingers. "Olé," he said.

"Mexico?"

"That's part of it."

The border was a little more than a hundred miles south of Rincon, and it ran for a hell of a distance. There were lots of good things available in Mexico that in the States were illegal and sometimes very profitable. All of them dangerous.

"What are you handling?" He poured his beer slowly, tilting the glass to control the head. The first sip was tasteless, cold enough to make his teeth ache.

Lee smiled at him, his thin mouth cocked in that tight wise-ass smirk that always made Pike want to clout him. "Well, Jon, old buddy, it's like in the spy movies where the hero gets the assignment and then he asks what it's all about and the boss tells him he doesn't really need to know. Need-to-know, that's the rule, right? You don't need to know." He nodded twice. "And neither do I."

Pike put his glass down very slowly. "Are you serious?"

"A gasser, huh? Don't that kill you, buddy?"

Not me, buddy, Pike thought but did not say. Not me, old friend of my Army days. Maybe it will kill you, but I'll make damn sure it doesn't kill me.

The beer had warmed from his hand and had a little more flavor now. He drank half the glass. "So now we've had the joke," he said carefully. "When do you go into your dance?"

"You don't like it, huh?" Lee laughed at him. "Well, Jon-boy, that ain't the worst of it. Not only I don't know what, I don't even know how. Or when. Now how do you like that?"

He held his eyes coldly on Lee's strained red face, waiting for the witless laughter to stop. He wasn't yet angry, but he could feel the first

26

rising heat. He spoke in a lazily calm voice, sounding almost amused because that helped him with the control problem. "You make me very curious, Lee-baby. Why did you bother writing to me? This is home ground for you, isn't it? What's wrong with the local talent?"

"Aah." Lee slashed a thick hand through the air near Pike's shoulder. "Jerks. They all want to be tough guys. Not a brain in a carload. I just figured you might not be fixed up permanent yet. This is pretty good stuff I'm talking about, buddy. You can take it from me."

Pike took another sip of beer. It was just the right temperature now, and he could feel the chemicals stinging his throat. "Are you going to tell me anything more?"

"Nothing much to tell," Lee said earnestly. He locked his big hands around his glass, almost hiding it. "We make a regular trip twice a week down to Puerta del Lago in Old Mexico. Some bad roads, and the trip back is fast and rough, so I need a man to spell me and help out. That's the job. That's exactly all there is to it. Anything more has to come from the boss." Lee drained his glass and set it down with a click. "You know how it is."

"No. I don't know how it is. I don't even know if I want to find out. But let's go talk to him."

Lee snickered quietly. He sucked at a small chunk of ice. "Don't have to go nowhere," he said indistinctly. "He's right here." He chewed the ice and swallowed. "Said he'd give us a few minutes to catch up on old times. I figure he just wanted to get a look at you. Sorta size you up."

Pike turned silently on his heel and surveyed the long room. He could scratch the men standing beside him at the bar. There were two doubles and a triple, all busy selling themselves. Near the side door were four under-age boys with highly visible Coke bottles on their table and a flat pint circulating invisibly from hand to hand underneath. Beyond them two mixed couples were engaged with drinks and low-voiced conversation. And Lee's boss in the far left corner.

There was no mistaking him. He was a big one, wedged uncomfortably tight in a padded captain's chair, leaning forward with thick forearms flat on the table and watching them with calm speculation through a haze of cigar smoke. Spanish, obviously, Pike noted, not one of the long-legged, long-nosed riders of horses but the mountain breed, those solid square-built tireless walkers, prodigious eaters, deep-voiced singers of melancholy songs. His massive head was lowered into heavy shoulders, inclined slightly forward so that his eyes were barely visible.

"Let's have a word with him," Pike said abruptly. He pushed away from the bar and crossed directly to the corner table, not waiting for Lee.

27

He stopped and stood there until the man looked up. Close up, he was older and softer than Pike had thought, those wrestler's shoulders padded with easy living, the broad face jowly and glistening as if it had been lightly oiled.

"I'm Jon Pike," he said. He put out his hand, knowing the man was just far enough away so that he would have to come to his feet if he wanted to take it.

Deep-socketed eyes moved slowly from Pike's hand to his face. Then the man balanced his cigar on the edge of an ashtray and pushed himself up, grunting, from the chair.

"Nacho Cordero," he said in the low rumbling voice that Pike had expected. His hand was wide, heavily veined, hard under Pike's fingers.

"Jesus, Nacho," Lee said quickly from behind Pike. "He just come right over without saying a word. Didn't even—"

"Sit down," Nacho said. "Both of you," he added without looking at Lee.

Pike hooked a chair with his foot and sat beside Nacho, back against the wall. Lee perched uneasily on the edge of his seat, looking from one to the other with a slightly puzzled, suspicious scowl.

"This's my old buddy Jonny Pike. From the Army," he said. "I told you about him, Nacho."

"Sure you did." Nacho tapped an empty beer bottle on the table to signal the waitress. "What are you drinking?"

"Nothing for me," Pike said. He didn't want to drink any more of that chemical slop, and he wasn't at all sure he was ready for a social session with these two.

Nacho glanced at him slowly, half smiling. He showed the girl the label on his bottle and waited while Lee ordered another double. "Going pretty strong on that stuff, aren't you?" His voice was quiet and not critical, but something in it stung Lee. He shifted his chair back irritably.

"My day off, right? So I like to slop it up a little. What of it?"

Nacho shrugged. He swung his heavy lowered head toward Pike. "Lee tells me you and him made out pretty well in the Army. That right?"

Pike sat well back in his chair, head slightly cocked, relaxed, with both hands cupped easily over the carved endpieces of the armrests. He looked evenly at Nacho without answering.

Lee scuffed his feet along the bare floor, tucking his boots under his chair. "Old Pike," he said with a short quick laugh. "Always figuring the odds. I told you how the MP's busted our racket at Sill and jailed half a dozen guys. Me and Pike and another guy managed to duck the court-martial, but they clobbered us anyway. Couldn't prove a damn

28

thing, but that didn't bother them the least little bit. They busted us down to basic rifleman and shipped us off to a headquarters outfit headed for Vietdamnam and I tell you I was pretty happy to get there too. I was just afraid those guys might change their minds and put us behind bars instead. So off we go, a couple of infantry dogfaces. We are stationed at Pleiku, pulling perimeter defense for the air base, and I'll be damned if old Pike doesn't get close to somebody at base headquarters and wangle a goddamn transfer and wind up in the base motor pool. I'll bet you didn't last a full week in that outfit with me, did you, Jon-boy? You should have seen him, Nacho. Tailored uniforms, got his four damn stripes back, jazzing around in a souped-up Honda, got his own hootch and a pretty little gook to play house with, and he's really living fat while I'm out there in the damn boonies waiting for some Cong to take a shot at me." Lee snorted, waggling his head. He snatched his drink from the waitress' tray and took a quick gulp. "Beats the hell out of me, buddy. I never could figure how you pulled it."

Pike smiled thinly, watching Lee's flushed, overly expressive face. And I sure as hell will never tell you, old buddy, he said in his mind. Lee would never follow it anyway. He'd see the risk involved. That would be enough to chill his guts, but he would never understand the cold calculation, the careful, measured approach that set up the deal just right, and made it work.

"When I come out for R and R," Lee was saying, his thin voice rueful and slightly mocking, "this son of a bitch is chief POL clerk for the base motor pool. You got any idea what that means?"

Nacho shrugged, half smiling. "I don't even know what POL means."

"Petroleum, oil, lubricants," Lee told him.

Nacho nodded knowingly. "Did all right, did you?" he asked Pike.

"The way Lee tells it I must have made a million," Pike said easily. "I don't remember it like that."

"How was it?"

"My records always balanced," Pike said in a patient voice. These guys are a couple of clowns, he thought with an edge of contempt. Did they really expect a confession? "Every drop that came into my storage area was accounted for. Every drop. Of course," he poked a tongue in his cheek, pushing out a domed peak. "I did hear there was a lot of pilfering down by the docks. Maybe that's what Lee is thinking of, but that had nothing to do with my operation."

Lee snickered. "Balls."

And balls it was, Pike agreed silently, but that's my story, old buddy, and it's the only one you'll ever hear from me.

He had made the endless tedious trip back to the States by boat after his tour was up, wearing the same pair of fatigue pants all the time, never taking them off even to sleep. A neat, polite little Vietnamese tailor had made a lining for them of soft strong silk, fashioned into small pockets that were just the size and shape of United States' currency. The evenly distributed mass of hundred-dollar bills was bulky, crackly, and stiff for a while, but as sweat and body heat softened and molded them, they became an unnoticeable part of him. Not quite fourteen thousand dollars, and when he had changed the last of the bills just a month ago, it still retained a faint whisper of that familiar old sweaty reek.

"So Lee tells me you'd like to work for us," Nacho said abruptly, as if he'd had enough casual chatter and now it was time for some business talk.

"He said there might be a job for me."

Nacho poured the last of his beer into his glass and drained it. "I run a wholesale produce business," he said. "Vegetables, fish, some meat. Lee makes a regular run twice a week down across the border to Puerta del Lago with a refrigerator truck for fish, mostly shrimp. It's a long haul, gets kind of boring, I guess, so I let him pick whoever he wants for a relief driver, someone he can get along with. As long as the man is qualified, I mean."

"It's a good deal, Jon-boy," Lee said earnestly, as if Pike had to be persuaded against his judgment. "Thermo-Queen box on a six-ton Jimmy. It's no bomb, but it's got a pretty fair charge even with a load. And Mexico! Wait'll you get a taste of that Mexican tail, man. We lay over two nights a week. And we could take a day off down there once in a while. Get in some of that great deep-sea fishing."

"You want it?" Nacho said, ignoring Lee.

"Depends what's in it."

"You got the right licenses?"

"For everything the Army had."

"You can make bond okay? No bad spots on your record?"

"Nothing." Not on any official record anyway, he thought.

"You single, no dependents, like Lee?"

Pike hesitated, then nodded. It wasn't exactly true, but it was nothing he wanted to discuss with Nacho.

"Then you'll take home a hundred and sixty-seven, thirty-two, every Friday, just like Lee."

Pike slowly drew his arms back and sat forward. "Lee sort of gave me the idea that there might be a little something more than that in it."

"Then he gave you the wrong idea." Nacho let out a sigh, then slowly smiled, shaking his head. "You know how Lee gets when he starts to tell a story. Can't guess where he'll end up. You ought to hear the ones he tells about you and him in the Army, how you were living like a couple of millionaires." He cocked one eyebrow at Pike, giving him a moment to answer if he wanted to.

Pike was beginning to understand. Nacho was a pretty sly fellow, he suspected. He let his face show nothing of what he was thinking.

"I think Lee likes this job because it gets him down to Mexico so often. He gets wallowing around in that sweet local ass and he forgets his own name. I'm too old for that stuff these days, but I remember how it goes. Fringe benefits, like they say."

"Nothing more to it, eh?" Pike asked carefully, watching Nacho. "Just the straight job, trucking fish and nothing more?"

"You don't even want to think about anything else," Nacho said in clear, sharp warning. "They got eighteen kinds of cops patrolling that border. Any one of them would cut your balls off if they thought you were bringing in anything on the hot list. I might even do it myself."

"And if there should happen to be anything else, just sort of by accident," Pike said quietly, "it wouldn't have a thing to do with you?"

Nacho flashed a quick rosy smile. His broad face widened in fleshy loops that jiggled slightly as he chuckled. "You see how it is, eh? My business is trucking fish, and I expect to be in that business for a long, long time. I'll never let anybody get me hooked with a smuggling rap."

Pike nodded calmly, his narrowed eyes never leaving Nacho's. He played the amiable, aging fat man very well. You had to look sharp and fast to spot the shrewd, careful operator hidden in all that cheerful blubber. I'd like a piece of whatever he's got, Pike thought, but I don't think I want any part of what Lee's got. Nacho was clever enough to set Lee up and probably ruthless enough to let him go down the drain if that was the way it worked out best.

Pike brought his feet back under his chair, ready to rise. There was nothing in this for him.

"Of course," Nacho said in a quietly amused tone, "you might get as much fun out of this job as Lee does. You hear him tell it, all kinds of wonderful things happen, just like he was back running a juicy racket in the Army. Like he'll tell you he finds an envelope in the mail about the middle of every month. Thick envelope like a little book. Five hundred dollars in twenties. Doesn't know where it comes from. Can't even guess. Five hundred dollars for absolutely nothing. What do you think of that, eh?"

Pike relaxed and sat back. "Pretty wild story," he said in a mild voice. "Hard to believe."

"Now don't get me wrong," Nacho said quickly. "I believe it. I've known Lee all his life. He grew up in my neighborhood, used to go to school with my own boys. Anything he wants to tell me is something I want to believe. But you try telling a story like that to someone else, say a hard-nosed suspicious cop, and how far do you think you'd get?"

Pike nodded appreciatively, smiling faintly.

So Lee Wallis, red-faced, grinning, happy Lee Wallis was the decoy, the clay pigeon sailing up there in the clear blue sky for anyone to shoot down. And whenever that happened, however it might happen, Nacho Cordero would be absolutely in the clear. No involvement whatever. He was willing to pay out a thousand a month in overhead expenses, and presumably he was making a good profit, so that must mean he was bringing bulk shipments of high-grade heroin across the border, because no other contraband would have a big enough markup in the retail market. None of that troubled Pike, or even interested him very much, except for the question of the risk. He was being asked to join Lee on the hot seat of a light truck loaded in some secret compartment with a hugely profitable shipment of drugs. Was five hundred a month payment enough to justify that kind of risk?

It might be. For a short time. Say a month. Just long enough to collect one of those anonymous letters in the mail. If I should get busted with Lee before then, I could prove that I was a new hand on the job and knew nothing about any smuggling racket. It could work. It might be worth the risk for a month. And if in that time I can find out just what the real setup is, how Nacho runs his racket, where the weak spot is, then I just might be in a good position to cut myself in for a small piece of the real action. Then I could stick around for a while longer.

Nacho smacked both hands decisively down on the table, making it rock. "Well, time for me to be getting home for lunch. I can't sit around all day drinking like you young fellows. So, Jon Pike, if you want the job, Lee can show you where to pick up the local licenses and a border permit and take you down to the office and run you through the paperwork." He tossed a bill on the table and told Lee to settle for the drinks. He nodded once to Pike. "Nice to have met you."

Pike rose with him, shook hands, smiled politely, and said nothing. He stood there watching the heavy man move through the long crowded room toward the door. Then he sat again and looked at Lee Wallis, raising one eyebrow.

Lee snickered again, nervously. "He's really full of that mysterious shit, right? But there is one smart old boy, I'll tell you. Nobody is ever going to walk in on Nacho Cordero when his pants are down. He doesn't look like much. Looks like a fat stupid slob, as a matter of fact, but I never once saw him get the short end. He always comes out on top."

32

"Known him a long time, have you?"

"He told you—I practically grew up in his house. I went to school with Ramon, his oldest boy. Nacho was running a truck farm then, raising early lettuce. He always made money, even in bad times. Nacho got a little expansion going during the war, began buying crops in the field, that kind of thing. Took some awful chances, from what I hear, but everything worked out just fine. Nowadays he's got a big operation going, and he's got his finger in just about ever' damn thing. He's got automatic laundries and drive-in movies and liquor stores and supermarkets and pieces of this and pieces of that till a man can't tell what-all he has got. And he runs ever' damn bit of it himself. No managers, no partners, just Nacho Cordero."

Pike nodded. That fitted with his judgment of the man. "Now tell me about that envelope every month," he said.

Lee grinned hugely, spilling his cigarette from his mouth and catching it with a quick stab. "Comes in regular—you don't have to worry about that. Around the fifteenth, day or two either way. Made you prick up your ears a little bit when he told you, didn't it?"

"You don't worry about it?"

"Worry about what?" Lee snorted. "You don't see that big picture, buddy. Sure, Nacho is covering himself, what do you expect? He's a prominent man these days. He's not a spender and he doesn't go for the flash, but he's got it plenty solid where it counts. And on top of that he's building up some real political clout. Half the families of South Rincon are on his payroll. You think he can't deliver a nice little block of votes any time he wants?"

"So?"

"So he's our protection, man! Can't you see that? As long as he's in the clear, he can lay down some pretty good smoke for us if anything goes bad. And you don't have to look at me like I'm some kind of stupid asshole. I know things can take a tricky swing any minute. But as long as Nacho's out there, covering himself, he's going to be in a position to move to cover us if we ever need him."

"How long have you been making that run?"

Lee shrugged. "Little over a year. Well, how about it? I told you it was a good setup, right? Are you in?"

Pike was in no hurry to commit himself. He picked up the five-dollar bill Nacho had left and handed it to Lee who shoved it carelessly into his shirt pocket and lifted his glass, tilting his head well back. He froze in that position and slowly grinned, looking over Pike's shoulder.

"Well, well," he said quietly. He waved a hand overhead. "Over here,

33

Angel-baby." He lurched to his feet, stumbling back a few steps to catch his balance.

Pike could smell her before he saw her. Heavy expensive whorehouse musk. Then from the floor up, tiny pointed black shoes near the leg of his chair, sleek, taut dancer's legs in a smoky film of nylon, short black skirt, very tight red sweater with two points bulging the knit so far that he could see her bra was black lace. Then Pike got to his feet and she tilted her thin pointed face to look up at him. A long heavy fall of Indian-dark hair, small plump mouth pursed in a secret kissing smile.

"This's Jon Pike, Angel," Lee said, reaching for her. "Old friend from the Army."

She turned large darkly bright eyes on Pike, focusing on him completely as she would on any new man, holding him in a brooding, questioning stare.

She was very young, Pike could see, probably still in high school, but the air of smoldering challenge, the blatant offering, suggested a sexual maturity that had little to do with age. She moved the point of her tongue out of the corner of her mouth, flicking it as if searching for a lost crumb. "I could eat you up," she was saying in a private language that needed no words.

It was all so obvious and overdone that Pike had to fight to keep his face straight. She was presenting herself as a hard-core sex bomb with the fuse set for instant detonation. But even with the phoniness, she might be the real thing, Pike suspected. Just looking at her made him horny. He had to remind himself that she was trouble, the kind of trouble he had to keep well clear of.

"Hello, Jon Pike," she said in a husky whisper, her voice artificially lowered, a voice learned from the movies.

He took her warm weightless hand in his briefly. "Angel, huh? That really your name?"

"Angela, really," she whispered.

"Angela Morales," Lee said quickly, scowling at Pike.

She turned then to Lee, as if she had just remembered he was there. "Let's go," she said abruptly, her voice sharper and thinner. "You shouldn't have made me meet you here."

Lee chuckled. He made a big chest for her and grinned happily. He was just the guy tough enough to make his broad meet him any-damn-where he said. And, by God, she'd better be on time, too.

"Her old man's a bank dick," he told Pike. "Struts around with a gun on his belt and thinks that makes him tough. Angel's still a little baby doll in pigtails as far as he's concerned. That right, baby doll?" Lee snickered and moved a hand across his mouth. "Good thing he don't know you the way I do."

"Come *on*, Lee."

"Now don't get nervous, Angel. Nobody's going to bother you."

Angel moved to face him squarely, tapping a small handbag swiftly against her leg. "You think you're so damn tough," she said in a quick sharp burst of anger. "You want to find out what tough is, you just let my old man catch me in here with you. Now come *on*. I won't say it again."

"Well, you get the picture, Jon-boy. See you around."

"What about those local licenses I need?"

Lee waved a casual hand. "Hell, can't expect me to waste my whole day-off on you, buddy. We'll handle it tomorrow. Tell you what, I'll pick you up, okay? Then we can stop on the way down. That do you?"

Pike wanted to object, but seeing Angel, he knew Lee was hooked for the day. And he could hardly blame him. He gave Lee his address, making him repeat it to make sure it registered.

"That's a real lousy neighborhood, Jon-boy. About two jumps away from a slum. I can find you something better than that. You must have a pretty bad case of the shorts, huh?" He grinned again, liking the thought that Pike might be having money troubles. "You want me to let you take a few bucks?"

The offer was made to impress the girl, Pike assumed, and he shrugged it off. "Just making the money stretch a little further," he said easily.

"No way to go, man," Lee said, shaking his head. He dumped money on the waitress' tray. "You want to live it up, go for the plush, baby. You don't want to kick off with your jeans full of loot you didn't have time to spend, do you?"

The last of the big-time spenders, Pike thought sourly. A true-blue outasight jerk. He didn't seem to realize he was giving the girl large expensive ideas. Pike winked at her with a sober solemnity that made her giggle softly against Lee's shoulder.

"What time tomorrow?" he said.

"Early start, buddy. Be ready for me by seven, no later." Lee scooped up his change, measured out a tip that brought no thanks from the waitress. "You'll be coming in with us, then? Pretty good deal I fixed for you, huh?"

I'll be coming in with you, Lee-baby, he thought coldly, but maybe not in as far as you expect. I'll try a month, maybe less if the action looks sour. You're not going to box me in any easier than you would Nacho Cordero.

35

"Sure," he said. "Thanks." He took Angel's hand again for a warm moment, shared a few comments with her in her private language, then turned away.

He didn't find the answer in a month. He never did find an answer that completely satisfied him, but it wasn't because he hadn't tried.

The Cordero operation lay just a few yards off the main highway running south from Rincon. It had once been a small ranch. The adobe ranch house was now the main office. The high angular horse barn with its lean-to attachments served as the motor maintenance section. The rest was new. Broad expanses of prefabricated metal-and-glass sheds stretched back from the highway in a circle, connected with busy loading platforms by a gravel road.

"Big deal Nacho's got here, buddy," Lee said, and Pike agreed that it was impressive. They climbed out of Lee's low white Corvette and Pike waited for him to lock up. Today Lee looked like a recruit for Hell's Angels in a shiny black leather jacket with chrome studs, tight black pants tucked into black buckled motorbiker's boots. He wore a flat-topped bad guy's black Stetson with the brim nipped up sharply at the sides. Pike, in his faded jeans, nondescript gray zipped jacket and baseball cap, was the poor boy of the team. He hadn't even thought to bring sunglasses, and the pair he had picked up at a drugstore counter would never compete with Lee's enormous blue-tinted airman's shades.

While the preliminary paperwork went on, Pike had plenty of time to stare out the office windows, watching trucks wheel in from the highway loaded with field produce—lettuce, onions, radishes—the early spring crop that would bring very good prices in northern markets. There was nothing fake about this side of Nacho's business and the produce moved steadily through the processing lines, being washed, sorted, graded, wrapped, packed in lightwood crates or slatted hampers or molded paperboard or plastic, all ready for display in your friendly neighborhood supermarket.

Finally he was ready to climb up into the cab of the GMC beside Lee and lean back as the big truck rolled out through the gate.

"We got a late start this morning, but it won't make much difference. Just stop someplace different for lunch, is all it amounts to. You better let me take that first stretch down to the border and through Sagrada and then you can spell me. It's about three-fifty to Puerta del Lago, down through Santa Rosa and Benicarlo. Doesn't sound like much, maybe, but a lot of it is secondary roads and you'll know you've been working before you drive it many times. Secondary Mexican roads develop new potholes every day. And there aren't any fences to keep the livestock off the roads.

36

You're apt to find a herd of cows sleeping on the road in some sunny hidden little curve. You run into something like that unexpectedly, buddy, and you're going much over thirty and you can scratch one damn expensive truck. Nacho pays us to get that truck down there and bring it back. Message clear?"

"Got it."

"And the traffic is wild in the towns. A Mexican likes to aim straight at you, and he sort of likes to look the other way, but he's watching you out of the corner of his eye and at the last minute he'll chicken out and swing over, if he times it right. Trouble is, he don't always get the timing right. It gets real hairy, buddy, if you're not used to it. So we watch it all the time, and we take it nice and slow. Right?"

And slow it was. Ten hours for the southbound trip, allowing a lazy hour for a lunch stop and a snooze on a warm sandy hillside.

Pike liked the country. It was flat scorched land with mountains far away, and closer the rumpled contours of shrub-pocked foothills that changed from harsh gray-white to soft pink-purple as the sun moved from morning into afternoon. Rain squalls swept the wide valley like ragged curtains, slowing the truck to a crawl through the sheer impenetrable weight of falling water. Then the sun baked them again.

Lee took the wheel again just before they came into Benicarlo, showed Pike his favorite bypass route, then switched back again and slumped in the passenger's seat, his badman's hat pulled down to the top level of his sunglasses.

"Okay, you roll it on down through Cienfuegos and then wake me up," he said, yawning. "It's a bitch to work your way through Puerta and you'd never find Cordero's wharf in a million years."

Pike did not argue. He could smell the moist scented tropical fragrance five miles away from Puerta, and he pulled up to let Lee take the truck in through the town. They swung sharply north to make a preliminary stop at a small beachside posada.

"Not much of a pad," Lee said, swinging down from the driver's seat. "But it belongs to Nacho's cousin, and we get a cut rate. The food's cheap and not bad."

The owners knew Lee and welcomed him. He and Pike checked in with a minimum of formality, left their overnight gear, and went back to drive along the curving beach road to the wharf where they were to leave the truck for the night. Ahead of them the southern horizon was jagged with the broken outlines of high-rise luxury hotels against the sunset glow.

"Won't be anybody here at the wharf this time of day," Lee said as he set the brake. "Fish business is early business. But the boats will come in before sunup in the morning. They've got a key for the box, and they'll have us loaded up by seven o'clock. Then all we have to do is check her out, collect the waybills, and gas up for the trip home. Okay with you?"

"The box has got a hell of a lot of road muck on it," Pike said, giving Lee a sincere frown. Lee just snorted at him.

"I still don't like it," Pike insisted. "We ought to hose it off at least. Leave it to dry overnight and somebody's going to have to use a scraper on it. Do you think we ought to bring it in that dirty?"

"Hell with it," Lee said lazily. "I'm heading back for the posada. You want to be the big motor-pool operator, you just go right ahead. Scrub her down all you like and lots of luck to you. Me, I want that hot shower and a clean shirt and a long cool drink in the patio. Come on now, Jon-boy, cut the bullshit."

"I'll just hose it off a little," Pike said.

"Hose yourself off." Lee slammed the cab door, checked to make sure it was locked, and stalked off down the road. After a few yards he stopped and looked back. "Find your way okay?"

"Sure, don't worry about me. I'll just be a minute."

"Outa your fucking head, buddy," Lee muttered. He turned away again.

Pike watched him out of sight before he moved. He had worked out a program that just might give him the answer to Nacho Cordero's operation. He found the freshwater hose used to sluice salt off fishing gear and connected it to a tap at the side of the shack that guarded the entrance to the wharf. He worked quickly, cleaning the truck, inspecting it as he went. He knew as much about bodies and engines and frames as any working mechanic, and he was sure he could spot any modifications or additions, no matter how cleverly they might have been made. He swabbed a soft leather lightly over the hood, then unlatched the hood and checked the engine, ducking underneath for a look at the mounting while the hood was up. Not a thing. And he knew he wasn't being fooled. Absolutely nothing.

The design of the refrigerator box was new to him and he took a careful time with it. The paint was glossy as porcelain, chipped only in a few places where stones had snapped up from under the tires. The forward end was a solidly welded unit, but each of the long, high sides had two panels (inspection ports? Pike wondered) that were pinned with rows of star-headed screws. All of them had been opened at some time and now the screwheads showed only a few flecks of white paint. Pike wiped them clean, making sure they were completely dry. Then he took out the small squat jar he had prepared the night before. Originally it had been a child's pastepot, a screwtopped jar with a small stiff brush suspended inside, fixed to the center of the lid. Now it held white paint, much diluted with turpentine. When he stroked the brush along the rows of screwheads, he could see the film of watery paint running smoothly down, clogging the inset portion of the screwheads but not very noticeable on the flat part. He ran the damp leather down to pick up the excess paint.

That film of thinned paint would dry very quickly. The panels of the box could still be detached with no trouble, but a star screwdriver would first have to gouge out the new paint. From now on Pike would know if the panels had been opened, would be able to guess why, should be able to figure out when and where. A useful first step, he thought. He ducked down to the two spare tires that rode flat under the rear of the box. They would make very poor stashes for contraband, even more obvious than the inner curves of the bumpers, but just for luck Pike dabbed two flat globs of paint on each, in the deep narrow grooves between rubber and steel rim. The paint seemed a little too bright, so he dusted a sprinkling of beach sand over the blobs and then slowly straightened to ease his back.

That was about all he could do at the moment. The interior of the box was out of reach. The understructure he would check when he had a better light.

He coiled the hose and returned it. He hung the leather to dry on the front bumper. He measured two lengths of his shoe from the front corner of the shack, then one length straight out and got down on his knees to scrabble a pit big enough to hold the fat little jar of thinned paint. He was whistling softly, cheerfully as he walked back up shadowed beach toward the posada.

He had his chance to inspect the underside on the return trip. While Lee Wallis was snoring after lunch, Pike took the big six-volt emergency flashlight from the toolkit and slid quietly under the truck. He went slowly and carefully. He found nothing. He squirmed out from under the truck and put the flashlight away before he beat the thick dust from his clothes and went to shake Lee Wallis awake.

On the next trip to Puerta he would climb out of bed before the workmen were due at the fish wharf and get down to the truck before they could start loading. They wouldn't object or question him if he said he wanted to inspect the interior paneling. He would have the paint pot ready, and in less than a minute he should be able to smear the loaded brush over all the likely spots. And then he would watch.

If Nacho Cordero was smuggling contraband inside the framework of the truck, then Pike was fairly sure he could pinpoint the hiding place the next time it was used. Of course the truck was carrying almost a full load of frozen shrimp packed in lightwood boxes. But it would be a fantastic risk, Pike felt, to try to hide anything in the cargo. Surely the border inspectors would check the load—wouldn't they? You'll have to watch that very carefully, he warned himself. Don't miss a move they make.

The border crossing, as far as the Mexicans were concerned, was a brief and casual ceremony. Lee took his plastic folder of invoices and permits into the small shabby office, slipped two ten-peso notes inside the folder, and politely turned his back while the clerk swiftly riffled the papers.

He held the folder ready on his lap as he drove the short stretch over bumpy railroad tracks and pulled in for inspection under harsh glaring lights on the American side. Pike watched the routine closely, and when it was over, he knew that only a dedicated idiot would ever try to smuggle anything inside those boxes of frozen shrimp.

The border guards checked the cab, understructure, bumpers, spare tires, and all the complex piping inside the box. They compared the load with the waybills, then selected at random three boxes of shrimp for a closer look. One man pulled on long rubber gloves and sifted patiently through hard lumps of icy shrimp. Only three boxes were checked out of seventy-two, but the random pattern of selection made it a mathematical certainty that any contraband would ultimately be discovered. Nacho Cordero might be willing to take reasonable chances, but he would never buck odds that long.

"Real active today," Lee grumbled. "Made us half an hour late." He put his papers back in the glove box and gunned the high-sided truck out onto the highway. "Some days they're happy to look at one box. Once in a while they'll just wave me through. And once they opened ever' damn box in the load. Never know what the bastards are going to pull next. Anything to keep you off-balance."

So the stuff, whatever it was, could not be hidden in the cargo. Which meant it had to be in the truck.

But he couldn't find the hiding place.

Now in his quiet dark apartment he was stretched flat on the lumpy bed, scowling up at the faint shadow patterns made by the vague moonlight coming through shaggy pepper trees. He drew in deeply on his hand-rolled cigarette, holding the smoke as long as he could without straining. Then he let it out in short even bursts through his nose. He wasn't high or anywhere near it, but his mind was freewheeling now, just

40

skimming along the ridges of ideas, not troubling with any dreariness of step-by-step analysis. But the basic problem nagged at him. He couldn't leave it alone.

Pike knew himself to be intelligent above the normal range. He had known that for a long time. There wasn't anything he couldn't learn if he wanted to know it enough to put his mind to it. That was the problem for him—wanting to know. Most things were either too easy or weren't worth the trouble. He had been tested over and over again in high school and later in his one disastrous year of college. He always scored in the upper two percentile, once even racking up a perfect score and then being put through the squirming misery of repeating the test in a different form because none of the battery of psychologists would believe that a perfect score was possible.

That repetition had been what kicked him off the whole thing of college. But now that he was remembering it honestly, he could see the fall was bound to come anyway. The work bored him, being largely a rehash of high school courses. After he had read the basic textbooks and most of the collateral material, he could probably have passed the exams and gone on to something more interesting. But waiting months until the end of the term meant he forgot most of it, forgot even to show up for some of the exams.

That was before he discovered pot. Until then he was still in his beer and whiskey period, drinking like a man with a square asshole. Out of boredom largely and a routine sort of rebellion that had become almost reflexive.

So the Army had scooped him up while he was still wasting time, and then he wasn't bored anymore because it took all his wiliness and ingenuity just to keep out of trouble. But after basic training he had solved it pretty well. He learned how to maintain a very low silhouette, sidestep all the areas of inevitable trouble, and locate the sources of profit that exist on every Army post. Most of all he learned never to stick his neck anywhere in view; leadership is for generals and other losers.

So why is it he couldn't figure out how Nacho Cordero ran his racket? The man was cunning and careful as a weasel, but he was operating an illegal business that involved a lot of other people. Just by definition it had to. How did he manage to keep every little bit of it completely out of sight?

The money was coming in on schedule. Twenty-five bills banded together inside a fold of cardboard and sealed in heavy manila paper. Pike had taken the package with him on the next trip, asked Lee to fix it with the office so they could take their usual day off in Puerta del Lago, and the next morning walked into town before Lee was out of bed and opened a checking account in the Banco de Crédito de Sonora with his deposit which had now become almost six thousand pesos, what with deductions for exchange and handling.

Even if he could not find out how or where Nacho Cordero hid the contraband for the border crossing, Pike was sure that Lee Wallis had been picked as the pigeon who would take the hard rap if the operation blew up. Lee, strutting in his tailored Roy Rogers outfits, lighting his Marlboros with a gold Dupont, timing himself with a gold Rolex, roaring through the sunny afternoons in his super-charged Sting Ray Corvette, secondhand, sure, but still an elegant and expensive piece of machinery. Lee was an obvious pigeon.

Okay, let Lee play the pigeon. Pike would be the fox. He would have a good deep burrow to hide in and a couple of wide-open escape routes well in mind. So he was never going to let that extra money change any of his normal routine. He would live on what he made as a trucker and let the rest mount up in the Mexican account until he decided it was time to cut out. By then he should have a fair little wad. Maybe pick up a used Volks camper and cruise down through Mexico and see how it is when the golden grass comes sweet and easy. But as long as he stayed in Rincon he was going to play it very square, and he knew it was about time to start edging away from Lee Wallis. No more of that old-buddy jazz. From now on, just two guys who happen to be working together, pushing the same truck. But after working hours—nothing. Let Lee go on collecting all the attention. Pike was going to make sure none of the glare bounced off on him.

But that was for the future, and it didn't get him any further with the real problem. He tried to puff his dead cigarette into life, then rolled in the bed, fumbling for matches on the night table. It was good grass, nicely cured and sweet, and he hadn't rolled the stick too tightly, but he could not keep the damn thing lit. So next time you'll winnow the stuff, he reminded himself, spread it out on a sheet and pick out all the seeds and stems and the hard dry bits. Of course you'll lose about a third of the bulk, but what's left will burn like a Chesterfield. And anyway you should be able to find plenty of the good gold in Puerta if you ask around, so you don't really have to hoard it anymore. He struck a match and heard a small hard-shelled bug go scuttling noisily somewhere along the linoleum to escape the flare of light.

He drew in the smoke heavily, feeling slow red pinwheels turning pleasantly in his head. So the hell with Nacho Cordero, he thought in a tired sort of resignation. It turns out he's a lot smarter than you figured, and that's a fact you'll just have to learn to live with.

42

He was aware of quiet rustling sounds from the ragged garden outside, prowling cats muttering to themselves, a thin scratching of dried branches across the screening of his open window, swishing gently like a trap drummer flicking his steel brushes in a lazy, broken rhythm. He tried his cigarette again, cursed softly and reached for another match. And froze where he was, right arm straining across his body, off-balance, almost tipping out of the narrow bed.

He heard the whisper of sound again, a soft scraping on the hard ground of the garden path. He rolled from the bed, stayed on hands and knees, and crawled swiftly and silently across the chill linoleum to the bathroom cubicle. He still had the cigarette in his mouth. He raised his head above the toilet bowl and spat the cigarette into the water. He rose immediately and pulled the chain. And blew out a tight lungful of pentup air in a soft explosion.

Bad time to be interrupted. The defenses are lowered, the responses dull, the alarm system is slow to open the valves and start pumping the adrenalin that lets you move fast and surely enough to save yourself. It could have been a very bad moment, catching him just after one stick had sent him dreaming.

One stick! It bombed in his head. *One.* So where is the second one? He snapped on the overhead light, not caring who might see him, thinking only of that other tan-paper cigarette lying on the bedside table. He snatched it up and turned in a tight spin toward the bathroom. And stopped when he heard the voice and recognized it.

"I can smell it," she said quietly. "As soon as I came out of the house I could smell it."

The girl from the big house. Paca something. Short for Francisca, she had told him. Sullen little foxy face, big eyes, tiny pointed chin. And a tightly muscled ass that romped like kittens playing under her thin dress.

He took in a quick relieved breath. He smoothed out the crumpled cigarette and grinned suddenly. Well, why not? A stick of grass never put him in a particularly horny mood, but why be unfriendly?

"Come on in," he said softly. "I don't mind sharing. Not with a friend." He snapped off the light and moved in his bare feet to unlatch the screen door.

"She can't figure you out." The girl's voice was almost a whisper in the darkness as she sat on the edge of the bed beside him.

"Tough." Pike shifted a bit and offered her another puff. The second cigarette was burning more evenly than the first, and going faster, with both of them working on it.

43

"Can she smell the smoke up at the house?"

"No, don't worry about it," Paca said dreamily. "I got a little whiff of it when I came out. But that old woman never goes out at night. The darkness scares her, I think. But don't let her find any in here. She searches."

"There's nothing for her to find."

"I know." She giggled quietly. "She looks every morning. And comes back looking mean as Judas. She can't find a thing. And that funny mail you get. That really bothers her. Most people in a place like this never get any mail."

Pike listened carefully then, concentrating. But after a short while he decided she wasn't prying. She didn't give a damn about the mail. Too bad it was attracting attention, but it didn't matter; it was the right kind of attention. So if someone were to ask the landlady, "Tell me, Mrs. Snooper, you say there was a lot of mail? Just what kind of mail?" And the old bitch would duck her head and chew her lip and agonize for a moment and then shrug angrily. "*I* don't know. There was just a *lot* of it."

Exactly. The place to hide a letter, so Mr. Poe has told us, is in a stack of other letters. So Pike had bought cheap introductory subscriptions to two weekly magazines, sent for every free catalogue offered in the papers, mailed himself envelopes stuffed with blank paper, at least two of them each week. So when that fat little envelope with twenty-five bills inside had come to the house, it was just another piece of "funny" mail for that nutty lodger out in the garden apartment.

"What if she spotted something she didn't like? Would she call the cops?"

Paca laughed softly. "Not her. She'd be afraid. She called them once. She saw a gun in a man's suitcase. Turned out he was a private cop, working out at the racetrack. She almost lost her license. She wouldn't call the cops again, not if she found a machine gun in your bag."

Pike let out a quick, easy laugh. He knew there was nothing in the apartment that needed hiding, but the idea of being constantly watched disturbed him.

The girl tapped his arm, asking for the last drag of the cigarette. He held it for her, cupping fingers around her small thrusting mouth. Then he took a quick little pull himself and snuffed the end in the ashtray. "Back in a minute," he said quietly. He went in to dump the ashes and butt in the toilet and make sure they were flushed away.

When he came back, the girl was lying at a long angle across the bed, humming softly to herself. He took her arms to lift her up against the

44

pillows, swinging her legs to the far side of the bed. "Hey," she muttered. "Hey now," she said more clearly, with a little flare of fear. She began to push herself upright.

"Don't fight," Pike said in a soothing tone. He pushed her gently back. "Nothing to worry about. You don't want to fight." He unbuckled the belt of his jeans, dropped them to the floor, and kicked them away. He cupped his hand under Paca's head, cradling it, as he slipped down beside her.

She squirmed away, pulling against him strongly and he had to tap her. But only lightly and only once. Then she understood and it was all right. She was a good willing girl.

At the midway stop coming back from their next trip to Puerta, Pike swung himself underneath the truck again, using the big flashlight to check for any changes. There was fairly fresh grease hanging from the lubrication points, but everything else was just the same, still coated with old impacted dirt. By now he was beginning to suspect the truck might not be involved at all. He would inspect it once or twice more, and then to hell with it. Nacho was just too tricky for him.

He pulled himself out from under the truck, braced a hand to shove himself to his feet, and looked across a sandy pebbled stretch to see Lee Wallis watching him intently, still sprawled in a shady spot, comfortably relaxed, with his ankles crossed, hands locked behind his head. But he wasn't sleeping now. Perhaps he hadn't been sleeping at all.

Lee cocked a thin knowing smile. "Drop your watch?"

Pike stood up and moved at an easy pace around the side of the truck with the flashlight. "Steering linkage," he said. "Didn't like the way it felt." He put the big flashlight back in its bracket and rattled tools as if he had just dropped a couple of wrenches in the box.

Lee was waiting for him, ready to swing up into the cab. "You sure do worry about this truck, don't you?" He flashed a big grin.

Pike shrugged. "Maintenance," he said and climbed up to the passenger's seat.

He was expecting more comments, but Lee was strangely quiet all the way back to Rincon. He kept his transistor going most of the time, rock and western stuff, which was all that he could get. The hard, driving, incessant beat made conversation impossible and that, Pike thought, was what Lee wanted. His inner warning system was sending little prickles along his nerves.

He was driving when they reached the warehouse compound and swung in, backing around so the big doors at the rear of the truck were lined up flush with the loading dock.

45

"Jon-boy, you mind waiting for them to unload tonight? I got a big date. Like to take off fast if I can."

"No sweat," Pike said easily. "Where you going?" he asked, not caring, just curious to see if Lee would take an extra moment for a friendly gesture.

"Jaycees spring dance tonight," Lee said. "Very large deal. Nacho is chairman this year. Going to be a long hard night, I can tell you, boy. Good thing the weekend is coming up. I'm going to need some sack time." He rolled the window up on his side, held the latch down, and swung the door shut to lock it.

Pike got out on his side and went back to jump up to the dock and unlock the box for the handling crew. Then he ambled very slowly to the end of the loading platform, casually bouncing the keys in his hand. From there he could see the nose of Lee's white Sting Ray parked in a far corner of the motor maintenance area. And by turning half right he could see the driveway that led to Nacho Cordero's office.

He leaned against a corner of the building. Behind him he could hear the quick brisk sounds of the loading crew stacking cases on their dollies. And then he saw Lee come out of the washroom door. He was moving lazily, stretching at every other step, working his big-muscled shoulders as if he had a cramp. He picked at a greasepacked thumbnail for a moment, then got out his keys, unlocked the door and reached through to open the other one to let the stale hot air blow out. He cranked down the window on the driver's side, taking his time, moving as if he knew he was being watched and wanted to make it very clear that he was a relaxed fellow, nothing on his mind but getting home for a hot bath and some party clothes. Then he climbed in and gunned the Corvette. He was still accelerating when he passed the turn to the office driveway. He slipped without a pause into the sparse traffic of the highway and slammed the speedy little car into high gear, noisy cutouts farting and blaring with excess power. The message was clear. Lee was telling him that he was no fink.

Pike walked back when the handlers had finished with his truck. He went casually inside the open reefer box for a quick inspection. His carefully painted screwheads were still unmarked. Some had been lightly scratched by the shifting of boxes, but the paint in the deeply inset heads was still solid, unbroken. So it was another dry run.

He snapped the lock and went forward again to drive the truck around to the parking lot. He reached in through the dispatcher's window and stuffed invoices and the truck keys in the slot of a locked box, and then he was finished for the day.

He stopped briefly in the washroom. No hot water at this time of day,

46

but he stripped off his sweated shirt and scrubbed himself with a wad of paper towels soaked under the cold tap. And he took a minute to scrub his hands with the gritty lava soap that removed dirt and skin impartially. He went out the door pulling on his shirt.

He stopped short when he saw her waiting and then realized that he had been aware of her for some time. That strong almost choking musky scent penetrated even through the carbon and petroleum stink of the garage. It suited her, he thought, that stuff distilled from the glands of small predatory animals. In a way it defined her. She made him uneasy, and he did not like the fact that she could do this by just being here.

She was half sitting on a mechanic's bench, stroking slowly through her long straight hair with a short-bristled brush that looked like a bed of fine nails. Her head was bent low, and she looked up at him through that dark mist and very slowly, privately, smiled at him. "Didn't expect to see you here," she said in her soft breathy movie-taught voice. "Where's Lee?"

"Took off early." Pike finished buttoning his shirt and eased his belt so he could jam the tails in his jeans. "Big date, he said. Not with you?"

"Hell yes, it's with me," Angel said sharply. "Son of a bitch. What am I going to do now? I was going to ride back with him."

Pike looked at her carefully. Didn't expect to see me here, eh? And where the hell else would I be this time of day? And where were you, you tricky clever little Angel, when Lee Wallis roared that Corvette of his out of here a couple of minutes ago? Hiding somewhere until he got clear?

"Bus stops at the gate," he said. "Pretty slow trip, though."

"What about you?" Angel dropped her brush in a soft leather shoulder bag and zipped it shut. "Haven't you got any wheels?"

Pike laughed softly, almost to himself.

"What's so damn funny?"

"Wheels," Pike said easily. "Yeah, I've got wheels. Two of them. Didn't Lee tell you?"

"Lee never talks about you. What do you mean—a motorbike?"

"Secondhand Harley. Real tear-ass bike. Gets all the way up to fifty once in a great while."

"Shit," Angel said bitterly. "Wouldn't you know it?" She slid from the bench and smoothed both hands down her hips.

Great disappointment, hearing about the bike. Sure it was. That's why she just happened to come dressed for bike riding. Tightly fitted black stretch pants lashed inside soft ankle boots. An overly fussy pink shirt, ruffled like a samba dancer's. Pink was not her color, if it was anybody's, but nothing could make Angel unattractive.

So she was making an offer, putting herself in the right spot at the right

47

time and leaving it to Pike to go on from there. In spite of his normal
wariness, Pike felt a rising excitement. If he took a serious hack at her, it
would probably mean a fight with Lee, but maybe that fight was long
overdue anyway.

"I can give you a lift home, if you don't mind the pillion. It can be a
rough ride." His voice sounded a little thick and he coughed to clear his
throat.

"Won't be the first time," Angel muttered. She drew a long gauzy
white scarf from her bag and looped it in a complex way that completely
covered and controlled her long hair. She came closer and took Pike's
arm warmly in both hands, squeezing lightly. "Well, I'm glad you're
here, anyway. I'd hate to have to walk." She moved beside him,
sidestepping in short little strides, holding his arm close.

"Wait here. I'll bring it out." He went down along the side of the
garage, pushed the big dusty bike off its mount, and rolled it back toward
Angel.

"God, that is a piece of junk," she said, making a tight scornful mouth.
She moved in a slow half-circle, looking it over, liking it less and less.
"You and Lee are going across that border four times a week every week.
Seems to me you ought to be able to find some way to swing a little profit
somewhere."

Pike stopped and stood very still. He looked at her sharply. That
slanting, knowing twist to her mouth, why was that familiar? And
answered it immediately. Lee Wallis. That was as close as she could
come to aping his smart-ass smirk. Not very close, actually, but Pike
understood what he was seeing. So Lee had been dropping those sly little
hints, had he? "Lots of good loot down there for a guy knows his way
around." Was that how it went? Goddamn that stupid childish son of a
bitch!

Pike fought back a surge of hot anger. He held his face expressionless,
then slowly raised an eyebrow and tried to look surprised. He even
managed a plausible short laugh. "Don't even think about it," he said.
"If you could see the kind of inspection we go through every trip, you'd
know we couldn't even sneak in a hunk of bubble gum."

"I'll bet." Angel shrugged. "Well, you start this piece of junk and then
I'll get on."

Pike straddled the bike and stamped it into life. He revved it a few
times to get the tired old four-stroke engine churning noisily.

Angel slung her bag, mounted the pillion, and slid well forward. She
locked both hands hard over his belt buckle.

Pike gunned the bike out to the perimeter road, shifted into second,

48

and rolled it to the highway. "I don't know where you live. How do we go?"

"You're not taking me home," she said quickly. "Boy, that's all I'd need, for someone to tell my old man I came home on a strange guy's bike. No, you let me off where I can catch a Number Seven bus. Go right here as far as Peeble's Tastee-Freeze, and then jog left a couple blocks to Amarillo. That way nobody's likely to see me."

Pike swung the bike into the highway traffic and worked up through the gears, very conscious of Angel's breasts moving warmly against his back, her legs touching his in an easy back and forth rhythm. Her hands unlocked slowly from his waist, then both thumbs hooked deep under his belt. Long inquiring fingers stretched flat on his belly, tapping out an erratic little tune.

He followed her directions, moving north along a narrow two-lane road toward the old part of Rincon which was now mostly the Mexican-American section. Sparse clusters of small houses gradually concentrated into dense shoulder-to-shoulder units of whiteplastered adobe and brick, set flush with the streetline. Sidewalks here were broken, and most of the streetlamps had lost their glass.

"Here," Angel said abruptly. "Pull around the next corner and let me off."

Pike slowed for the turn, slipped the bike easily right, and stopped on a crumbling berm just off the paving.

Angel swung down smoothly. She stood with one hand on Pike's shoulder, shaking him impatiently. "You don't really think I was there by accident, do you?"

"I was wondering."

"Why didn't you ever call me, all this time?"

Pike shrugged.

"Lee doesn't own me," Angel said quietly. She had her breathy voice back now, almost whispering. "Nobody owns me, Jonny Pike."

"Okay."

"You coming to the Jaycees tonight?"

"Not invited."

"Invited? Shit! Two bucks at the door, that's all the invitation you need. So come, huh?"

"Can't make it."

Angel eyed him carefully, not quite frowning. "You giving me the brush?"

Pike grinned and shook his head. "Not me. But let's try something a little more private. I don't like those big dances."

"Who does? But if you say no, then nobody invites you. So what are you doing Sunday?"

"You tell me."

"You know El Pinar, the big grove out near the fairgrounds?"

"I can find it."

"My class at Rincon High is having a picnic there Sunday. I have to go, but I don't have to stay. So come pick me up about three o'clock. Okay?"

Pike nodded slowly. "I'll try to make it."

"You be there. You'll be glad you came. I'll make you glad you came."

Angel turned slowly, pivoting in a tight circle, then stopped facing away from him. Her hand touched his shoulder and slipped down slowly along his chest to his beltline, and the fingers opened flat and were against him, then moved quickly lower and constricted in a slow pulsing rhythm that made Pike stiffen. Angel patted him, once, expertly.

"Sunday," she said. "Three o'clock." Then she was gone, hard heels making crisp little sounds on the paving. In his mirror Pike watched her walk back to the bus stop. He stayed where he was for a long moment before he started the bike again.

Shortly after noon on Sunday Pike was stretched out lazily in a frazzled wicker chair in his apartment, bare feet up on the bed, the plug of his transistor stuck in his ear like a bean. He was listening to an organ program from one of the churches, slow powerful chords that rang and echoed in his head. He had the volume turned so low that the deep tones were like another pulse. He was listening hard and enjoying the long involved progression that was like a musical form of mathematics. He was also very conscious of the time.

He had come awake early that morning, saying "three o'clock" in his mind. And after that he was finished with sleep.

But he still couldn't make up his mind whether it would be worth the grief. He didn't give much of a damn for Lee Wallis, but until he had actually decided to dump the job, it seemed a little foolish to pick a fight with him. Maybe Angel would be worth the trouble. Maybe. She talked a good game and she made some tricky moves, and it just might be okay. But she's trouble. She's a troublemaker and she likes making it. Hell with it. Wait and see how you feel when the time comes. He closed his eyes and let the heavy somber music flood his brain.

He heard the screen door rattle and looked up to see a tall lanky man in a rancher's hat standing there, blocking the light and throwing a long shadow into the room. He could see the man's lips moving, but with the plug in his ear, he heard nothing.

50

Unhurriedly Pike reached across to the table, located the volume switch of the transistor and turned it off. He took out the earplug and put it down carefully.

"Your name Pike?"

Pike nodded.

"Like to talk to you for a minute."

Pike brought his feet down, pushed slowly up and leaned forward far enough to slip the catch. Then he sat down again, straighter now, with his feet on the floor.

The man was too tall for the low-ceilinged room—a skinny, awkward man with stringy muscles visible under the tight shirt and pants that looked like some sort of uniform. As he came closer, Pike could see he was wearing a small round badge on his shirt pocket, a star the size of a silver dollar set in an open circle. He took off his pale stained hat, forked a hand through a mat of dusty gray hair, and then settled the hat on his head again, tipped casually back from his long, narrow, weathered face, the sort of face you associated with western movies—calm, gray-eyed, impassive, wide mouth tilted by a slightly ironic quirk. He looked friendly, sympathetic, understanding. Too much so, Pike guessed. He would probably be the one who played' the good guy when they were whipsawing a suspect at the county jail.

Pike folded his arms easily and leaned back, looking up, with his head slightly cocked, waiting.

The man waded through the scattered sections of the Rincon *Record* that Pike had dropped on the floor after reading. He pulled a straight chair away from the table and sat across from Pike.

"Name's Malcolm," he said in a slow easy drawl. "Deputy Sheriff. You're Jonathan R. Pike."

Nothing in Pike's face changed, though tension suddenly knotted his belly. He nodded again, studying the man closely.

"You applied for a bond through Southwestern Mutual, they say. I'm supposed to check up, ask a few questions. Just routine. Nothing a little frank talk won't take care of, a little goodwill on both sides."

Pike smiled thinly. Malcolm was pretty good, he thought. Looking at him, you'd swear he was busting out all over with goodwill. He watched Deputy Sheriff Malcolm steadily, letting the silence build up. Then, when he saw Malcolm shift impatiently and open his mouth to speak, Pike said, "Bullshit," in a quiet tone.

Malcolm stiffened. His long face darkened slowly. Pike could see the goodwill ooze away, the suspicious, half-contemptuous cop look come into the long horsey face. Better. He looked more natural that way.

51

"The bonding company asked you for a check. That much I'll buy. The rest is Mickey Mouse."

"What are you getting at?" The deputy's voice was hard now, all pretense at friendliness forgotten.

"I was about to ask you the same thing. The bonding company asked you to check your records. So you sent back a negative report because my name doesn't figure in them anywhere. And as far as your office is concerned, that's the end of it. So just what are you getting at, sheriff?"

"Deputy," Malcolm said, correcting him automatically. "We get a lot of requests for information. I understand you also applied for a border-crossing permit?"

"So I did," Pike said. "I applied to the federal government, and if they asked you for anything, it was just exactly what the bonding company asked for. You must have sent in your reports a month, six weeks ago. So what are you here for, sheriff?"

"You're a pretty cute little fellow, huh?" Malcolm brought his boots down to the floor and leaned forward. "How come you know so much about police reports?"

"I don't know anything about the police. But I've made bond before. The investigation is routine, sheriff. There's never any mystery about it."

Malcolm nodded slowly, his big mouth pulled down at the corners. "We got a big county here," he said, trying to get back to his friendly tone. "Pretty soon we are going to have a quarter million people, but we still can't get authorization for any more deputies. So we have to work overtime and Sundays, and we still don't get caught up. But sooner or later we get around to checking out every stinking long-haired drifter who comes into our county."

Pike leaned back and laughed silently. "You've got the wrong man, sheriff. I had a bath this morning. My hair isn't much longer than yours. I'm no drifter. I've got a steady job, the rent's paid. I've even got a few bucks in the Valley National. I'm a respectable citizen, sheriff."

"Where did you come from, Pike?"

"West Coast."

"And before that?"

"East Coast."

"And you're not a drifter?"

"Certainly not, sheriff. I'm just looking around, trying to get ahead, settle down, make good. Man can't just sit still and hope things will come to him. He has to get out and scuffle. That's the American way." Pike kept his face straight, speaking very earnestly, but he could see that Malcolm was getting progressively angrier. Better not goose him too much, he thought.

"How do you stand with the draft?" Malcolm demanded.

"We're all square. I'm an honorably discharged veteran."

"Let's see something that says so."

"I don't exactly know where the papers are, sheriff. But I can produce them if I have to. When some authorized person asks for them."

"You don't think I'm authorized?" Malcolm's big knuckly hands clamped hard together as if to keep them from Pike's throat.

"I don't know, sheriff." Pike showed him a worried, thoughtful face. "I just don't know what to think. You come in here Mickey-Mousing me, what am I expected to think? Why don't you show me some of that goodwill you were talking about? How about if you try leveling with me? What is it you really want?"

"You don't know who I am?"

Pike shook his head.

"Never heard my name?"

"No."

"Thought maybe Lee might have said something, the way you were acting, all that smart backtalk."

"No."

"Lee's my sister's boy. She worries all the time that he might be going bad, company he's keeping lately. I try to help out where I can."

Pike nodded soberly.

"He's into something, I know that. His big fancy car, all that money he's flashing around. What the hell is it, Pike?"

"I don't know, sheriff." Pike spread his hands. "I don't know he's into anything. It's not my business what he spends his money on. He works for it, doesn't he?"

"You're his friend. Old Army buddy, right? He got you the job with Cordero, didn't he?"

"Sure, but we're not all that close. He's just a guy I knew in the Army. He told me about this job and it sounded okay, and I've always wanted to see this part of the country."

"And that's all there is to it?"

"As far as I'm concerned, sheriff. I can tell you I'm not mixed up in anything and I'm not going to be. I don't believe Lee is either. I never saw any sign of any funny business."

"You guys stick together, don't you?"

"Well, hell, sheriff, Lee's a sort of friend. You don't expect me to start inventing things about him, do you?"

"Now it's my turn to say bullshit," Malcolm said in a quiet menacing tone. "You little assholes think you can get away with anything these days, don't you? You don't kid anybody, Pike. And Lee don't kid

53

anybody either. I came here meaning to ask for your help, give me a hand straightening that boy out. But I can see I'm wasting my time. You're as bad as he is. But before I go, I just think I'll knock a whistling fart out of your smart ass, teach you how to talk when you're asked a civil question."

Malcolm planted his big boots squarely and came to his feet. Pike looked up at his hard tight face and was careful not to smile.

"If you held a gun on me, you just might cut it, sheriff. But I don't think you want to go around beating up on people when witnesses are watching, do you now?" He shook his head. "Look behind you, sheriff."

Malcolm whirled, too quickly for his eyes to change focus. Pike knew he would be registering a delayed image that would seem to be movement.

"My landlady," Pike said. "She's a snooper. You've got a file on her. She's always out there hiding in the bushes whenever I'm in. She likes to know what's going on. See her, sheriff? She'll be just over there under the big pepper tree by the gate. Go ask her what she heard you say you were going to do to me."

Malcolm slowly straightened. He stayed where he was, facing the shadowed screen door. He lifted off his hat, using both hands, and settled it in its usual line low across his eyebrows. Then he half turned to look at Pike. "I'll be taking an interest in you, Pike," he said in a thickened tone. "You can, by God, count on that. You tell Lee the same goes for him."

"You think he doesn't know?"

Malcolm hesitated, hand on the latch, then decided he'd had enough. He went out and let the screen door slam on its spring behind him.

Pike came quickly out of his chair to stand in the doorway where he could watch Malcolm going up the wobbly flagstones of the garden walk toward the big house.

He wondered if the old bitch or the girl really had been out there somewhere. Didn't matter. He didn't know and what was even better, Malcolm didn't know. But Malcolm probably knew all about Mrs. Snooper, had probably checked with her before coming back to see Pike.

Pike went outside into the hard bright sunlight. The constant wind was broken by the house and the dense trees, and the air seemed still and dry and warm. Perfect day for a picnic, he thought suddenly. And laughed.

Okay, Lee, he said in his head. It's your own goddamn fault. That crazy vindictive uncle of yours has cut my safe time down to a nub. He's reaching out for you, and that's okay with me, old buddy, old Army pal. But the trouble is that while Uncle Malcolm is reaching for you and

54

getting all out of breath just thinking about what he's going to do to you, he is very likely to stumble over me and accidentally give me a mortal kick in the balls. I don't want to take a chance on that, so I guess my days with Cordero are numbered. Like maybe until I collect one or two more of those thick little envelopes through the mail. Just about that long.

So we don't exactly have to be friends anymore, do we, Lee, old buddy? So how about if I wheel my bike down to that piney grove where the high school class is having a picnic and take a hack at that little Angel, see how she comes on? Why not? All your own fault, Lee-baby.

He couldn't believe she was that strong. Those slim legs were a tight fierce clamp around his middle and she was lifting him. *Lifting* him. He felt his bare knees rising from the dense mat of pine needles, and he dug hard with his feet, driving forward and in, deeper and deeper.

"Hard," she whispered hoarsely. "Hard."

A furnace breath whistled in his throat. He locked his hands under her shoulders and pulled her closer.

"Haah!" Her head strained back, mouth half open and tight with effort. That raw harsh cry softened abruptly. She slumped. Girl puppet with the strings cut.

Pike arched his back, stiffened, and slowly rolled away. He was breathing with his mouth open, sucking for air. He opened his eyes slowly then, looking up through the heavy mottled shadow of the pine trees. They were in a cave, dry and dark and secret, the hidden space close to the thickened bole that was completely shielded by drooping branches that touched the ground in a dense circle around them. Angel's secret place. He lay very still, listening to the noisy thump of his heart. Layered pine needles made a soft gritty sound, and he knew Angel had shifted toward him. Then he felt her hand.

She smelled much better now. That choking thickness of musk was tempered now, sweetened by the richness of heated female and sexual effort. "That's how I am," she whispered in her movie-star's thready voice. Her small hand tightened on him. "You're the same."

"Dead, if that's what you mean." Pike tried to swallow. His throat was too dry for talking.

"Not yet. God, not yet!" She was up on her knees then. Her shadow fell across Pike's face. Both hands busy now.

Pike straightened a cramped leg. He tried to ease his back. Crazy bitch. Three times, charging like a bull in rut, and she's still looking for more. Let her work. She'll see.

55

Dead, he said to himself. The cupboard is bare, Angel-baby. Let's take a little rest. He sighed out a long breath. He roared in pain and shock when she dug a double handful of viciously sharp fingernails deep into his upper leg.

He came surging up, still bellowing, raging now. He swung as hard as he could in that awkward sitting position. His knotted fist caught Angel on a padded hip. She twisted on her knees, fell heavily on her shoulder, and tried to roll away. He pushed up on one hand, swinging at her again, but she was away by then, facing him on hands and knees, sharply pointed breasts swinging free, small plump mouth wide and thinned with excitement.

"Look at you!" she whispered. And she was exulting. "Just look at you now!"

He stopped where he was, letting himself down on his elbow. And looked. And there it was. Pike. A long-handled weapon with a stabbing point. Aimed straight up.

"That's how you like it, isn't it? Why didn't you say?" She came toward him on her knees. "Why didn't you say? You think I care? I can take anything you got. Anything. All of it."

Pike stared in amazement. But not for long.

Lee Wallis was still sulking. He wasn't complaining, no loud grumbles about Pike cutting in on his girl, nothing like that. Just the surly sulks. Grunts for necessary answers but no comments offered on any subject.

Pike ignored him, spoke little and politely, and enjoyed the quiet. Everything considered, Lee Wallis with the blackass was better company than Lee Wallis trying to be entertaining.

Pike was dozing lazily when Lee drove the big rig in through the warehouse enclosure and backed it up to the loading ramp. He shook himself awake and went around to open the box.

The boss handler flagged him before he could turn away. "Nacho wants you," he said. "Up at the office."

"I'll stop on my way out."

"Said right away."

Pike shrugged. "So I'll go right away."

The office was less than a hundred yards inside the ring of warehouses. Pike walked up the unpaved driveway, kicking powdery dust high with each step.

The chattering girls in the big outer office fell silent when he opened the door. Pike bowed solemnly and set off a gale of giggles. He pointed at Nacho's closed door, lifted an eyebrow in question, and went forward when one of the girls nodded.

He knocked twice, waited a beat and went in.

Nacho Cordero was sitting behind a gray steel desk piled high with papers and bound ledgers. He was wearing an open-necked white shirt, and he seemed even larger than Pike had remembered, probably because he took up so much of his chair, big chest looming out of it like Santa stuck in the top of a chimney. His head came up slowly. He took a freshly lighted cigar from his mouth and balanced it precisely on the rim of his ashtray. He pushed himself up with a grunting effort, using both hands, and then walked around the desk toward Pike.

"You wanted to see me?"

Nacho smiled amiably. Then, with no flicker of warning in his eyes, no change of expression, he clubbed Pike below the ear with the side of his fist. Pike felt his head lift off and slam against the floor, skidding along the baseboard. It seemed minutes later when his body followed the head, falling in a tangle of arms and legs that knocked over a light chair and wound around it. He rolled up to his hands and knees, dazed, gulping for air. He pulled the chair away, let it go, then snatched it up again. Bentwood chair, lightly varnished, woven cane seat. Lion-tamer's chair. Pike got one foot flat against the floor, balanced on one knee, and thrust the chair blindly forward, legs first. His eyes were blurred, unfocused. Then he heard Nacho's voice, and it seemed to come from a long way.

"My uncle used to break mules. He always started out by slamming a two-by-four over the brute's skull, just to get his undivided attention."

Pike could see him then, hazily, a thick bear-shaped outline. He was standing in front of the desk, leaning slightly, one hand flat on the top.

"Got your attention, did I?" He watched the chair closely, and what Pike was doing with it, then nodded, recognizing that Pike's posture was defensive. "So put down the chair and sit on it."

Pike stayed as he was. Two or three feet to the left, he was telling himself. The big window. It's screened, but you can get through it okay if you give it a good belt with the chair. Swing it first at Nacho and, when he ducks, head for the window.

Then Nacho turned away, moving in that ponderous mincing gait as if his feet hurt. He went back to his chair, lowered himself carefully. Pike watched him, unbelieving, as he picked up his cigar, blew softly on the end, and put it in his mouth.

"Sit down," Nacho said again. He reached forward on his desk, pawed through papers, picked up something small, and tossed it toward Pike. It sailed up in a slow lazy arc so that Pike could judge it easily enough to get his left hand under it as it fell. He kept the chair aimed at Nacho and flicked a quick glance down at his hand. A small squat jar, caked with sand around the lid. It took him a moment to realize what he was seeing.

57

Then he put the chair down and used it to lever himself to his feet. He stood with his hands braced on the curved back.

"I hired you to drive that truck," Nacho said quietly, "not paint it."

Pike nodded, puzzled now. Nacho didn't sound angry; in fact, Pike suspected he might be secretly laughing.

"You think you can sneak around down there in Puerta and nobody sees you? Why, man, half those people are some kind of cousins of mine. They work for me. They see somebody fooling around with that truck, they want to know why. Anything happens to me, they're all out of work."

"I should have known," Pike said slowly.

"That goddamn paint. Man, that really had them worried. Nobody could figure it out. I had to tell them myself when they phoned me. We had those panels off half an hour after you painted them, just to make sure you hadn't decided to set yourself up in the smuggling business. Then I had them painted again. And I made sure people watched every step you took from then on."

Pike was numbed as much by what he was hearing as the solid punch he had taken. What a clumsy operator you are, he told himself bitterly. It's a real pleasure to work with a bright one like you. You thought you were outsmarting Nacho, and it turns out the old man has been leading you by the nose all the way.

"I had Ray Guerra and his boys trailing you every minute you were in Puerta. It's a lucky thing for you they stayed close. They know every *contrabandista* in northern Mexico, and if you had said just one word to any of them, even just hello, you'd still be in Mexico. You understand what I'm telling you?"

Pike nodded again, sour with defeat.

"When I ask you a question, I want you to say something back to me." Nacho's deep voice was still easy, almost amused, but his eyes were narrowed, watchful still.

Pike coughed his throat clear. He fingered the aching tenderness under his ear. "I follow you," he said.

"You took that crack on the head pretty good," Nacho said cheerfully. "When I was your age, I could hit a man hard enough to keep him down for a while. Hell of a thing, getting old." He leaned back comfortably, blew a long streamer of smoke at Pike, and put the cigar aside. "So tell me what you thought you were doing with that paint. Huh? Why the paint?"

Stupid question, Pike thought. You know damn well why the paint. "Curiosity," he said. "Thought I might spot something."

After a thoughtful moment, Nacho nodded, "You know, I think I believe you. I can see how you were figuring it. You still got the idea I'm running something in that truck?"

"I thought you might be."

"And what do you think now?"

"I've stopped thinking," Pike said heavily. "I'm all out of ideas."

Nacho smiled slowly. "You're lucky, you know that?"

"I'm getting the idea."

"You come close to getting yourself in real trouble, making people worry about you and the funny kind of life you live. You come into Puerta, park the truck, get cleaned up, go have a couple beers and dinner and practice that very bad Spanish on the girls at the posada. Then you go for a walk on the beach and maybe have a smoke, right?" He lifted a big hand to stop Pike before he could answer. "Smokes I don't mind. I'll take a smoke once in a while myself. Long as you don't carry the stuff over the border. So then you go up to your room, play a little music and read a goddamn book and go to sleep. Now what kind of a way is that to behave? No wonder people get worried about you. There's Lee out on the town, catching all the new acts in the clubs, checking the whorehouses every night. And there you are, flat on your ass in bed. With a goddamn book. What's the matter? You don't like Mexican girls?"

Pike almost laughed. All that careful planning and snooping, setting clever little traps for Nacho and all the time there were two or three guys trailing him and reporting every move he made. Jesus, what a jackass.

"The Mexican girls are great," he said, trying to keep it light. "I love them all. But I've been trying to build up a stake. I hit here flat busted and owing money."

"What I figured," Nacho said agreeably. "I had a boy check over that lousy cheap pad where you live and he says you're clean, no signs of any kind of spending at all. Even do your own cooking, don't you? And that bike you bought is the cheapest set of wheels you could get anywhere. So now we stop worrying about you." He held Pike in a steady, sober stare. "You understand what I mean?"

"I think so."

"Tell me."

"You're saying I've been a small nuisance to you, sort of like an itchy place on your back. But now you've scratched it and it doesn't itch anymore."

Nacho scowled at him. "You read too many books," he said. "Okay, you got the idea. So get back to work."

"I still work here?"

Nacho pretended surprise. "You want to quit?"

"No."

"Then get back to work." He dropped his foot to the floor, turned to his desk and picked up his cigar. "Drive," he said over his shoulder. "Don't paint."

Pike moved clumsily, still slightly numb in his mind. He had been ambling along at his own comfortable pace, pretty well pleased with how things were going, and then he had slammed head on against a solid brick wall with no warning. He was furious with himself but, even more, was astonished to know how stupidly overconfident he had been. He shook his head angrily. So Nacho is ten times smarter than you expected him to be. But he wasn't all that smart. He had help and you know where he got it.

Pike went faster now, hurrying back toward the parking lot, then slowing when he saw the blunt nose of Lee's white Sting Ray still in its slot. He detoured through the garage, found a foot-long screwdriver with a tape-wrapped handle on a mechanic's bench, and took it with him as he went toward the washroom door, holding it in his left hand by the heavy tang, the handle thumping against his leg.

He could hear Lee snorting and wallowing in a basin of water. He leaned against the wall. His heart was pounding noisily, too quickly. He made himself breathe in deeply. No hurry now. He'll be along. He crossed his legs and folded his arms, keeping the screwdriver out of sight against his side.

He didn't use the side of his fist. He knew he could not hit with Nacho's ponderous force. He let Lee come level with him, unsuspecting, cocky, moving with a confident bounce. Then he swung a hard-knotted fist, hitting Lee just under the ear, a little forward of where Nacho had tagged him. Lee spun away, choking. He slammed a shoulder against the wall and came off it sagging, both arms raised at a strange angle, open hands lifting toward Pike.

Maybe he was finished. One punch might have been enough, but he was coming forward and Pike couldn't take any chances with that big trained mass of isometric muscle. This wasn't a sporting contest; this was punishment. He hit him with a second merciless punch, swinging freely with a big windup, harder than the first. He aimed at the slight soft bulge over Lee's ornate silver belt buckle, but as he was swinging, Lee was turning, and the fist landed soggily deep just above Lee's right hipbone.

Lee huffed a blast of air, clamped both hands where it hurt and rocked back against the wall. He slid slowly down as if his knees didn't work anymore.

Pike stood over him, keeping the weighted screwdriver ready. It was just insurance, but until he knew how Lee would react, he meant to have it handy.

A skinny grease jockey in dirty blue coveralls rounded the corner of the shed and skidded to a halt just behind Pike. He made a quiet strangled sound deep in his throat and turned wide soft brown eyes toward Lee. Then he was caught by Pike's coldly violent stare and he went away, quickly and silently.

Lee was on his knees now, bracing himself with both hands on the gritty floor, his head low, hair hanging in his face.

Pike rubbed the tapered handle of the screwdriver roughly along the back of his neck, then tapped him lightly several times. "That's what I got from Nacho, fink," he said easily, relaxed now and breathing smoothly. He rapped Lee's head with the screwdriver again. "Just returning the favor, fink."

Lee wobbled his head. "Sick," he muttered. He tried for air and moaned when a muscle spasm caught him. He pushed himself up, still groaning, clawing at the wall for support. He coughed heavily, wincingly. He hawked deep and spat out a rubbery string that slapped back against his chin and hung there.

Pike watched him closely, but there was nothing left, no threat. Lee was finished. Those well-exercised muscles were there to back up a mean, ugly temper, to dominate a loud bullying talk session, full of menace, but not for fighting. Not today. He stared up at Pike in dull apprehension, eyes sick and frightened.

"Jesus," he said. "You really hurt me, buddy." He felt his side with delicate fingertips. "I think you broke something."

"You'll live," Pike said with no interest.

"Didn't think you could hit that hard." He looked at Pike warily, uncertain about the next move. He shivered violently, surprising himself. "Sick," he said softly. "You better help me out to the car, old buddy."

Old buddy, Pike repeated in his head. Does he really think it was an old buddy who decked him a minute ago?

Lee held out his left arm, elbow crooked, asking for help. Pike shook his head, then stepped quickly forward and took the arm high up under the armpit where he could keep Lee away from him in case he had belligerent ideas. But there was nothing left in him. He moved with slow dragging steps, making Pike work to keep him on his feet. By the time they reached the Corvette, Pike was taking most of his weight.

Lee stood with both hands on the top of the car, gulping air noisily through his mouth. He rolled over to free his right hand and dug for his keys. He had to fumble, and when he brought out the keys he handed them to Pike.

"You'll have to drive, buddy. I don't think I can make it." He rubbed a hand across his face and moaned again.

"Hell with that," Pike said roughly. "I've got my bike here."

Lee bent over the car. "Please, Jon-boy. I'm real sick." He looked up at Pike without moving his head. Under the dark tan his face was a dull sickish yellow. "Just run me down to the Old Forge, huh? Get a couple drinks in me, I'll be okay. We can come back for your bike. Okay, buddy?"

"Get in," Pike said wearily. He slid into the driver's seat, put in the key, and waited for Lee to claw his way achingly around to the other door. He got in stiffly, falling back, head lolling against the backrest.

"What you hit me for, old buddy?" he asked in a small thin voice.

"What you fink on me for, old buddy?" Pike said savagely.

"Jesus. Don't even remember. That goddamn Angel." Lee closed his eyes, gulped down a surge of nausea, and leaned forward to cup his face in his hands. "Let's get a drink, huh? I'm bad sick."

Pike checked through the gears before turning the switch. The car was strange to him, over complicated, he thought. He slid the seat back as far as it would go and scanned the dashboard dials.

"It's lively," Lee mumbled. "Go easy till you get the feel. She'll take off on you."

Pike discovered what he meant on the short lap down to the highway. The Corvette was too eager. Sting Ray was a good name. It swirled out from under him, and he had to hit the brake hard to keep from plowing into a truck passing on the highway.

"Told you," Lee muttered into his hands.

Pike drove cautiously then, staying in the right lane and keeping the car in second. He barely touched the accelerator, but the motor surged faster than he wanted to go. He was ready to quit when he came to the parking space of the Old Forge and rolled off the highway.

Lee struggled for a handkerchief in his hip pocket, scrubbed it hard across his face, and gently dabbed it at his eyes. He rolled it between his grimed hands and then let it drop to the floor between his feet.

"Mess," he said thickly. "Goddamn Angel. Why in hell do I get so hot about that bitch? Fucking gang-bang whore. Hundred guys wouldn't be enough for her. So why should I get sore when my good old buddy cuts himself a slice? That's a funny thing—what makes a guy sore. You know? What the hell am I mad about? That bitch fucks anything stiff enough to get it in."

62

"That's why you finked on me?" Pike didn't believe it, couldn't believe it, but something about Lee made him unsure.

"Joke, huh?" Lee almost sobbed. He lay a hand heavily on Pike's leg. "Really had the hots for that little bitch. Anything she wanted, just had to ask. Ask, hell. I used to go around looking for things she might like. Paid forty bucks for a scarf I saw in a window. Forty bucks for a scarf! About a yard of silk in crazy colors. Just because it looked like Angel. Real asshole I am, huh?" He shook his head in bewilderment. His hand clamped tightly on Pike's leg. "Sorry, Jon-boy. Really mean that. Must have been out of my fucking mind, do a thing like that."

Pike scowled at him. Lee was trying to please, to ingratiate himself. For what? It didn't make sense. A guy clouts you, one thing you can be sure of, he's no friend. So why try to be friendly afterward? He'd heard all that bullshit about how a good thumping fight is supposed to make two guys friends for life, but Pike didn't believe it for one goddamn minute. Any time he fought somebody, he was out to do some real damage. And win or lose, some of that murderous intent stayed with him from then on. Hell, the only reason to fight is because you hate the son of a bitch, right? So why in the hell would you want to be friends afterward? Bullshit.

But there was Lee staring at him with that dopey lost-dog face, trying to make his good old buddy understand how it was. He deserved what he got. Okay. So now they were square. Time to forgive and forget. Right, old buddy? It made Pike want to kick him.

"Let's get that drink," he said heavily.

Lee needed Pike's hand to get out of the car and his shoulder for balance, but he moved under his own power, wobbling a little. He let Pike open the door and then led the way toward the long dimly lighted bar. The Old Forge had been a good place once when the motels along the southern highway had been new and competitive, but in the last few years business had been moving north and east of Rincon, and now the Old Forge was overly large for its place and time, going shabby and beginning to smell of stale beer and the sick spew of wine-drunks.

"Double Old Granddad," Lee told the bartender. "That's what I feel like right now, an old granddad." He nudged Pike to make sure he got the joke and snickered to point it up.

"Beer," Pike said.

"Hell, you don't want to drink that slop," Lee said with an edge of his old style. "Give my buddy a double, too," he insisted. "On me, Jon-boy. On me. Drink up."

Pike shrugged. Hell, why not? He could use a solid drink. He took a long pull of the icy beer to clear his throat, then downed half the warm whiskey in one gulp.

Lee drained his glass and slid it toward the bartender. "Let's have another right away. On the rocks this time."

It was a good time of day for a drink and the Old Forge was doing a fair business. There was a free-standing fireplace in the big area behind the bar, a circular table around it, and deep low double seats, all of them occupied. A nice civilized murmur of cocktail-time voices, and a soft ripple of Mexican music riding over it.

"Fucking mariachis," Lee muttered. "Sound like a pack of goddamn Swiss yodelers." He picked some coins off the bar and moved very stiffly down toward the selector box. He punched it several times and came back grinning. "Tex Ritter, boy. 'Streets of Laredo.' Real music for a change."

Pike stared at him. Crazy son of a bitch. Who can figure him? He reached for the second drink and pushed the beer aside. That boiler-maker route was too rough. The whiskey was enough. Cracked ice had chilled the drink just right, and when the glass was empty, Pike sucked up a mouthful of tiny chips.

"Let's go get my bike," he said.

"No hurry, Jon-boy. I'll take you back. Let's just have another one. It's doing me a world of good, I'll tell you. Feel like a new man. Weak as a two-day-old baby, but all new." He snickered again, a wave of good feeling relaxing him, making him very cheerful now that he and his good old buddy were friends again.

Pike let the bartender make him another. Why not? He wasn't in any hurry; he just wanted to get the hell away from Lee Wallis. The guy was a shade too nutty for his taste. But the whiskey was good, the best. And Lee was paying.

"Drink up, Jon-boy."

Pike nodded. He lifted his glass, tilted it slightly, silently, toward Lee and drank up.

Pike came awake all at once, surging up from a tangle of sheets, sitting upright before his eyes were open. His naked chest was running sweat, his heart pounding fast and hard.

He couldn't remember the dream; he never could, but he could remember the panic. He rolled his tongue around in his dry mouth and tasted himself. The slow sick throb of a blistering headache began to pound behind his eyes.

That goddamn whiskey. Must have been more than a year since he'd

64

taken on that much. Grass is easier on you, better all round. Whiskey is a crazy man's high.

He was going to have a bad day, he knew. Red spots were forming and shifting in the air and the headache had a good grip now. He pushed himself to the edge of the bed and swung his feet out onto the cool linoleum and sat up slowly, carrying his head carefully in his hands.

He was wearing a tight pair of shorts that bound at the crotch and for some reason, some drunken reason, one rumpled sock on his left foot. He could see black jeans wadded on the floor near the bed. No sign of shirt or loafers.

He looked around warily, expecting the worst. He couldn't remember anything yet. It was too early. Later it would come to him in little flickers of memory, and by sundown he would have it all. That's how it usually worked. And coffee would help the process, speed it up a little. He batted a zooming fly away from his face, then noticed that his screen door was standing wide open, flat against the wall, its closing spring broken.

Pike pushed up from the bed, held to the footboard to steady himself, and reached out to shut the door. Through the dirty haze of wire mesh he could see his cranky old Harley lying on its side in the garden dust outside.

So I went back for it, did I? Glad I did something right last night. But why the hell did I bring it in through the gate? I'll bet I tore half the fence down getting it in.

He refused to think about it. Coffee, then a long shower, a shave, some clean clothes, all the routine civilized gestures. Then you'll be ready for it when you begin remembering what happened after that third drink. Or the fourth, or fifth, or however many you slopped down last night.

But he was not ready for it. He was sitting in a tired, aching slump, hands linked around his third cup of coffee, clean now, freshly dressed, shaved down to the blood, haggard and shaky and half sick. He was staring out at the canted wheel of his motorbike, knowing that he should get out there and prop it on its stand and then go see just what damage he had done with it last night.

He watched the two pairs of dusty pointed-toe boots that passed on either side of his bike and came toward the door. He watched them with no response, no intimation whatever. He looked up dully when Deputy Sheriff Malcolm pushed open the broken screen door and came in, followed by another man who looked much like him, same big hat, same badge and semi-uniform. Both of them were wearing gunbelts today, holsters empty. The guns were in their hands, pointing at Pike.

He listened to them, not believing anything they said, holding the coffee cup under his chin in both hands, elbows on the table, so they could see he was peaceful. But he wasn't yet remembering. Still too early. He'd had one little flash about staggering out of the motor maintenance area, pushing the bike and laughing like a wolf. Laughing why? Still too early for that.

But Deputy Malcolm could fill in the gaps. He was eager for the chance. Pike didn't argue with him. Pretty soon he would be remembering for himself and then he would give him an argument. Right now all he could do was listen, not believing a word of it.

"Murder," Malcolm said to him, voice harsh with restrained anger. "Brains pounded out of her head, face smashed till you couldn't recognize it."

Murder? Pike shook his head, setting off a blaze of pain. Wrong man, sheriff. Not me.

"Angela Morales," Malcolm said then, and his voice hit Pike with a sickening impact.

He stared at Malcolm, shocked into silence, suddenly frightened, belly knotting in icy lumps.

He couldn't find his loafers anywhere. They waited while he dug out his good shoes, the soft low-cut Italian moccasins, the last of the good things he had given himself during that last good time. Then they clamped handcuffs on him and took him away up through the bare neglected garden past Paca and the old woman who stood back at a safe distance. Out to the street, over the crazily broken sidewalk to the black sedan marked with the seal of Rincon County.

Pike took in a long slow breath just before they shoved him into the back seat.

III

---◄◉►---

COOL early morning wind boomed along the terraces of the house, clanking the pinned-back shutters, snapping the curtains at the open window of the room where Gordon Guthrie was sitting at a long worktable in a pool of brilliant light thrown by a wide, green-shaded overhead lamp. He was drafting a trial plan, the roughest sort of preliminary sketch, referring constantly to the long detailed statement that his client, Jonathan Pike, had made to the sheriff's investigators.

This was the best time of day for him, these two or three morning hours before the house was awake, when he was concentrating well, getting through a sizable workload without the distractions of telephones or office traffic.

He drew a light pencil stroke in the margin of the statement and leaned back in his chair to stretch, feeling tendons creak with the strain. He was a large, rough-looking man, awkwardly tall, with heavy sloping shoulders and very large hands and feet. He took in several deep lung-clearing breaths and bent forward to the table again. Another hour should see it in shape, he thought.

He was searching the statement for Pike's exact wording when the door opened noisily behind him. He did not even scowl as he looked up. Six o'clock. That would be Jumbo then.

"You got in late, Gordie." The voice in the darkness rasped with an early morning harshness. "You working too hard?"

"Not hard enough, Jumbo."

A chair scraped back along the rough floor tiles and settled facing his table. Then his father pushed a birdbath-sized mug of coffee toward him, shoving papers out of the way. Jumbo's coffee, fresh-roasted, fresh-ground, fresh-perked, with a sifting of sugar on top, served in hefty portions over an inch of dark Mexican rum. Gordon Guthrie had grown up on that brew, though the rum had not been added until after he had come home from the Army.

"Elena made a cake yesterday," the heavy voice said. "You miss it?"

"And everything else last night. All I wanted to see was that bed."

"Good cake. Birthday cake," he added with no emphasis.

"Oh, hell, Jumbo. I forgot all about it."

"Well, why not? It's your birthday. Nobody says you have to make a big thing out of it. I just figured a man's thirtieth calls for a drink or something. Kind of expected you."

Gordon sighed quietly. "Sorry. Didn't even think of it."

Jumbo reached to the floor and swung a heavy cowhide briefcase up to the table. He placed it precisely in the center of the circle of light. "Happy birthday," he said dryly.

"Well," Gordon said, trying to sound pleased. "Thanks, Jumbo. Thanks very much. It's a beauty."

It was a good piece, he could see. Heavy rich belting leather, darkly oiled, expertly stitched and mitered at the corners, solid brass fittings with a durable carrying handle that would take a lot of punishment. And a small pair of gold G's stamped under the lock. "Very fine stuff," he said, running a hand along the top. He lifted it to his lap, being careful not to disturb the arrangement of his papers.

Jumbo took his mug into the shadows and returned it after a noisy swig. He sat with his hands loosely around the mug, well inside the pattern of light.

Gordon looked at the hands, as he was meant to, at the seamed and wrinkled, horny, scarred flesh with the one little finger that would never bend stuck out now like the comically elegant finger of a tea drinker. Old Jumbo, his whole fighting, working life was there to be seen in those broken hands, permanently stained around the nails with heavy grease that came from Jumbo's work at Butler and Barlow's Premium Dairy where he was now foreman. Production manager, he liked to say, but he always laughed when he said it. His hands were witness to the mangling injuries that come to any heavily experienced professional working at his hard trade. He was the man who could coddle and coax and tease and bully the dairy's antiquated, obsolete boilers into complaining but dependable service, adjusting the tired and frazzled parts so that production never entirely broke down. Jumbo was proud of what his hands said about him and always scornful of any man whose hands carried no scars.

68

"Thirty years old," he said gloomily. "Man has to think about that. Nobody's going to live forever. When you thinking of getting married?"

Oh, Christ, Gordon groaned inwardly. Old Jumbo always thought he had been so very clever when he managed to work around to his favorite subject. "God knows," he said easily. "I'm too busy right now."

"Not too busy to go prancing around with those mean little dark girls out at the racetrack."

He probably meant the one with the long oily hair who followed the quarter-horse trials, Gordon figured out after a moment. She really was mean, too, knowing and vicious, expert, with strange interior muscles that drained a man to the bottom.

"She wasn't so very dark," he said easily. "More of a middle blonde. Anyway, she's gone with the racers."

"You still looking serious at that big-shottedy girl?"

Big-shottedy. That took a little work. A big shot to Jumbo was any man who willingly shaved more than twice a week. Big-shottedy girl. Who could that be? Claudia Farrall possibly. Daddy Farrall was about as big a shot as they came in Rincon.

"Her daddy doesn't like me," he said. "He's got big ideas for his little girl. Anyway she's too rich for my blood." But she's the one I'm going to marry, he promised himself. And screw Daddy and anyone else who didn't like it.

"Nothing wrong with your blood, boy," Jumbo said fiercely. "Maybe you wasn't raised fancy, but you was raised good. And your mother was as good blood as you'll find anywhere. She was a Breckinridge, she was, and there ain't no better blood than that."

"Didn't mean it that way, Jumbo," Gordon said with no heat. "Just that her daddy's rich and we don't exactly move in the same world."

"Her daddy's a goddamn crook. Ain't a two-bit real estate swindle in Rincon County but what he's got a finger in it."

Gordon grinned. "The Rincon *Record* wouldn't agree with you, Jumbo. Just last week they were calling Roger Farrall a 'farsighted real estate developer.' They seem to think he's a real asset to the community."

Jumbo made a hawking sound of disgust in his throat. "He's a crook," he said again. "So what are you going to do about the girl?"

Gordon took a limp sack of tobacco from the table, slipped a sheet of rice paper free of the pack. He crimped the paper lengthwise with three fingers, teased open the drawstring of the pouch, and sifted a small amount of tobacco into the trough. He was pleased to see that his fingers moved with no tremor, no sign of the rising irritation he was trying to control. Even Claudia didn't yet know of his plans for her, and he sure as

69

hell did not intend to spill it to Jumbo and have him spread it all over town. He flipped the paper tag of the string up to his mouth, caught it between his teeth, and drew the noose closed again.

"Well, I'll tell you, Jumbo," he said in a slow drawl. "I think maybe I'll just run her back into the bushes some dark night and see if she's got the kind of stuff I want in a wife."

Jumbo made a rough, strangled sound, then forced a thin chuckle. "You could do worse. You going to smoke that cigarette or you just going to sit there waggling it at me?"

Gordon scratched a match on the underside of the table and lit the skinny cigarette. Two puffs, one to light it and get a taste, then one long satisfying lung-filling drag, and he was finished with it. He dropped the butt in the ashtray before it could sting his fingers.

"Don't hardly seem worth the trouble," Jumbo muttered. He smacked his hands together decisively and got to his feet. "Looks like you still got quite a lot of work ahead of you. They finally letting you handle something by yourself?"

Gordon made a brief ugly sound. "Not a chance. I still have to carry that old bastard Delancy on my back."

"Goddamnit, son, you don't want to talk about your boss that way. He's famous man. Why, I heard stories about him—"

"He's worn-out old fart who should have retired years ago," Gordon said angrily. "I thought he was going to after he was so sick last winter. But no, back he came, gaunt as a dry-pastured horse and just about as much use. Jake Prinz still carries a good load and Billy Gaines pays his way by bringing in a pile of business, but old Delancy isn't worth a damn. He's going to get us all in a real mess someday."

"Jesus, boy!" Jumbo shouted. "I wish you wouldn't beller at me. I swear that big ugly voice of yours would knock down a brick wall. It makes my ears ache."

"Sorry," Gordon muttered. His enormous voice was a constant hazard. When he remembered, he could hold it to a decently muted volume, but sometimes it got away from him and he could see people wincing, almost in physical pain. Men often considered his voice a mark of aggression, a driving challenge that brought Gordon into contention more often than he intended.

"Just whisper," Jumbo growled. "I don't know how you can get along with people in that office if you blast away at them like that. You want to be careful. First thing you know you'll scare off all the songbirds. Well, time for me to be getting. You want to ride in with me?"

"No thanks, Jumbo. I phoned Nico Kronstadt. He's picking me up at the gate."

"Nico, huh? He's a good boy. You give him my regards. Be like old times, you two riding in together, I guess. When do you think you'll be getting your car back?"

"Hard to say. They'll tell me sometime today. They may have to send to El Monte for some parts."

"You really smashed the living hell out of that rear end. How in the world did you manage to do so much damage?"

"Goddamnit, Jumbo, how many times do I have to tell you?" He did not trouble to moderate his tone, just let the big voice soar angrily. "I did not wreck my car. It was that drunk cowboy tailgating me. He hung on my bumper for twenty miles, just playing games, roaring up close enough to give me a little bump, then dropping back and coming at me again. He had a souped-up T-bird and I couldn't run away from him. I just got tired of it. I picked my spot and hit the brake hard and he flared off like a duck, tried to swing out around me. He clipped my rear end, and we both went spinning off. But I got the flat desert and he got a good deep ditch. And that is one cowboy who is going to be watching how he drives from now on. After he gets out of the hospital."

Jumbo grinned at him, his flat harsh yellowish eyes lit with a meanly humorous glint. "Yes, sir, ever'body just better clear the way when Gordie Guthrie hits the road. Hell among the yearlings. Blood on the moon. Powder River."

Gordon shook his head slowly, feeling morose and seeing shadows in his mind and wishing he hadn't ever tried to explain anything to Jumbo. It always ended the same way.

He could vaguely see his father's large bulky outline moving away.

"Jumbo," he said abruptly.

"What you want, boy?"

"Just wanted to say thanks for my birthday present. It's exactly what I wanted."

Jumbo came back quickly, his broad red face thrusting down into the pool of light, spread now in a wide rosy grin. "Why, I'm just pleased, Gordie. I told that little feller at Jordan's Saddlery that I wanted the very best, but you never know." The smile stretched his mouth open, showing pungent strands of winesap tobacco he had tucked in his cheek to insulate himself from the sour-milk stench of the dairy. "I just hope it brings you good luck." He shook hands formally. "Happy birthday, son."

"Thanks, Jumbo. I'm sorry I missed the party."

"Nah, nah." Knotted hands batted impatiently at the air. "You got the right idea, Gordie. You just stay with it. Plenty of time to play when you get where you want to go."

Wherever that is, Gordon thought. He was used to Jumbo's abrupt changes of mood. Just at this moment he knew Jumbo would be remembering how proud he was of his lawyer son, how much he bragged of him down at the dairy. But that would wear off pretty soon and then they would be back to normal. "Okay, Jumbo," he said.

Gordon gave himself another hour in the quiet of his house, then stacked his notes tidily together and read through them once more. He had the sort of mind that could absorb a mass of detail and retain it with complete accuracy for short periods, never more than two weeks. A useful ability and one he had learned to trust. He ripped the ten legal-sized yellow sheets down the middle, wadded them and dropped them in the wastebasket. When he got to his office, he would dictate his trial outline in two or three uninterrupted hours and never need to check a single reference.

He packed the Pike statement and his blank notepads in his glossy new briefcase and went into the bathroom to shower and shave and make an official start to his day.

He crammed a necktie in the side pocket of his gray linen jacket, slung the jacket over his shoulder, and set off down the rocky footpath that led directly down the long slope of foothills to the gate and boundary fence of his father's homestead. People still tended to disbelieve him when he told them how Jumbo had taken up his full section, one square mile, under the homesteading act only thirty-some years ago. Homesteading sounded like something out of the dim dark dawn of pioneering times. Few people knew, or would even believe, that there was still plenty of land available, though most of what was left was worthless and almost inaccessible.

But Jumbo had lucked onto this pocket of the Great American Desert, found the not-very-deep but never-failing source of water up the bare talus slopes just twenty miles west of Rincon and then had sense enough to keep his mouth shut about it until he hired a lawyer to show him how to process his claim.

After he had brought in the water and dug the tanks to hold it, he had worked a full hard year, using local laborers he hired for a dollar a day, to build the house, the first he had ever owned. The roof-supporting vigas had been cut from the pine groves high in the mountain canyons, the adobes dug, mixed, shaped, and sun-dried in the open flats, kilns built to bake the *tejas* for roofing and floors and outer terraces. He had made a good house, wide and low and cool and graceful in the Spanish-Moorish tradition of the land.

Gordon balanced his loaded briefcase on top of a gatepost and swung up to the top rail of the fence and perched there as he had when he was a boy, waiting for Nico Kronstadt to stop by and give him a lift into school. He sat facing away from the road so that the bright morning sun was on his back. Looking up the slope, he could see Jumbo's house outlined on its high ground against the sky, looming massively like a ship cresting a wave.

This was the area the scientists called the upper *bajadas,* that wide strip bordering the base of the foothills. The earth is washed from the weathered mountains, loosely packed and full of stones. Not growing country, not ranching country, but the earth retains what little water it gets, holding enough of Rincon's ten annual inches of rain to give the saguaro and cholla and prickly pear and paloverde a livable atmosphere. Here the giant saguaro lived for centuries, grew as high as fifty feet, spreading wide shallow root structures just below the surface, seizing and keeping the rain as it fell, storing as much as two tons of water inside thick waxy green skins. They stood widely separated to give each a guaranteed source of water. Walking among them was not a wilderness scramble but a pleasant easy stroll through a desert park where every element is separately valued and given its rightful space.

Gordon rolled one of his toothpick cigarettes and hunched down comfortably on the fencerail, content and alert as a lizard on a warm stone. He could hear Nico Kronstadt coming a long way off. He was still driving that square-built, high-sided old station wagon made by the Checker Cab people, a durable gray-green monster the color of sagebrush after a sandstorm. It had a motor that developed twice the power the builders had intended, but it still looked and sounded like a rattling bucket of iron bolts. Gordon slid off the rail and took down his briefcase.

"Rincon Raiders ride again," Nico called from the open window. Gordon grinned, pleased to see him again and feeling much better for no reason at all.

They had been together for four years at Rincon State, both of them in prelaw, and for three of those years had been regulars on the football team that called itself the Rincon Raiders. Gordon "Go-Go" Guthrie, the big ungainly pass-catching end whose huge hands could smother a football. Nico Kronstadt, speedy, shifty running back, explosive on a broken field. They had probably not been as good as they thought they were but plenty good enough for the small-college competition of their league.

Gordon went around to the passenger's seat, tilted the adjustable back, and ran the seat back as far as it would go.

"Drive." Gordon flipped a lordly hand.

73

"As you say, sir." Nico backed expertly to the gate, reversed direction, and headed back along the scraped-earth township road. Half a mile ahead he picked up the graveled county road at Puma Canyon and from there was able to drive a little faster.

"Nothing changes out here, does it? This road's as bad as it was ten years ago."

"No money out this way, just us poor homesteaders," Gordon said lightly. "Now you could do something about that, Nico. Have one of your rich uncles tell the county commissioners to get some paving crews working on this side of town."

Nico made a slight sound in his throat and frowned at the rutted roadway, making it clear that he was too busy driving to answer. He always shied away when anyone began talking about money.

Nico was the rich boy of the world Gordon Guthrie had grown up in. Officially he was Nicanor Davila de Merida Kronstadt, one of the forty or fifty living descendants of Red Axel Kronstadt who had been one of the legendary figures of the old territory. According to the stories, Red Axel had stood seven feet tall, three hundred pounds of limber gristle, with bristling hair and beard as bright as a burning bush. He had drifted down to the desert country first with the fur-trapping mountain men on a trading expedition and later returned as a teamster when the northern beaver had played out. He made a lot of money hauling supplies and equipment for the mines and set himself up in fine style, and later married the daughter and heiress of the Conde de Merida, holder of Alta Loma, one of the sizable Spanish land grants. Red Axel had sired a baker's dozen of sons and not one of them had looked anything like him. All were small by comparison, barely six feet; all were dark, slim and quick, and unmistakably Spanish. And, four generations later, Nico was holding to the pattern. In spite of the Baltic name, he was entirely a Davila de Merida, slender and graceful as they all were. Alta Loma was still theirs but swallowed now inside the huge Crown Ranch that took up most of Alta Loma County and a good stretch south into Davila County. It was the southern part that had Mount Kronstadt six thousand feet above the desert floor and almost solidly copper. That was home base for the Crown Copper Company, the parent unit for Corona International which leased and operated the South American mines that now brought in most of the Kronstadt money. Of course Nico was not the sole heir to all that, but even after splitting with fifty others, he would still have enough to give the tax people warm little tingles whenever they thought of him.

The money troubled him and he tried not to think or talk about it, and very little in his life-style suggested that he was not living on his salary alone. Even in college he had been careful not to let the money show. He liked living out at the family ranch, and that meant he had to commute almost sixty miles into Rincon every day, but he never drove a car that looked expensive.

Thinking back, Gordon could see that the years at Rincon State must have been a constant trial for Nico. The family wanted him brought up as a local boy, familiar and comfortable with the normal life of Rincon. But he had probably had a lot more fun when he went on to Harvard Law where he could spread out a little bit without anyone noticing. Gordon often wondered why he had come back to Rincon after that. He had been one of the editors of the Law Review, so he would have been offered some good spots in the big Eastern law shops where he could now be working on important projects instead of hacking around as a junior associate at Kellogg and Sampson.

For a time after he came back to Rincon, Nico had been one of the bright young men in the county attorney's office, full of zeal and a youthful determination to make the law function better and more simply than it ever had before. Inevitably, it seemed, he would become county attorney, then run for governor, and after that, who could say? There were few limitations for Nicanor Davila de Merida Kronstadt. But something went sour and after a year he left the county attorney for private practice. All he would say was, "Prosecution just doesn't seem to be my area of the law."

Gordon wondered if Kellogg and Sampson came closer to what Nico was looking for. It didn't seem likely and Gordon could not understand why he stayed with it. Given Nico's background and his backing, Gordon knew he would never have wasted ten minutes working in Rincon.

"What have you been doing lately, anything interesting?"

Nico shook his head, half smiling. "What a question," he said, almost sighing. "Yes, of course it's interesting. But essentially, contract law is precision nit-picking. It has its dull moments. Maybe I should switch over to litigation and get in on some of the action."

"It's just the county attorney's office in reverse, Nico. You wouldn't like it any better. Anyway, only low types like me get involved with criminal law. No, you stay where the big money is. Only the really bright boys get invited to work on contracts."

"Come on now, Gordie," Nico said sharply. "Why are you always playing this hick-town gallus-snapper bit? You edited your Law Review. I was only one of thirty others at Harvard. So how did you get so stupid all of a sudden?"

"Worlds of difference between Harvard and Rincon State."

75

"Not that much. You had your pick of jobs. Why did you take Gaines, Prinz and Delancy? Why did you decide to specialize in litigation? Nobody pushed you. You could have had any job you wanted."

"No," Gordon said flatly. Old Nico was sometimes not very bright. Gordon Guthrie could get a job all right; any new young lawyer with a good law school record is going to be offered work, particularly if he has shown that he can carry a load. But Nicanor Davila de Merida Kronstadt is something else. Potentially he is money in the bank for any law firm that takes him on. Corona International covers some two hundred separate corporations and from time to time every one of them needs legal advice. You think some of that business isn't going to gravitate to Nico's law firm? That meant a nice increase in profits for Kellogg and Sampson, and they were probably feeling grateful enough to make Nico a full partner long before his turn would normally come due.

"You downgrade yourself, Gordie," Nico said seriously, glancing at him quickly. "If you really want to move over to contracts, you can come with me right now. Kellogg and Sampson would jump at the chance to get you."

"Forget it," Gordon said promptly. "I was just bitching. No, trial law is my meat. That's why I went for Gaines, Prinz—because they had the right spot open and I thought they'd give me a crack at something good right away." He sighed heavily. "What a mistake that was. I didn't know old Delancy was going to hang onto every decent case. He insists on handling it all himself, but he can't—or won't—work on the preparation. He's screwed up two of my cases in the past six months, two I'd worked damn hard on. But it's too late to make a move now. I've got too much time invested."

Nico turned with a serious frown. "Haven't you ever thought of going out on your own?"

Gordon snorted. "Of course I've thought of it. Who doesn't think about it? But I've sort of drifted into a bad habit. I'm used to eating three meals a day. No, I couldn't swing it on my own. I'm not well enough known to pull in the business."

"You might think of moving over to the county attorney's office for a few years," Nico said, trying to be helpful.

"That's another dead end. You know damn well how Dave Burrell grabs off all the good stuff for himself. He's the original career-prosecutor. He handles everything that makes a headline. I could work there ten years and I'd still be a full-time nobody. I'm better off where I am. And anyway, I'm no politician. It's all I can do to get along with my friends, and sometimes I don't get along too well with them."

"A true statement," Nico said soberly. "Just what I tell everybody. That Gordie Guthrie is one rough, tough, mean son of a bitch."

"You know it, Nico. Maybe I should have stayed in the Army. I probably hit my peak as a drill sergeant. Missed my big chance. I had everything going for me. And nobody ever asked me to lower my voice. They liked hearing me bellow."

Nico chuckled quietly.

Gordon stretched and rolled his head on the backrest to look at Nico. "I'm getting stale," he complained. "Old Delancy has been riding me pretty hard. What say we take a day off and go fishing?"

Nico snorted. "I'm locked in tight for a month."

"Have to figure something," Gordon said. "Have you seen Claudia lately?"

Nico's eyes flickered from the road to Gordon for a swift second. His answer took a little longer. "Last night, as a matter of fact," he said. "Family dinner sort of thing. She looked fine. Great. As usual."

"As usual." Gordon lay back, enjoying the thought.

Nico slowed gradually for the turn off the unimproved gravel road onto the state highway heading toward Rincon. He ran straight across the intersection toward a circular drive-in restaurant at the junction.

"Let's get some coffee. We've got time. And I have to hit the john for a minute."

Gordon sat irritably at the counter staring down at a cup of weak coffee he did not want. He made it a habit to be the first man in the office every morning. He liked that solitary half hour or so when he could read his morning paper in peace and get his day organized. But Nico, of course, would be used to wandering in at any reasonable hour. Nobody would ever be pushing him or wondering if he was carrying enough weight.

He got up abruptly and went out to the car and pulled his gray linen jacket out through the open window. He smoothed his crumpled necktie and half stooped to use the side mirror to get the knot in place. He put on the jacket, brushed his hands down the front to knock out the creases, and went back inside, ducking his head just in time to miss the doorframe.

He was just too damn big, that's all there was to it. The world was organized for people half a foot shorter. For Gordon, nothing was comfortable. Beds were too short; the relationship between desk and chair was never right; clothes, even the most routine clothes, had to be custom-made. It wouldn't be so bad, he thought, looking at his reflection in the shiny chrome of the coffee urn, if he was handsome. But he really did look like a drill sergeant, and not the kind of sergeant who is going to become an officer either.

It was seeing Nico again that did it, roused up the old competitive thing that had always been between them. Whatever Nico wore was, instinctively, inevitably, the right thing to wear. And whatever Nico did, he was never going to have to worry about failure. He had too much going for him in every area. Just looking at him made Gordon realize how far he still was from the goals he had set for himself in law school.

He scooped up an abandoned coffee-stained copy of the Rincon *Record* and spread it out on the counter. He rolled one of his matchstick cigarettes, bending low over the counter, elbows on his knees. He skimmed the headlines and found the item he wanted. A four-column box below the fold was headed, EARLY DATE SET FOR "ANGEL" MURDER TRIAL. It carried a chin-up determined picture of David Calder Burrell, Rincon's county attorney. Little David, Gordon thought sourly. He was announcing the news, a little late as usual, that James Oliver Delancy, Esq., partner in the celebrated law firm of Gaines, Prinz and Delancy, had accepted the court's appointment as defense attorney for Jonathan R. Pike, twenty-three, young dropout drifter accused of the rape-murder of Angela Morales, fifteen, in the picnic groves of El Pinar on Tuesday night, May 25. Mr. Delancy had agreed that an early date for trial would be set after he had an opportunity to review the case.

Review the case, Gordon said to himself with a wry twist of humor. For James Oliver Delancy, Esq., you can read Gordon Breckinridge Guthrie, Esq., and you'll be a little closer to the facts of that review.

"The 'Angel' case?" Nico said, reading over Gordon's shoulder. "Are you working on that one, Gordie?"

"It's all mine. Except for what little Mr. Delancy may want to handle."

"I wondered who would get it. I knew Gene Salazar had it originally, but he told me last week he was withdrawing."

"Well, he stayed on it long enough to collect a fee, and that's more than we'll ever see. Pike's ex-boss hired Salazar, but he quit the case. He had it all fixed for Pike to cop a plea, and when Pike told him to shove it, smart little Gene pulled out."

"A plea? Dave Burrell offered a plea?"

Gordon turned to look at him. "Well, maybe he didn't exactly offer a plea, maybe he had to be talked into it. But I'll bet the talking didn't take ten minutes. A plea is always better than a trial. No case is ever so good that you can be absolutely sure of winning it."

"Yes, sir," Nico said mildly.

78

"Laying down the gospel, was I?" Gordon lifted one hand and shrugged in apology.

"I was surprised. I would have thought Dave had an airtight case. Didn't he take a confession from Pike?"

"No. What he got was a statement," Gordon said. "Unsigned. But useful. And he can establish a long line of circumstantial evidence. Also, Pike was fool enough to lie eighty different ways at the beginning of the interrogation. No, Little David has a good case, but he would still be smart to let Pike plead guilty to second-degree and take a life sentence."

"But it was an atrocious crime and Pike is clearly guilty." Nico colored slightly, realizing what he had said, and hurried to cover it. "I mean to say, don't you think he's guilty?"

Gordon shook his head sadly.

"The man hasn't been tried yet. How can you say he's guilty?"

Nico turned to signal the waitress and order a cup of coffee. When he looked at Gordon again, he let out a small soft sigh.

"I was forgetting, wasn't I?" he said very quietly. "It is very easy to forget presumption of innocence in a case like this. I was thinking of what he did—of what was done—to that fifteen-year-old girl, and all of a sudden I don't want to hear anything more about the killer's legal rights. I just want to see him punished. An eye for an eye. The Old Testament is still a powerful influence, isn't it?"

Gordon shrugged. "A lot of people feel that way. Sometimes I think they may be right. And sometimes I know they are wrong as hell."

"Sad," Nico murmured. "All that law school training and I still haven't learned to keep my feelings to myself. Not yet. I'm not at all sure I could defend a man unless I was completely sure he was innocent. I don't see how you can. Unless"—he swung sharply back to Gordon, struck with a new thought—"unless you believe Pike *is* innocent?"

Gordon dropped his cigarette and scrubbed at it with his shoe. "I don't think in those terms, Nico. It's a waste of time. According to our statutes, there are thirteen grounds for justifying homicide. Thirteen. But how many people know that? Most people charged with a crime don't know enough about the law to tell me whether they are guilty or not. They simply don't know. So I don't ask. It's my job to defend my client. I'm not asked to judge him. What's more, I'm not allowed to judge him. That's for the jury."

"But—" Nico hesitated. "Oh, hell. You're right, of course, Gordie. I was overstating. But it's going to be tough for you this time. You've got a bad case and a bad client, and I think you know it. I was having lunch with Gene Salazar when he was still representing Pike and he was just shaking his head. He said Pike was a strange one, couldn't figure him. Sharp enough, understood everything Gene was telling him, but he didn't seem worried enough. Unnatural self-control. Closed in on himself. Gene said he never could get through to him. Now what can you do with a client like that?"

Gordon grunted into his cup.

"Worst of all, Gene seemed to feel there was a clear pattern of violence in Pike's background. Usually that sort of sociological jargon leaves me fairly cold, but if Gene is right, then you may have some real trouble ahead."

"Not because of his background," Gordon said flatly. "The remote past is not evidence. Anyway, plenty of ugly customers manage to get through their lives without killing young girls. No, David's got plenty of evidence against Pike without digging into his past."

"Doesn't it worry you at all, Gordie?"

"Frankly, I'm a hell of a lot more worried about Delancy. An uncooperative client with a bad reputation isn't going to be half as much trouble as a tired old man who won't work hard enough. I can handle Pike. He doesn't worry me a bit. It's Delancy I'm scared of."

Nico made a noncommittal sound and picked up his cup.

"Gulp it down, Nico," Gordon said impatiently. "I want to get to the office some time before noon."

He had filled four belts of the dictating machine, briefly sketching the details of the prosecution's case against Jonathan Pike, then outlining a proposed trial plan, emphasizing the weak points, identifying the areas for effective rebuttal, suggesting targets of opportunity where the prosecutor's assumptions might be effectively challenged.

It was ten o'clock now, the magic hour at Gaines, Prinz and Delancy when it was possible to find a senior partner at his desk. Gordon scooped the four plastic belts into an envelope and dropped them off at the typists' room as he went down the long echoing linoleum-floored corridor toward officers' country.

He passed through double swinging doors padded in red leather and studded with patterns of bright brass nailheads. Then he was moving silently over thick nubbly neutral-gray carpeting along a hallway painted a soft silvery gray and hung with black-framed prints of courtroom scenes by Daumier and Hogarth and the anonymous satirists published by *Spy*.

Gordon's office was an eight-by-twelve cubicle that contained a simple steel desk, one comfortable chair that he had bought for himself, an open bookcase, and one extra straight chair that was seldom used. Junior associates did not require space for visitors. Where he was now, in the domain of junior and senior partners, a great deal of money and thought had been invested to create an atmosphere of aristocratic but austere dignity, not a sense of reckless luxury, merely the discreet and appreciative use of the very best materials and design. Clients were expected to know without being told that the sort of people who worked in such an atmosphere required, and deserved, exceptional fees.

James Oliver Delancy, as founder and senior partner, needed a suite of offices large enough and furnished suitably to reflect his position and responsibilities. As the partner directing the bulk of the trial work, he needed space enough in his office to accommodate the very sizable numbers of people involved in complex trials. And because of the volume of that traffic, his office entrance was situated nearest to the small elegant reception hall.

Gordon passed through the door to Delancy's outer office. There were flowers; the walls were hung with pictures of Mr. James Oliver Delancy, showing him on intimate terms with notable types whose faces were all familiar. The magazines on the low tables near the long brocade couch were the lighthearted sort a client could riffle without distraction. Gordon always felt awkward here, as if he had stumbled accidentally into a room reserved for expectant mothers.

He waited silently in front of Miss Madeline Dorelli's desk until she put down her busy pen and looked up. Miss Dorelli was entirely a devoted and concentrated legal secretary, making as much money as Gordon, and earning it.

"Do you have Mr. Delancy's daybook there, Miss Dorelli? Can you tell me when he's got me scheduled today?"

Miss Dorelli eyed him over the rim of her half-glasses. "But you are not in the book today, Mr. Guthrie."

"Hell," Gordon muttered. Delancy probably forgot all about it. "We're defending Jonathan Pike," he explained carefully. "Maybe Mr. Delancy didn't mention it. I've dictated a report he will be getting later this morning, and then I imagine he'll want to see me, so maybe you can find me some free time somewhere."

Miss Dorelli was guardian of Mr. Delancy's tightly scheduled and expensive time. Something more than Gordon's matter-of-fact explanation would be needed before she shook up the schedule.

"I doubt if there will be any free time today, Mr. Guthrie."

Gordon drew in a long slow breath and spoke very quietly. "I think Mr. Delancy will want to make time. He gave me the case yesterday and asked for a preliminary report as soon as possible. I saw Pike for a few minutes last night and I'm going down now to talk to him again. I'll be back around noon. Or if Mr. Delancy wants me sooner, you can reach me through the sheriff's office. You have the number?"

"I can find it, Mr. Guthrie," she said, picking up her pen, "if I need it."

"Thank you." Gordon backed out, feeling the flare of that old useless, tiring anger.

Since he was near the reception room he went out through the front entrance rather than the steel fire door that was handier for the associates' wing. From here he could ride the express elevator and get down twenty-three stories to the street much faster, and right now he wanted to get out of the Gaines, Prinz office fast, before he said something very rude to somebody. But even in his vile mood, a portion of his mind noted that there was a new girl on the reception desk. Showgirl type, as they all were, this one long and lithe and palely blonde, hair like a metal cap under the soft overhead light. Investigate, he told himself. Or maybe not. Maybe not—maybe it's time for Claudia.

He went along the wide palm-lined streets in a better humor now, moving through a thin scattering of morning shoppers. The sun was bright and its sharp unrelieved light broke in reflected dazzles from display windows and plastic storefronts and the tiny flecks of mica embedded in the sidewalks. He stopped for the light at the corner, waited until the WALK sign clicked on and crossed diagonally when the traffic stopped at all four corners.

He was in cool shadow now, going along a narrow passage that had once, in Rincon's earliest days when it had been a small Spanish presidio known as San Marcos del Pueblito de Rincón, been a main thoroughfare. It led toward what had been the Plaza de las Armas where an understaffed Spanish garrison had once paraded. Now the town is called simply Rincon and the Plaza is Courthouse Square. It was elevated slightly above the surrounding streets and almost completely filled by the low simple white building designed in the classic Spanish-Moorish pattern as a hollow defensive square, the sections at front and rear rising four stories and the connecting units just two stories. Gordon went up the slight slope, in through the arcade entrance to a narrow colonnade that ran along the inside walls. Tiled walkways radiated from a central pool and fountain. It was always cool here, even on the most scalding days, and the stone benches of the garden were favorite spots for outdoor lunching.

The courthouse was much too small for the county's expanding business. Most of the departments had been shifted to across the street to a new office building that was much like every other office building in town. But the courts, the judges, the county attorney, and the sheriff had all managed to hang on in the old courthouse, fitting themselves in somehow, although the sheriff had to move his jailhouse to larger quarters on the top floors of the new building. His headquarters, his communications center, records and interrogation rooms, were still in the courthouse. So was a small block of six cells used mostly to house prisoners during trial. That was where Jonathan Pike was now, because the prisoners in the new jailhouse had taken a high moral stance against murdering rapists and had damn near rioted. Pike might have been lynched, the sheriff said, if he had been left there overnight.

Gordon went around the long way through the narrow shaded colonnade, heading toward the far front corner where an oil-stained cement ramp led down to the rear entrance of the old jailhouse.

He pushed open the door into the small lawyer's room but stayed where he was in the hallway, waiting for Pike to come up to him. In the poor jailhouse light Pike was a dim figure in the narrow corridor, walking with a slight list because the thick squat deputy escorting him had a hand wedged high under his left armpit, holding Pike just a little off-balance so that he would never have a chance to grab for the pistol that swung loosely under the deputy's arm.

"Are you Mr. Guthrie?" the deputy asked. Then, before Gordon could answer, he said, "Sure you are," in a brisk, positive voice. "Recognize you now. Go-Go Guthrie, right? Won a couple bets on you when you were playing ball. Going to be representing this young man, are you?"

"Probably." Gordon took the deputy's outstretched hand and, just at the last possible moment, remembered his name. He was Archie Romeral, Rincon's near-famous bowling champion, a powerful low-slung man with a square dark brooding face like an Aztec idol. "Nice to see you again, Archie."

"Pleasure, counselor." Romeral edged Pike in through the open door and let him go. "I'll be just outside. Knock when you want out." He closed the door and rattled the knob to make sure the door was locked.

"Have a seat, Pike." Gordon went around the long steel table and took one of the hard straight chairs at the end. "We didn't have time for much more than hello–good-bye yesterday, but we can cover some ground today."

Pike sat warily, stiffly upright, using only the outer edge of the seat. He was fresh from a hot shower, skin pink and slightly moist, hair still damp and holding the toothmarks of the comb. He smelled of strong soap and the harsh sort of disinfectant used in the jail. He folded his arms and looked at Gordon.

Handsome kid, Gordon thought, studying him silently. Well-built, too. Carries himself like a man in good shape. Hardly the sort who would have to use muscle to score with the girls. But you never know.

He said easily, "My name's Guthrie, in case you've forgotten. Gordon Guthrie. You're Jonathan Pike, but I don't suppose anyone calls you Jonathan, do they? What is it? Jon? Jonnie?" Pike shrugged, his face showing no response. "Jon is all right. Or Pike. It doesn't matter."

"The lawyer the court appointed to defend you is James Oliver Delancy. I'm one of his assistants. Our firm is called Gaines, Prinz and Delancy."

"Okay," Pike said. He did not add "So what?" but it was implied.

"My job is to help Mr. Delancy prepare your case for trial. We'll be spending a lot of time together, so we might as well get acquainted."

"Why?"

Gordon looked at him for a long quiet moment. At least the kid isn't scared, or stupid. He shoved his chair back and turned away so he could cross his legs. He brought out his flattened sack of tobacco and slipped a sheet of rice paper from the folder. He watched closely what he was doing, though he could have rolled a cigarette in the dark.

"No special reason," he said with a slow strained patience. "We don't have to be friends. It doesn't make much difference to our problem, but Mr. Delancy and I already have enough enemies on the other side, all the prosecution people. It makes it easier if all of us on this side are on good terms, but it isn't actually necessary. Have it any way you like."

"I didn't mean to be hard-nosed about it," Pike said slowly. He put his hands down flat on the table and shifted back in the chair. "I was just thinking about that first lawyer who came to see me. Salazar. He spent a lot of time playing buddy-buddy. Until I told him I wasn't going to cop a plea. Then he wrote me off fast."

"I don't know anything about that." Gordon licked his cigarette, hung it in a corner of his mouth, and brought out a pack of matches. He struck one and held it in midair. "Sorry. Didn't think to ask you. Don't suppose you want one of these?" He nudged the tobacco sack toward Pike before he lit his cigarette.

"Thanks. I don't smoke."

Gordon finished the cigarette as quickly as always and dropped the butt on the floor. "Don't smoke," he repeated with a quiet emphasis. "Tobacco, you mean?"

Pike looked at him tightly, openly suspicious now. He leaned back in his chair, head tilted, one eyebrow cocked.

84

"They found that bag of pot hanging in the trees." Gordon spoke with a slow forceful calm, driving it home. "Didn't you know?"

"I don't know anything. They won't let me see the papers in here. I don't know anything about bags of pot—in trees or anywhere else."

Gordon let out a gusty sigh. "This won't get us anywhere, Pike. We'd better set up some ground rules before we go any further. You don't have to tell me anything. You can sit there and ignore my questions, if that's what you want to do. But one thing you'd better get through your head. I mean right inside where you live. Don't lie to me. That's all. Tell me, don't tell me. That's up to you. But don't try to bullshit me."

Pike lifted one hand and let it drop in a quick contemptuous gesture.

"Personally I don't give a shit how you handle it," Gordon went on, an edge of anger in his heavy voice. "Lie as much as you want, if that's how you get your jollies. But this is a fact—a hard fact—if you let Mr. Delancy go into that courtroom with a defense plan based on lies that the county attorney can shoot down, can actually prove to be lies by solid evidence the jury will believe, then you are committing suicide. Is that plain enough for you? Do you understand what I'm telling you?"

"You're clear," Pike said calmly.

"So let's try again. We were talking about a bag of marijuana. Tell me or don't tell me. But if you say a word, make it the truth."

Pike's face was blank, masklike. He stared at Gordon silently, considering his answer. Then he shrugged and said, "It's mine."

"Okay. It's nice of you to say so. There just happen to be four good sets of fingerprints—yours—on that plastic bag. Still it's nice to know you're leveling with me about something." Gordon smiled at him, but his smile was hard, not friendly.

"You're a sarcastic son of a bitch." Pike's eyes were the colorless gray of spring water. They reflected shading but had none of their own. He spoke through lips that barely moved.

"How we get along," Gordon said harshly, "is entirely up to you. I told you that. You're the client. You set the tone of this relationship. Except for one thing. You are not going to turn that tongue on me, sonny. You remember that. Unless you want to walk away with a fat lip."

Pike's eyes flared wide in quick response. He measured Gordon carefully, gauging height and weight, guessing at his readiness to follow through. Slowly he nodded, and for the first time there was no hint of mockery in his expression. "You really lay it right out there on the table, don't you?"

"I'm here to prepare your case for trial. Now tell me what you want. Do we go on shadowboxing, or can we settle down to some work?"

"Let's try working." Pike almost smiled.

"Okay. Here's the first question. The obvious one. Did you kill Angela Morales?"

"No."

Gordon's head snapped up quickly. He didn't try to hide his surprise. "I warned you—"

"I'm not lying," Pike said flatly. "I didn't kill her."

"You told the investigators you hit her several times."

"But I didn't kill her. She was still alive when I left her at El Pinar."

Gordon scrubbed a hand across his forehead, pinched at the bridge of his nose hard enough to bring tears. "I'm going to say it just once more. After that, you're on your own. Don't lie to me, Pike. If I ask a question you don't want to answer, just say so. But don't lie."

"No, I won't lie to you, Mr. Guthrie. I did not kill Angela Morales. Killing is stupid. I'm not stupid."

Pike said this with absolute conviction, Gordon felt, as if he believed it. For a moment Gordon was ready to believe it too.

"Okay, let's move on. I've read through the sheriff's transcript. You made a lot of confused and contradictory statements during your interrogation."

"Lies," Pike admitted. "Mostly they were lies."

"Okay. The sheriff expects people to lie to him. That's why he takes you over and over your story until he gets a version he likes. But what about the final statement?"

"It's mostly the straight stuff. I left out a few things."

"Good enough. Later on we'll be going over it word for word. Right now let's just hit the high spots. Two points bother me. First, you did go back to that grove in El Pinar, didn't you?"

"Yes, somewhere around three o'clock, I think. To find my shoes."

"Shoes? What happened to your shoes?"

"I don't know. I couldn't find them anywhere. That's why I went back."

"And the murder weapon? Where did that come from?"

Pike shook his head. "I couldn't tell you, Mr. Guthrie. I don't even know what it was."

Gordon stared in obvious bewilderment. "You don't know—"

"Nobody ever told me. They just said the girl was dead, beaten to death, they said, and torn apart inside some way."

"It was all in the papers," Gordon said, his voice carrying a clear note of warning. "I saw at least three different pictures of it."

"They won't let me see any papers in here," Pike reminded him. "Even that guy Salazar wouldn't bring me any."

"Forget Salazar. He's out of this case. Angela Morales was beaten to death with the butt of a heavy-duty screwdriver. It was a little more than a foot long, black friction tape wrapped around the handle. Does that sound like anything you know?"

It was a long moment before Pike said, "Why didn't they tell me?" in a quiet wondering tone.

"You recognize it?"

"I think so. It could be one from the garage where I worked."

"Cordero's? That's not a garage."

"No, but they have a pretty big motor-maintenance section. That's where the screwdriver came from, I think."

"Think? You don't know?"

"No, I can't be sure it's the same one. I don't remember what happened to it after—" Pike let his words drift away to silence. He swung his head toward Gordon in a quick, decisive movement. "I'd better tell you how it went. I didn't even know they meant the screwdriver when they were questioning me. Somehow I got the idea she was killed with a rock."

"Apparently a rock was used too. But afterward. The medical examiner says the screwdriver was the murder weapon." Gordon made another cigarette, taking a moment to think. "Okay, let's go over the whole thing. Keep it simple. We'll have plenty of time later for the details."

"I can't figure that screwdriver, Mr. Guthrie. I don't remember what happened to it. I had a kind of fight with Lee Wallis—" He broke off abruptly. "You know who Lee Wallis is?" When Gordon nodded, he went on. "Lee's got a little reach on me and a lot of heft, all those goddamn mail-order muscles, and he can be a mean bastard, so I didn't want to take any chances he'd get his hands on me. That's why I picked up the screwdriver. Just in case. Turned out I didn't need it. I belted Lee solid a couple of times before he could get set and that was it. Lee got sick and chickened out. He was puking his guts up. I had to help him walk over to his car. Later on I drove him down to the Old Forge for a drink, and I guess somewhere along the line I got rid of the screwdriver. I can't remember."

"This is the same night?"

"Same night. We'd just got back from Mexico. After the fight Lee was feeling sick and he slugged down double bourbons awful fast. He was putting on the big buddy act and setting them up for me. Let bygones be bygones, all that crap. After a while it got pretty drunk in there."

"You're not going to tell me you don't remember what happened because you were too drunk?"

"I'm trying to tell you the truth, Mr. Guthrie," Pike said quietly. "I'm still a little hazy on some points, but I've got most of it clear in my mind. Took me a while before I remembered. The sheriff's people were pounding on me pretty hard, and I had a hell of a hangover and I couldn't get my head working. But later on I got it straight."

"How did it go?"

"Well, we hung around the Old Forge for quite a while. And then we headed down to Biggie's Bonusburger for some food. Lee picked up a bottle of Jim Beam at the package store next door, and by the time we were finished eating we were in the bag pretty far. That's when Lee got the big bright notion about Angel. We were going to pick her up and teach her a lesson. Lee was very strong on giving her a good lesson, he said."

"What kind of lesson?"

"Lee was really pissed off, you know? That's what the fight was about earlier. He knew Angel was putting out all over town, but he got mean as a snake about her giving me a piece."

"I'm not following you very well," Gordon complained.

"Well, by God, it does sound sort of funny when you think about it. There is Lee ready to cut off my balls because I took a hack at Angel, and after I belt him a couple, he's all over me, slobbering about what great death-defying buddies we are. Buys me more drinks than a sane man would want, and then gets this wild notion to pick up Angel and take her out to some quiet place and give her the word." He glanced at Gordon, suddenly cautious. "I must have been out of my fucking mind. I didn't even like the bitch. I knew what she was like. A real ball-breaker with a mean streak as wide as Lee's."

Gordon could hear the convincing note of truth in Pike's voice. He could believe Pike had not liked the girl. He was not yet ready to believe he hadn't killed her.

"The girl's dead," he said coldly. "I hope you haven't been talking about her like that to anyone else."

Pike looked at him scornfully, not quite sneering. "I told you, Mr. Guthrie. I'm not stupid."

"You were that night."

Pike nodded. "Okay." No argument.

"Let's get on. You went to pick up the girl. Then what?"

"Lee had this tricky way of letting her know he was outside waiting for her. He'd drift by and turn around in the driveway across the street and flash his headlights up and down three times and then drive around the corner and park until Angel made up some excuse or just ducked out the back door when no one was looking."

"Well, that answers one of my questions," Gordon said. "So it could not have been a prearranged meeting."

"Just spur of the moment. But Lee had the signaling arrangement all set. He used it a lot, I think."

"Then what? You took her out to El Pinar?"

"Finally, yeah. But I'd left my bike at Cordero's and we went there first to pick it up. Angel raised hell about that." Pike smiled thinly, remembering. "There was a pretty big night crew working and Angel was afraid somebody would recognize her, so she scrooched down in the Sting Ray, back behind those bucket seats. Don't know how in hell she managed. Afterward, I trailed them out and Lee headed for El Pinar."

"And Angel came willingly?"

"Sure. Hell, she was a hot little kid, always willing."

"Why El Pinar? That was a hell of a long drive."

"Yes, but that's what Lee wanted. He knew I'd laid her out there once after a picnic, so that's where he wanted to take her for the big lesson."

"And you went along with all this?"

"Yeah," Pike said in a wondering tone. "Went along, hell! Why try to dress it up? I was just as hot as Lee. And skunk-drunk. When you were in the mood for it, that Angel was a choice cut. You just look at her and your balls start dancing a jig."

"So you gave Angel the message. How did she take it?"

"Bad. Very bad. She didn't want any part of it. Kept saying she'd tell her old man. I remember that all right. She must have said it a million times. Her goddamn old man. She had to be worked over pretty good before she'd shut up about him."

"Who worked her over?"

Pike shrugged. "I'm not holding out on you, Mr. Guthrie. That part of it is still vague. I remember Lee swung in and parked in a big grove. He socked her one just as I was coming up on my bike. Angel jumped out of the car and tried to run. I had to chase her a hell of a way. I hit her then, I know. But I didn't really want to hurt her and I don't think I did. She squirmed around quite a bit, yelling at me and trying to kick me. So I had to quiet her down. When she was quiet, I ripped off her pants and put the boots to her right where she was."

"Let's clarify that one," Gordon said quickly. "You mean you screwed her, I take it. Or did you really kick her?"

"Well, later on, yeah. But right then I was more interested in screwing." He hesitated. Then he added, as if this was a fact that Gordon couldn't be expected to know. "So was Angel. She was a girl who liked her sex rough."

Pike sat hunched easily over the table, hands locked in a loose knot. His flat voice was toneless, metallic, almost without resonance. Gordon could see no element of strain or remorse. None of this was especially painful to Pike, Gordon realized, certainly none of it was particularly shameful. He watched Pike carefully, making sure that his face showed nothing of what he was thinking.

"Go on," he said.

"Well, after that, Lee took a hack at her. And then we all went back to the car and passed the bottle around for a while and Angel began to get a little high. She turned on the radio and wanted somebody to dance with her, but she didn't get anywhere with that one. She began bitching and moaning again, worrying about how she was going to get back in her house with her pants all ripped, and what her old man was going to say, and all that crap. She went a little wild there for a while and Lee slammed her a few times, just teaching her a lesson, he kept saying. He's real hot for teaching, that Lee."

"And this went on how long?"

"Can't be sure. I don't even remember how we came to break it up. Angel was dancing around, pulling at me, and I gave her a good kick in the ass and she went running again. I kicked at her again, I remember, and sent one of my shoes sailing up somewhere. Loafers, you know, moccasin-type. They come off pretty easy. So I went scrambling around looking for it. For a while I thought I'd found it. I mean, at first that's the way I remember it, but I guess I was wrong. I could hear Lee off in the bushes with Angel all the time I was looking for my shoe. He was sort of snickering and telling her not to answer when I was calling them, so I just said the hell with it and got my bike and went home."

"That was the first time?"

"Right. I parked out back of my place and that's when I noticed I didn't have any shoes on, when I started walking over that damn sharp gravel. But I went on anyway, crippling along, and made myself a smoke and then I was going to go to bed, but I kept thinking about those shoes for some drunken reason. They seemed to be important somehow, couldn't get them out of my mind. So after a while, an hour or so, I went back, still in my sock feet, not even thinking that I had another pair of shoes there in the apartment. Drove back in my socks and tried to find my shoes. No flashlight and the moon wasn't very bright, and I was still about as drunk as I've ever been in my life. But I went over that ground pretty good, hands and knees most of the time."

"Was Lee still there? And Angel?"

"Lee's car was gone. I looked around for a while, and then I got the idea that my shoes might be in his car, so I drove over to his house and got there just about a minute after he did. He was sitting in the car, finishing off the bottle. He helped me search the car, and then he said he'd come back to the grove with me and help me look some more. Couple of drunks staggering around in the piney woods looking for a pair of ten-dollar shoes by moonlight. Goddamn comics. But it seemed sensible enough then."

"What about Angel? Where was she?"

"I never thought to ask. I guess I figured Lee had taken her home. Then when we got back to the grove, there she was, drunker than we were, stumbling around just as much. Lee wanted to take another hack at her, but I was too tired. I'd smoked down that joint, and it was making me peaceful and dreamy and all I wanted was bed. I had a kind of fight with Lee, I remember. By that time I'd forgotten about my shoes, I guess. Lee caught me a good lick when I wasn't looking, sent me on my ass in a mess of dried bushes."

"That's how you got the scratches?"

Pike shrugged lightly. "Could be. Might have got them from Angel. She was flashing those fingernails pretty fierce for a while there."

"Okay. Then what?"

"Then nothing. I was feeling too peaceful to fight. I just crept out of those bushes like an Indian and snuck over and got my bike and went on home."

Gordon leaned back, stretching. He had a hundred questions in mind, but he didn't want to risk putting Pike on the defensive this early. Try another tack.

"We are still talking about Tuesday night?"

"Right."

"You were arrested the next day. When? Around noon, wasn't it?"

"Little later, I think, but not much."

Gordon took a moment to make sure he was remembering just how it went. "As I recall, the papers said that some unknown woman phoned in a tip about you earlier that morning. The cops didn't think much of it until those boys running a rabbit hound found Angel's body about nine thirty or ten o'clock Wednesday morning. Then they remembered that anonymous call and came for you. Did you know about that?"

"Not at the time. Somewhere along the line somebody said something about an anonymous call. Asked me if I knew who had made it."

"Did you?"

Pike shook his head. "Couldn't even guess."

"You never thought it might have been Lee Wallis? Or someone he knew well enough to make that call for him?"

Pike's pale eyes narrowed, and for a moment Gordon thought he was frightened at the possibility. Then he straightened and flashed that slanting insolent smile. "There's a fink in the house somewhere, but I don't think it's Lee. He's too involved in this himself."

"Maybe." Gordon moved one hand quickly, brushing it away. "Well, we can't solve that one here. We'll find out soon enough. Let's move along. The sheriff's men brought you downtown and you started right off telling them a pack of lies. Why?"

"Well, that's a little hard to explain. They had me rattled, I guess. I wasn't in very good shape then, and they were pushing me hard. I was just trying to sidestep."

Gordon blew out a quick breath. "Why did you wait so long before you told the straight story? How long was it you were trying to peddle those lies to the sheriff? About three days?"

"I guess so. I don't remember exactly. That was a hazy time for me, Mr. Guthrie. Those guys never let up. No sleep, no food, on my feet all the time. You know how they operate. They just kept hammering at me."

"And then finally, after all the hammering, you admitted you went back to El Pinar that second time, and then they let up on you. Is that the way it went?"

"I don't know how they figured it. Maybe so."

"The first time around you didn't mention Lee Wallis. And you kept him out of the story until your final statement about three days later. Why?"

Pike's mouth twitched in a faint secretive smile. "I made a mistake," he said simply. "Something I didn't figure right."

"That's no answer," Gordon said sharply.

"I think," Pike said with slow deliberation, "I just think we'll pass that one for now. Maybe I'll have a better answer later."

"That won't do," Gordon said. He could see Pike's chin lifting in defiance and went on quickly. "I'll have to know sometime."

Pike turned his pale eyes away.

"I'm the only one who can help you now," Gordon said earnestly. "Maybe you expected Lee Wallis to do something for you if you kept him out of your story for a while. I think you know that didn't work, if that's what you did have in mind. It came out a little different from the way you hoped, didn't it?"

"It did?" Pike's face was blandly watchful. "How?"

"When you finally got around to mentioning Lee Wallis, the sheriff's investigators checked him out, of course. But you gave him two days' free time. His car had been steam-cleaned, inside and out. There was no way to tell anything about the clothes he wore that night. The ones he showed the deputies were all right, no bloodstains, nothing out of the way. No bloodstains on his shoes either. Of course, by that time he had a lawyer and there wasn't much the sheriff's people could do about it. Young Mr. Wallis was not cooperating, on advice of counsel. You did him a good turn, Pike. But he left you in the soup."

"He did?" Pike half-smiled, but the tired, bored lift of his eyebrows was a strained and obvious gesture.

"There was blood spotted on the legs of your jeans and on the foot plate of your bike. Your blood type, but also Angel's. And they found your shoes, Pike. Didn't anyone tell you? Not out at El Pinar. Not in Lee Wallis' car. Right outside your own doorway, in a big tangle of dried rose bushes."

Pike wasn't even pretending boredom any longer. His eyes fixed intently on Gordon's face. He seemed not to be breathing.

Gordon nodded. "Yes. Plenty of blood. And something worse. One little fleck of tissue, barely big enough to make a good specimen for the microscope. Brain tissue, Pike." Gordon kept his voice low, like a hidden weapon held in reserve. "Angel's brains on your shoes, Pike."

Pike stared numbly.

"You figured something wrong when you kept Lee Wallis' name out of your original story. And you're figuring something wrong now if you think you can hold out on me. It's too late for that, Pike, way too late." He pushed his chair back and rose. "You think about it. You've got a lot to think about. I'll give you some time. But you be ready to talk to me when I come back here tomorrow. You understand what I'm saying?"

Pike sat locked in a still, inward-looking concentration. He did not answer.

"You understand me, Pike?"

Slowly Pike nodded.

Gordon signed out in the attorney's book at the front desk. The duty sergeant read the entry upside-down and shook his head gloomily.

"Got a real bad boy there, Mr. Guthrie. Won't be around much longer, I'll bet you."

Gordon put the pen down. "We'll see," he said easily, meaning that he was not going to discuss his client's business with an outsider. "Mind if I use your phone?"

The sergeant pushed it forward and moved away a few steps to suggest an area of privacy.

Gordon dialed a familiar number, asked the switchboard girl for Miss Dorelli, and spoke in a mild, quiet voice when Miss Dorelli answered.

93

Mr. Delancy would try to squeeze him in for a few minutes at five o'clock. It was a *very* busy day for Mr. Delancy. Miss Dorelli advised young Mr. Guthrie to put everything down on paper and possibly Mr. Delancy would find time to read it over this evening.

Gordon thanked her politely. He put the phone down with care, tempted to throw it through the plate-glass window. Five o'clock, for Christ's sake! Delancy wasn't in court today, so he would be having a convivial two-hour lunch with his cronies at the Bench Club. By the time Gordon got to him he would be well past the occasional sharpness of mind that still came to him in the freshness of the morning hours, fading slowly as the day wore on. At five o'clock he would be unable to concentrate on what Gordon was telling him. He would not even care. Gordon would have to try, though, and in the meantime he might as well have a good lunch too, and see if he couldn't find a few cronies for himself. One female crony anyway, the one he had in mind. He thanked the sergeant and pushed through the swinging doors into the bright hot sunlight.

He ran a few quick steps to catch a Route Sixteen bus as it was pulling away from the stop across the street from the courthouse. He stayed forward, standing just behind the driver where the breeze created by their movement made a small pocket of coolness.

He held the chrome post in both hands and pushed back hard, straining his shoulder muscles, easing the tension that had been building up since he had first seen Jonathan Pike. But nothing could relieve the sense of depression that moved sluggishly like a shadow in his mind. The prosecution's case against Pike was solid, buttressed by hard evidence, shored up by a plausible chain of circumstantial evidence. Any faint chance the kid might have in the courtroom would depend on a tightly planned, imaginative, hard-driving defense that disputed every prosecution move, and a quick, agile shiftiness, an up-on-the-toes readiness to leap at any possible opening.

And Gordon Guthrie did not believe that James Delancy was up to it. He had been a demon defender in his great days, one the prosecutors hated to face in court. There was nothing fake about the man's reputation. But since his illness, the juice had been running thin, the once-hot fire could still give off a little heat, even shoot off some sparks from time to time, but you couldn't count on it any longer. You never knew when he was going to be totally ready for a case, eager, completely in control, and when he was going to fumble automatically through the ritual, droning out the responses that ceased to have any meaning for him, like an actor bored with a part he has played too many times.

Put it out of your mind, Gordon told himself. You can't do anything about it now. Wait till you see Delancy this afternoon. Who knows, he might even decide this is the one he'll let you handle all the way.

Gordon snorted lightly, deriding his hopes. He stooped to look through the windshield to see where they were.

The bus swung slowly through the narrow streets of the old part of Rincon, stopping often in the downtown district of department stores and hotels and banks and movie houses, less often after they cleared the railroad tracks and were in the more open area of used car lots and drive-in restaurants and supermarkets. When they passed the city limits to the north, the driver moved out illegally to the center lane and went faster than he should have, passing isolated clumps of new pastel houses gathered like bright clutches of Easter eggs around a shopping center or a new school. Out here there were still a few of the old adobe houses spreading over acres of ground, most of them derelict now.

Then they turned sharply east into the low foothills, and here the houses were larger, farther apart, recently and expensively built after the fossil water had been tapped thousands of feet below the desert floor. Here too were the new hotels. Gordon touched the driver's shoulder and swung down the high gritty steps when they stopped at the gateway to the Coronado.

The hotel was set back a hundred yards from the road and Gordon walked slowly up the driveway in the hot sun. In the noontime light the high, aggressively designed building looked much like a large carved chunk of strawberry ice cream that has melted slightly and begun to run. The center portion was a bright towered cube. From it ran low flowing wings that were mostly glass with pale pink tiles along the roofline.

He went into the hushed chill lobby and straight through to the doors that led out into the flagstoned patio and the swimming pool beyond. The gardens were spectacular here but always slightly irritating to Gordon because none of the plantings belonged in this arid setting. The lush blue grass and contorted box sculpturings and pampered plots of brilliant tropicals all needed artificial shade and a flood of water every day. And for what? Gordon scowled at the extravagant fakery and moved even faster, along the shady side of the pitch-and-putt golf course to the tall line of Lombardy poplars that marked the rear boundary of the Desert Valley Tennis Club. Hell of a long roundabout way to get here, he was thinking. He'd forgotten how hard it was to function in Rincon without a car. Have to remember to find someone to give me a lift back to town.

He went down the shady avenue, stripping off his jacket on the way.

His collar and cuffs were unbuttoned, his necktie hanging free as he came in through the back door and down the corrugated ramp to the men's locker room. Then, without stopping, he came back up again and went through the lounge to look out the big picture window at the four tennis courts closest to the clubhouse, those that were constantly shaded. All in use, of course, because the other six courts farther out in the mouth of the canyon were in the full sun, murderous to play on for more than a few games. By early evening the mountain shadows would begin to sneak across the canyon, touching the other courts with the startling impact of a shower of very cold water. But until four or five o'clock only those four courts would be usable. And they were jammed. Impatient knots of people in white tennis shorts, bouncing balls irritably, jogging in place, swinging mighty overhead smashes through the empty air, were waiting at each of the wire gates, ready to pounce as the players on the courts reached game points.

Claudia would be out there somewhere, Gordon suspected, but from this distance he could not be sure. Hell with it, he muttered to himself. He wasn't going to buck that mob today. He went back, stripped off his clothes and hung them in his locker. He pulled on a faded pair of swim shorts and moved barefoot toward the door, picking a fresh towel from the bin as he passed.

The club's pool was small, a hundred feet by twenty, with a single low board that didn't have much bounce. Anyone who wanted something more challenging could walk back to the Coronado and use their Olympic-sized pool. Gordon went in a slow careful circle around the rough tiles beside the pool, stooping sometimes to peer under low umbrellas, checking the people on sunning pads and couches, those sprawled on the burned-out Bermuda grass, the hardy drinkers collected at the long outside bar, the few swimmers. He nodded, grinned, waved, occasionally said something to people he knew, but he did not stop. No sign of Claudia. Try again later, he told himself.

He moved up to the deep end of the pool, dropped his towel, and went in a lazy dive into the clear area under the diving board. He swam ten easy laps the short way, staying under water as much as he could, just porpoising along with little effort, letting the coolness soak in. He went deep on the last lap, kicked off lustily from the bottom, and came surging up, shedding water like a surfacing whale, shoving with both hands off the lip of the pool as he rose so that he came out standing upright in one smooth movement.

He could feel the water drying on his skin even as he was slicing it away with the edge of his hand. He scrubbed his head with a towel, hung it around his neck, and moved back under the shade of the roof where a dripping olla full of the club's celebrated mint-tinged iced tea was always hanging from its decorated cord. He dipped out enough to fill a paper cup, drank some, and took the sloshing cup with him. He found a long sailcloth-covered sunning couch beside the pool and dragged it back into the shade, swinging it around so he would be able to see anyone making the turn toward the women's locker room. He stretched on his back, knees high, took a swig from the cup, and then balanced it on his bare chest, liking the small patch of chilly damp it made.

He closed his eyes, letting out a long quiet breath, and then opened them again when he felt someone sit with a thump on the foot of his couch. A man, he could see that much. But the bright sun behind gave him only a blurred silhouette. Short, broad, high-shouldered, a frieze of spiky hair standing on end. Then he spoke and Gordon knew him.

The Honorable David Calder Burrell, Rincon's county attorney. Little David, the Giant Killer. He was not one of Gordon's favorite people, but he was a colleague and Gordon had worked with and against him many times and had learned to treat him with a certain wary respect. They always pretended a casual friendliness which neither of them felt.

"Still winning, David?" He drained the paper cup and put it on the grass under the couch.

"They make me run for it these days," Burrell said, speaking in short bursts as he strained for air. He propped two cased rackets against the side of the couch and sat back, flapping his damp shirt away from his chest. "But mostly I can still take them. None of these people realizes that a trial lawyer has to stay in top condition, just like a professional athlete."

Gordon snorted quietly. No matter what job he had, David Burrell would be the same dedicated health freak, forever preaching the organic gospel. Two fast sets of tennis before lunch every day. Ten furious laps up and down the pool before dinner. A complexly programmed diet. He did keep himself in remarkable shape for a man past fifty, Gordon had to admit, but his success in the courtroom had little to do with his physical condition. Burrell's meticulous trial preparations were the product of long concentrated hours at his desk. There was no other way and lithe springy muscles didn't help him a bit.

When David came into court he was a tireless, aggressive prosecutor, always driving, conceding nothing, content only with total domination. His excessive energy, all that radiant good health, could be very tiresome, but Gordon was never tempted to underrate him because of that.

"Sheriff tells me you're catching for Jim Delancy on the Angel case." Burrell was speaking more easily now, his normally light quick voice riding with a clarity of tone that would carry through the largest courtroom.

"In our shop," Gordon said lazily, "we call it the Pike case."

Burrell made a smothered sound like a series of broken hiccups, his way of laughing. "Whatever you want to call it. You might tell Jim that I'll be seeing Judge Pontalba this afternoon. I think we can count on clearing the calendar so that we can go to trial on the twenty-fifth. No later than the twenty-seventh, anyway."

Gordon sat up slowly. He swung his feet to the grass. "The twenty-fifth," he said carefully, not believing a word of it. "Of what month?"

"Hmmm?" Burrell scrubbed a towel roughly over his head. He shifted from Gordon's couch and found a low sling chair. "What were you saying?"

"I asked what month you had in mind."

"Is that supposed to be a joke?" He scowled to show he was in no mood for jokes. He had a good face for scowling, wide and high at the forehead, pale freckled skin that flushed easily, long muscular jawline narrowing to a pointed chin. The heavily marked lines around his mouth deepened when he set his lips in a down-turning curve.

"You mean this month? Less than three weeks from now? Do you really expect Mr. Delancy will agree to that?"

"Agree? Of course he'll agree. He has already agreed. It's just a matter of finding a place on the calendar. What the hell has got into you, Guthrie?" He pulled his chin tightly in toward his chest, glaring suspiciously at Gordon through a tangle of pale eyebrows. "Or is it Delancy? Did Jim change his mind?"

"I haven't seen Mr. Delancy today. But I know he won't go along with you."

"Aaah!" Burrell let out a long relieved breath. He nodded wisely. "Well, you just take it easy on that, young fellow. Give Jim my message and see what he says."

"There's too much to do before we'll be ready for trial," Gordon said in a patient, controlled voice. "I don't think we can be ready by the twenty-fifth. In fact, I know we can't."

"Do the best you can," Burrell said with no interest. "This isn't one of those cases where pretrial preparation is going to mean anything to you. Your man is guilty. He killed that girl. He raped her half to death, and then he tore her to pieces and beat her to death. He actually beat the brains out of her head. And he's going to hang, I promise you that. No defense attorney in the world could get him off."

Gordon swung in a slow stiff movement to face Burrell, seeing the tense, feisty stance of the man and wondering why he was speaking with such a depth of personal involvement. "What are you so hot about?"

"Don't you know anything about this case at all?"

"I've seen the sheriff's report. And Pike's statement."

"That should be enough. I didn't have to show you that statement, you know. I could have kept it back for the trial. I just sent it over as a courtesy to Jim Delancy, so he would know what to expect."

"It was a pretty detailed statement," Gordon said, as if he were making a damaging admission. "If Pike gave you all that, how come he didn't sign it?"

"Who knows? He's an insolent son of a bitch, one of those cocky bastards who thinks he knows it all. Probably he thought he was outsmarting us by not signing."

"But he did identify it, I understand?"

"Page by page. At the last minute he decided he wouldn't sign, but he read it all through, the whole thing, and he didn't object to any of it. Three witnesses saw him. I was there myself. Pike said the statement was accurate. He didn't ask for any changes."

"You're sure it was a voluntary statement, are you, David?" Gordon said, just to give him something to think about.

"You really are snatching at straws, aren't you?" Burrell leaned back, grinning at him. "Forget about the statement. We won't even need it. But don't get the idea you can keep it out. Pike's interrogation went strictly according to the rules, right out of the police manuals. No coercion whatever."

"Balls," Gordon said flatly. "I've read those manuals too, so don't give me that crap, David. I know what they say, that it's okay to use any psychological pressure short of outright torture. Isn't that right, David? You stripped him, didn't you? You made him answer your questions while he was wearing nothing but a damp towel, or something like that."

"A blanket, as I recall," Burrell said, still smiling. "Just routine. You know that. The lab boys had to inspect his clothing, didn't they?"

"But somehow it so happened that you didn't get his clothes back to him for a couple of days, did you? And you sort of forgot to give him any food. And you got so interested in the questioning that you didn't let him rest, just kept running relays of cops in on him until you broke him down. That's not coercion?"

"The courts have ruled it isn't." Burrell was sitting upright now and watching Gordon with a new interest.

99

"No lawyer to help him, to tell him he didn't have to answer any of your questions," Gordon went on, heated in spite of himself. "Forget what the courts say, David. Do you really believe that's fair?"

"Certainly it's fair," Burrell said quickly, positively. "There was pressure on Pike, plenty of pressure. Some from the investigators, but mostly from Pike himself, from his own guilty conscience. He knew damn well he was guilty, and when he got tired and couldn't think of any more lies, he began telling the truth, some of it anyway. Without that pressure he'd still be lying to us."

Gordon looked at him coldly. "Who the hell are you to say he's guilty? Are you setting yourself up in the punishment business? You're not the judge, David; you're the prosecutor."

"Don't turn that big ugly voice loose on me, Guthrie. I have to make these decisions. I'm The People."

"Jesus," Gordon said softly.

"I never prosecute anyone unless I'm sure he's guilty. And then I go all out. None of this 'innocent until proven guilty' business for me. Pike's guilty. I know he's guilty. And I'm damn well going to make the jury know he's guilty before I'm finished with him."

Burrell was leaning forward, smacking a tight bony fist into an open palm, hitting himself solidly in a slow pounding rhythm, holding his bright hard eyes on Gordon.

It's a personal thing with him, Gordon thought suddenly. It's not just another murder trial, one more scalp for Little David's trophy case. He really wants to hang Pike. I suspect he'd fix the noose himself if they'd let him. Pike was insolent and abrasive all right, the sort of man anyone would love to smack solidly in the teeth. But David Burrell must have seen hundreds like him in the past. What was there in Pike that made David go shrill and shaky?

"You were awfully lucky on this one, David. Getting onto Pike so early."

"Smart detective work."

"Helped by an anonymous phone call. If you hadn't been tipped to Pike, you'd have backtracked the dead girl, looking for her boyfriends. Chances are you'd have reached Lee Wallis and been satisfied."

"Not a chance," Burrell said flatly. "We got the right man. The phone call speeded things up, that's all."

"Have you been able to trace the woman who made the call?"

"Not yet."

"Are you trying?"

"Why hell yes. She'd make a good witness if we could find her. That call came in before anyone knew anything about a body. She said, 'Jonathan Pike killed someone last night.' That's all, but you can guess how much I'd like to ask her how the hell she knew he killed somebody."

"Maybe he didn't."

Burrell snorted angrily. "Stop smoking that stuff, boy, it'll rot your brains. Your man is guilty as hell. And he's going to hang."

"You sound awfully damn sure of yourself," Gordon said in a thoughtful voice. "But a little while ago you offered Gene Salazar a deal for a guilty plea. What made you change your mind?"

"I didn't offer a deal," Burrell said sharply.

Gordon waved that away. "We won't quibble. Let's just say you agreed to a deal. If Mr. Delancy and I came to you now, would you give us a deal? Manslaughter, say, for a guilty plea?"

"No."

"Second degree?"

"No."

Gordon stared at him blankly. Deals yesterday but no deals today. Why the change? What had happened to make his case against Pike look so much stronger? And as always happens, just defining the question was enough to suggest the answer.

In the space of time between the deal with Salazar and the present moment, only one new element had entered the case. Lee Wallis. Pike had named Wallis as an accomplice after he had shielded him for two or three days. And in that safe time Wallis could have destroyed any evidence linking him with the rape-murder of Angela Morales. But the sheriff's people had kept after Wallis for a week. They must have got something useful from him. His name was prominent on David Burrell's list of witnesses for the prosecution. So Lee Wallis must have made his own separate deal, Gordon suspected. Which could explain Burrell's new confidence in his case.

He pushed stiffly up from the couch, went back into the shadows, and dipped out two cups of iced tea from the olla and brought them back. He held one out until Burrell noticed it and reached up.

"You sound pretty sure about Pike," Gordon said with no emphasis.

"I'm sure." Burrell cleared his throat noisily.

"If it's all so cut-and-dried, then maybe you'll let me see your file, get an idea of what we're up against."

Burrell took a deep breath. "We have a policy of full disclosure," he said, looking away from Gordon. "You know that."

"Which means you'll hand us the file on each witness when you put him on the stand and then the judge will give us about half an hour with it. What good is that?"

"It's exactly what the law requires. Standard procedure. What more do you expect?"

"I don't know," Gordon said. He sat down facing Burrell. "But why fight us so hard, if you've got it in the bag? We're taking this on for free, you know. Court-appointed counsel. So we'll be billing the county for expenses. Why should Rincon County pay for two separate investigations? Waste of money, isn't it? Might even be illegal. I think I'd better ask the Supreme Court for a ruling on that."

Burrell erupted in a chuckling burst of hiccups. "Might stir up a pretty lively debate. That's a nice tricky idea, Guthrie. You go right ahead. It won't get you anywhere, but give it a try anyway."

"You wouldn't care to think about it? Lots of merit in the notion, David."

"Not a chance."

Gordon smiled at him slowly, knowingly, thinking of Pike's slanting insolent smile and trying for something of that quality. "So you aren't so sure after all, eh, David? Pike just might slip out of your bag, right?"

"Goddamn you, Guthrie," Burrell said in a thin, carrying voice, "I don't have to take this shit from you. What the hell do you know about it? When did you ever run a trial? I have to be ten times the lawyer you and Delancy are. It's that simple. If your side can persuade just one man out of twelve to see it your way, then you win. At the very least you get a hung jury. But the only way I can win is to get all twelve on my side. And yet you still expect me to help you?"

"I just wanted—"

"What do I care about your wants? I only get this one crack at that murdering son of a bitch. There is no appeals structure for the prosecution. If you lose this time, you can appeal, over and over for years, maybe even get a new trial. But if I lose, that's it. The end. So I don't lose. I can't afford to. I won't give you a damn thing the law doesn't say I have to give you. I've got Pike sewed up. I've got him by the balls. And I'm going to see that he's executed for murder."

He got up abruptly, swung around, scooped up his cased rackets, and moved off quickly along the tiled walk. After a few strides he looked back, made a small shrugging gesture and lifted his glass of iced tea. He nodded to Gordon, hesitated as if he meant to say something, then turned again and went away.

Gordon watched him out of sight, shaking his head. David Burrell was moving in a lithe easy trot along the edge of the pool. He took the five tiled steps to the men's locker room in one short bound. Lots of bounce in the old boy. But what about the rest of it, Gordon wondered. What the hell was all that? A sick mind in a sound body? No, not that bad, probably. But bad enough. Plenty bad enough for Jonathan Pike.

He stretched out again on the long shaded couch, locked both hands behind his head, and closed his eyes.

He felt her hand move in a firm sensuous stroke up the side of his head, pushing his thick coarse hair up in a roached mane, then smoothing it back again, brushing it away from his forehead.

"I knew you were here somewhere," she said in a quiet dreamy voice. "I always know when you're around."

He believed it. She had all the natural animal graces. Why shouldn't she have the animal talents as well? He tilted his head farther back, but he could not see her.

"Where were you? I looked around."

"I was hiding behind the bar. I just didn't want to see David Burrell today. I'm beginning to hate him."

Gordon chuckled easily. "Your old tennis partner? I thought you two were the champs."

"Not anymore," she said firmly. "Never again. I told him I won't play with him ever again. And I told him why."

"Forcefully, I'll bet."

"You can depend on it. Little David, the fighting DA, charging around the courtroom like a fizzing skyrocket. And he's just the same on a tennis court. Chop, chop, chop, all the way. And if he gets the chance, he'll bury the ball in your gut. A real competitor. All he cares about is winning. Where's the fun in that? Tennis is supposed to be fun. For David it's kind of warfare."

"That's just the way I play."

"No, that's not the way my Gordie plays." Her long strong fingers dug into the tension points above his ears. "You whale the daylights out of the ball and you're lucky if it stays in the same county, but you don't try to blast people off the court. There's a big difference. David is a bully."

"And I'm just a big good-natured fun-loving kid." He reached up and pulled her down beside him.

She was a rare one, physically perfect in the sense of total genetic felicity, all the elements combining in beautiful precision. You did not think of the elements separately, the dark-blond hair that never shaped her head ungracefully, the eloquent paleness of sea-blue eyes, the swift and lively emotional responses a wide, mobile mouth could demonstrate. Never separately, one by one, always the totality, the quick, solid, shocking impact that could stop the heart.

103

He would never be used to it. He still stared, as he always stared, fascinated by the glowing skin so finely textured that it seemed a special substance, something created for Claudia alone.

"Don't look at me like that, Gordie. Not here." She put a hand on his ankle and gripped hard. "God, you're big. You're so much bigger with your clothes off."

Gordon grinned wolfishly.

"I'm so glad I saw you here. I have to tell you—" She broke off and came quickly to her feet in a lithe quick swirl that pulled the lines of her tennis dress tightly against her body.

"You don't really want to eat here, do you?"

"Wouldn't think of it."

"Hurry then."

"My cowboy lover." Her eyes were bright with affectionate mockery. She licked the side of the cigarette she had made, sealing it carefully. She placed it in the center of Gordon's mouth. She sat back then, braced against the far bedpost, and crossed her legs, stretching slowly and luxuriously, graceful as a tiger relaxing.

The tanned sleek body was perfection too, the skin silky and surprisingly warm under his fingers. Those lucky genes, he thought again. He watched her curl herself into a loose lazy circle at the foot of the bed.

They were in the small bedroom of the guesthouse hidden in an acacia grove a hundred yards behind Claudia's house. They had come in the back way as always, run her car quickly under cover, and unearthed the key buried near the second step at the front door. It was quiet here, shaded always and even darker now with the curtains tightly drawn.

Gordon was thinking of the other times he had been here with Claudia, remembering with clarity and sharp pleasure. Especially those brief and savage moments when he was completely master, commanding totally. And defeated just as surely in a surging, heart-stopping climax that broke over him like a tidal wave. She was eager, lustful, inventive, bringing him again and again to a renewed strength he would have sworn was impossible.

And now she lay in a lithe spent coil, smiling serenely up at him, head cradled in her arm, hair brilliant in the soft light.

"Who was that old western movie star who was always rolling those very thin cigarettes? Silent movies. I was trying to remember." She spoke with her mouth warmly against her arm and he had to strain to hear.

"I'm not much of a movie buff." He scratched a match underneath the bedside table and rolled up to light his cigarette.

"He was a fierce one," she insisted. "Hard thin face. Very cold eyes. Wore sleeve garters."

Gordon laughed easily. "That did it. The sleeve garters. It was William S. Hart."

She patted his knee lightly. "I knew you would remember. I count on you remembering things. William S. Guthrie. Little skimpy toothpick cigarettes. Do you really like them, Gordie?"

"Sure. I don't fiddle around with cigarettes. Couple of puffs is all I ever want." He scrubbed out the butt to show her what he meant.

She lifted up an arm to brush a fan of hair back from her face and turned slightly, just enough to see the small clock on the night table. Her voice was a quiet laziness, but Gordon could sense that she was organizing herself for movement. "Damn, almost one thirty. And I have to be in Portola this afternoon." She yawned slowly, her mouth frankly wide, tongue fluttering, not troubling to shield it. "Was it sweet today, Gordie? I really wanted it to be stately and elegiac, but it got away from us, didn't it?"

"Elegiac?" Gordon said, alerted as if he had been stung. "Sure you've got the right word?"

"That's why I was so pleased when you came to the club today. I didn't know exactly when I'd see you again. And I knew I had to see you."

Gordon pushed himself up against the headrest to see her better. She was still smiling, gravely now. Was he just imagining that she looked sad?

"Nico didn't tell you, I know. I talked to him this morning and he said he was going to tell you, and then at the last minute he just decided he'd keep it private as long as he could. Even from you."

"Nico?" Gordon said carefully. "You and Nico?"

"Last night," she said with a slow smile. "Just for families last night. But it will be in the papers this afternoon. That's why I was so glad you came to the club today. So I could tell you myself. So we could say good-bye."

"Sure," he said in a voice he did not recognize. "Good-bye. A great thing for us to say."

It meant nothing to her, he realized. Or very little. Claudia was being kind, gentle, and generous. There was a sort of horrible innocence about it, Gordon could see. Her emotions were not really engaged. Probably no one would ever touch her so deeply that they could do to her what she had just done, effortlessly, to Gordon.

I was about an inch away from asking her to marry me, he

remembered with a wild silent rage. Thank God we didn't get that far.

He was working hard to control himself, but under it all he was wondering if his surprise was the real thing. Shock, of course. The shock was real, almost comic in its timing. Like the man dying of thirst in the desert who stumbles on the hidden pool of water, drinks deeply, and lifts his head, exulting, sure now that the luck has turned, the future bright, and then sees the coiled rattler just seconds before it strikes him in the throat.

He had never had many illusions about Claudia, he tried to tell himself. He knew she was as self-loving and vain as a Persian king, totally Claudia-oriented. So why the surprise?

Poor Nico. Congratulations, Nico, best of luck, you rich, elegant, handsome son of a bitch.

He watched her roll from the bed. She picked up her rumpled tennis dress and pulled it on carelessly.

"I must run, dear Gordie." She arranged her tumbled hair quickly with her fingers.

Gordon pushed himself up, slowly, stiffly.

Gordon drew in a quick breath and let it out audibly. He crossed his legs the other way, made a fast grab at his stack of file folders before they could slide away, and settled them on the chair beside the couch. Miss Dorelli glanced up, managed a small sympathetic smile, and went on with her work.

It was nearly six o'clock now and still Delancy had not found time for him. Gordon had crammed his long afternoon with work—committees, conferences, telephone calls, correspondence he had been putting off, reviews of pending work, all the busy details that can distract a lawyer and often make it impossible for him to do any serious thinking. But today it had been very welcome, that endless parade of nit-pickery that left him no time to think of himself or of what was happening to his private world.

But he had been waiting here in Delancy's outer office since five o'clock with nothing to do.

"Colonel Bannister stopped in without an appointment," Miss Dorelli had explained. Colonel Bannister was a rich and argumentative land developer, always at odds with his neighbors and the government. He was a valued and profitable client. And one of Delancy's oldest friends. Time could always be found for Colonel Bannister.

Miss Dorelli rolled the sandwiched papers and carbons up out of her typewriter, lifted the first sheet, and pushed her chair back. "I'll just take this in to Mr. Delancy and remind him you're still waiting."

"Thanks," Gordon said. He rolled a quick thin cigarette and had it lit before Miss Dorelli left him and finished before she returned.

"A few minutes," she said. She took a large lizard handbag from her bottom drawer and went out into the corridor.

The inner door opened at last and a short bulky man came backing out, chortling and making a wide expansive gesture with a big hat. Delancy joined him in the doorway and shook hands formally.

"I'm sure we're on the right track, Phil."

"You always know what you're doing, Jim." The bulky man tapped his hat against Delancy's chest and swung away. He slammed the outer door behind him.

Delancy looked at Gordon long and hard, frowning slightly as if trying to remember who he was. Then he nodded and turned back to his office, leaving the door open.

James Delancy was long-boned and thin, faintly stooped in a scholarly way, and very pale in a country where almost everyone is tanned. His head was narrow and big-nosed with a high-domed skull touched lightly with a brushing of silky gray hair. His upper lip was unusually long and tended to sharpen to a V when he smiled.

He was not smiling as he went to sit in his high-backed chair, looking up with tired hooded eyes at Gordon. "I'm afraid we will not have much time, Gordon. Mrs. Delancy is entertaining this evening. What do you have for me?"

Gordon brought a chair closer. He pulled out a sliding shelf from the front of Delancy's desk and piled his papers there. "Pike is the subject, sir. Jonathan Pike. You have my report?"

Mr. Delancy lifted bony shoulders in a slow shrug. "I glanced through it. Hardly a finished piece, is it?"

"It's the preliminary report you asked for, sir," Gordon reminded him. He'd been right; the old man was rambling, forgetting things.

"Quite so," Delancy said absently. "You've been very quick with it. But do we need a conference on it just now?"

Mr. Delancy had an overly precise way of speaking, forming each word carefully with a lot of lip movement. It made Gordon very tired sometimes.

"It's a question of priorities, sir," he said forcefully, commanding Delancy's full attention. "I have to know the targets. First point: Pretrial motions. What do you have in mind, sir?"

"You might tell me what *you* have in mind, Gordon." Mr. Delancy pinched his mouth into the wry V-shaped smile.

"David Burrell wants to go to trial on the twenty-fifth. Did you know that, sir?"

"Yes, we talked of it."

"That won't do, sir," Gordon said flatly. "It doesn't give us enough time."

Mr. Delancy sighed. "It does no harm to cooperate with the county attorney from time to time, Gordon."

"In this case it does," Gordon insisted. "Anyway, what's the hurry?" He didn't have to ask; he knew. David wanted to strike while the case was still hot. Didn't Delancy know that? Or didn't he care? "The county attorney gave us a list of twenty-nine witnesses in the Pike case. We can't possibly investigate all of them in less than three weeks."

"We must do the best we can, Gordon. I have already agreed with Mr. Burrell that we would be ready for trial on the date he set."

"It's a mistake, sir," Gordon said, quietly stubborn in the face of the old man's growing irritation. "At least we should object. We should inform the court that Pike's right to a fair trial is being endangered by unreasonable haste. Throw it right back in Burrell's lap."

"I think not, Gordon. What else do you have?"

"I hope you'll reconsider, sir." Gordon said, knowing that Delancy would listen to no more on the subject just then. "The next question ties with the first—change of venue."

"I can hardly ask for a change of venue when I have already agreed to a trial date," Delancy said stiffly. "Even if I did, what would be the value?"

"The obvious one," Gordon told him with careful patience. "In another jurisdiction we would stand a chance of getting a better jury. We would be drawing from people who haven't seen so much of the local press and television reports. They were brutal, Mr. Delancy. Do you remember them?"

"Not clearly, I'm afraid." Delancy rubbed his eyes with a long-fingered hand. It trembled a little. "I've had other matters to think about, you know." It was a mild, almost vague reproof.

Not clearly, Gordon repeated to himself. Not at all, I'll bet. These days Delancy's memory was erratic at best. Sometimes it simply didn't function at all.

"In the first few hours after he was arrested they had Pike tried, convicted, and sentenced to death. The Rincon *Record* said that he confessed. That was a lie. Pike never confessed. He didn't even sign the statement that he made. But the *Record* still says he confessed. And the local television was just as bad. They had cameramen out at El Pinar when Pike was showing the sheriff where he had parked the night of the crime and where he left the girl—alive. But that's not what the commentator said. He told his audience that Pike was reenacting his crime. He did not mention that Pike denied killing the girl." He paused, trying not to push the old man too hard. "In my opinion, sir, we could never get an unbiased jury in Rincon County."

Delancy's response was querulous. "If the publicity was universal, I'm sure the whole state felt the same impact. It would not have been limited to this county alone. In any event, David Burrell would never agree to a change of venue. He wants to try this case himself."

"Mr. Burrell's wants are not the only important elements." Gordon was careful to speak quietly. "We have to think of our client first. Even if our application for change of venue is denied, we'll still have it in the record and that can be important for appeal."

"We will see," Mr. Delancy said in a tone that indicated the matter was closed as far as he was concerned. "What else?"

Gordon took a quick calming breath and held it for a moment. "Polygraph," he said then. "I'd like to give Pike a lie detector test."

Mr. Delancy shook his head irritably. "You know that I am no believer in the value of such tests, Gordon. In any event, Pike would probably refuse."

"If he did, that would tell us something useful about him, wouldn't it?"

"And it would tell Mr. Burrell as well. No, Gordon, that won't help. Polygraph evidence can be admitted only with the county attorney's permission, which we would never get. And the expense, in any case, would be prohibitive."

"I think it's worth it, sir."

"I can't agree."

Gordon drew a hard slashing line across his notepad.

"If we'd had this case from the beginning," Delancy said with a sudden, unexpected vigor, "we might have tried for 'not guilty by reason of insanity.' Considering the nature of the crime, that might have been the best solution."

Gordon looked at him, his expression carefully blank. A few years ago one of James Delancy's most famous cases had been won on the basis of a dramatic and successful plea of insanity. He is living that one again, Gordon thought.

"Yes, sir," he said. "If we'd had it from the beginning. But not now. Anyway, Pike would never agree. He claims he is innocent. He wants to go to trial."

The old man sighed. "What else?"

"I will need authorization for other expenses," Gordon said. "How far can I go with private investigators?"

"Investigators? What is it you want to investigate? Aren't the facts clear?"

Gordon shifted irritably. "No, sir. Not clear enough. I would like to get a good man working on Lee Wallis to find out exactly what kind of story he sold to the sheriff, maybe get some line on how to break him when he gets on the stand."

"You can't do that yourself?"

"Wallis won't talk to me, sir. I'm not even sure an investigator can get to him, but we have to try." Gordon edged forward in his chair. "This is a tricky problem and I think the whole case may hinge on it. The situation is that Lee Wallis has managed to turn himself from a prime murder suspect into a witness for the prosecution. He was able to do this because Pike didn't mention his name in the early days of the investigation and that gave Wallis time to juggle any evidence that might have linked him to the girl's death. Somehow we have to show the jury that Wallis is still a prime element in the case. By rights he should be a co-defendant. Why isn't he in there with Pike? The jury is going to see Pike in handcuffs, guarded by deputies with guns. But Wallis is going to be free as the air, testifying for the prosecution. Naturally, the jury is going to think Wallis is probably telling the truth, because if he wasn't, he would be in jail like Pike. You see where that leaves us? What it amounts to is that the prosecution is vouching for Wallis' honesty, accepting his version as the straight gospel and asking the jury to believe him."

Mr. Delancy raised his thin shaky hand again and wiped it across his chin with a faint rasping of dry skin. "You are not suggesting that Mr. Burrell has made a deal to exonerate Lee Wallis?"

"I don't say it's quite that bad," Gordon explained. "The fact is that the investigators got to Wallis too late, because Pike gave him all that free time, so now David Burrell is making the best of a bad situation by using Wallis to nail Pike."

"And we do not yet know what sort of story Wallis has told the prosecution? Is that the position? Is that why you want to hire private investigators?"

What else have I been saying for the last ten minutes? Gordon thought sourly. Aloud, he said, "Yes, sir. Exactly. David Burrell is very confident about his chances now he has Wallis for a witness. You will remember that Burrell was willing to make a deal with Gene Salazar when Salazar was representing Pike?"

"So I heard."

"I ran into David today, and just as a 'try-on, I asked him if he'd make

110

the same deal with us. Guilty plea to manslaughter or even second degree. He turned me down flat."

"And who authorized you to make such a suggestion?"

Gordon grinned quickly. "I was just kidding him, Mr. Delancy. I wouldn't say a thing like that seriously. But David was plenty serious when he said no. It's obvious that he's a lot happier about his case now than he was at first. And the only thing that has changed is that now he's got Wallis for a witness. So Wallis has to be the key."

"It would seem to follow." Mr. Delancy was not pleased with it, but he accepted the reasoning. "Very well. Hire the investigators for a few days and see what can be developed in that time. But be prudent, Gordon. Our client has no money and it is not likely that Rincon County will allow unusual expenditures."

"I'll hold it down," Gordon said quickly. He had won something, anyway. "Now, about the jury panel?"

Mr. Delancy lifted one gray eyebrow.

"One hundred and fifty names on the panel," Gordon reminded him. "We'll have to check them out. We can't just go in there blind."

"No," Mr. Delancy said flatly. "You may send for the credit bureau reports and look at the police records, but we cannot afford a full investigation of that many people." Mr. Delancy closed his eyes. "What else?" he asked in a tone that meant he wanted to hear nothing else.

"I'll have to find out why Pike didn't implicate Wallis at the very beginning, why he didn't tell the truth about that night, if he was going to say anything at all. Well, I can handle that tomorrow. I think we may be able to work up a few surprises for Burrell, if we have any luck."

"I'm sure you will, Gordon," Mr. Delancy said with his tight *V*-shaped smile. "Keep me informed. Daily reports." It was clear dismissal.

Gordon choked back a surge of anger. He had a dozen more points to discuss.

But Mr. Delancy was finished for the day. His narrow chest rose and fell with a slow regularity that was much the rhythm of sleep. Gordon looked at the worn old face and told himself he should be more understanding, develop a sympathetic and helpful attitude when the old man was tired. But he felt only frustration and anger. He had never worked with James Oliver Delancy in his great days. He had never seen him explosive with energy and enthusiasm. He knew only this slow-minded cautious old man and felt him to be an impediment and a menace.

"Yes, sir," he said heavily. He got up and went out quickly.

* * *

III

It was past midnight when he swung the rental car in through the gates of Jumbo's homestead. He ran it in a few yards and then turned off the scraped roadway and parked. The rental car was a veteran Ford with a very noisy rear end and he didn't want to wake up the house by grinding it up the long slope. He cut the lights and reached back for his loaded briefcase.

He was learning how to handle things now. Just a matter of taking it an hour at a time, keeping the mind wholly occupied. Then the shadows moved back, and for long stretches of time he could pretend they weren't there. So he had put in a pretty good evening's work. Sandwiches and coffee in the law library on the same table where the librarians had collected all the references he had asked for. It had taken three hours of careful reading and two more for drafting, but he had come out of it with a good tight brief for Delancy. Now all he had to do was persuade the old man to use it. To lean the full weight of his prestige behind it.

It wasn't any sense of personal involvement with Pike or his welfare that was stabbing at Gordon. It was simply, he tried to tell himself, a matter of professional pride. He considered himself a good trial lawyer, hell of a lot better than Delancy or anyone else at Gaines, Prinz. And he'd be damned before he'd let that old man stumble through a lackadaisical defense and send his client down the drain just because he had made a thoughtless, almost reckless agreement with the county attorney about the trial date and was too muleheaded to admit his mistake. Somehow Gordon had to find a way to get through to him.

Naturally David Burrell wanted to rush Pike to trial while public interest in the case was still high. But when he pushed for an early trial date that did not allow the defense adequate time for preparation, he made a serious mistake. Not just a human mistake, but a legal error. Pike had a right to object and his counsel had the duty to speak for him. And if the court insisted on pushing them, an appeal should be filed immediately. The same went for the matter of change of venue. Every literate person in the county had read again and again those inflammatory newspaper stories. Even those who couldn't read had seen the television reports. All of these things said flatly that Pike was a confessed murderer, that he had confessed to what was probably the ugliest and most mindlessly brutal murder Rincon had ever seen.

The flood of prejudicial publicity had poisoned the air. A fair trial was close to impossible. Again Pike had the right to object and his counsel had the duty to speak for him. And if the court overruled them, an appeal should be filed immediately. All that was part of the basic, logical progression of a good defense lawyer's preparation for trial, and Gordon

Guthrie promised himself he would find a way to make Delancy see the light.

His brief should help, he thought. He had written it with an eye to persuading Delancy more than the court. And when Gordon showed him the exhibits he had in mind, the kinescopes and transcripts of television broadcasts, the blowups of newspaper front pages, even Delancy should be able to see he could have himself a fine dramatic session in court, and also strike a shrewd blow for his client.

Gordon stopped halfway up the long slope, shifted his briefcase from hand to hand. It was a dark night and he was going mostly by feel. He could sense but not see the loom of Jumbo's house. And he could smell the vagrant sweetness of the night-blooming *reina de la noche* that brought sharply into his mind a flickering vision of Claudia. He pushed it away quickly and firmly. Nothing there for you, boy, he told himself. Forget it. Or remember it and cripple yourself. Take your pick.

He stayed where he was to roll a cigarette and then went on around the house to the back door that was closer to his room than the front entrance.

Just short of Jumbo's open bedroom window he heard the soft caressing clap of hand on flesh and he froze in position, one toe barely touching the ground. A body shifting heavily made bed springs complain. Jumbo coughed, cleared his throat with a soft crash, and chuckled.

"Don't tickle me, little girlie," he said in a hoarse whisper. "I don't need no tickling."

Bare knuckles rapped lightly against the plastered wall near the window, then both bodies moved in joined rhythm, slowly, slowly, then accelerated, picking up the beat in long throbbing urgent intervals.

Gordon eased his weight back onto his other foot and drifted away across the bare earth, circling away from the window, making no sound, going lightly around to the front door. He let himself in silently and went down the hallway to his room without turning on any lights.

I hope that was Elena in there, he thought. I just hope it wasn't some raddled beer-hall bimbo he latched onto somewhere last night, with too many drinks in him. At such times Jumbo was not choosy; almost any available female would do. But afterward he had to pull himself out of bed in the early morning, head hurting in hard sickening pulsations, stomach lurching, to fumble into his clothes, get the bimbo up and dressed somehow, and try to smuggle her out of the house before anyone saw her. It just wasn't worth it any longer. It took too much out of Jumbo.

Gordon undressed silently, letting his clothes drop on the floor. He peeled the covers back from his bed, sat for a moment, then got up and prowled, naked and barefoot, down the hallway to the huge dusty sitting room they seldom used. He found Jumbo's store of Mexican rum in an open bookshelf, picked a bottle that had been opened, and went quickly back.

He piled both pillows against a wall and sat high in the bed. He tasted the rum, swallowed a little, then tilted the bottle and drank until he was out of breath. He leaned back then, panting, sucking in huge breaths, feeling the fumes bubbling in his brain.

Long day, he told himself. And for most of it he had been fighting back a surge of hot angry frustration that damn near choked him. Hell with it. Let that be the watchword. Hell with all of them.

The lightened square of his window began to move, changing shape and size and color. He drank again as long as he could and then rolled over, meaning to set the bottle on the floor. He felt it tilt, heard it thump and roll away. He let it go. Hell with it.

They were waiting for him just inside the small lawyer's room. Gordon dropped his heavy new briefcase on a chair, nodded once, and immediately stripped off his crumpled linen jacket.

"Sorry I'm late," he said in a slow thick voice. "Archie, can you send out to Mama Montoya's for coffee and a sack of *buñuelos?*"

"Glad to, counselor." The deputy closed the door behind him and gave it a shake to be sure it was locked.

Gordon sat heavily, reached over to open his bag and take out a long yellow pad. He leaned back and looked at Pike who was perched on a far corner of the table, arms lightly crossed, his coarse denim shirt pulled tightly across his shoulders and back, fitting as snugly as if it had been shaped for him. He was poised and alert and a little too sure of himself, Gordon thought. I just hope he doesn't try to hand me any more of that cocky bullshit today. I really am not in the mood for it.

"I told you yesterday." He stopped to cough his throat clear, and when he spoke again his voice was sharper but still rough. "I told you what I wanted from you. You aren't going to waste any more of my time. Let's get started."

"What's chewing on you?" Pike cocked an eyebrow and almost grinned.

"I'm tired," Gordon said heavily. "My head aches. I've got a lousy hangover, and I am plumb out of patience."

The day had begun badly and so far there were no signs of

improvement. He had slept too long and heavily, had pushed himself soggily out of bed to find that Jumbo had made a late start that morning too. So there was no coffee. Then he had cut himself shaving and noticed it only after he had dribbled blood on his shirt and had to go back for a fresh one. And then the elderly rented car had refused to start, so he had manhandled it out to the road and waited there until a trucker came along to give him a push. This made him late for his appointment with the Rincon Investigation and Security Associates. And that preliminary conference had been blurred with misunderstandings until he had finally made them realize that Lee Wallis was not likely to talk willingly. They would have to be fast and shifty, double-team him, and try to push him off-balance. First with a comfortable fatherly type who would put it to him in a quiet, straightforward approach.

"You've already told your story to the sheriff and the county attorney. You'll be telling the world when you take the witness stand. So what's wrong with telling us? You haven't got anything to hide, have you? Of course not! So how about it?" That approach wasn't likely to work, but you're starting with mighty little and you have to try everything.

Follow up with the youngest operative on the staff, a recent graduate of the Army's CID school, who was just a few years older than Wallis. He could track his man and try to get close to him when he took time out for a drink. Back-stopping him would be a tough little monkey-faced girl with a spectacular body who could be called in if Wallis showed any sign of interest.

That was the best program they could work out. Thinking about it as he left the office, Gordon had felt morosely convinced it was going to be a sorry waste of time and effort. So he had been late getting to the county jail. Still no breakfast, still dull and tired, fogged with hangover, ready to blast the first man who stepped in his way.

Gordon took a deep slow breath. He locked his hands on the table and made himself speak calmly and without anger. "A little while ago the county attorney was willing to make a deal with you, let you plead guilty to second-degree murder."

"I wouldn't make any deal," Pike said sharply. "It was all Salazar's idea. He didn't even ask me. And when I turned it down, he ran out on me."

"I know all that. The important fact here is that David Burrell was willing to make such a deal. Now he isn't. I tried it on him yesterday. He didn't even take a minute to think it over. Just gave me a flat, fast refusal. Why did he change his mind?"

"How could I know?"

"Think about it. In the beginning he was ready to talk deal. But now he is absolutely sure he can get a first-degree conviction. Why?"

Pike shook his head a scant inch each way, watching Gordon intently.

"The physical evidence hasn't changed or improved," Gordon said, thinking out loud. "So it has to be a witness, someone whose testimony is now a lot more useful than it seemed to be at first. What witness, Pike?"

Pike did not try to answer.

"It has to be Lee Wallis," Gordon told him. "Nothing else makes sense. Lee Wallis, your good friend. It seems obvious that your good friend made a good deal with Burrell. You can blame yourself for that one. You blocked for him just long enough to let him get clear. And to stay clear, he's going to help the prosecutor dig your grave."

"Are you guessing?"

"I'm reasoning from the available evidence."

"If you're not guessing, then you are scaring the shit out of me."

"High time, too. You'd better be worried, Pike. You've put yourself in a real box. I'm trying to get a line on the testimony we can expect from Wallis, but I'm not too hopeful. We may have to wait till he's actually on the stand."

Pike nodded slowly. "I could probably guess what he's likely to say."

"I imagine you could. You and Wallis are the only ones alive who know exactly what happened that night. We'll be going over the whole thing again, step by step. But for the moment, let's stay with Lee Wallis. Tell me why you covered for him."

"I didn't." Pike got up from the table. He used his foot to hook a chair away from the wall. He sat, not quite facing Gordon. "I really wasn't thinking about Lee just then."

"Then who—" Gordon stopped himself. A third person? He let the new possibility move through his mind like a drifting trace of smoke.

"What do you know about Nacho Cordero?" Pike asked in a casual tone. "What kind of reputation does he have?"

Gordon gave himself a minute to consider. Ignacio Cordero, head of a large Mexican-American family long resident in Rincon. Prosperous, with a lot of varied interests, not yet an element in Rincon's power structure, though he might, Gordon felt, exercise a certain political influence in his own strongly Mexican-American part of the county. His reputation? Commercially it was excellent, of course. And personally? Nothing against him that Gordon knew.

He was about to answer when the deputy tapped on the door behind him and pushed it open. The deputy stood aside, professionally wary, and gestured for a trusty in jailhouse denims to enter.

116

"Black, with sugar. That okay?"

"Thanks, Archie, just right. I'll settle up on the way out."

"No hurry." He locked them in again and took his post in the hallway.

Gordon shoved one of the covered cardboard containers across to Pike and tore open the grease-spotted paper bag, spreading it open like a tray. Pike prised off the lid of the coffee cup and took a cautious sip. He glanced curiously at the mound of brown misshapen lumps on the paper.

"Mexican kind of doughnut." Gordon bit into one, spraying crisp flecks over the table. "Called *buñuelos*. Around here we all grew up on them. Try one. They're good."

Pike shrugged and picked up a small lump. He bit into it with obvious suspicion, then slowly smiled after he swallowed the first bite. "They are good. I never had these before."

"Home-type grub." Gordon wolfed down several quickly, before his coffee was cool enough to drink. He took half the cup in one long swig and sat back, heartened by the sweet scalding brew with its faintly bitter undertaste of chicory. He rolled one of his thin cigarettes and lit it when he had finished his coffee. He filled his lungs with a deep inhalation, blew out a long dragon's breath of smoke and dropped the stub into the coffee cup.

"Needed that." He stretched wide and then sat back and crossed his legs. "Nacho Cordero," he said, getting back to business. "The newspapers would call him a prominent Mexican-American businessman. Credit to the community. Civic-minded. Charitable. Good family man. Church-goer. Good credit risk."

Pike ducked his head and spoke without looking at Gordon. "So if someone told you that Nacho Cordero was a big-league drug smuggler, what would you say?"

Oh, my Christ! Gordon groaned in his head. Drugs. That's all we need to blow this case plumb to hell. Just mention the word in the courtroom and you are buying Pike a nonstop ticket to the death house.

"I hope," he said very slowly, waiting until Pike lifted his head, "I hope to Christ the subject never comes up. If it does, it isn't going to do you one bit of good."

"I know that," Pike said impatiently. "I can see how it would work against me. But you'll have to know about it. Because that's why I told the sheriff as little as I could for as long as I could. I wanted to give Nacho time to help me. I thought he'd want to do a hell of a lot more for me than he did."

"Why?"

Pike stared at him for a long moment. Almost absentmindedly he began tidying the table, wadding the greasy paper, nesting the cups together, dusting crumbs onto the floor. He shifted his chair slightly so he was facing the side wall. "I've been thinking about how to lay this out for you. It isn't easy, so maybe you'd better let me take it straight through and then you ask questions."

"Go ahead."

Pike took his hands from the table and laced them tightly over one knee to make sure there would be no nervous jittering. He began by telling Gordon about his first meeting with Nacho Cordero, and the never-quite-stated offer of an extra five hundred dollars a month for the run down to Puerta del Lago with Lee and the fish truck.

He could see no response from Gordon. The big young lawyer sat hunch-shouldered, both hands idly turning a limp sack of tobacco. He made only an occasional note on his pad, but Pike sensed that he was memorizing every word.

Pike went through it carefully, detailing every move of his search for the answer to Nacho Cordero's smuggling racket. Gordon snorted quietly when Pike remembered the scene in Nacho's office when Pike's jar of watery paint had been returned, together with a monumental boff on the chops.

Just what connection did the truck, its two drivers, and those twice-weekly trips to and from Puerta del Lago have with Nacho Cordero's drug smuggling? The question had plagued Pike for months. The answer is none. None whatsoever.

And the next question presents itself immediately. If Nacho was not using the truck as a carrier of drugs, why then is he willing to pay out a thousand dollars a month to the two drivers? What did Nacho think he was buying? A couple of not-too-expensive decoy ducks, that's what. Decoys fancied up in bright eye-catching plumage, ready to be thrown to the wolves any time there was a suspicion of heat coming Nacho's way.

It would be no trouble kicking them over, not with the help Nacho had at both ends of the border run. All he had to do was to say that those two wild young hoodlums, both with bad records in the Army, had gone into business for themselves without his knowledge. He would be shocked, disappointed, sad. And very helpful to the authorities.

Who would believe denials in the face of Nacho's solid position in the Rincon community? And, of course, all those witnesses he would have on hand. What chance would they have—a clown like Lee and a solitary drifter like Pike. Hell, taking that extra money made them feel guilty even when they weren't.

After a little time off, waiting for the heat to simmer down, Nacho would be back in business again, safe as ever. His insurance would have paid off. Worth every cent of a thousand a month.

And how *was* the stuff coming across the border? Well, between Texas on the Gulf of Mexico and California on the Pacific coast the border is a mighty long stretch. At all the official border crossings you are aware of high woven-wire fences impressively mounted on heavy galvanized pipes and topped with those flaring aprons of barbed wire that make climbing all but impossible. It is obvious that the gate, guarded and patrolled by the federal police of both countries, is the only way through. And so it is—at that place.

But there are other places. In remote areas you will find that the border fence is often only a couple of strands of sagging barbed wire, little more than a legal statement. At those places you stoop and spread the strands apart and duck through. There is not much likelihood that you will be caught, or even seen. Especially if it is night and you know the terrain as well as all those obliging "cousins" of Nacho's—and you know that other protective "cousins" are busy making sure there aren't any curious eyes around to see you. The border bit is a breeze.

So Nacho has been finding it for some time now. Some long time. And the additional protection he gets from his two decoys in the fish truck is just an added—and very enjoyable—element of sureness.

Pike went silent, staring at the drab-painted wall. Gordon fashioned a toothpick cigarette and lit it as Pike swung around to face him.

"After Angel was killed and the sheriff picked me up, I took a chance on Nacho. I figured then that he thought of me as a part of his team and he would help me. I was thinking that all I had to do was keep my mouth shut and give him time to get me out, at least send me a lawyer to help me."

"You took a big chance. What did Cordero actually do for you?"

Pike shrugged. "Just sat on his fat ass and let me take my lumps. He sent Salazar and at first I thought the guy was on my side. But he came and went a couple of times and never really talked to me until after the sheriff got a statement that satisfied him. Can you imagine that? My own lawyer?"

Gordon could not imagine it. There were lawyers who did not care to make enemies in the sheriff's office by pushing too hard, but Salazar was not one of them. And if he had been hired to protect Nacho Cordero as well as Pike, then he would have been battering on that jailhouse door with his heaviest weapons, making sure he got to Pike before he made any damaging admissions. The fact that he had not made that maximum effort suggested to Gordon that he had not been greatly worried about Nacho Cordero's position.

"They mousetrapped you," he said flatly. "You might have hurt Cordero if you'd leveled with the sheriff at the beginning. But it's too late now. If there was any evidence that would have pointed to Cordero, it might have been found the day you were arrested. There is no chance now."

"Why not?"

"You said it yourself. If you had talked, the worst you could have done to Cordero was put him out of business. It's obvious now that he put himself out of business temporarily as soon as he heard you were arrested. So he doesn't have to worry about you. Or help you."

Pike nodded soberly. After a moment he let out a long audible breath. "I'm afraid you're right. That's the way I would have played it, in his place."

Gordon dropped the stub of his cigarette and stepped on it. He tore off the top sheet from his notepad, folded it, and put it in his pocket. He put the pad back in his briefcase and then slowly got to his feet and reached for his jacket.

"Lee Wallis may have had sense enough to keep his mouth shut about this drug traffic too. Maybe they scared it out of him, but maybe not. If any of this comes out in court, it could be very bad for you. Do I have to explain that or do you understand?"

"I think I understand. It's not much of a character reference. Makes a bad impression on the jury."

"It's worse than that," Gordon said heavily. "Tell me this. Did Angela Morales know anything about Nacho Cordero and this drug business?"

"Angel?" Pike lifted one eyebrow and then slowly shook his head. "She knew Nacho, of course. She knew we worked for him. The rest, no. Not from me. And I don't think even Lee was that big a fool. But what's Angel got to do with it?"

Gordon propped his bag on the back of a chair and leaned on it with both hands. He waited for Pike to look up at him. "If the prosecutor hears anything about drug traffic, he might find a way to use it against you. He could suggest to the jury that the real reason you killed Angela Morales was because she knew about it and threatened to inform on you. At the moment he is going for first-degree on the basis of rape-murder. That's not going to be easy for him to prove. But if he can insert this drug-traffic issue into the trial, he has two shots at the same target. An unscrupulous prosecutor could kill you with that one. David Burrell is not an unscrupulous prosecutor, but I wouldn't want to put too much temptation his way. He is determined to convict you. Sometimes I think it's a personal thing with him."

"Damn right it is!" Pike said in a voice that had suddenly gone thin and tight. "That bastard is out to kill me. When he was questioning me, he would get all white and shaky. A couple of times I thought he was going to take a poke at me. He had to get up and go away for a while. I don't know what it is with him, but it's personal all right."

Pike squared his shoulders and sat straighter in his chair. He seemed oddly young, Gordon thought. As if, for the first time, he realized the danger and was beginning to be frightened.

"Why do you think that is so?" Gordon asked. "Was he like that from the beginning of the interrogation or did something happen later to make him take a personal dislike to you?" A new thought came and his voice hardened with it. "Did you give him that smart-ass treatment you gave me?"

Pike drew a breath. "Maybe," he said warily. "Yes, I guess so. He kept bugging me and I was too tired to know what I was saying." He looked away, eyes shadowed with the memory of that bad time.

"What did you say to him?"

"He kept on and on about what happened to Angel. About how torn up she was. About all the blood and the ugliness. Over and over. He was stamping up and down and waving his arms, like a hambone actor chewing the scenery. Finally I asked him what he thought he was doing? Trying to scare me with that Fighting DA act, shouting and poking his finger in my face? I told him to go get a job on television. A couple of guys in the room laughed, and Burrell got even redder in the face than before."

"Jesus," Gordon said softly. They were almost the same words that Claudia had used about Burrell, and he knew how much she had stung him. Pike had hit him in his most vulnerable spot—his image of himself as a devoted public servant. And coming from a suspect being questioned for a brutal murder, a sneer like that would scald Burrell to the bone. No wonder he acted as if he hated Pike. He probably did.

Pike caught something of Gordon's feeling. "What can we do about it?" he asked.

"You could pray," Gordon suggested. "And I'll get back to work. There's a hell of a lot to do between now and trial day."

And there was still a hell of a lot to do, Gordon was angrily aware, as he rose with Pike and Mr. Delancy and waited for the judge to seat himself in the courtroom where Pike was going on trial for his life.

They were not ready for trial. For Gordon the situation could be put that simply. James Oliver Delancy had not agreed.

"We have a gentleman's agreement with Mr. Burrell and I do not intend to break it. We will go to trial on the twenty-fifth, as agreed." And Mr. Delancy had formed his thin V-shaped smile. "I have read your reports carefully, Gordon. Can you honestly say that spending more time or money would bring us any substantial benefit?"

And that had made Gordon even angrier, because the cagey old bastard may have been right. Lee Wallis was the key and Lee Wallis was out of reach. Gordon knew that only too well.

Wallis still worked at Cordero's, but he no longer made the Mexico trip, probably because David Burrell wouldn't let him leave Rincon until the trial was over. Now he was one of a three-man team servicing one of Cordero's local delivery routes. He lived quietly at home, seldom going out, and when he did leave the house, he always had three or four of Cordero's people with him. They did no public drinking except for an occasional beer. They went to drive-in movies, night baseball games, bowled a few frames at one of the neighborhood alleys. They were not interested in conversation, free drinks, or any of the available girls they saw here and there. Lee Wallis was talking to no one but David Burrell. Frustrated, Gordon could only rage.

The other witnesses had not been so elusive, but less than half of them were willing to help the defense prepare for trial. More time would have given Gordon a chance to work on them. More time might have given him an opening somehow with Lee Wallis. But there was no guarantee.

Not that Pike seemed visibly worried about the trial, or anything else. Gordon had come to the courthouse early that morning, giving himself time for a brief conference with Pike, thinking he might need some steadying, a little touch of reassurance before going into the courtroom.

Pike was waiting for him in his cell, fully dressed except for his cashmere blazer, closely shaved, hair freshly trimmed. He was stretched full-length on his cot, hands above his head and linked comfortably on the bare ticking of his pillow, ankles crossed. He seemed well-rested and relaxed, curiously composed for a man about to go on trial for his life.

He looked like a capable, controlled, intelligent young man, a promising junior in advertising or insurance or the training program of one of the major corporations. Looking like that might help him with the jury, Gordon thought. When David Burrell began talking about ravening mad dogs and blood-spattered rapists, the jury would turn to Jonathan Pike, look, and wonder if he could possibly be the man the prosecutor was talking about. But he was perhaps too calm, too self-contained. This sort of cool composure in these circumstances might not seem natural or credible.

"Well, you're looking okay," Gordon said, trying for a cheerful tone. "I guess you won't be needing any pep talk from me."

Pike's mouth slanted in a quick half-contemptuous smile.

"Thought you might like to know what to expect when we go up to the courtroom. Have you ever seen a trial before?"

Pike shrugged. "In the movies. Television."

"Then you know the pattern. This will probably go just about the same. A trial is a ritual. It doesn't vary much. It isn't allowed to vary much." Gordon dropped his briefcase to the floor and leaned back against the cell door.

"I want to warn you that you will have a deputy sitting just behind you, and there will be plenty of curious reporters around. So be careful what you say. I'll give you a pad and pencil for notes, but I don't want you doodling with them. Sit as quietly as you can, no fidgeting. Pay attention to everything that goes on. When there is a witness on the stand, look toward him, but don't stare at him and don't scowl if he says something you don't like. And if anyone cracks a joke, you don't laugh or smile. This trial is a serious business. You are sober and concerned. You are a young man unjustly accused of murder, and you know the good people on the jury are going to find out that a mistake has been made. And you are going to do everything you can to help them find out. Do you get the picture?"

"Sure."

"Then get that goddamn wise-ass look off your face," Gordon roared suddenly. "And keep it off. You let that jury get the notion that this trial doesn't mean anything to you, by Christ, they'll convict you just to let you know how serious it is."

Pike grinned. "I get the message. Loud and clear. Especially loud. Boy, you could knock a hole in the wall with that voice."

"Just so you understand," Gordon said more easily. "Today we start picking a jury, twelve people who are going to decide whether you live or die. From now on we are playing for keeps."

"I understand." Pike swung his feet to the floor and rose quickly. He slid the knot of his blue-and-white striped tie into place and reached for his blazer.

He was a little overdressed, a shade too elegant for summertime Rincon. But it wasn't only the costly raiment, Gordon thought; there was actually something basically disturbing about Pike that made him uneasy. He just hoped the jury would not feel the same way.

And now, toward the end of the first day of trial, Gordon's uneasiness was still with him, only its focus had shifted from Pike to Delancy.

The day had started badly. When James Oliver Delancy got to his feet to take on the first challenge, Gordon had to fight down the feeling of apprehension that had plagued him since the first time he had talked to Delancy about Pike's defense. He told himself again that he was jumping at shadows, that for all the great changes his illness had brought, Delancy was a wise old head, a shrewd and experienced defense attorney. He had picked hundreds of juries. He would know that this was the most critical phase of any trial, the point where his case could be lost beyond recovery. There was never any assurance of winning, of course, even if a defense attorney could select his ideal jury, but defeat was certain if he picked a bad one.

The first prospective juror was Frederick James Engel, a beefy, quick-moving, purposeful man, fifty-one years old, bushy black hair, blue jaw. He had a cheerful glint in his eye. A reformed rogue, Gordon guessed, and he liked him on sight. Mr. Engel was now section manager for Trans-Western Moving and Storage, having been promoted after fifteen years on the trucks. He backed into his chair and crossed his legs and gave Delancy an easy, confident smile as the old man came forward.

Gordon didn't pay much attention to the preliminary questions. He scanned his information sheet on Fred Engel and slid it under his file. The man would be a good juror for the defense. He had lived a rough hard life. He would remember his own bad times and know how much a man needed good friends and plenty of luck to pull out of them. He would not be shocked to hear that a man might take on a little too much booze after a long day. And hearing about the marijuana smoking wouldn't bother him either. A young man like Jonathan Pike would not be totally strange to Fred Engel. And the fact that Engel was a Jew might also be an asset, for he would have his people's blood-knowledge of misery and oppression. He was not likely to accept the official word of authority as the gospel truth. He would want solid proof. All told, Engel would do very well.

And then Gordon realized with a growing puzzlement that Engel wasn't doing very well at all, not with James Oliver Delancy. He could hear the old man's voice rising sharply.

"You do?" Delancy said in an incredulous tone. "Please tell me about that, Mr. Engel."

The big man shrugged easily. "Nothing to tell. I just know Mike Morales from the bowling league. South Rincon Chamber of Commerce League. We run off the games every week at the Charro Bowling Alleys. Mike bowls for his bank team and I've played against him six or eight times this year."

"Are you on friendly terms?"

"I wouldn't say friends. We've bowled together, that's all."

"Do you know Mrs. Morales?"

Engel shook his head. "Never met any of his family."

Delancy stepped back and studied him for a long moment and Gordon wanted to shout, "Take him." Engel was just what they were looking for. His very casual acquaintance with Angela Morales' father meant nothing.

But it did to Delancy. "The defense will excuse Mr. Engel," he said, seeming pleased with his skill in spotting a poor risk.

From that moment Gordon watched and listened intently, trying to chart Delancy's approach. He was working through the list of talesmen almost as quickly as the county attorney, and that was always dangerous. David Burrell didn't have to worry about finding money for investigators; he had a complete file on every member of the jury panel. He had consulted those detailed reports to preselect his ideal jury. He knew the ones he wanted. He even had his alternates picked.

Burrell's questions were brief, almost perfunctory—occupation, years on the job, marital status. Any juror he didn't want was tested with a few sharper questions to establish cause for excusing him. If that didn't work, Burrell would exercise one of his twenty peremptory challenges and wave the man from the stand.

For the defense the problem was a lot more complex. It is not just a question of this man or that. Out of the mass of unknown, unpredictable human beings on the panel, the defense counsel has to pick the wise, the understanding, the just, the compassionate. And he has to make his judgments in too little time, with too little solid information.

Where the prosecutor would welcome retired policemen or military officers, the defense would challenge without a single question.

The prosecution believes that men are generally less emotional than women, less reluctant to punish, so they don't choose women. The defense prefers women, when possible, unless they are spinsters, because neither side wants spinsters of either sex. The prosecution does not care for people from minority groups, unorthodox religions, unstable employment backgrounds. The defense usually finds them completely acceptable.

During the jury-selection process, the defense has its first good chance to reach the minds of the jurors, to condition them for the testimony to come. Delancy was not seizing that chance.

Gordon sat very still, mouth clamped hard, not looking at Delancy but following every word with cold concentration. One fist pounded slowly, painfully, against his leg, out of sight under the table. And each time Delancy dismissed a prospective juror after a few routine questions, Gordon winced.

He knew that in Delancy's place, he would have been charging at them from the very beginning. The entire panel was right there, seated in the front rows of the courtroom. He could reach them all, now. A question asked of one was heard by all. And the questions would have been pouring from Gordon in a relentless, overpowering torrent.

The answers would not be important; the questions were everything. Using them, Gordon would have defined the ground rules of the trial, emphasizing them over and over so that every juror would know what was expected of him. He should be told that the entire burden of proof lies with the prosecutor. It is the prosecutor who must establish his case beyond any reasonable doubt. The defense isn't required to prove a thing. The defendant comes into this courtroom an innocent man. He is presumed to be innocent and it is your duty to accept that presumption. It's up to the county attorney to prove him guilty, and I tell you here and now, sir, he can't do it if people like you will just exercise the good common sense that God gave you. You are willing to do that, sir, aren't you? Of course you are!

And Gordon would have been hammering at them, over and over, about the doctrine of reasonable doubt. He would be telling them in a powerful, carrying voice, that reasonable doubt means just that, a doubt for which you can give a reason. A doubt that won't go away. One such doubt and the defendant must be found innocent. And I promise you that before this trial is over you are going to have so many doubts in your mind that you will have a hundred good reasons for setting the defendant free.

But James Delancy was doing none of this. His old man's voice was barely audible in a courtroom that was noted for its excellent acoustics. Gordon stiffened angrily, trying to send mental messages through to Delancy. Then he noticed Pike turning to stare curiously at him and he forced himself to sit still.

After all, he reminded himself, Delancy wasn't making any serious mistakes. He wasn't scoring many points for his side, but the three jurors he had accepted so far seemed to be okay. All were married men in their middle fifties, slow-moving, comfortable sort of men with nothing of the fanatic about them.

So, he warned himself, let's not be so goddamned self-righteous. The old man isn't doing such a bad job. He doesn't have a lot of excess energy to spray around the courtroom these days, so he is pacing himself for the long haul. He knows what he's doing. He's been doing it for a long time. Just stop second-guessing him and see if you can't be some help around here.

He handed Delancy the sheet for Mr. Karl Erich Handschler after skimming it quickly. No problem there. Mr. Handschler was a senior accountant for the Mesa Land and Title Company, stalwart of the Reformed Lutheran Church, member of the State Republican Central Committee. A perfect juror for the prosecution. Just the kind they liked. Pillar of the community, a man who would fearfully detest every aspect of someone like Jonathan Pike. Gordon watched him march like a soldier to the chair, sit square-backed, thin-lipped, and disapproving, convinced the defense attorney would probably challenge him without questioning.

But Delancy seemed to approve of Mr. Handschler. This was the sort of man he played with in bridge tournaments, competed against in desultory foursomes at the Rincon Country Club, disputing savagely in five-cent Nassaus. Delancy knew people like Handschler and felt at home with them.

Gordon listened, hardly believing what he was hearing, as Delancy shared a pleasant little chat with Handschler. Even with that much warning, he was astonished when Delancy gave a quick little nod, pursed his *V*-shaped smile, and announced Mr. Handschler acceptable to the defense.

Pike had his pale, rarely blinking eyes fixed hard on him, Gordon could see, and he was careful not to show anything of what he was feeling, though he was raging in his mind. What was wrong with Delancy? Had he forgotten he was in a courtroom?

When the next name was called, Gordon slipped the reference sheet out and went through it carefully, letting Delancy wait. A thirty-six-year-old research chemist, unmarried, Protestant, Democrat. Unacceptable on two important counts. Just to make sure Delancy did not miss the point, Gordon took out his heavy pencil and scrawled a large black "NO" across the upper right corner. He stretched across in front of Pike and held the sheet tilted for Delancy to see.

The old man bent to read it and straightened abruptly. His thin gray eyebrows flared. He darted a quick scowling glance at Gordon. He did not touch the sheet. But he excused the juror after a brief courteous exchange.

The judge tapped his gavel lightly. "It is nearly five o'clock, gentlemen. I think we have done fairly well for the first day. Let us try to complete the jury tomorrow. We will be adjourned until nine thirty tomorrow morning."

Gordon nudged Pike to his feet, and they waited with Delancy until the judge left the podium and disappeared through the door to his chambers.

"Now, young man," Delancy said, his voice thin and sharp, "you will please be good enough to tell me—"

"One moment, sir," Gordon said hastily. Reporters had surged forward when the judge left the courtroom and were struggling against the crowd in the central aisle. Gordon took Pike's elbow and walked a few steps away with him.

"You don't like the way he's picking that jury, do you?" Pike watched him closely, suspicious as an animal sensing an unseen danger.

Gordon made himself smile and he hoped it came easily. "It's always a problem picking a jury. You can never be sure. Now, before you go downstairs, I want to remind you about the press. They'll be trying to get to you. They may even manage to reach you in jail. Just remember to say nothing. Tell them Mr. Delancy is doing all the talking. Okay?"

Pike shrugged. "Sure. What would I tell them anyway?"

Gordon signaled the deputy to take charge of Pike and turned back to intercept the first of the reporters. "The defendant will not have anything to say to any of you," he said, using his heavy, dominating voice that could be heard out on the street. "I've told him not to talk. Any comment will come from Mr. Delancy."

The old man was ready for them. He waved a thin languid hand, in a brushing-away-the-flies gesture. "You know better than that, gentlemen. We do not want to try this case in the newspapers. I may have a word for you from time to time. At the moment, nothing."

But while he was talking, most of the reporters were already drifting across the courtroom to where David Burrell was speaking rapidly, tracing broad gestures with both hands, drawing quick bursts of laughter from the reporters nearest him. Obviously David was willing to try his case in the newspapers any time. And if he had been in Delancy's position, Gordon would have been out there competing with him all the way.

Mr. Delancy was latching his slimly elegant briefcase with hands that trembled slightly.

"What was it about that man that prompted you to write me that message?" He sounded tired and slightly hoarse, but Gordon could hear the controlled note of anger in his voice.

Propriety outraged, he told himself. You should have been a lot more cautious in telling him what to do. So watch yourself. He just might kick you off this case if he thinks you are getting too big for your saddle.

"Sir, the man is a scientist. He works with abstracts, not people. The

128

odds are that he would not be sympathetic to a man like Pike. And he is a bachelor at thirty-six. That suggests he isn't an impulsive or warm-hearted person. It seemed to me that he would be an unacceptable risk for us."

"All of that information was on the sheet you prepared?"

"Yes, sir."

"And you thought I would be incapable of reading it, or understanding what it meant?" Mr. Delancy straightened stiffly, his chin coming high so that he was looking squarely at Gordon.

"I was trying to be helpful, sir," Gordon said. But that wasn't going to be enough, he could see. "I'm sorry if I seemed—presumptuous."

"You were trying to make a critical decision without consulting me." Delancy's voice was still quiet, but the tone had a cutting edge. "There will be decisions to make during this trial, many of them, and all of them will be made by me, and only by me. I hope that is clear, Gordon. I will not warn you again." He turned quickly, without giving Gordon time to respond, and went up the aisle, his hard heels making brisk angry clacks in the emptying courtroom.

Gordon unknotted the fists that had begun to ache with tension. He reached down for his briefcase and began loading the stack of files spread across the table.

He almost jumped when an open hand smacked against his shoulder.

"My God, Gordie, you're twitchy as a wild horse. And old Delancy is just as bad. He almost knocked me down on his way out. What's the matter with you two? The first day of trial and your nerves are already hanging out."

Gordon forced a tight smile. He was faking a lot of responses lately, and if this lousy day went on much longer he suspected he just might wind up slugging somebody. But he smiled for his friend and after a moment it became the real thing.

"Sorry, Nico. One of those days. Did you see much of it?"

"Didn't see any of it. Couldn't get in. As far as Rincon is concerned, this is the trial of the century. Anybody who wants a seat had better get here at dawn and sweat it out. You're worried already, are you?"

Gordon closed his loaded bag and picked it off the table. "I always worry," he said. "I just have time for a quick drink before I get back to the office. Join me?"

"Glad to. That's what we came for." Nico moved aside to reach the gate in the railing and swing it open for Gordon.

"We?" Gordon looked at him carefully, remembering suddenly, and was surprised that he had almost forgotten. Maybe a day's hard work actually was good therapy.

Nico was unusually elegant for a working-day lawyer, he noticed. There was a festive air about him. Smoky-gray shimmering mohair suit, richly subdued necktie in several shades of silver, ice-blue silk shirt with large onyx cuff buttons. As always, he made Gordon awkwardly aware of outsized clumsiness, of grotesquely large hands and feet. He buttoned his wrinkled linen jacket and smoothed it with one hand, feeling the dampness of his soggy sweated shirt against his skin.

"Claudia's waiting outside," Nico said unnecessarily. "She didn't want to come in."

I'll bet she didn't, Gordon thought with some bitterness. I'll bet Nico had to skull her before he could get her anywhere near me. Or maybe not. He was forgetting about Claudia. She was capable of a total focus, an inward concentration so intense that she could wipe from her memory anything she might not want to remember, anything that might dim the gloss of perfection. She just might have the least little bit of trouble putting a name on that big gangling fellow coming toward her along the bare echoing courthouse corridor. Nico waved at her and pushed Gordon ahead.

She was waiting just inside the south entrance. The afternoon sunlight came in broken reflections through robusta fan palms and lit the weathered old stone of the courthouse in a soft golden glow. In that light Claudia was radiant. Simple sleeveless shift of coarse raw silk in a mottled ivory design, silver cord sandals, and something new in the way of hairstyling that gave her two densely contoured wings swooping down from her smoothly candid forehead, the streaky blond striations of her hair pointing up that illusion of layered feathering. She smelled of flowers in a warm sun, and something else, an essence of animal perfection, sun-heated and self-adoring. Strong silken muscles moved sweetly as she reached up to Gordon, pulling him down so that she could kiss his cheek in a quick, casually affectionate gesture.

"We were going to take you to lunch, but Nico said you wouldn't come."

"I never have time for lunch when we're in court." His voice sounded strange to his ears, thick and slightly hoarse.

"But you can manage time for a drink." Nico put a hand on his shoulder, urging him forward. Claudia took his free arm and half-ran with him down the shallow steps to the street, almost knocking over a television reporter who was moving quickly forward, microphone waggling overhead.

130

"Give us a second, Gordie." He inserted himself expertly between Claudia and Gordon, signaled his cameraman, and pushed the button at the base of his microphone.

"Mr. Gordon Guthrie, who is assisting Mr. James Oliver Delancy in defending Jonathan Pike, charged with the rape-murder of Angela Morales. Mr. Guthrie, after the first day of trial, how do you—"

"Knock it off, Joey." Gordon swept one hand in a cut-off sign for the camera. "You said it yourself. I'm the junior in this case. Mr. Delancy does the talking."

"And he isn't saying a word. He just skipped on by without looking my way."

"So go home."

"Now come on, Gordie. What do you think? Have you got a chance? How do you see it?"

"I see it the way Mr. Delancy sees it."

"Shit." The reporter switched off his microphone. "Fat lot of help you are."

"Tough. What are you looking for anyway? What do you expect to get?"

"Just the usual. We shot some good crowd scenes this morning. Little David is coming down to give us a statement. It'll edit out to maybe a three-minute clip for the nine o'clock."

Gordon nodded and turned away. Nico had his arm again before he had taken two steps.

"Damn it, Nico, I'm due back at the office. I haven't got time for—"

"A quick drink," Nico insisted. "We won't keep you long. I have a very important question to put to you, Gordie."

Gordon shrugged helplessly. "Okay, but let's get out of this neighborhood. Too many reporters around here."

"The Territorial Hotel is the best spot. And it's on your way." Nico dropped back as they moved along the busy sidewalk, Claudia still gripping Gordon's arm as if she thought he might run away.

And I should be running, he thought. I don't know what the hell I'm doing here, but I know it's a bad idea. Nico probably has me tagged as one more in that long list of Claudia-losers, another of those half-hearted, indecisive suitors who, after that first moment of chagrin, is going to take it all with good grace and settle down as a close and dear friend of the new family. And obviously Claudia had said nothing to make him change his mind.

He let Nico order scotch all around, then asked the girl to bring him a large glass of ice water as well. He scooted his padded chair back from the low table to make room for his legs and turned slightly to find enough light to roll a cigarette.

The bar was cool and dim, almost deserted. Pale blue fluorescent lights broke dazzles off the polished plastic tabletops. Over the whisper of canned music Gordon could hear the quiet rattle of ice, the swish of the siphon as the bartender made their drinks. Claudia was watching Nico with a still solemnity and he reached quickly across the table to touch her hand.

Nico bent his long narrow patrician head toward her, and Gordon could see Claudia's warm wide mouth part slowly in a secret smile. They looked great together, he admitted grudgingly. They'll make a fine breeding pair, probably throw some champion pups. He felt a sudden ugly flare of resentment and made himself back away from it quickly. Sour-dog Guthrie, he jeered at himself. Can't bear to see a friend happy, can you?

But it wasn't just that, he told himself. Not just being a bad loser. Who in hell would want to be a *good* loser, for Christ's sake? No, it's something else. Something I lost in this deal. I can't put a name to it and I don't want to think about it just now, but it's gone, I know that. And I don't believe Claudia had a right to take it, unless she meant to keep it.

When the drinks came, Gordon gulped his glass of cold water in a quick draft. He lit his ready cigarette, burned it down to his knuckles in two drags, and snuffed it out. Then he was ready for a drink. He tilted his glass of scotch and soda in a brief salute to Nico.

"All the best. Have you set a date?" The scotch was pungent and rich in his mouth. That good mellow twenty-five-year-old, of course. Great to be a Kronstadt, eh Claudia?

"We were thinking of the tenth," Nico said happily. "My grandfather's birthday. The old gentleman is pretty excited about it."

Claudia turned toward Gordon so swiftly a pale wing of glossy hair swung across her face. "He's letting us take his yacht for as long as we like. Imagine! Hawaii! Tahiti! Hong Kong!"

Gordon flashed a quick unbelieving stare. The Claudia he knew was not a gushing, ecstatic burbler, and she didn't give much of a damn for rich men's toys. She had plenty of her own, actually. By Rincon standards she was fairly rich herself. A "big-shottedy" girl, as Jumbo had called her. Of course, in Kronstadt terms she was only a step or two above the poor little matchgirl, but since when did that sort of nonsense trouble Claudia, or even interest her?

Nico laughed softly, leaning back. "I keep telling her she won't stick it out beyond Catalina. This famous yacht is a creaky old interisland schooner. It's duded up pretty fancy, but it's slower than a rowboat. It carries a crew of six and there is never a minute of privacy or peace. But yacht is a magic word, I guess."

"Be supercilious, if you like." Claudia pulled a face, mock-haughty. "But we never had a yacht in my family and I want to go cruising like the rich people."

That's more like it, Gordon thought. The satirical tone was clear enough, he would have said, but Nico paid no attention. He responded seriously, as always.

"Of course," he agreed. "It might be fun for a while. We'll see."

"And Nico's Uncle Juan is giving us an airplane for a wedding present." Claudia sounded breathless, as if she were marrying into the Santa Claus family and had just realized she was going to get to drive those flying reindeer. "An airplane!"

This time the mockery was clear enough even for Nico.

"Uncle Juan is a goddamn troublemaker," he said, and he did not sound amused. "He spends all his time in Rio these days and he hardly ever gets back here. He just doesn't remember what it's like."

"But what does that—"

"Let it go for now, Claudia," Nico said with an edge to his voice. "I can't control the impulsive old gents in my family. You are likely to get a lot of comical gifts before you're finished. But what Uncle Juan is forgetting is that there isn't an inch of uncultivated ground at the home ranch. Does he really think my grandfather is going to plow under fifty acres of good alfalfa just for a landing strip? He'd plow me under first."

"Oh, I don't think he—"

And that is about enough of this crap for me, Gordon thought. If Claudia keeps working that needle, she just might find that Nico isn't as tame as he looks. Anyway, it has nothing to do with me.

"Tell him to get you a helicopter," he said impatiently. "Well, thanks for the drink, Nico. I have to be on my way."

"Wait, wait, wait." Nico snatched at his wrist. "I never did get to the point. Miss—" He lifted his head for the waitress. "Another quick round here, please. Sit a minute longer, Gordie. Got something to ask you."

Gordon let his heavy bag down to the floor again and stayed where he was, poised on the edge of his seat, ready to go.

"All this wedding-present chatter and I forgot what I wanted to say. The wedding, Gordie. I want you to stand up with me. I need some friends on my side. The whole family is going to be there, some of them I haven't seen since I was a boy. And Claudia's got a mob of strangers coming too. So I need help. A friendly face. You'll do it, won't you, Gordie?"

133

"Stand up with you," Gordon repeated slowly. "What does that mean?"

"Best man."

"For Christ's sake, Nico. You've got the wrong guy. I'm no good at that stuff. Hell, I'd probably lose the ring at the last moment. No, I can't do it."

"Don't answer so quickly." Nico leaned forward, frowning earnestly. "I want you there, Gordie. I told you, I need some friends around. I know you don't go for these cutaway affairs, but—"

"Cutaway? I haven't got one."

"On me," Nico said quickly. "Bridegroom's treat. My tailor will do us both. Come on, Gordie, be a sport."

Gordon snorted angrily, but he kept his mouth shut and gave himself a moment to think. Claudia was watching him, quietly intent. Apprehensive? Gordon wondered. Her eyes seemed to be pleading, he thought, but she said nothing.

Claudia wouldn't want him there any more than he wanted to be there. But what about Nico? They had been friends for a long time, and when he asked Gordon to be his best man, Nico was saying something about that friendship and its meaning to him.

The waitress distracted him when she placed fresh glasses on the table. Gordon gulped his drink quickly. Claudia had not moved. Her eyes still tracked him.

It would be uncomfortable for her, maybe even embarrassing. Too bad. To hell with Claudia. To hell with me, too, for that matter.

"Be glad to, Nico," he said with all the sincerity he could manage. "Thanks for asking me." He put his empty glass down and left before anyone could answer. He went stomping down the street in a steaming temper, mopping his face with a handkerchief that was already sodden. He was behind schedule and running sweat like a broken faucet and was solidly furious with himself and everyone he had so far met in this long disastrous day. When a stout little man darted out from the shade of a shop-window awning and touched his arm, Gordon was, for a trembling second, on the verge of hitting him. And then the quick grace of humor saved him. Even when you have only five minutes to catch your plane, you still have to stop for the red lights. Even when you are hungry enough to bite a chunk off a live wolf, you still have to wait a decent time until everyone else at the table has been served. Gordon pulled in a long breath and forced a smile for the man who had seized his sleeve in both hands.

"You are looking very bad, Gordon. Terrible," the small man said in a tone of outrage.

"What?" Gordon blinked at him. "Mr. Arkin. How are you? What did you say?"

"You look terrible, Gordon. Just look at you." Mr. Arkin turned Gordon's arm upward and ran a stubby finger along the worn seam of his sleeve. "This suit is at least three years old, no? Look at the buttonholes. Like open mouths of babies."

Gordon laughed helplessly. Mr. Arkin was an old friend.

"It is nothing to laugh at, Gordon." Mr. Arkin was righteously stern. "How long has it been since you ordered a new suit? You don't know, eh? I will tell you. Two years, Gordon. That is ridiculous for a young man in your position. You must pay more attention to your appearance. It is most important for a young lawyer."

Gordon sighed. He shifted aside, trying to move along. Mr. Arkin skittered beside him, holding his sleeve in a death grip.

"I haven't time just now, Mr. Arkin. Maybe later."

"Time? Time for what? I know your measurements. At your age you don't change that much. I will cut and baste two new suits and let you know when they are ready to try on. If you are too busy, I will bring them to your office. Agreed?"

Gordon muttered under his breath. "Okay, okay. Two more like this one. Gray linen with the nylon in it."

"Gray? Why always gray? I have a very nice piece of beige linen-weave Tergal. About the color of your hair. It will make a change."

"Okay, okay. One gray, one beige."

"And also, just for you, I have a bolt of white Moygashel, just in from Ireland. That you must have too."

Gordon stopped short. "I don't even know what Moygashel is, Mr. Arkin." This was crazy. He had work to do; he couldn't waste time like this.

"Linen. Genuine Irish linen, the best. Soft like silk. Treated so it doesn't wrinkle. It is beautiful, Gordon, and for you it will not be too expensive. I make you a nice price. So we say three, eh?"

"But I don't wear white linen, Mr. Arkin. It gets dirty in five minutes."

"So in the cool evening you take a young lady out to dinner and to dance, eh? For this you need a nice white linen, no? So we say three."

"Okay." Gordon gave up. "Let me know when you're ready for me."

"You will thank me, Gordon."

"Yes, thanks very much," Gordon said absently. He pulled his sleeve from Mr. Arkin's grasp and went along the street toward his office, blowing out a long patient breath. He was going to be a very well-dressed fellow pretty soon. A new cutaway from Nico's New York man and three new workaday suits cobbled together by Mr. Arkin. And that is a clownish combination that defines me pretty well. How does that line go? Tragedy tomorrow, comedy tonight. So just go on taking yourself so somberly serious and see if someone else doesn't sneak up on your blind side with another sharp pin.

He shifted his heavy bag to his other hand and moved along more slowly, keeping to the shadows, feeling easier within himself, almost lighthearted. Almost.

Pike's trial moved slowly through the opening stages. Too slowly, Gordon thought. He suspected that David Burrell was deliberately drawing it out, that he was needlessly elaborating routine exchanges, maintaining a constant and often artificial tension that was visibly tiring Delancy, bringing him at the end of each long day's session near to the point of exhaustion. Yesterday he had wavered, almost stumbled as he started down the courthouse steps with Gordon and had gladly taken Gordon's arm and held onto it tightly until he had eased himself down in the back seat of his car. The old boy was really beat. I just hope he got plenty of rest last night. It's a cinch he got more than I did.

For the past five nights Gordon had been averaging three or four hours a night in one of the cramped attic rooms close under the sweltering slate roof of the Bench Club. Miserable quarters, but the people there were very good about hauling sleep-sodden young lawyers out of bed in time for their morning appointments. Lack of sleep did not bother Gordon; the dullness of his mind and spirit came from a grinding sense of frustration, an angry, impotent resentment that soured him, because he knew now that Delancy was never going to allow him any active part in the trial. The old man was used to playing the star part. The only assistant he would accept was someone to shift the scenery.

But he might change his mind, Gordon told himself, trying to cheer himself up. If Burrell wears him down just a little more, he may think again about letting me carry some of the load. I could have helped him. Given a chance, I could have picked a better jury, and I could certainly have prepared them a hell of a lot more too.

Realizing the serious mistake he had made with Mr. Karl Erich Handschler, Delancy had gone more carefully in selecting the rest of the jury. Until the tag-end of the third day when he had fumbled again in passing Mr. Iko Murikato as the eleventh juror.

Afterward Gordon had furiously underscored three items on his information sheet with savage black penciling and smacked the sheet down in front of Delancy when the old man came slowly back to the defense table and slumped in his chair. Gordon stabbed a blunt finger at the sheet, forcing Delancy to follow. *Japanese-born.* Naturalized now but born and brought up in an atmosphere of unquestioning authority-worship. Mr. Murikato owned and operated Sayonara Nursery Gardens and daily shipped planeloads of cut flowers to West Coast markets. *Rich man,* Gordon emphasized with a stab of his thumb. Rich men do not make good jurors for the defense. Worst of all, as far as the trial was concerned, Mr. Murikato was the father of twin girls. *Two fifteen-year-old daughters.*

Delancy sighed quietly. When the court rose he left without speaking to Gordon.

So they had Handschler and Murikato, two very bad ones for the defense. And only one that looked particularly good. Juror Number Nine. Evans O'Neill, thirty-two-year-old English instructor at North Rincon Consolidated High School. Married, no children. Young enough, experienced enough. He should be able to understand something of Pike's background and motivations. At least it was possible to hope.

The rest were so-so. No way to tell about them until the jury cast its votes. Given his choice, Gordon would have excused four of them and taken the others only under pressure.

That was the jury that would try Jonathan Pike for murder.

Gordon came into the cool empty courtroom and went slowly down the bare dusty aisle to the defense table. He turned as a uniformed bailiff's assistant came through the side door with three thermos carafes of water and doled them out, one first to the judge, then one each for counsel.

"Feels good in here," Gordon said. "You fellows finally got the air-conditioning working, did you?"

"Hoo-boy." He held up crossed fingers for Gordon to see. "Something about the compressor, they say. It starts off fine in the morning, but just when the sun gets to burning, it wants to dribble off. Don't know what the hell's wrong with it."

Gordon tipped his briefcase and slid out a stack of fat file folders.

"Judge Pontalba is gonna raise some dust if that thing kicks off again today."

Gordon grunted. He sorted the folders into four stacks.

The bailiff shambled away, stroking a dustcloth as he moved up behind the bench to polish the judge's working space. He shined the small rosewood gavel, poised it above its block and looked out across the empty courtroom. "Y'all be in order now, y'hear?" he said very softly. He nodded once, satisfied, and tapped the gavel. "Gonna be a hot-hot day," he muttered as he came down and passed Gordon. "You want to learn to take it nice and easy, young man."

Twenty minutes to go, Gordon noted. Minor court officials were drifting in. The bailiff placed his Bible on a shelf near the witness stand and stood there absently rubbing his cloth over the gold-embossed cross on the leather cover. The court stenographer came in more briskly, going directly toward his desk, arms loaded with his stenotype machine and boxes of folded paper tapes. Two big-hatted gun-toting deputies clomped up the aisle to the main entrance, swung both wings of the door open and latched them back, and then took their posts outside, blocking away the mass of spectators waiting impatiently in the corridor. One of them touched the brim of his hat when a small hunch-shouldered man came bustling through, leaning heavily to one side under the weight of a crowded canvas carryall. Mr. Ellery, senior clerk at Gaines, Prinz and Delancy.

Gordon got up quickly. "Here, let me take that, Mr. Ellery." He moved a few steps up the aisle and swung the bag easily up to the table.

Mr. Ellery leaned on the back of a chair and fought for breath. "Don't know what gets into these messenger boys these days. Always late. Can't depend on any of them."

"Thanks for bringing the stuff yourself, Mr. Ellery." Gordon un-strapped the carryall and lifted out half a dozen fat bound volumes. He kicked the bag out of sight under the table.

"I'll be stopping for the transcripts of yesterday's testimony," Ellery said. "Would you like me to bring you a copy, Mr. Guthrie?"

"Just put one on my desk, please. I'll look at it tonight."

"Very well. Good luck to you and Mr. Delancy."

"Thanks. We can use some."

Gordon took a blank sheet of paper and tore it in narrow strips. He opened a file folder, turned to the page that listed his citations and checked the first one. After that he didn't bother. He could trust his memory well enough to find the right page in each volume and insert a slip so that he could locate it quickly if the judge were to ask Mr. Delancy to substantiate any of his references to past decisions. He stacked the books on the table. Still ten minutes until the starting gun. He could take time for one last cigarette.

He went out through the side door and crossed to the window that looked out onto the central patio where long-term county prisoners were weeding the flower beds, trimming grass along the walkways, scrubbing the small ornamental fountain, going about their work slowly to make it last the whole day. Gordon sat on the windowsill and fished out his sack of tobacco.

Two young lawyers he knew casually went past him, both of them stretching their necks to read from the same paper-covered volume. It looked like a trial transcript, Gordon thought. Probably yesterday's testimony in *State v. Pike*, he suspected. And when he heard one of the lawyers whistle softly and saw him shake his head, he was sure. That would be the medical examiner's report which had opened yesterday's session. Very bad. He didn't need a transcript to remember how bad it had been. Almost as hard to take as that earlier time when Angela Morales' mother was on the stand.

Of course a prosecutor has everything going for him in the early days of a trial, and it is his business to give the defense some very bad times indeed. And David Burrell was not missing any chances. His opening statement had been a model for the textbooks, brief, concise, deliberately undramatic. David was too wily a prosecutor to expose his trial strategy to the defense by an overlong opening.

The People, he said gravely, would prove that Jonathan Pike, and Pike alone, had murdered fifteen-year-old Angela Morales in the groves at El Pinar after brutally beating and repeatedly raping her. Burrell would be speaking to them again about the legal meaning of rape-murder. At this moment it was enough to say that the facts of this atrocious crime fitted precisely the statutory definition of first-degree murder. The People would prove that Jonathan Pike had committed first-degree murder. The People would ask the death penalty.

"Pike, and Pike alone." Gordon printed it in large letters on his pad and shoved it across to Delancy. He did not need the note to remind himself, but he wanted to make sure that Delancy understood the significance. This was the first and would probably be the only clue that they would get from Burrell about the general thrust of Lee Wallis' testimony. Those few words made it clear that Wallis was going to deny being present that night at El Pinar with Pike and Angela. He might even have an alibi arranged. That was a possibility that Gordon wanted an investigator to check out immediately. Delancy nodded shortly and returned the pad.

Gordon then offered Delancy the folder containing the opening statement for the defense. Five-and-a-half pages that he had sweated to reduce from twenty. And a top sheet with key-word reminders typed in oversized capitals. Delancy rose without touching it.

"The defense will reserve its opening statement, your honor," he said.

Gordon made a startled sound that brought Pike's head swinging sharply around toward him. He managed a smile and rubbed his throat as if he had been smothering a cough.

Last night Delancy had been planning to follow Burrell immediately. He had complimented Gordon on his draft, even tried out a few of the good phrases. Why had he changed his mind?

It is normal procedure for the defense to wait until the prosecution has presented its entire case before making a statement of intent to the jury. But in Pike's trial, they had decided to jump in right away to counteract the effect of Burrell's opening. They would lose nothing by it. They had so few witnesses scheduled to appear for Pike and they would take so little time on the stand that Delancy's opening and his summation would come too close together. They would almost overlap. One might blur the meaning of the other.

Why had Delancy changed his mind? Unless—and a fearful possibility struck Gordon like a blow—unless he was now planning to put Pike on the stand. If that were so, he would be wise to reserve his opening. Was it that?

They had discussed at length the matter of putting Pike on the stand. Gordon thought that Delancy realized how tricky a witness Pike could be and how unpredictable the jury's response. As a man on trial for a particularly brutal, emotion-charged murder, Pike was almost too self-composed, calm, seemingly unconcerned. The jury would not know how hard-won the composure was. They did not know the boy.

Burrell probably could not rattle Pike on the stand if Pike had been properly coached ahead of time. That was not the danger. The danger was Pike himself, his air of challenge, his personal sureness that could translate as insolent, smart-ass cockiness. And if it did, it would repel any jury trying to reach the truth about the killing of Angela Morales. Or so Gordon felt.

Delancy had agreed with him when they'd talked about it. He had even volunteered one of his very few personal observations about Pike.

"He is a strange one, Gordon. He behaves like a man who never had a friend and never expects to have one. He has a rare talent for locating the point of vulnerability, flicking a raw nerve that you did not even know was exposed."

So Delancy had noticed that. Gordon was a little surprised. Delancy did not seem to be noticing much of anything these days. But hearing that, Gordon felt sure that the old man would never allow Pike on the stand. He had put that problem out of his mind. Too soon, perhaps.

He was so intent on the problem of Delancy's sudden decision, that he paid little attention as Burrell called his first witnesses and began to lay the factual groundwork for the trial.

A large aerial photograph of El Pinar was put in evidence. On it a succession of deputies pointed out exactly where they had found pieces of torn and bloodied clothing, an empty cracked whiskey bottle, a melon-shaped blood-encrusted rock, and the long heavy tape-wrapped screwdriver that had come from Cordero's garage and now looked as if it had been dipped in discolored rust-red paint.

Burrell took a long and careful time with the girl's clothing, unfolding each piece slowly as if he had never seen any of it before, inspecting the rips and stains and shaking his head in wonderment, standing always directly in front of the jury box. He repeated the same procedure with each of three witnesses from the sheriff's office and by the time he was finished with them, most of the jurors were skidding their eyes away and looking slightly sick. Pike sat stiffly, not moving, hands clasped hard together on the table. Gordon heard him swallow dryly, making an audible click in his throat.

Burrell left his exhibits in plain sight on the clerk's table as he turned to escort Angela's mother from the door of the witness room. And after one brief look at her, Gordon knew this was the point David had been building toward, the dramatic explosion that would drive home to every juror the human meaning of Angela's terrible death. Until that moment they had been considering official, almost impersonal evidence. But no more. This woman before them was the victim's mother. The torn and bloodied flesh of Angela Morales had once been part of the flesh of this woman. Living proof that this crime was a human horror, the source of human grief, and a human cry for justice.

And there isn't a damn thing we can do about it, Gordon thought. David is going to bring this court to a goddamn emotional frenzy and we just have to sit here and take it. All the exhibits have been identified over and again, but David is going to repeat the whole ritual, lingering over the details until that woman breaks down in a nerve-racking storm of scalding tears, screaming her torment and calling on God for a savage vengeance.

Mrs. Morales moved heavily toward the stand, looking blindly past Burrell. Her short body was broad and powerful, thickened by childbirth and hard work, shapeless in a black dress that nearly touched the floor. She had the broad square face of the Mexican-American, darkly sallow, the nose slightly flat at the bridge, eyes opaque, almost unfocused. She took the oath with a calm dignity that made Gordon hopeful for a moment, but then she leaned immediately forward, gripping the railing of the witness stand with wide stubby hands, clenching them so hard that veins stood out like heavy cords. Her face was impassive, enduring, but a swift wild pulse beat visibly just beside her right eye.

Burrell began very quietly, with the expected questions, and Mrs. Morales gave a mother's answers in a reasonably steady voice. Yes, Angela was fifteen. She was the youngest of four daughters; the others were now married and gone away. She was not doing well with her studies, but it was good for a girl to go to school. Her Angela was very popular, had many many friends, was always going somewhere with young people. But she was also a good girl, obedient and dutiful. Mrs. Morales had not known that Angela had left the house on the night she was killed. When she found Angela's bed had not been slept in, she did not raise an immediate alarm because she was afraid Angela's father might be very angry to hear she had been out all night. He was a good man, a loving father, but very strict. So she had waited until after he left for work and then she had searched the neighborhood, asking for Angela. She did not find her. After a long time she came home and waited. Now she would have to tell Angela's father. But the man from the sheriff came first.

All the time she was speaking, Mrs. Morales kept looking toward the table spread with Angela's torn clothing. She sat tensely upright when Burrell turned for the first piece. Yes, the little sleeveless red sweater she had bought herself as a present. She would know it anywhere. The flat velvet slippers were very expensive, Italian, she thought. Angela had saved a long time for them. There had been a scarf too, crazy colors of red and pink and orange. Angela had loved it and worn it a lot. But that had never been found, as they knew. She had told the police about it and they had searched, but the scarf had not been found.

Jonathan Pike shifted his steady, expressionless gaze from the woman's face and made a note on the pad in front of him. It was his first.

David Burrell was now holding up a pair of thin black skin-fitting stretch pants.

Well, yes, that is the sort of thing young girls wore these days, Mrs. Morales was saying, even her Angela.

Burrell held the fabric carefully in both hands. Watching him, Gordon was sure that he had rehearsed this move often, because the pants now seemed whole, not really damaged, merely dusty and slightly stained. Then with no warning Burrell shifted his grip, letting the torn front panel fall away toward the floor.

Mrs. Morales drew in a wild sobbing breath. She reached out with both hands and Burrell draped the bloody violated fabric over them and stepped back, giving her a moment to inspect it, giving the jury an unobstructed view of the woman's dreadfully contorted face as she turned the cloth this way and that, as if trying to make it whole again.

"Can you identify the garment as Angela's?"

Mrs. Morales did not look up as Burrell took the torn stretch pants from her. Her head rose and fell once. Burrell stopped on the way back to the table and told the reporter to let the record show that she had signaled yes.

He came back carrying scraps of torn black lace and silk. He was too slow to keep Mrs. Morales from rising and snatching them from him. She stood behind the low railing still and brooding as a stone statue. She wadded the tattered silk in her hands. A low anguished moan began in her throat, then rose to an animal wail. She turned a flat hating stare toward Pike.

"He raped her. He beat her. He killed her. Why? Why?" Her voice soared and broke like a flawed trumpet, cracking with tension. Both short hard hands hooked into claws. She darted down the steps, brushing past Burrell.

The bailiff and two armed deputies jumped toward the defense table, forming a barricade before Mrs. Morales could cross the room to where Jonathan Pike sat, suddenly pale and frozen. The woman stopped. The murderous impulse left her as quickly as it had come.

"He must die," she said in a slow, reasonable voice. "He is not like other people. He must die so that he can never do to other girls what he did to my Angela." Then she slumped suddenly to the floor, the sturdy worn body striking with a painful sound. It was as if the entire courtroom had drawn in a long silent breath.

After Mrs. Morales had been sent home in a county ambulance and the courtroom was again in order, David Burrell apologized to the judge. He said he would have no more questions for Mrs. Morales, but if Mr. Delancy wished to cross-examine, he was sure that Mrs. Morales would be sufficiently recovered by tomorrow and able to answer.

Delancy rose in wrath like a stern preacher rebuking a presumptuous congregation. "The defense," he stated in a voice that shook with anger, "will not subject that poor grieving lady to one more moment of senseless torture on the stand, your honor. She should never have been called here."

Gordon was proud of him. And Burrell had sense enough not to object.

At the recess Gordon walked down to the cell block with Pike, knowing he was still shaken.

"Scared me for a minute there," Pike said in a low, wondering voice. "She moved fast."

"Surprised everybody."

"Not Burrell," Pike said flatly. "He wasn't surprised. He had plenty of time to stop her. Didn't you see him sidestep?"

"No."

"It's a wonder he didn't hand her a knife while she was going by. That bastard is out to get me." He ran a hand quickly across the back of his neck. "How do you figure? Is it going sour for us?"

"It always looks bad at this stage," Gordon said, giving it the old pro's matter-of-fact tone. "The prosecutor has everything his own way right now. Nothing we can do about it. Our turn comes later."

Pike leaned against the steel wall and folded his arms. He studied Gordon carefully. Slowly he shook his head.

"I saw you writing a note in court," Gordon said. "Anything I should know about?"

"It might be." Pike handed him the folded sheet he had torn from his notepad. At the top was one word, "Scarf," followed by a jagged line of question marks.

"Angel's scarf? The one her mother says was lost?"

"She was wearing it that night," Pike told him. "Lee gave it to her. Said he paid forty bucks for it. Angel wore it all the time. I didn't know it was missing until I heard Mrs. Morales on the stand today. Do you think it means anything? The fact that it's missing?"

"I doubt it," Gordon said slowly. "It might have been useful information if we'd known about it earlier. It's too late now. If Wallis took it, he's had plenty of time to get rid of it. If anyone else found it, he probably just stuffed it in his pocket and gave it to some other girl."

Pike shrugged. He crumpled the paper in his hand.

Mrs. Morales had been the most damaging witness so far, but the medical examiner's report was almost as bad for Pike because the jury was no longer being told of that impersonal object known as "the body" but was now compelled again to think of Angela's murder in human, personal, gruesomely physical terms.

Dr. Allen McCann, professor of pathology and county medical examiner, was a calm, dispassionate man, experienced and confident enough after hundreds of trial appearances to present his report to the jury in simple nontechnical language that seldom needed interpretation. No part of his evidence was slanted toward dramatic emphasis, but the impact on the jury was severe. Gordon noticed them looking away, occasionally darting quick speculative glances at Pike as the doctor was testifying.

Dr. McCann had examined the body where it was found at El Pinar, had pronounced Angela Morales dead, and had later performed a detailed autopsy in his laboratory. He had found her skull to be totally crushed. The cerebral cavity was almost empty, with hardly any brain tissue still in place. The right eye completely destroyed. Both lower and upper jaw fractured. Nose broken and smashed flat against fractured right cheekbone. Upper right front teeth missing, all others so loose they could be removed with fingers. Left arm fractured twice between wrist and elbow. Right hand and wrist shattered. Right elbow broken. Both buttocks showed multiple bruises and deep lacerations. Vagina and vulva bruised and swollen, some sign of bleeding. Anal aperture severely torn, rectum deeply bruised, some bleeding. Both vagina and rectum showed traces of semen. Blood-group tests established that the semen had been emitted by a male of Group O. Victim's blood type was also O. In addition there were multiple contusions and lacerations over entire body, most noticeably on both upper thighs. Death had been caused, the doctor concluded, by a total crushing of the skull with a resulting decerebration.

There was a curiously long silence when he had finished, as if the jury needed time to accept as reality the picture of Angela Morales his calm impersonal testimony had created.

"A few brief points, Doctor," Burrell said then. "You told us about the right hand and wrist, both crushed, completely shattered. I wonder if you could explain to the court how that could have happened?"

Delancy stirred in his chair, but he did not rise.

"I can't be sure, of course," the doctor said. "But it seems to me that the right hand must have been braced against a firm surface which would have intensified the impact of repeated blows. At least that would be one explanation of the severe damage."

"If Angela Morales had tried to fend off her attacker," Burrell suggested, "if she had held her hand up, pleading, and if that hand were struck with a heavy weapon, driving it against the side of her head, then we could expect that—"

"Oh, I don't think so, your honor, if you please." Mr. Delancy came to his feet at last, leaning on a corner of the table. "Dr. McCann is an expert witness and must be allowed a certain range of speculation, but we are now drifting toward total imagination. I don't think it should go any further, sir."

Judge Pontalba nodded gravely. "Mr. Burrell?"

"I will withdraw the question, your honor. I think the jury has a sufficiently clear picture. Now, Doctor, I show you these two objects, State Exhibits Twelve and Thirteen, and ask you to examine them and tell the court if in their general size and shape they are consistent with the weapons that brutally beat the life and brain from the body of Angela Morales?"

Delancy sighed, began to rise, then sank back and let the doctor answer.

"I couldn't say definitely, Mr. Burrell. Any heavy object without sharp edges might have been used. The condition of the body makes it impossible to tell."

"But these objects, this long, blood-encrusted screwdriver that weighs eighteen ounces, and this smooth-surfaced rock weighing twenty-one ounces, are not in any way inconsistent with the weapons used to kill Angela Morales. Is that true?"

"They are not inconsistent."

Burrell took a long moment to return the exhibits to the clerk's table, making sure the jury saw them clearly once more.

"Now, Doctor, one last point. You told us you found traces of semen in both vagina and rectum. I want to be sure we all understand you. Semen is the male sexual fluid emitted during orgasm. Is that an acceptable definition?"

"It will serve."

"Having found semen present in the body of Angela Morales, you would then conclude that before her death she was forcibly raped, sexually violated?"

"No, sir," Delancy said promptly. "I must object again, your honor. The prosecutor knows better than that. This witness is not qualified to draw such a conclusion. No witness is. He may testify to the evidence of sexual intercourse, but the question of rape is one for the jury alone."

"Angela Morales, your honor," Burrell said forcefully, "was brutally murdered before her sixteenth birthday. Anyone committing sexual intercourse with her, with or without her consent, was committing rape. It is as simple as that."

"No, sir," Delancy insisted. "Now it is Mr. Burrell who is improperly drawing conclusions. And they are conclusions extremely prejudicial to the defendant. I ask that the question be disallowed and struck from the record."

"So ruled," the judge said. "Continue, Mr. Burrell."

"Your witness, Mr. Delancy." Burrell turned away, well content. The jury had understood the meaning of that interchange and that was all that he wanted.

"No questions for this witness," Delancy said.

Gordon had expected nothing else. In murder trials most defense attorneys prefer not to point up the meaning of the medical evidence by additional questions unless it is absolutely necessary. But earlier Gordon had proposed two lines of questioning for the medical examiner and even though Delancy had vetoed both, he still believed the answers could have scored for their side.

The semen the doctor had tested, for one. Group O was the most

146

common blood type; the majority of the people in that crowded courtroom almost certainly carried Group O blood.

A question, doctor. If I told you that two separate, totally distinct male sources supplied those traces of semen you found, you would not say that was impossible, would you? Of course not, how could you?

For the same reason Gordon would have taken answers from Dr. McCann about Angela's shattered right hand and wrist. The medical evidence showed that the most severe damage had been inflicted on the right side of the girl's head and body, which suggested that the murderer might have been left-handed. Any faint clue pointing to a left-handed murderer was bound to be helpful to a right-handed defendant. He should have gone for the answers. He was thinking of the jury, left at the end of this day's session with those gruesomely detailed mental images of the battered, violated, murdered young girl. All of them had been looking somberly in Pike's direction when the court adjourned.

Every seat in the spectators' section of the courtroom was filled when Gordon came back in. He went quickly across the bare floor and took the chair next to Delancy.

"Good morning, Gordon. Splendid day." The old man was looking brisk and cheerful, with a note of healthy ruddiness in his face. He probably walked over from the office, Gordon guessed. A good night's rest really had done him a world of good.

"Morning, sir. First thing this morning David is going to identify his photographs and try to get them in."

"Yes?" Delancy seemed only mildly interested.

"Here is a list of citations for objection that we discussed the other day. The usual ones."

"And we will get the usual decision, I expect."

Gordon frowned slightly. "Maybe so," he said, half irritated. "But we have to try. David had some hellish big enlargements made of those photographs. They look like movie posters. In living color. Now, in any human terms, those blowups are downright prejudicial, and it's up to us to say so."

"Of course." Delancy pursed his prim little angular smile: the wily old veteran being gently amused at the zeal of his youthful junior. Gordon's scowl deepened. "However, you must remember that trial courts have admitted all sorts of gruesome pictures, enlarged and in color, and have always been upheld on appeal. Don't be too hopeful, Gordon."

"Sooner or later, Mr. Delancy, the way things are shaping up, some court of appeals is going to reconsider this whole question, really go into the question of prejudice deliberately created by a prosecutor, and when they do, we'll see them throwing out half these horror pictures the prosecutors are always sneaking in. We have to be ready for that. This might be the decisive case, the one that changes the rules. We have to get our objections on the record."

He was speaking too loudly, he realized. Burrell and two of his assistants were looking across, half smiling. Gordon felt his face go hotly flushed.

He slid over to his outside seat when Pike came in with his guard. Pike moved at an easy relaxed pace, looking casually around the crowded courtroom as if he, too, had come to watch the show and didn't think much of it so far. He nodded to Gordon and took the center chair. Delancy gave him a chilly good morning.

"Want to talk to you," Pike said in a quiet undertone. "Got an idea."

"At the break." Gordon nudged him to his feet as the judge came through from his chambers.

Judge Pontalba stood in front of his high-backed swivel chair, surveying the court. He looked tired and pale. At that moment he very closely resembled James Oliver Delancy, Gordon thought. The judge was considerably younger, but he too had the smoothly polished cap of thin gray hair, the long, narrow, sharply defined features, the same air of weary politeness. He said good morning in a thin hoarse voice, told the court reporter to note that defendant was present with counsel, and then signaled Burrell to get on with the day's work.

The first three witnesses were technicians—the sheriff's crime photographer, one man from the photo lab, and another from the Desert Valley Photographic Studios who had made the color enlargements. One of Burrell's assistants took them through their testimony. They spoke knowingly of color values, dye transfer prints, relief images, scale values, tonal balances, and Delancy let them ramble, saving himself for the moment when Burrell offered his seventeen pictures in evidence.

The preliminaries ended with the civilian technician identifying the eight identical sets of prints he had developed from the official negatives. One package went with a flourish to defense counsel, another was handed up to Judge Pontalba.

"I think this would be a good moment for our morning break," the judge said. He turned a thin smile toward Delancy. "I think the jury may anticipate a longer break than usual. I expect that Mr. Delancy will have something to discuss when he returns."

"I most definitely will, your honor," Delancy said with a brisk forcefulness.

148

Gordon got up and leaned over Delancy's chair. "Pike wants to talk to me. I'll check the pictures when I come back."

They went together quickly down the circular metal staircase to the jailhouse corridor below and along it to the small room reserved for lawyers and their clients.

Pike unwrapped a stick of chewing gum and folded it into his mouth.

"You be sure to get rid of that before we go back," Gordon said sharply.

Pike looked at him scornfully, his mouth working lazily. "I'm not stupid, counselor."

"Okay, what's on your mind?"

"I got an idea last night. Couldn't sleep much, just walking up and down in that damn cell, I got to thinking about what you said, how the cops got onto me so fast. I've been wondering about that."

"So have I."

"Sure. I went back over that Tuesday night, trying to remember every movement. It seems I see it clearer every time, new little details."

"And what did you remember this time?" Gordon tried to sound interested, but he was beginning to question the value of Pike's selective memory, and something of that feeling was evident in his voice.

Pike shot a suspicious glance at him. "I'm not boring you, counselor? Keeping you from something more important?"

"Don't be so goddamn touchy. Get on with it." He took out his sack of tobacco and eased the drawstring.

"Well, I was about half asleep, I guess, staring up at that damn light they never turn off, and I was thinking about the first time I came back to my place that night. You remember?"

Gordon nodded. He licked his cigarette to seal it and hung it in a corner of his mouth.

"Every other time I thought about it, I was always remembering myself being alone. I pulled in and braced my bike out in the back road and came in through the garden gate. I remember making myself a stick and smoking it down, staying outside, sitting under that big pepper tree and feeling pretty good. But last night when I was thinking about it, I got the hazy notion there was someone else with me. And that's what gave me the idea about that anonymous phone call."

"I'm not following you very well."

"Well, it isn't anything definite. Nothing I could actually swear to, but I seem to see that girl from the main house. The maid. Skinny little girl named Paca. I think maybe she was there that night. Then I remembered that the cops said it was a woman's voice on the phone and I just wondered—" He shrugged and sketched a brief gesture with one hand.

"Paca," Gordon said thoughtfully. "I talked to her earlier, and to that landlady of yours, Mrs. Seltzer. Just routine. They didn't have much to say about you except that you were a stand-offish type and hardly ever talked to anybody. I didn't get the idea that either of them had it in for you, though."

"Maybe not," Pike said. "Just a notion that came to me. I thought it might be worth checking."

Gordon sighed, letting out the rest of the cigarette smoke. He dropped the butt to the floor and stepped on it. "Yes, I'll have to talk to her again. It's too risky not to. But I wish I could just ignore the whole thing."

"Now I'm not following you. I thought—"

"You didn't think long enough," Gordon said heavily. "Suppose the girl did make that phone call. Don't you remember what the anonymous caller told them? She called the sheriff's office substation at seven thirty-two Wednesday morning. She spelled out your name, made certain they had the address right, and then said 'he killed someone last night.' There hadn't been any deaths reported Tuesday night, so no one paid much attention. Just another one of those nut calls they get. The duty sergeant made a routine report, and they might have sent a deputy around to look at you in a day or so. But then those boys found Angela's body and the cops came a-helling to grab you. All because of that phone call. Now are you getting the picture, Pike? Do you see why I hate the thought of talking to that maid out at your place?"

Pike shook his head.

"She said you killed someone. So you might have said or done something that Tuesday night that set her off. What was it? Any idea at all?"

"I don't remember. I just can't bring it back. I'm not even sure she was there. Maybe I just dreamed it."

"And maybe you did do or say something that sent her right to the police. That's what I'm afraid of. I don't even want to find out, but I'll have to talk to her. I'd like to forget it, but if my guess is right, and Burrell's investigators get to her first, she could turn out to be one hell of a witness for the prosecution."

"Jesus," Pike said quietly.

"Were you on bad terms with the girl?"

"No, nothing like that. I thought we were friends."

"If she's the one who set you up, boy, you must have given her a pretty good reason." Gordon shook his head. "This girl could be real trouble. Even worse than that damned drug-smuggling business."

Pike spat the wad of gum into his hand and plastered it to the underside of the table. "I don't suppose you were able to find out much about that, were you?"

"Now how in the hell could I find out anything?" Gordon demanded angrily. "I didn't dare make a move. I can't even go to the Narcotics Bureau and ask a few discreet questions about Cordero. If just one small hint reaches Burrell, he gets some solid ammunition to shoot at you. If he could show the jury you were mixed up in a drug-smuggling operation, hell, I don't even want to think about it. That marijuana is bad enough. If Burrell heard anything about narcotics, he'd wind up making you into some kind of drug-crazed maniac. We'll just have to hope that Wallis doesn't bring it in. He should know that any mention of drugs would ruin him too, but there's no way of telling what he's going to say when he gets on the stand. We'll just have to wait and see."

"And this business of the maid. If I remembered it right, if she really did make that call, then it just makes everything worse for me? Is that it?"

"Doesn't have to be," Gordon said with more sureness than he felt. "She might even know something that could help us. I'll try to get to her during the noon recess. Let's get back now. I want to get a look at those pictures before we start arguing."

Gordon was braced for them, but he had not expected the photographs to be so graphic, so horrible in their impact. Delancy pushed the stack toward him when he came back with Pike. The old man's hand was trembling slightly, and his wide lipless mouth was pinched in a harshly compressed line.

The pictures were a shock, an offense, gruesomely detailed. The ugliness of white splintered bone, long glossy strands of thick black hair caught in jagged lumps of rough gray stone, bruised pulpy flesh, and the glaring brilliance of blood that was the dominant note in all the pictures.

"Jesus, we can't let him put these things in."

Delancy tapped the pictures shakily into line and turned the stack face-down. He shook his head in a dazed movement.

The clerk's gavel cut off conversation, but murmurs continued, especially from the first two rows in the public area that had been set aside for the press. Judge Pontalba rapped his gavel vigorously when he came up to the bench. "You are reminded that court is in session. Please be quiet."

David Burrell took a folder from one of his assistants and turned back the cover. He skimmed quickly over his list of countercitations and

151

rebuttal arguments, leafing rapidly through half a dozen pages to refresh his memory.

The judge broke the seal on his wide flat envelope and shook out the prosecution's enlarged photographs. "Let us give ourselves a few minutes to see what it is we will be talking about," he suggested. "Do we all have exactly the same selection of photographs, Mr. Burrell?"

"Exactly the same, your honor. Each is numbered on the back for reference."

The judge put on his reading glasses. He drew the pictures closer and bent over them. It was a strange moment, Gordon thought. The courtroom was totally silent. Everyone sat quietly, watching Judge Pontalba.

The judge studied the first picture for a long moment and then slipped it off to expose the second. Suddenly he made a raw, rough sound deep in his throat. Then he rose quickly and almost ran down the four steps that led to the door of his chambers.

Gordon sat as stunned as the others. Then he saw the opening the judge had given them. He tapped Pike's shoulder.

"Shift chairs." He rose quickly, bending over the back of Delancy's chair. He took Pike's seat when it was clear.

"That cooks David," he said urgently, pitching his voice as low as he could. "He can't get those pictures in now. If one quick look makes the judge vomit, how can he possibly send them to the jury?"

Delancy looked at him coldly. "The judge's reactions are not pertinent, Gordon. The jury is not present."

"That doesn't matter," Gordon insisted. "We are still in session. The judge didn't recess. He just ran. Look at the court reporter. He's got both hands ready on that machine, just waiting for somebody to say something. It all goes on the record. That's what I'm trying to say, Mr. Delancy. Now is your chance."

Delancy rose stiffly without answering, and when Gordon glanced at the bench and saw the judge standing there, he got up too and made sure that Pike was on his feet.

Judge Pontalba swallowed heavily. "My apologies. Mr. Burrell. Mr. Delancy. Shall we continue now?"

"Certainly, sir." Burrell moved briskly toward the bench, notes ready in his hand.

Delancy composed his mouth in that quirky little smile that was his inevitable preliminary to agreement. But before he could speak, Gordon smacked his hands together sharply.

"Could we have five minutes, your honor?" he said in a voice that shook the walls. "On a matter of great importance?"

The judge turned his drawn, half-sick face toward Gordon, blinked once as if he couldn't remember who he was, then looked at Delancy. "Mr. Delancy?"

The old man straightened to his tallest height. "I must ask the court's indulgence, your honor. If I might have a moment with my young and very eager assistant?"

The judge smiled thinly, understandingly. "Five minutes then, Mr. Delancy. And please make it clear to Mr. Guthrie that there will be no more such interruptions."

Gordon leaned along the table toward Delancy, trying to ignore the quick flare of anger that made his voice ugly. For the second time in his life he touched the old man, taking the delicate bird-boned wrist in a quick hurting grip.

"It has to be said, don't you understand that? The court reporter has to hear you say it before he can put it in the record. You've got to get up there and—"

"Come with me, Gordon." Delancy wrenched himself free and went quickly toward the side door, almost stumbling in his haste. He moved down the outer corridor a few steps, then turned and glared up at Gordon, coldly outraged. "This is the third time you have intruded upon me in this courtroom, and it will be the last."

"Mr. Delancy, don't you see we have to—"

"Please don't interrupt me, sir!"

Gordon jammed hard fists into his pockets and prayed for a magic wand that would transform him into the quietly confident, poised, coolly assured young assistant that Delancy so very much wished him to be. But now, meeting Delancy's bleak stare, he knew that he seemed only clumsily insistent to the experienced old man, infuriating in his stubborn intensity.

"You've defended hundreds of cases like this, Mr. Delancy, and of course you recognize this opportunity as clearly as I do. I'm sorry if I made a big dramatic scene out of it. When I have your experience, maybe I'll learn to play it a little cooler."

Delancy showed him a thin little smile. "Very well, Gordon. Let's return."

"About the judge, sir?"

"What about the judge?"

"Goddamn it, sir!" Gordon exploded, his carefulness forgotten. "All you can see is that I'm intruding in your trial. What about our client, for Christ's sake? What are you doing for him? Don't you see the opening the judge gave us? You saw Judge Pontalba when he looked at those pictures. He was physically sickened. He went through a sort of emotional storm that sent him puking right out of the courtroom. You saw him. All you have to do is get that reaction into the record. Then if he overrides your objections and lets those pictures go to the jury, you've got a terrific point for appeal. You can't let this one slip by, too, Mr. Delancy. It's too important."

"Slip by, too." Delancy repeated Gordon's words in a thin choked voice. "*Too?* Do you think I have let other opportunities slip by in this trial, Mr. Guthrie?"

The icy bite of the old man's voice brought Gordon up short. He realized only then that he had offended in the worst possible way, touching Delancy on the raw quivering nerve of his professional pride. He could have chopped his tongue off, but it was too late now for apology.

"I didn't mean to say that, sir," he said with complete sincerity. "I'm afraid I was pushing too hard. The point is, sir, and I think you should consider this very carefully, that we may have a matter of reversible error involved here. If you make a point of getting the judge's reactions noted in the record, then we could—"

"And how does one do that? The judge is not a witness."

"Do you have to ask me how to do it? You go back in there, go right up to the bench, and say, 'With the court's permission, your honor, I wish the record to show that the trial judge's physical response after a brief inspection of these inflammatory and prejudicial photographs which the prosecution wishes to enter in evidence was so severe that the judge himself was sickened and compelled to desert the bench.'"

"And I would then be held in contempt."

Gordon stared at him, astonished. "So what? He won't remove you while the trial is in progress. And you wouldn't be saying anything that wasn't true. You're just saying that the emperor lost his pants. And everybody in the courtroom saw him lose them. What if he does cite you? Are you so tender you can't stand a little disapproval from the bench?"

"You are being impertinent, young man."

First Gordon, then Guthrie, now young man. I wonder if he thinks I give a shit what he calls me.

"No, sir," he said patiently. "I am being your assistant. It is my duty to give you all the information I have that will help the defendant. So I am telling you now that I believe the judge will be committing reversible error if he admits those pictures. Provided you have put his physical reaction into the record."

"Reversible error is not a possibility."

154

"You can't be sure of that, sir. I think we could build it up high enough to get a new trial out of it."

"A new trial? Why should I want that?"

"We would go into a new trial knowing exactly what kind of testimony to expect from Lee Wallis. We would have time to check out every detail. That's just one of the benefits. I'll bet David has got half a dozen nasty little surprises ready for us. He'll have to spill his whole case now, and then we could slaughter him in a new trial."

"This is ridiculous," Delancy said testily. "The only trial that interests me is the one going on right now. Which you are needlessly delaying."

"Needlessly!" Gordon heard his voice soaring again, but he did not try to hold it down any longer. "I'm trying to talk sense to you. Get after the judge. Nail him while you have the chance."

"You obviously understand nothing of the courtesy an attorney owes to a presiding judge. There are a great many lacks in your store of information, young man. Manuel Pontalba is a fine man and a fine judge. He is always careful to protect the rights of any defendant in his courtroom. I would never think of attacking him in such a fashion."

"But that's not what I—"

"Furthermore," Delancy went on harshly, "if you had an ounce of compassion, you would have sought for a personal, a human, reason for the judge's response to those pictures. If you had asked me, I could have told you that Manuel Pontalba's youngest daughter is only a few years older than Angela Morales and he might well have made a momentary identification of his daughter with that unfortunate girl. Now, sir—"

As he spoke, Delancy was backing away. His breath came rapidly and his thin face was dangerously flushed. He raised a long bony finger with slow deliberation and stabbed it toward Gordon. "And now, young man," he said in a judgment-day voice, "you will listen to me. You are relieved as my trial assistant. You will go from here directly to your office and wait there until I send for you."

"Sir!" Gordon protested. "I—"

"Immediately, sir." Delancy brought his narrow shoulders back in a stiff brace. "In the meantime I will be thinking about your future position in Gaines, Prinz and Delancy. You will wait for me to call you and you will talk to no one until then. I have made myself clear, I trust?" He nodded curtly, sure that he could not have been misunderstood, in language or in meaning.

Gordon watched him march briskly toward the courtroom door. He stared after him, dazed, not believing it had actually happened, until the attendant swung the door shut behind Delancy. He slumped heavily against the wall, looking blindly down at the scarred and dusty floor, shaking with a sick fury that caught him like a sudden onset of fever.

He cursed himself, his wild intemperance that had given Delancy a valid excuse for pushing him out. He could be no further help to Jonathan Pike, who needed all the help he could get, God knows. And now, he thought, I am supposed to consider myself in professional disgrace. If Delancy has his way, I can see how it will go. From now on I'll be getting those dreary penny-ante assignments that drain time and energy to very little purpose. All my work will be questioned over and over until I'm ground down so far that I'll send in my resignation. I think that's what Delancy has in mind for me.

He straightened himself stiffly against the wall. He pulled his chin hard back into his neck, tightened his belly muscles, and made himself draw in a long deliberate breath.

But it's not going to happen that way with me, he promised himself. No matter what Delancy thinks. In a shop like Gaines, Prinz and Delancy, a senior partner cracks a very long whip, but surely Delancy's credit would take a sudden drop if his partners knew how poorly he was handling the Pike trial.

To hell with Delancy, he told himself forcefully. He's not going to send me off to my desk to count my thumbs until he's ready for me. I've put in a hell of a lot of hard work on this case, much more than Delancy even knows about. It's my case as much as his, and I'm not going to let him fire me off it.

His mind seemed to be working with a cold white clarity. He caught a flash of the future. He could see what was going to happen now and he knew what he had to do about it. He nodded to himself, easier in his mind now, calmly determined. He knew what he had to do. And Delancy was not going to stop him.

He waited where he was for a few minutes, smoking a cigarette and giving himself time to grow quieter. Then he moved up to the turn of the corridor and went left toward the main entrance to the courtroom. He tapped one of the deputies on the shoulder.

"Just want to stick my nose in for a minute," he said in a whisper.

The guard shook his head dubiously. "Don't know if you can make it, Mr. Guthrie. We're jammed pretty tight." He pulled a wing of the door open and Gordon could see what he meant.

The twelve-foot clearance between the rear wall and the last row of solid oak bench-seats was packed almost solidly. I wonder what the attraction is for them, Gordon thought. There's nothing to see and damn little to hear. They'd all be better off staying home and watching television. He leaned all his weight slowly forward, making room for himself.

He could see easily over the heads of the people in front, but he could hear only vague murmurings from the direction of the bench. Delancy and Burrell were at side-bar, their heads very close to Judge Pontalba who was leaning toward them. At that distance their voices were all but inaudible.

But Gordon did not need to hear them to know what they were saying. Delancy would be offering *Janovich v. State* to remind Judge Pontalba that trial courts traditionally are allowed complete discretion in admitting or excluding prejudicial or gruesome pictures and that Judge Pontalba therefore need not feel that he was in any way bound by previous decisions. The judge would hear him out, politely attentive, would then turn to Burrell and let the prosecutor remind him that in the case cited by his learned colleague, the trial court had, in fact, admitted the disputed photographs.

Delancy would then shift his ground to *State v. Campéon*, as they had planned, would also refer to *Henderson v. Breesman*, a civil case that might be helpful in his argument. And, as expected, David Burrell would admit that in those trials, photographs had indeed been excluded, but only because it had been established that the photographs showed a changed condition in the body of the victim or in other physical evidence. However, he would go on to say, citing *Young v. State* and *Browning v. State* as his authorities, that photographs showing changed conditions could be allowed in evidence if the changes were not considered detrimental to the defendant.

And anyway, he would say, beginning to get a little heated, what is it that Mr. Delancy is claiming here? Does he contend that these particular photographs show some changed condition? If so, what? They were, after all, taken at the earliest possible opportunity, by trained professionals. What more does he want?

And that would be it, probably. Delancy could only retreat to eloquence, pleading as persuasively as he could that these glaringly colored enlargements were prejudicial by their very nature. No appeals court had ever reversed on the basis that enlarged photographs or color photographs were not properly admitted, but a forceful argument could still be made, if Delancy had the heart for it. He could remind Judge Pontalba, man to man, of his own physical reaction and ask him if, in his heart, he genuinely believed a jury could look at those pictures without being sickened.

Maybe the old boy was being very forceful up there, charging like a warrior-knight, daring all for his almost lost cause. But Gordon did not believe it. Nobody at the bench was raging at the law's rigidity, pleading for a measure of human compassion in a case where a young man's life was at stake.

Another moment and Delancy returned to his place beside Pike.

Gordon knew the answer then, but he waited to see it for himself. The jury was summoned, seated with the usual muffled commotion. David Burrell picked up four sets of the enlarged photographs and approached the bench. Gordon backed to the door and turned away. The photographs were in.

Four news photographers, barred from the courtroom, swung toward Gordon as he came out. None of them tried to stop him. They had all the pictures of Gordon Guthrie they would need.

Gordon paused in the shaded entry looking out across the sun-glaring plaza, seeing heat-shimmers rising off the pavement. He could feel the sweat spring up in heavy beads the moment he moved into the sunlight.

He went along narrow Spanish-planned streets for several blocks to the wide cool entrance to the Ford agency garage. He was nearly deafened by wild strident Mexican music as he came down the grease-stained ramp. He spotted the blue-coveralled mechanic taking his ease in the back seat of an open convertible, transistor bellowing an inch from his right ear. Gordon slapped the hood twice sharply and, when the mechanic looked up, covered both ears with his hands. The heavy dark-skinned man grinned, lazily thumbed his nose, and then swung the same hand across to turn off the radio.

"Don't like good music, huh?" His very white teeth seemed enormous, jutting out of a wide mouth.

"I know when I'm licked." Gordon gestured toward the back of the garage. "Did you get my car fixed yet, Juanito?"

"Sorry, Gordie." The mechanic opened the door and slid out. "That goddamn El Monte agency. They still haven't sent that bumper section. Say they'll have to get it from Los Angeles."

"Well, hell," Gordon said impatiently, "I'll just take it as it is then. I need some wheels."

"Cops might not like it, you not having a whole bumper, but I guess they won't do too much to you if they catch you. It's back here." Juanito led the way, talking over his shoulder as he went. "How's the case going? Looks bad for your boy Pike, huh?"

"Early days yet, Juanito. Don't believe everything you hear."

"I saw that guy Burrell on television last night. He seemed awful damn sure he's got your boy by the balls." Juanito looked at him slyly, half maliciously, hoping for a response.

Gordon shrugged.

"Doesn't bother you much, huh? You think you'll get him off anyway, do you? Guy kills a little Spanish-blood girl and who cares? Plenty more where she came from, right?"

Gordon stared at him. "What the hell's the matter with you, Juanito? Pike says he didn't kill the girl. Don't you think we should give him a chance to tell his story before we hang him?"

"Oh shit." Juanito wiped a heavy-knuckled hand across his mouth. "I don't know why I get so pissed-off about that little tramp anyway. It's just people talking about her like she was a two-buck whore who got what was coming to her. Hell she *was* a whore. But I still get the black-ass when somebody else says so." He shook his big head, wondering at himself.

"You knew her?"

"Sure. I think she's some kind of far-back cousin. Known her since she was a baby. Beautiful little girl she was, too."

Gordon stopped with his hand on the door of his car. "I thought she was always pretty careful about her reputation. Scared of her father and what he would do to her if he heard anything."

"Old Mike Morales is *muy duro*, all right. He did everything but lock her up. But he's a dumb shit. I could name a dozen young studs who've been in her pants. She was a real fun-girl, from what I hear. But what do you care? None of that stuff helps your boy, does it?"

"No," Gordon said heavily. "It doesn't matter whether the girl was willing or not. She was only fifteen, so it was still rape. No, telling the jury about the girl wouldn't help Pike very much. Might even hurt him."

"What I figured." Juanito tapped Gordon's chest with the back of his hand. "Well, hang in there, champ."

"You bet," Gordon said. "What about the car? Do you want some money now?"

"Hell." Juanito hesitated. "I don't know, Gordie. The boss isn't here today. Suppose you just sign the worksheet."

"Okay. Tell him I'll come in tomorrow and settle up."

He swung in behind the wheel, turned on the ignition, and listened to the motor. Sweetly tuned, it burbled quietly, then roared with surprising power when he fed it more gas. He pulled the stick shift into first and let out the clutch when Juanito signaled the way was clear.

*   *   *

159

The place where Pike had been living until he was arrested lay beyond the old section of Rincon in a quiet, dying neighborhood of too-large houses that could not be sold and were not worth proper maintenance.

Gordon parked outside the large grimy white house and sat there a moment, wondering why Pike had chosen to live in such a miserable place. He'd been paid fairly well, and if he really did get that extra five hundred a month he talked about, then he could have afforded something a lot better than this. Maybe, like so many other young men, Pike thought of his pad merely as a place to sleep and store his clothes. Real living went on somewhere else. And maybe, Gordon suspected, Pike had a taste for squalor.

Worn bricks in the front path were tilted at crazy angles across the yard of burned-out Bermuda grass. The three steps up to the broken terrace were lined with pots of unpruned geraniums.

Gordon remembered that the bell did not work. He knocked lightly on the door. A lock chain rattled and clanked as the door snapped open. She was taller than he had remembered but just as scrawny, her gray hair still strained hard into a tight bun, her thin mouth pinched tightly, eyes narrowly suspicious. Gordon offered her a wide friendly smile that brought no response.

"Gordon Guthrie, Mrs. Seltzer." When she did not answer, he brought out his wallet and produced one of the business cards the office furnished him. "I was here before."

"I remember you." Her voice said the memory was not one she treasured. She ignored the card. "What do you want now?"

"Just a few questions." Gordon worked to keep the smile in place.

"I am tired of questions. I am tired of all of you asking questions. I'm supposed to cooperate with you, but nobody ever talks about you cooperating with me. The sheriff keeps my garden apartment locked up for two weeks and I can't rent it and I lose all that money, and who cares? No, I don't want to answer any more of your questions."

"I am very sorry about the apartment, but—"

"And when they found that sack of marijuana, the way they took on, you'd think I had something to do with it. Well, I'm not helping any of you anymore." She began to swing the door and Gordon moved forward quickly before she could close it.

"I am sorry you had a bad time, Mrs. Seltzer. Police investigations are upsetting for everybody. I don't like bothering you again, but this is pretty important."

"What is?" she asked coldly.

Gordon hesitated a moment. He looked down the long dim hallway behind Mrs. Seltzer, wishing the maid would show up and save him the trouble of asking for her.

"There is some question about the exact timetable of events the night Angela Morales was killed—"

"I don't know anything about that," she said swiftly, ready with her denial before he had finished. "I've said it over and over. I hadn't even set eyes on that man Pike for days before it happened."

"What about your maid?" Gordon asked. "She might be able to help me."

"Paca?"

"Could I ask her? It won't take long."

"No, you can't," Mrs. Seltzer said flatly. "She's gone."

"Gone? Where to?"

"Who knows where girls like that go?" she demanded. "Who knows where they come from, for that matter?"

"But she can't just disappear."

"Why can't she?" Mrs. Seltzer was beginning to enjoy herself now. Gordon's obvious perplexity made her mouth twitch in a mean little smile. "She left about two–three weeks after Pike killed that Morales girl. Those deputies kept on and on at her, and I guess she just had enough finally. Probably scared."

"But didn't she tell you where she was going?"

"Just said she was going home to her sick mother. No warning, no notice, nothing. Just 'I'm leaving.' Well, she had two weeks' pay coming, and I told her she would have to wait until the end of the month if she expected me to pay her. But she just left, big as you please. You'd think money didn't mean a thing to her."

"She went home, you said, Mrs. Seltzer. Do you have her home address?"

"I never asked her for it. I can't keep track of these girls. Paca's the fourth one I've had this year. They never stay."

"Paca's real name is Francisca Guitterez, isn't that right?"

"Something like that," Mrs. Seltzer said grudgingly. "I can't speak those Mexican names."

"Guitterez is a pretty common name in Mexico. Did she ever mention the name of her hometown?"

"I don't remember. She told me she used to work for some American family down there. That's how she picked up her English. But I don't know where it was. On the seacoast somewhere."

"Does the sheriff know she's gone? Did you tell him?"

"Of course he knows. Those deputies came out here a dozen times after she left."

"And that's all there is to it?" Gordon asked. "She just walked out, left no forwarding address, didn't say a word, just left, and nobody cares enough about it to ask questions? That's hard to believe, Mrs. Seltzer."

"Don't you call me a liar, young man. You just get out of here. I don't have to talk to you." The door banged shut, the chain rattled into its slot.

Gordon turned away. He was still holding the card he had offered Mrs. Seltzer. He crumpled it slowly in his hand.

The cool bright reception room of Gaines, Prinz and Delancy was almost deserted as Gordon came hurrying through. He flipped one hand toward the new blonde at the desk, admired the way the small directional spot glazed her polished hair. He still hadn't found time to check her out, didn't even know her name. He'd have to give her some serious effort as soon as he got Pike off his neck.

He turned toward Delancy's office and went in without knocking. As always Miss Dorelli let him wait while she finished the line she was typing.

"Mr. Delancy was looking for you at the noon recess, Mr. Guthrie," she told him in a disapproving tone. "He was surprised to find you were not waiting for him."

"Had a lot to do," Gordon said easily. "I'll catch him when court adjourns. I wanted to see you."

"He was quite angry, Mr. Guthrie. He said—"

"I'll wait for him to tell me." Gordon cut her off with a forcefulness he had never used before with Miss Dorelli. Maybe he would have to take his lumps from Delancy, but he would be well and truly damned if he'd take any at second-hand from his secretary. "I have a confidential report for Mr. Delancy. It's not the kind of report I want to give to one of the girls in the typing pool. Too much likelihood of gossip, and we couldn't afford that. Can you take it?"

Miss Dorelli was trying to freeze him with the chilling glare of her eyes.

"It's something Mr. Delancy should know about for the trial," he said. "You'll understand when you hear it—" But he had lost her. This time his sigh was more a groan of exasperation. "Well, the hell with it. I'll wait and tell him myself later on."

He swung toward the door, had his hand on the knob when she called. "Sit down, Mr. Guthrie. I will take what you have."

Gordon dictated a detailed account of his talk with Pike during the morning break and his later conversation with Mrs. Seltzer. When he had it finished, he took a moment to roll a cigarette.

"Is there more, Mr. Guthrie?"

"A little more." Gordon tried a smile to ease the chilly atmosphere. "Summation. Recommendation."

The smile didn't work with Miss Dorelli any more than it had with Mrs. Seltzer. Gordon dropped it and went on in a businesslike tone.

"First question: Is Pike telling the truth about remembering that Tuesday night meeting with Francisca Guitterez outside his apartment? I think so. In spite of all the liquor he drank that night, and the marijuana, he has shown a remarkable accuracy in the details he has so far remembered.

"Second question: Was it the maid Francisca Guitterez, also known as Paca, who made that anonymous telephone call that directed the sheriff to Pike? My vote is no. For two reasons. We know she left Mrs. Seltzer's house and we can assume the sheriff is not looking for her, because he would let the newspapers know if he was seriously trying to find her. So the sheriff probably has no interest in her, present or absent.

"Also, I think I can guess why the girl left as soon as the investigation tapered off. Remember the five hundred dollars in twenty-dollar bills that Pike told us he got every month in the mail? What if one of those packages came in after Pike was arrested? And what if the girl opened it, saw what she had, and rat-holed it away until it was safe for her to leave? There are places in Mexico where five hundred dollars in cash is a fortune.

"So where does this leave us?

"First, I suspect we had better be prepared to see David put that mysterious phone-calling woman on the witness stand. The sheriff isn't showing much interest in tracing Francisca Guitterez, which suggests to me that he already has a line on that unknown woman.

"The alternative possibility is that the unknown woman made that phone call because Lee Wallis asked her to do it—maybe bribed her to do it. Wallis would have the most solid motive for directing early attention toward Pike, and he may very well have seized his chance. If that is the case, then I don't expect that we will ever know anything more about the woman, because Wallis has had plenty of time to get her out of reach of the sheriff or anyone else.

"So we are right back in that same position we were in when Pike told us about the drug-smuggling racket he suspected Cordero was running. We can't investigate the maid, Paca, any more than we could investigate Cordero. We can't take the risk of alerting David by any sign of unusual interest. It's a case of damned if we do, slightly less damned if we don't. Not a very favorable position, but at least now we have a little better idea of what to expect."

Gordon rose, stretching. "Just the ribbon copy, I think, Miss Dorelli.

If Mr. Delancy wants duplicates, you can run them off on the Xerox."

Miss Dorelli made a note on her pad. She did not look at him.

"Thanks very much," Gordon said. "Please tell Mr. Delancy I will be waiting in my office until he's ready for me."

At seven o'clock he was still waiting.

If court had adjourned at the usual time, Delancy should have been back in his office by five thirty. Of course he would have notes to give Miss Dorelli, letters to sign, other clients to consider, but an hour and a half, for Christ's sake! What the hell was he doing?

Gordon was ready to go in there slack-shouldered and contrite, slink into that luxurious office and perch on the outer edge of his chair and thank the old man for a big tasty portion of crow baked in a humble pie. He had stepped far out of line in that bad-tempered session with Delancy and he expected a certain unpleasant retaliation. But what was Delancy waiting for?

He had been able to keep himself occupied earlier, knowing Delancy was busy in court. In spite of his instructions, Miss Dorelli had sent him a carbon of the report he had dictated to her. Office rules called for a stated distribution of copies, and Gordon Guthrie was not man enough to make Miss Dorelli break the rules.

He had locked the report away in his file cabinet. While he had the drawer open, he had skimmed through the thick collection of carbons of other reports and briefs he had sent to Delancy in preparation for the Pike trial. Four hundred pages, he guessed. I wonder how many of them the old man bothered to read?

The thinnest and least satisfactory was the file on Lee Wallis. Two weeks of work by three investigators and Gordon now knew nothing more about the man than he had at the beginning. It was possible to anticipate the general lines of the testimony he would give on the stand. There were only a few important areas he could admit knowing about. But where and when would he begin to slide away from the truth?

Gordon sighed heavily. Of course Wallis was going to deny any involvement in the death of Angela Morales. David Burrell's opening statement to the jury had hinted strongly at an alibi for Wallis. So Gordon had a few clues, but not nearly enough to plan a strategy for cross-examination. In the end it would come down to a matter of dominating the witness. You would have to overpower him, tear apart that innocent image he was trying to present as the truth. And then break the man himself. Delancy knew how to do it, had done it often. All it needed was implacable determination to apply the steady, relentless pressure of raw force.

164

Delancy knew all that. And he should have known that, since his illness, he simply did not have that vitality, the energy that would keep him charging at Lee Wallis until he found the crack that would shatter him like a flawed diamond.

And that will be enough of that, Gordon warned himself. Stay off that one. It's Delancy's case and he has made it awfully damn clear that he means to run it his way. So stop telling yourself how much better you could do it. Of course you could break Lee Wallis faster and more completely than Delancy could ever manage. But you'll never get the chance, so forget it. You keep on like this and you are going to wind up storming in there and giving the old man another lecture on trial management. And then, my friend, you really will be through here, forevermore.

Gordon snorted. Seven twenty, he noted, and that was cutting it a little too fine. Delancy never stayed in the office after seven thirty. He might come back for a long night session, but he made a point of getting home before eight o'clock unless there was a very considerable emergency.

Gordon swung his feet down from his desk with a crash, turned off the lights, and slammed his door hard to make sure it was locked. He went down the corridor in long quick strides, then purposely made himself slow down.

Easy does it now, he reminded himself. Nice and easy. You are the eager, well-meaning young hero sauntering down for a warm little heart-to-heart with your fatherly old adviser. He may have a few stern words for you, but it's all for your own good, and under it all you will be able to sense the affectionate concern in that gruff fatherly voice.

Gordon grinned at the thought. Then he set his face in sober lines and opened the door to Delancy's office. And he stood there with his mouth open like a bumbling young cowboy on his first trip to a fancy house. The place was empty. Miss Dorelli's desk was tidied and locked, her electric typewriter bedded down for the night.

Gordon went slowly across the outer office and poked his head around the edge of Delancy's open door. After a long still moment he turned away. He closed the hall door behind him very quietly, as if he were leaving a room in which someone had just died.

Gordon got out to open the gate that led to his father's place, drove through, and climbed out again to latch the gate. He drove around the back of the house and rolled in beside Jumbo's dusty old pickup under the carport. He sat there for a while before he pulled himself heavily out of the car and swung the door shut.

Coming slowly around to the front door, he caught a glimpse of Jumbo through the lacework of brittle sparse bougainvillea that shielded the sunward end of the terrace. He stopped abruptly, then shrugged and went on.

Jumbo was fresh from his evening bath, dressed in clean faded khakis, his big bald head gleaming. He was stretched almost full length in a woven rawhide sling chair, his bare toes waggling luxuriously in the coolness. He lifted a long tubular glass, rattled the ice, and stared at Gordon over the rim.

"You look about six inches shorter. Somebody been pounding on you?"

Gordon made a weary gesture. He brought a matching chair closer to Jumbo's drinks table and eased himself down slowly. He swung his feet up, used one hand to spring his tight collar and the other to pick up a glass. He dropped in two ice cubes from Jumbo's insulated bucket, took half a sugar lime and squeezed it dry, and then half-filled the glass with pale Mexican rum. He topped it up with soda and stirred it with a finger.

"You bring your dirty shirts? Elena was asking."

Jesus, Gordon groaned in his head. Dirty shirts! "Didn't think," he said mildly. He drank the whole glassful in one long thirsty swig and put it down on the table with a small careless clatter. He leaned back and half-closed his eyes. It was very good out here in the beginning twilight when the bare tawny earth went orange and purple in the shadows and the scalding heat eased off toward a cool evening freshness.

"Nice tonight." Jumbo let out a quiet breath. He reached toward the table with one hand. Gordon could see the scars and breaks on that hand as it wrapped around the base of the rum bottle, the little finger that would not bend prodding toward him like an accusation.

That little finger was a reminder of the days when Jumbo had been running a donkey engine for the Mesa Copper Company. He had been young then, a brawling, tireless bucko full of boiling juices, saddled with three small boys, motherless after the birth of the last and best of them. The accident had been a cave-in that had killed twelve other men. But Jumbo had come out of it with a broken arm and collarbone, a permanently straight finger, and a bone-deep determination never to go underground again.

And which of those whitened, crisscrossed scars represented the succession of poorly paid, futureless jobs he had taken after he came down-mountain to Rincon, uneducated, unskilled. "Strong, willing, stupid, and honest," he always said when he was remembering that bad time.

166

The job at Butler and Barlow's Premium Dairy had been Jumbo's salvation. He hated it with a strong man's unwavering loathing. He constantly wore a plug of molasses-flavored chewing tobacco in his jaw when he was working, trying to dampen the stink of milk souring in its various degrees. He scrubbed himself rawly pink every evening when he came home. He tried every variety of bath oil and scented soap. He never drank milk, refused butter, despised cheese. But he had kept the job because he needed the money for his family, and now he would probably never leave it.

"I was thinking about the house," Jumbo said, his voice low in the evening quiet. "Man has to think. Nobody's going to live forever. I think about the house. I built ever' inch of this house. Not much money but a lot of sweat."

And some blood, Gordon suspected.

"I been thinking about you and Bruce. You reckon Bruce will ever want to live here again?"

No, Gordon said in his head but did not say it to his father. No, Bruce is never coming back. He was the oldest and he had taken the worst punishment because he could understand something of what was happening. I had a fairly easy time, Gordon thought. And Ian rode free until he got himself killed. But Bruce was badly hurt.

Mostly it was the women. When they had been boys living with Jumbo in much more restricted quarters, the women had been very hard for them to understand. Hardest of all for Bruce who could remember his mother clearly and hated Jumbo because his father's human appetites had not died when his mother had died. Gordon had been disturbed, too, he knew now, but not as badly as Bruce. Ian, the baby, noticed very little. But for Bruce they had been terrifying because even then he could sense the basic instability of the family and knew that each woman Jumbo found during one of his periodic raging drunks could be a serious threat. What a hell of a life it must have been for Jumbo, Gordon thought suddenly.

"I don't know," he said softly. "Bruce is pretty well set, I think. He's got that good job in the refinery and he's married to that New Jersey girl and what with the two kids—"

"What I thought." Jumbo's voice was somber, heavy with some private mourning. "So last night I got to figuring. I got a little money, you know. I'm a sly fellow and I stick some down a rat-hole from time to time. I was thinking, if it was all right with you, why I'd leave the money to Bruce and you could have the house and land. How would that sit with you?"

167

Gordon understood what he was trying to say. He could hear the unspoken, unspeakable appeal, and he wished that he could respond with the quality of acceptance and affection that Jumbo wanted and needed. They had reached their compromise, he and his father, after he had come home from the Army. They could speak now with decent regard for each other's opinion. They remembered now to be properly cautious about any blunt declarations of policy. There were no more brutal shaming fights, no voices roaring in thunderous insult. They were father and son, linked in the heart's blood, knowing what others would never know. But they were not yet friends.

"This is a good house, Jumbo," Gordon said carefully. "I wouldn't want to live anywhere else. But—"

"Sure, boy, sure," Jumbo said heartily. "I just figured, a man of property like me ought to start thinking about how he's going to leave his millions. You do want the house, Gordie?"

Gordon sat up to make himself another drink. Jumbo watched him closely out of the corner of his eye.

"I'd like to have the house," he said sincerely. "Thank you, Jumbo."

Jumbo, he thought suddenly. He had never been Father or Daddy or any of the names other kids called their fathers. Just Jumbo. Because Bruce had once brought a book home from school and Jumbo had read to them about the elephants, and from then on the name was fixed. Because he was the strongest and biggest and most dependable element in their lives. Until later, when he wasn't.

He had taught them to ride and care for horses, to locate the trout holes in mountain streams, to bait their hooks and head and gut their catch, to kill and scald and butcher their winter pig, to fight fair and to fight dirty, to build a good fire in any condition of wind and weather, to cook the basic northern Mexico foods they all liked best, to read for fun, to reckon a column of figures accurately, and, best of all, never to accept misfortune with philosophical understanding but to bellow and kick like a herd of outraged mules.

He had put them through school when other parents in his position were arranging jobs for their kids the minute they became fourteen. He had somehow managed decent denims for them most of the time, fed them adequately, whipped them when they lied or stole or were caught playing doctor with the neighbor's girls or palming their Sunday School nickels and dropping pennies in the plate instead. There had always been some sort of treat for birthdays and something under the scrub-pine Christmas tree. So why didn't they love him, knowing and remembering all that?

168

"Well, it's a relief to me, boy. I was worrying. I didn't know but what you might want to go off somewheres else, once you was married."

Here it comes again, Gordon warned himself. He grunted to discourage him.

"I was reading in the paper about Nico and that Farrall girl." He glanced slyly at Gordon. "Come as a surprise, huh?"

"You might say that, Jumbo."

"That why you're sittin' there like a sour old man, all hunched over, not even enough gumption to pour a drink?"

Gordon stared into those yellow-glinting goat's eyes, saw the bright malice clearly, and grinned silently, holding Jumbo's gaze until he forced him to look away.

Jumbo drained his glass noisily. He reached over for the rum bottle. "Never thought," he said slowly. "Back when you boys was little. It never even come to me that you was going to turn out the best of the lot."

Oh, God, Gordon groaned inwardly. Not again.

"I'm not," he said in a calm voice. "I'll run even with Bruce, I suppose, but you know damn well Ian was the pick of the litter."

A natural, as the athletes always said. Everything had come easily to Ian. Handsome, silver-blond, tall and strongly thewed, rhythmic and graceful as a Spanish dancer, with the reflexes of a startled panther.

Jumbo shifted irritably. His silence demanded proof and Gordon offered him a portion of the routine recital.

"You know the coach said he was the quickest, fastest big man he'd ever trained. A hundred yards in less than ten seconds and even in those days Ian was close to two hundred pounds. He could move better than anyone I ever saw."

"He wasn't much for smart, though."

"He was bored most of the time. Rincon State isn't much like Harvard, you know. But Ian could carry any load you put on him. I don't know what you have to learn before they let you fly a plane for the Navy, but I can't remember meeting any stupid fliers. It was all easy for Ian. Trouble is, he just wasn't lucky."

Jumbo made an ugly strangled sound. That last comment was not part of the agreed litany. They did not mention that Ian had been killed trying a stormy night landing on his carrier.

And they did not mention that Ian would not have come home either. Bruce had gone for that chemical engineering scholarship at Brown because Rhode Island was about as far as you could get from Rincon without leaving the country. He had written to acknowledge the small bits of walking-around money Jumbo had sent regularly but, except for that, nothing more than a hasty scrawl on a Christmas card. He had never been back since. His summer jobs had always been on the East Coast and he had graduated right into Richfield Oil's laboratory, got himself quickly married, and somehow, what with this and that and the kids and all, just never could find time for that long trip out West.

The Navy had given Ian his free ticket away from Rincon—and Jumbo. Gordon knew that he had planned to make it a career, just so he could stay away. So Gordon was the only one still at home, and if anyone had asked him why that was so, he could not have answered. Habit, inertia, not enough incentive for a major move, something like that. Something unsatisfactory like that.

Jumbo shook himself like a bear surging up out of water. "Well." He smacked a big hand decisively against his leg. "As long as you want the house. That's the main thing. Will you draw up the papers for me? Have you got time for it?"

"No problem." Gordon finished his drink and brought out his sack of tobacco. "I'm going to have plenty of time from now on, I think."

"What are you talking about?" Jumbo pulled his heavy eyebrows down in a suspicious scowl.

Gordon lit his cigarette and flipped the match across the terrace. "I think I've just been fired, or demoted, or something like that. I finally managed to screw myself good with old Delancy today. So I don't imagine I'll be around Gaines, Prinz and Delancy much longer."

"He fired you? He really did?" Jumbo didn't believe it.

"Not exactly. I mean, he didn't actually say the words, but that's what it adds up to. They never actually say it; that's not the way it works. They just start the long-drawn-out squeeze play to get me pissed-off enough to quit. It's a pretty effective routine. I've seen it work. Remember Jackie Kleinschmidt? He was out here a couple of times."

"Little fellow? Like a boiled shrimp? Pink hair? That the one?"

"He was a good lawyer and hard to discourage, but they decided they didn't want him and they squeezed him out in a couple of months."

"He was a gutless little shit."

Gordon shrugged. "It's heavy pressure, Jumbo."

"Are you scared of them?" Jumbo glared at him ferociously. "By Christ, you are!" He was amazed, then suddenly enraged. "I can't believe it! I plain can't believe it. A son of mine whining around like a little whipped dog because some big man speaks mean to him."

"I know what they can do, Jumbo. You don't. So don't give me any of that—"

He was leaning across to put out his cigarette. He had no chance when

170

Jumbo roared suddenly and lunged toward him. Jumbo's stone-hard open hand smacked against the side of his face and knocked him off the chair. He landed solidly on the point of his shoulder, felt his head scrape against the tiled floor as he rolled back.

Gordon shoved himself quickly to his feet. His knotted hands came up, his chin tucked in behind his shoulder, and he took that first automatic step forward, sliding in good balance, dazed but not hurt.

Jumbo snatched the rum bottle from the table and swung it high. "Come on, damn you," he yelled. "Gutless quitter. Come on. Come on. Can't take you with my hands anymore, but I can, by Christamighty, crack your goddamn yellow head wide open."

Gordon blew out a short angry breath. He let his hands drop. He felt sick with self-disgust. He shook his head at his raging father. "You're spilling all that good rum, Jumbo."

He turned on his heel abruptly and went into the house, going straight through to his bedroom, peeling off clothes as he moved. He took a long time under a cool shower, finished with the needle-spray running pure ice from the deep well. He was still shivering when he dried off and collected some fresh clothes. He loaded his pockets, carried jacket and necktie with him, and went slowly back out to the terrace.

Jumbo was sitting hunched on the edge of his chair, head in both hands. Gordon stopped beside him. "I owe you one for that, Jumbo," he said quietly.

The big bald head snapped up, sadness wiped away, the old habitual belligerence rising again. "Any time," he growled.

Gordon put one hand on his shoulder, feeling the hard tension under Jumbo's shirt. "Not what I meant. The clout on the chops is nothing much. I've had plenty of them. But not many for that reason."

Jumbo watched him, still suspicious.

"I guess there was a little self-pity splashing around a while ago. I pulled a bonehead play with Delancy, and he's going to make me pay for it. There's not much I can do about it; that's what makes me so mad. But I won't quit, Jumbo. You can count on that."

The old man's face tightened like a fist closing hard. He nodded fiercely twice, emphatically. Gordon smacked the big shoulder lightly and went on along the front of the house toward his car.

He cut his lights at the corner and drifted on a dead motor until he was slightly past the house and could vaguely see the dense shrubbery against the grape-stake fence at the back of the lot. Then he tapped his brake lightly and stopped.

He turned sideways on the front seat to stretch his legs as far as they would go. He took a small sip from the still half full bottle of whiskey, rolled a cigarette by feel, ducked down to light it, and then settled himself comfortably.

It was a pretty spectacular house, he thought, even in the dark. Fashionable in the modern southwestern way, low and sprawling, lots of glass and redwood and white plaster, set well back from the road on a stretch of dead-white sand studded with a scatter of pastel cactuses. There was a wide stubby ornamental palm tree in the center of the circular driveway. And in Gordon's direct vision was the service area with the kitchen where Jacob Prinz would come to make his own breakfast at six thirty as he did every morning of his life. Nothing to do now but wait.

He had done everything he could, he thought, and there was some satisfaction in knowing he was completely prepared. He had spent the night in the library at Gaines, Prinz and Delancy, ignoring the two other junior associates who were also plugging away at the reference books. He had brought the bottle of whiskey and a fresh sack of tobacco with him, and they were enough until some time after midnight when hunger pangs sent him out to the all-night counter at the Southern Pacific depot for two big bowls of chili and a stack of wholewheat toast. On his way back he had stopped off at the courthouse to pick up the transcript of the day's testimony in the trial of *State v. Pike.*

Beginning with the admission of those gruesome pictures of Angela Morales' body, it had been another bad day for Pike. Gordon read the transcript carefully. As he had expected, Delancy had made no official reference to Judge Pontalba's nauseated reaction when he first looked at those pictures. So there was no record for appeal. Delancy's objections had been standard and ineffectual. The judge had rejected them all.

After the jury had been given time to inspect the pictures—and knowing Burrell, Gordon was sure it had been a good long time—the prosecution had begun to develop its case against Pike himself.

The sheriff's chief deputy, Andy Venable, had been officially in charge of the investigation, and he was the witness Burrell used to tie the loose ends into a coherent pattern. He introduced the records of the anonymous phone call that had directed police attention toward Pike hours before the girl's body had been found. Delancy had pursued that one with real style and vigor. His questions took up ten pages of the transcript. He had covered the ground completely. And he came up with nothing.

It was hard to believe. After nearly two months of investigation and public appeal, the sheriff's office had no line at all on the woman who made that telephone call. They knew the maid, Francisca Guitterez, could have made it, and they knew she had disappeared. Why wasn't she offered as a scapegoat? The transcript offered no answer. Nobody seemed very interested in her. Nobody had offered any other prospect. Why not? Could it be because Burrell knew, or guessed, that Lee Wallis had arranged that anonymous phone call and did not want to discredit his own witness? That was a good possibility, Gordon suspected.

Burrell had spent the rest of the day's session introducing physical evidence. He had brought in a parade of technical witnesses from the sheriff's office and the state police lab to identify Pike's blood-spotted clothing. One of them had explained how he had washed Pike's head, hands, and feet in distilled water and had later identified traces of Group O blood in the water.

Burrell knew the value of a strong ending. He had saved the shoes for his last exhibit. He had let Venable tell the jury about the first useless search in El Pinar and the later successful one in the garden near Pike's apartment.

The green-plastic bag of marijuana had been brought in as a by-product of the general search, introduced almost casually, as if Burrell were saying "Yes, of course marijuana. What else would you expect from a man like Pike?" Gordon could almost see the jury's response to that. Delancy had objected, of course, but too late, so that discussion of his objection just gave the jury more time to look at the green bag and stare across at Pike and wonder just what sort of man they were dealing with.

The shoes had been wrapped in transparent plastic. The state police technician had marked the plastic wrapper to show where dried blood had been lifted for examination.

"Other than the spots of blood you told us about, sir, did you find anything else of interest on those shoes?"

"A very small portion of tissue was lodged in the welting between the upper section and the sole of the right shoe."

"Did you examine that tissue in your laboratory, sir?"

"I did."

"Please tell the jury what you found."

"It was human brain tissue, sir."

The transcript showed no pause here, but Gordon knew there had been one. That dead, shocked silence that is more eloquent than any sound. Burrell would have stood there, leaning intently toward his witness. And when he had heard the answer he would have stepped slowly back, nodding gravely, deeply saddened. Then he would have collected himself and gone on with his questions.

"The sheriff's office also delivered to your laboratory other fragments of human brain tissue and told you that those fragments had come from the body of Angela Morales. Isn't that correct, sir?"

"It is."

"Did you compare those fragments with the fragment you took from the shoe of Jonathan Pike?"

"I did, sir."

"Please tell the jury what you found."

"I found them to be identical, sir."

"Identical?"

"Yes, sir. Identical."

Delancy had had no questions.

Gordon drew a long breath and squirmed in his narrow seat. Come on, Jacob Prinz, he said in his mind, come on, dammit. Time to get up. Rise and shine. Greet the new day. And he saw the lights snap on just at the moment his wrist-alarm went off like a startled rattlesnake. He sat up so quickly he banged his head on the top of the car door.

The glow from the kitchen showed him the side path around the house. He walked along it silently, carrying four paperbound trial transcripts and a bulky file folder under his arm. He placed himself where the light from the rear window would show him clearly and reached forward to tap on the glass.

He could see Prinz standing at the stove in a white terrycloth robe, percolator basket in one hand, measuring scoop for ground coffee in the other. Prinz glanced up at the sound, squinted slightly to see who it was. He nodded twice, measured out three more scoops of coffee, put the percolator together, and plugged it in before turning toward the door.

Jacob Prinz was the scholar of the firm, the brains, everyone said. He looked like a retired wrestler. Wide heavy bones, thickly muscled, large bullet-shaped head with coarse hair that was now solidly gray. His face was strong and ugly, deeply seamed. He had a very fine, warming smile that always made Gordon feel good.

"Are you drunk, Gordon?" It was a question, not an accusation. He asked it in about the same tone he might have used to inquire about the weather.

"Don't think so, sir," Gordon said honestly. "I got through a fair amount of whiskey last night, but I don't think I'm drunk."

"This is my free time, you know. Best part of the day for me. I like to be alone."

"Yes, sir. I know. That's why I came."

Thick eyebrows knotted in a scowl as fierce as any Jumbo could have managed. "You deliberately came here, knowing—"

174

"I didn't say it right, sir," Gordon broke in hastily. "I meant I had to see you alone. And talk to you before you went to the office this morning. I knew I could catch you here in the early morning. I wouldn't have come if it wasn't important, sir."

Prinz eyed him carefully, looked at the mass of material Gordon was holding in his hands. He raised his shoulders slightly and let them drop. "Come in. I don't do business at home, but I can feed you. How do you like your eggs?"

"Thank you. Any way at all, sir."

"Sit over there." Prinz used a narrow spatula to point to a breakfast table set for one. "Plug in the toaster. Get out the bread and butter. There's jam in that cabinet. Green plum for me. Pick any you like."

Gordon tried only once to explain why he had come, but Prinz waved his spatula impatiently to silence him. "We'll eat first. Cups and saucers are over there." Gordon caught the first steaming whiff of coffee fragrance from the percolator and gave in willingly.

Prinz scrambled a panful of eggs with chopped onion and scraps of smoked salmon and heaped Gordon's plate. One taste and Gordon settled down silently to serious eating. Prinz poured his first cup of coffee and gestured for him to help himself after that.

"I like fiddling around in a kitchen," he said with a full mouth. "As long as I don't have to clean up afterward."

"You're a good cook, sir. As good as my father."

"Old Jumbo, eh? He cooks, too, does he?"

Gordon stopped a forkful in front of his mouth. "You know him, sir?"

Prinz loaded the toaster and reached for the plum jam. "Of course I know him. One of my first clients when I was a very young lawyer. Jumbo Guthrie. Never forget the man. Big brawling bastard. Voice like a bull moose. Temper quick as a scalded cat."

Gordon laughed quietly. "I guess you know him, all right."

Prinz shook his head. "Did he ever tell you about that case I handled for him?"

"Don't believe so," Gordon said politely. This wasn't what he had come for, but if a little old-times chatter was going to put Prinz in a good frame of mind, he'd go along.

Thinking back, Prinz slipped into the soft slurring tone of an earlier Southwest; his heavy voice lightened and took on a slight twang. "Jumbo slugged some old boy one night down at Hank's Busy Bee. That was the tough saloon in those days—girls, gambling, you name it. Any hard case needing a fight didn't have to do much looking. Busy Bee was run by a fellow named Kitchen, and I can tell you, boy, nobody ever made fun of that name. Didn't do it twice, anyway. He was a real nice fellow, couldn't ask for better company, but he sure did get mean when some liquored-up brawler busted his property."

Prinz waggled his head happily and bit off an enormous wedge of jam-loaded toast. He drained his cup and refilled it immediately. "That's why Jumbo came to me. Kitchen was suing him for damages, and Jumbo swore he hadn't busted a thing that night. I believed him. Any man believed Jumbo Guthrie when he swore to something."

Gordon nodded somberly. Jumbo could be very persuasive, he knew, especially when he let you know he was ready to fight if you wouldn't take his word.

"So I filed for him. We were going to trial in about a week, and I started talking to the people who had been in the Busy Bee that night. Then one day Kitchen came in and told me Jumbo had settled up, paid half what Kitchen was asking, and everything was clear."

Prinz gulped his coffee. "Well, I was mad. You can imagine. A client back-dooring me like that, settling without saying a word. So I braced Jumbo, and big as he was, I was about to slug him. Then he told me why he'd done it and I couldn't stay mad anymore. It seems he'd been fighting with a good old friend that night, fellow by the name of Modesto Guixart. Mule-breeder who'd just gone dead-bust, even lost the place he had down south of Sixmile. Jumbo figured he could win against Kitchen, but if he did, that would just lay the whole thing on Modesto's back, and that poor fellow just didn't have a solitary nickel to pay anybody. Jumbo figured he'd be shamed if he had to admit he couldn't pay up, so he just went around and made a deal with Kitchen and never said a word about it to Modesto from that day to this."

"I can see why you were mad," Gordon said.

"I stayed mad for a while, too," Prinz said, laughing now. "Right up till I made old Jumbo pony up ten bucks for my fee. He cussed some, but he finally paid. Fine old boy, Jumbo."

Gordon put his cup down solidly. And that will be just about enough of this crap, he thought.

"Mr. Prinz," he said in his courtroom voice. "That fine old boy, Jumbo Guthrie, knocked me flat on my ass just about ten hours ago."

Prinz stiffened. He chewed slowly, swallowed, and took a sip of coffee. His cold bright eyes steadied on Gordon.

"It was a full-arm swipe," Gordon told him. "And if you remember Jumbo, you can imagine what a clout it was. His own beloved unsuspecting son. You know why, Mr. Prinz?" Gordon leaned forward and Prinz caught something of his urgency. "Because I was going to quit

176

and Jumbo doesn't let people quit. I'd forgotten that. And I'd forgotten that I don't let myself quit either."

"Do you have a point, Gordon?" This was the dryly harsh legal voice now.

"My point is the trial of Jonathan Pike, Mr. Prinz. Have you been following it?"

"Only in the newspapers."

"Then maybe you don't know where we stand at the moment, how things are going for our client?"

Prinz shook his head. "Only in a general sense. Not well, I gather."

"Not well," Gordon said flatly. "Yesterday David Burrell stopped at the point where his next logical witness in the case is Lee Wallis. He's got the physical evidence in. He'll use Wallis to tie Pike to the girl, and after that he'll introduce Pike's statement and try to persuade the jury it's as good as a confession. That's the best way for him to proceed and I'm sure he knows it. That means Wallis will take the stand today. When Burrell is finished with him, we take over for cross-examination."

Prinz nodded silently, still watching.

"That's why I came here this morning, sir. I am convinced that this is the last chance we'll have to save Pike. If we don't break Wallis on the stand, Pike is finished."

"You have finally come to the point, have you?"

"I think you see the point as clearly as I do, Mr. Prinz. The point is James Oliver Delancy."

Prinz's entire body seemed to tighten. "I don't think you want to say anything more to me about that, Gordon." He spoke quietly, but his voice was heavy with somber warning.

Gordon spread his hands. "I have no choice, sir," he said simply. "I say it, or I quit. And I'm not going to quit."

"You realize that a law office is not disciplined in the military sense of the word," Prinz said. "But often the protocol is just as rigid. Think well before you say another word."

Gordon shook his head impatiently. "It's too late for that, sir. I spent the whole night with this problem, and at the end of it I knew there was only one thing to do. I came here this morning to ask you to persuade Mr. Delancy to withdraw from the Pike case. I do not believe he is capable of conducting that trial in the best interests of our client." And how stiff that sounds, he thought. How poorly it says what I want to say.

After a moment Prinz picked up his empty coffee cup, stared into it, and put it down again. "You are a bold young man, Gordon," he said thinly. "And something of a fool."

"That may be, sir. I know I've tied the noose and stuck my neck in it. And if I can't make you see what I mean, then I've hung myself. I know all that. What do you think I've been sweating about all night?"

Prinz shook his head as if he could not credit what he was hearing.

"Please listen to me, sir. I'll be brief. And then I'll leave it to you."

Prinz did not look at him during his explanation, but Gordon needed no encouragement. Long weeks of strain, of overwork and frustration, gave him impetus and even a certain eloquence as he outlined the blunders, the indifference, the forgetfulness, the sheer ineptitude that had crippled the defense of Jonathan Pike.

"So, that's it, sir," he said finally. "Mr. Delancy simply doesn't have the energy to fight a case like this any longer. With David Burrell prosecuting, the defense *has* to fight hard and constantly. Mr. Delancy knows that. I think if you were to put it to him, he would listen. But it has to be you."

"No," Prinz said with no hesitation.

"It's not just Mr. Delancy, sir," Gordon said urgently. "Or me. It's the life of our client. And the professional reputation of Gaines, Prinz and Delancy."

Prinz's head came up quickly. "What did you say?"

"Our firm, in the person of James Oliver Delancy, was given the responsibility for defending Jonathan Pike. You and I and Mr. Delancy himself know that he isn't physically capable of giving Pike an adequate defense. If you let him stay in there, knowing this, then it becomes the firm's responsibility. Is there any doubt about that?"

"That's enough, Gordon." Prinz's voice was stiff, cold. "What time is it?"

Gordon blinked. He pulled back a soiled cuff to see. "Seven thirty, sir."

Prinz rose slowly and cinched the belt of his robe again. "I must get dressed. I have a very busy morning. Jonathan Pike is not our only client, as you may remember. I'll see you in the office. Wait until I send for you."

"But, sir, I wanted to show you—"

"I said that was enough, Gordon," Prinz said again, more sharply. "It may well have been too much. I will talk to you later."

Gordon collected his bulky files and came to his feet.

Prinz opened the kitchen door, held it for him, and latched it firmly when Gordon moved outside. He was slow and deliberate, cautious as a man who has taken heavy punishment and does not quite trust his own control.

*   *   *

178

Gordon took time for a bath and shave at the Bench Club, got out his last clean shirt, gargled a lime-scented concoction that one of the stewards highly recommended for whiskey-breath. He sat over three lukewarm cups of drugstore coffee and pretended to read every page of the morning paper. Even so he was in his office before eight thirty, rolling cigarettes that scraped his raw throat, and very forcefully not looking at the phone on his desk.

Ten o'clock came and went and Gordon knew then that the decision had been made—and that he had lost. By now Delancy would be rising to stand behind the defense table with Pike beside him, watching as the judge entered from his chambers to begin the day's session. And sometime before the noon recess, Lee Wallis would take the stand.

When Jacob Prinz's secretary called him, he was tempted to ignore the call. But he answered, his voice dull and faraway. Yes, he would come at once.

Jacob Prinz had taken the corner office farthest from the reception hall where he would not be bothered by routine traffic. He had fitted it as a study with his personal library packed ceiling-high along two walls, four red-leather armchairs circling a low ebony table. He had his carved mahogany desk placed diagonally in the far corner between two blue-tinted windows. But most of his work was done on the sloping top of a scarred old stand-up desk just inside the door. It was there that Gordon found him.

Earlier that morning, wrapped in a bulky terrycloth robe, intent upon his breakfast, Jacob Prinz had been gruffly amiable, an approachable man. But the cold eye, the hard-set impassive face now told Gordon that all that had changed.

"Sit down, please." Prinz led the way across to his desk. He sat stiffly erect in a high-backed chair, hands cupped over the ends of the armrests as if he felt more sure of himself with something to hold onto. "I am going to forget that you came to see me this morning." His voice was flat, almost toneless, and quiet because he expected Gordon to be listening very carefully to every word. "I am going to forget the things you told me. I am also going to forget this conversation. Do you understand me, Gordon?"

"Not yet, sir."

Prinz nodded slowly. "Not yet," he said, as if to himself. "Yes, there is something more to be said, isn't there? So let me say it. James Oliver Delancy is a senior partner of this firm, a thoroughly experienced attorney, and my very old friend. I spoke to him briefly this morning. I do not intend to tell you anything of that conversation, but I will tell you that James Delancy is fit and vigorous, deeply concerned about the Pike trial, and eager to get on with his client's defense."

"That will last about an hour, as it does every morning," Gordon said in a slow even tone. He could see where Prinz was going, could guess what the end would be, but he was not going to roll over and play dead for the man. If Prinz wanted to cut a throat, he would have to swing his own razor.

"James Delancy assured me he is completely recovered from his illness of last winter," Prinz said as if Gordon had not spoken. "He is following a rigid and carefully planned regimen laid out by his doctor whom he sees twice a week. He is budgeting his time and his energy, concentrating everything on his client's defense."

"Maybe so, sir. But it is beside the point," Gordon said, stubbornly insistent. "I suggested that Mr. Delancy's failing energies might be the reason for his poor performance in the courtroom. I still think so. But the basic issue is that poor performance, not Mr. Delancy's state of health." Before Prinz could reply, Gordon went on quickly, convinced that he was digging his own grave and feeling strangely lighthearted now that the moment had come. "May I ask if you have read any of the trial transcripts, sir?"

Prinz stared at him for a silent moment, then shook his head.

"I'm sorry you haven't had time, because if you had you would see what I mean—the missed opportunities, the failures to follow promising lines of examination. The transcripts themselves don't read badly. What's in them is okay. The bad part is what's missing. I told you that Mr. Delancy refused to make any pretrial motions. He did not ask for adequate time for preparation, and he did not ask for a change of venue because of the inflammatory publicity that has been flooding this part of the state. Now you must have seen a lot of that yourself, Mr. Prinz. Wouldn't you have insisted on having the Pike trial moved somewhere else? Wouldn't you at least have tried?"

"I will not second-guess James Delancy," Prinz said stiffly. "And neither will you."

Gordon locked his hands together until the knuckles ached, trying hard to hold himself in control. "I am not second-guessing, sir. From the beginning I have been urging Mr. Delancy to make both those motions. I prepared a report on newspaper and television publicity that covers one hundred and six pages and has two hundred and thirty exhibits. And I am absolutely convinced that Mr. Delancy has never even looked at it. He made an absentminded agreement with David Burrell which set the date of the Pike trial far too early and left us with too little time for preparation. That worked to the detriment of his client, no matter how Mr. Delancy tries to justify it. When I pointed it out to him, he refused to listen."

He was getting nowhere, he could see. Prinz sat like stone. His eyes held Gordon's in bitter concentration.

"Okay," Gordon said heavily. "Maybe that one doesn't seem so important to you. But what about that jury? Any second-year law student would have challenged at least two, and maybe six, of the people Mr. Delancy was willing to accept."

Nothing. Prinz's short thick fingers dug deeper into the soft leather of his chair, but he showed no other response.

"I'll just remind you once more of Judge Pontalba's behavior when he first saw those pictures of the girl's body. He didn't even excuse himself. He just ran for his chambers. He was physically sickened. But he is Mr. Delancy's friend and colleague, so when Mr. Delancy was trying to keep those pictures from going to the jury, he made no reference whatever to the judge's reaction. And he should have, Mr. Prinz, friend or no friend. He should have fought for his client. You know that as well as I do. There are other examples I could point to." He paused, hoping for a response, almost any response. Then he shrugged. "All right, sir. I'm finished. If you aren't convinced, then I'll pack up and clear out of here." He was shaking now, but as long as he gripped his hands hard it didn't show.

Prinz swung his chair to one side, got up quickly, and went slowly down the length of his office. He stopped at his old-fashioned stand-up desk, stroked a hand along the sloping edge, then made a fist and smacked it down angrily. He turned to face Gordon. "You are every bit as impetuous and bull-headed as James Delancy said you were. What I see is that my friend and partner James Delancy is sixty-eight years old, much too old to enjoy having a young vigorous assistant pushing him at every step. It may be true that he has not entirely recovered from his illness. Can't you understand that he knows he is not at the peak of his powers, and that he worries about it? James Delancy is an honorable man, Gordon. He would never undertake a defense and give it less than his best effort."

Gordon made an impatient gesture. Delancy's honor was not at issue.

"Don't interrupt," Prinz said sharply. Then slowly he shook his head. "I didn't mean to bark," he said, his voice heavy with a kind of personal sadness.

What's troubling him, Gordon wondered. What is he talking all around and not saying?

"I don't say that you have done anything wrong," Prinz went on. "But the way you have gone about it is impossible to tolerate." He came back to his desk and leaned on it with both hands. "If it came to a choice between you and James Delancy, have you any doubt about how it would be resolved?"

Gordon looked at him coldly. "No."

"We don't want to lose you, Gordon. You've done good work here. You've shown considerable promise. Also you represent a serious investment in time and training that we would not like to throw away."

He straightened, went around the desk, and lowered himself into the big chair. He smacked his hands on the padded arms and changed the subject with startling abruptness. "William Gaines has just been given a trial date for *Schnelker v. Schnelker.* Do you know the case?"

Schnelker v. Schnelker. Gordon shifted gears in his mind. He knew only the office scuttlebutt. It was a bitter family dispute involving control of an interlocked group of land and cattle companies.

"It's a complicated mess," Prinz said, as if that was the sort of problem he enjoyed most of all. "It's likely to be in the courts for the next ten years. But William would like to bring it to trial two months from now if he possibly can. It will mean an enormous amount of preparatory work that must be covered in a short time. You work very well under that sort of pressure, Gordon. William and I have decided you might be the best man in the office to take it on."

Again he stopped Gordon before he could speak.

"James Delancy has more than once mentioned your skill and energy in examinations before trial. That is a valuable asset in criminal law but even more valuable on the civil side. In a civil case, EBT is make-or-break. You win or lose depending on how well you have tested your opponent's evidence. None of that will be new to you, except possibly in point of emphasis."

Gordon tried to understand what he was hearing. This was not the squeeze-out play he had expected. *Schnelker v. Schnelker* was a serious assignment. He looked again at Jacob Prinz, more than ever conscious of a quality of uncertainty, of things unsaid.

"William Gaines will probably find time to brief you thoroughly later this afternoon."

"And what am I to do about Jonathan Pike? Just drop him?"

"Jonathan Pike is not your responsibility, Gordon. James Delancy is his attorney, not you. He tells me that the trial will not last more than another two or three days. He can manage alone for that time."

Gordon shoved himself up in an awkward lunge and turned toward the door.

182

He blinked to see Prinz standing beside him, one hand on the tall scarred desk, staring at him with a puzzled scowl. The man must have crossed the room in one jump.

"Everything said in this room is to be forgotten. Is that clear? I will add one last confidential word that will also be forgotten. The senior partners of Gaines, Prinz and Delancy will be holding their quarterly meeting next month. One of the subjects on the agenda will be a review of the firm's retirement policy."

Gordon swung his big feet up over a corner of his desk and scowled at them. Then he grinned suddenly, sourly amused. This was the second time he had walked into the middle of an Old Friends Act and come out with fresh lumps on his skull. It was like the little kid whose cap is snatched by a gang of bigger boys. The cap goes sailing around the ring from one to the other and the little kid jumps after it, always a step behind, red-faced and squalling, not yet ready to start a fight he knows he can't win. Gordon remembered very well how it went.

Judge Manuel Pontalba was an Old Friend. Therefore James Delancy could not possibly embarrass him by taking formal notice of the judge's reaction to those pictures of Angela's mutilated body. Of course not. What are Old Friends for? And James Delancy was also an Old Friend. So Jacob Prinz could not tell him flatly that he was fumbling his job. Certainly not.

It was just too damn bad that Jonathan Pike didn't have any Old Friends on his side.

So now what, Gordon asked himself. And he heard no answer. Last night he'd felt pretty good, telling old Jumbo he was going to stick in there, give it another brave try. But in the bleak light of midmorning, the issues were not so clear. By offering to switch him to the William Gaines' side of the office, Prinz had blurred Gordon's resolve to force a decision about James Delancy.

So what are you going to do now? Go or stay? Open your own shop, without money enough for a decent library or even the basic furniture? Do your own typing? A one-man operation scrambling constantly for the rent money. Cheap divorces. Negligence suits for the people who are always finding flies in their pop bottles or hurting themselves on slippery staircases. Defending the petty embezzlers and hit-run killers for whatever fees the court would assign. A hick lawyer in the horse latitudes. Or stay and try to choke down the dead fruit they would be serving up every day from now on?

The phone rang then and Gordon snatched it, eager for any interruption.

"This is Reception, Mr. Guthrie. A young lady here wants to deliver a sealed message to Mr. Delancy. I thought possibly you—"

"Yes, I'll take it. Be right out." He locked his door and went loping down the hallway.

There were four people in the bright narrow hall. The receptionist nodded toward a slight dark-haired girl in a black pants suit who was standing rigidly facing a corner window, staring through the slats of the tilted blind.

"You have something for Mr. Delancy?"

She whirled so quickly that her handbag swung out and clipped Gordon lightly on the elbow. That small clumsiness almost broke her. She gasped. One hand darted up to cover her mouth. Tears formed in large dark eyes. A very nervous girl.

Gordon spoke slowly in a calm voice, hoping to distract her. "I'm Gordon Guthrie, Mr. Delancy's assistant. Mr. Delancy is in court this morning. If you'd like to give me the message?" He held out one hand, smiling reassuringly.

"There—there isn't any message. Not really. I just didn't want to tell her my name." She was speaking so softly that Gordon could hardly hear. "I'm Mrs. Jonathan Pike."

Mrs. Jonathan Pike? His *wife?* Then why hadn't Pike mentioned her when they were talking about his background? Gordon went over the details in his mind. Mother dead. Father remarried and totally without interest in the problems of his full-grown son who should be old enough to take care of himself. Elder sister married and living in Germany with her soldier-husband. No mention of a wife. Why not?

"I was just this minute going out for some coffee. Would you like to come along, Mrs. Pike? Just downstairs? We can talk there."

He could have taken her into Delancy's office or used one of the small conference rooms, but he suspected that Mrs. Pike would probably hold herself in better control in a public place with people around. He held the door and took her arm as she came through.

"I didn't know about you, Mrs. Pike." Gordon pushed the elevator call-button and turned back to her. "I would have been in touch if I had."

"Jonnie didn't say anything about me?"

"I guess he was trying to spare you."

"Or maybe he just forgot he had a wife."

Gordon stared at her. The girl was all surprises. She was acutely nervous, on the edge of explosion, but somehow Gordon got the idea that Pike was not her major concern.

She was very thin, cheekbones sharply prominent in a long narrow face that was made even more narrow by a straight fall of center-parted dark hair. Her eyes were unnaturally bright. Her mouth was wide, richly full, but tightened now as she looked up at him, half-defiant, half-challenging.

Gordon followed her into the elevator and rode silently down with her, wondering how he should handle this one. Her sudden unexpected arrival could not help Pike very much at this stage, but Gordon could think of a dozen ways she could hurt him, if that was what she had in mind.

The coffee shop downstairs was nearly empty. Two loners dawdling over their newspapers. Waitresses setting up for the noon rush. Gordon led the way to a remote table in the far corner and ordered coffee from the girl who had trailed them.

"Something to eat, Mrs. Pike? Toast? Pecan bun?"

She shook her head, looking down into her open handbag, rummaging deep. She came up with a plastic lighter and a crumpled pack of cigarettes. She flipped one out and had it lit before Gordon could find a match.

No wedding ring, he noticed. She had strong hands, slightly roughened, short-fingered, firmly muscled, with no adornment except an opaque ivory polish on nails that were filed very short. She wore good clothes, had carefully brushed that lustrous hair, carefully ironed the silky blouse, and taken special pains with eye makeup and nail polish. He'd bet she had told herself over and over just what she was going to say and how she was going to behave. And now the moment was here and none of it was any help to her. She blew out a soft streamer of smoke and flicked a quick wary glance at Gordon.

"How long have you been married, Mrs. Pike?" Answering a few routine questions should help ease her tension, Gordon thought.

"Two years, almost three," she said, not looking at him. "If you could call it a marriage."

"Are you from Pittsburgh, too?"

"Wheeling," she said, "West Virginia."

Close by, but in another state. That might explain why the Pittsburgh records had said nothing about Pike's marriage.

"Did you know him very long?"

"Not long. Not long enough. Dumb me, I had to go and marry him after a couple of dates. Like a dopey kid."

She must be all of twenty-one right now, Gordon thought. He was careful not to smile. "Tell me about it," he said.

"Tell you about what? What's there to tell? He was home on a furlough, and we met at some party and started going around together. My father didn't like him and his father didn't like me, so that was probably why we just drove over to Kentucky one night and got married. I can't think of any other reason."

"That was when he was in the Army?"

"Stationed at Fort Sill. I was going to pack up and go out there, but all of a sudden he got orders for Vietnam and he was gone in a week. He tried to tell me it was some kind of mistake in the office, but I heard later he was mixed up in some dirty racket and was lucky they let him off. He was always mixed up in something."

It's a good thing for Pike, Gordon was thinking, that this little girl hasn't been doing any talking to Burrell or the reporters. She'd get him hanged.

"A whole year and I'll bet he didn't write me two letters all that time."

"But he did come back?"

"Oh, he came back all right. Stinking rich. He made a fortune out there. Stole something, probably. Anyway, all he wanted to do was go off to New York or Miami or Las Vegas and live high."

"And you did?"

"For a while. Four or five months, maybe. I had a good job then, secretary to the assistant sales manager at Firestone, and I was in line for something better, so I didn't want to break off and just wander around. But Jonnie said he was going and either I came or he was cutting out. So—"

"And how was it? Fun?"

"Fun?" She seemed outraged for a moment, then shrugged and showed him a brief bitter smile. "I was going to say it wasn't, but who am I trying to kid? Sure, it was fun at first. Big hotels, nice clothes. We would rent a jazzy convertible and drive to all the good places. Who wouldn't have fun? But Jonnie was drinking too much. It didn't seem so much at first. Screwdrivers for breakfast. Bloody Marys for lunch. A lot of martinis and then wine with dinner. And Scotch and soda all night long. It just built up and up, I guess. Jonnie couldn't drink, it turned out. Pot, yes. He was okay on pot. But liquor, no. He just couldn't handle it."

So Pike had been telling the truth about that, Gordon thought, oddly reassured. He nodded.

"What happened?" he asked.

"He blew up," the girl said simply.

"He what?"

"You didn't·know about that?"

Gordon shook his head, wishing he didn't have to hear it now.

"It was in Miami. One night when I went to bed early. I was worn out, but Jonnie wanted me to stay up and see the floor show. I don't know what happened down there after I left, but he got into some sort of fight, insulted one of the guests, and they threw him out. When he came upstairs he was wild. He wanted to tell me all about it, and all I wanted to do was sleep. So it went on like that and one thing led to another, the way it does. And then he hit me."

Gordon's hands tightened. His face went stiff with restraint.

"He just went ape. He was a wild man. I didn't know who he was. I don't ever want to see anybody look at me like that again. I was really scared. I damn near screamed the walls down."

"What happened? Did he hurt you?"

"Scared me mostly. I had some loose teeth for a week or so and a lot of bruises."

"Was he arrested?"

"In Miami?" She almost laughed at him. "No, the hotel just wanted to hush it up. As long as I didn't want to charge Jonnie myself, they said they wouldn't. But we had to get out of the hotel right then. Four o'clock in the morning! I told them I wasn't having any part of that. I wanted a doctor and I wanted some sleep. So they let me stay. But they made Jonnie leave. They packed up for him and made him pay the bill and out he went. He could hardly walk straight, but he made it."

She leaned toward Gordon then, pushing her coffee cup to one side. "And that's the last time I ever saw Mr. Jonathan Pike. He left me a thousand dollars at the desk and that was that. Finished. Next I heard of him he was in jail for beating this girl to death. This Angela Morales. Did he really kill her, Mr. Guthrie?"

"He says he didn't."

"And what do you say?"

"I'm his lawyer. I'm on his side." Gordon watched her until she turned to look at him. "Why did you come here, Mrs. Pike?"

"What?"

"You could hurt him very badly if you told that story to anyone else. If people knew he had once beaten his own wife in a drunken rage, they might find it easier to believe that he killed Angela Morales. Is that what you want? Is that why you came here?"

"Oh no!" she said in a low fierce whisper. "I don't want to hurt him, Mr. Guthrie. I wouldn't do a thing like that. I just want to get clear of him."

"Clear of him? How?"

"When Jonnie was arrested, I had to leave home. Everybody knew about us, and I couldn't stand any more of it. All the talk. So I went to—somewhere else, and got another job. That's the good thing about being a secretary. If you know your job, you can go anywhere you like. I'm not going to tell you where I am now, Mr. Guthrie. I've got a lawyer who says he can file for divorce for me and keep everything quiet until the day the judge gives me the decree. Then I'm off again, back to my maiden name, and clear of Jonnie Pike. That's all I want, Mr. Guthrie. Just to forget I ever heard of him."

"All right," Gordon said. "That shouldn't be too hard to arrange. What do you want me to do?"

"Well, it's pretty obvious, isn't it? He has to know about the divorce. I want him to keep it to himself. I don't want reporters tracking me down. You just tell Jonnie to keep quiet, and so will I."

Gordon took a deep breath. "That's all?"

"Maybe it doesn't seem like much to you, Mr. Guthrie, but this is my whole life."

"I can see that, Mrs. Pike. Okay, I'll get to him as soon as possible. Where can I reach you?"

"You can't reach me. I'm leaving on the two o'clock bus, and I'll never be back. But you tell Jonnie what I said. I'll know if he keeps his side of the bargain. That's all I want from him."

"I can promise you he will, Mrs. Pike. I'll see to it. You are doing him a very large favor, and I'll make sure he understands that."

"Then that's all I want." She sat back in a tired slump, all vitality drained. Her narrow face was very pale. Slowly she collected lighter and cigarettes, dropped them in her bag and latched it. It took an effort for her to rise, and Gordon moved quickly to take her arm.

"No, you stay here, please, Mr. Guthrie. I just don't want any more of this. I'll say good-bye here."

"Very well. Good-bye, Mrs. Pike. And thank you. I'll say thanks for Pike, too, since he can't say it himself."

She brushed back a wing of her dark hair, looking up at him with a twisted little smile. "Tell him he's welcome. But don't make a big thing out of it. I just want to get clear of him. I think he really did kill that girl."

And maybe he did. The evidence certainly was not with him. But Gordon still did not believe it. He watched Pike coming along the jail corridor in a light bouncy stride, erect and confident.

The hell with the evidence. I still don't believe it.

188

"I thought you'd run out on me." Pike cocked an eyebrow, half-smiling.

Gordon moved back out of the doorway. "Mr. Delancy handles the trial work. I'm just an errand boy."

Pike came inside the small room and pulled a chair away from the table. "I'm beginning to get the idea he's not much of a trial man," he said slowly. "Does he really know what he's doing?"

"He's had a lot of experience." Gordon chose the words with care. "What's troubling you?"

Pike made a quick gesture with one hand. "I don't know. It was a judgment call, I guess. But I didn't like the way he handled the business of the shoes. He didn't ask any questions at all."

"What shoes? The ones you lost?"

"Sure. Those shoes are the only solid evidence against me. The blood spots on my clothes don't mean anything. They could have come from the bloody nose Lee handed me just before I left. Or the way I scratched my feet walking on that rough gravel. But the shoes are bad. I know damn well I lost them out at El Pinar. Somebody else must have bloodied them up and hidden them outside my place. That's the only way they could have gotten there. I kept trying to tell Delancy he should ask about fingerprints on those shoes. Somebody else moved them, carried them in his hands probably. So maybe there were fingerprints and the police found them and just didn't say anything about them."

Good point, Gordon thought. He nodded silently.

"Then there was the time-lag. The first time they searched my place they found that bag of marijuana and I had that hid pretty good. But it wasn't till two days later that they spotted the shoes in the rosebush. Did you know it took two days to find them?"

"Not until I read the transcript."

"Well, why did it take them so long? That's something worth asking questions about, isn't it? They found that marijuana right away and it was pinned up high and out of sight. The shoes were just thrown in that bush, but they didn't see them. Why not? Because they weren't there when the police searched the first time? Because somebody else brought them later on and dropped them where they would do the most harm? That's worth asking questions about, isn't it? But Delancy didn't even mention the shoes when he had that deputy on the stand."

That would have been toward the end of yesterday's session, Gordon remembered from the transcript. Burrell had been crowding in a lot of physical evidence and Delancy was probably just too tired and confused to keep track. Asking about fingerprints would have been a good move, well worth making. And the time-lag could have been built up into something effective, if it had been handled right. Pike was right when he said the shoes were the most damaging evidence against him. Delancy should have made a serious effort to minimize their importance. But there was no point in saying that to Pike. It would be easier for him if he could keep some belief in Delancy's competence.

A prisoner-trusty tapped on the open door and came in with a covered tray.

"Compliments of Mr. Delancy," Pike said with a thin smile. He peeled back a napkin and inspected an ornate club sandwich. He pried the lid from a container of chocolate malt. "The old boy came down here once and saw that horse-cock sandwich and sour coffee the jail hands out, and he set it up for me to order lunch from the drugstore." He picked up a quarter of the towering sandwich and bit off a huge dripping bite.

"Your wife came to see me this morning," Gordon said quietly.

Those very pale, almost transparent eyes swung quickly toward Gordon and held him in a flat hard stare. Pike chewed his mouthful slowly, giving himself time. He swallowed, wiped his mouth with a paper napkin, and pushed his chair back an inch. He smiled lazily, pointedly ironic and just a little contemptuous. "Katie? Well, well." He took another large bite.

"She didn't tell me her name."

Pike drank some chocolate malt. "Mary Katherine MacMahon, that was," he said lightly. "Broth of a girl. Had something to tell you, did she?"

"And you can be damn thankful she told me and not someone else." Gordon brought out his tobacco and busied himself with a cigarette so that he could turn away from Pike. Just one more of those sardonic little smiles and Pike would be picking himself up off the floor.

"And what does my unhappy marriage have to do with anything?"

"If you're lucky, nothing."

"Then why are we talking about it?"

Gordon lit his cigarette and spoke through a cloud of smoke. "She wants a divorce. She has a man who can handle it for her without any noise, as long as you don't kick up a fuss. I told her you wouldn't."

Pike reached for another wedge of sandwich. "Did you now?" he murmured.

"She is doing you a big favor, just by staying away from you. I thought you'd have sense enough to see that. Do you really want her telling people about how good you are at beating up girls?"

Pike snorted lightly. "I can see she gave you a fine story. It wasn't anything like—"

190

"I don't give a damn how it was," Gordon said hotly. "I don't want to hear about it. What about the divorce?"

Pike grinned, head tilted up at Gordon. "And if I say no, you're going to deck me. Right?" He laughed with genuine amusement. "She really did snow you, didn't she?"

"Are you saying no?"

"Now why would I do a thing like that? If little Katie wants to shake loose, let her go. I've got nothing against her. She was always a goddamn bore, but goodhearted. You know? Small-town girl. Wants a new house with a twenty-year mortgage. Husband who carries a lot of insurance and comes homes every night. Credit cards. Savings programs. All that crap. It never was my idea of living. I want something with a little more bite to it. Take a few chances. Live a little bigger than the next guy."

And you were doing so awfully damn well for yourself, weren't you, Gordon thought sourly. "Okay," he said. "I imagine you'll be getting the papers in a few days."

"If I'm still here."

Gordon looked at him sharply and slowly nodded. "There is that. How is it going? Where are you?"

"Lee Wallis," Pike said with a full mouth. "He took the stand about half an hour ago. He's just getting to where we left the Old Forge and went to get something to eat. He's got to start lying pretty soon if he wants to clear himself."

Gordon stopped him incredulously. "Just a minute. Didn't Burrell hand over his file on Wallis? You should know what line he's going to take."

"He gave Delancy a fat envelope. Delancy looked at it for a minute, but he didn't show it to me."

"Well, he'll have time to study it during the lunch break. Then he'll know how to handle Wallis on cross-examination."

"I hope so." Pike looked at him soberly, flat ice-gray eyes half-lidded. "Doesn't give him much time. He has to break Lee in little pieces, or I'm cooked."

"He'll take him." Gordon spoke as forcefully as he could, but he did not persuade himself.

Gordon sat hunched morosely in his cramped office, bent over three heavy cardboard cases that contained the file-to-date on *Schnelker v. Schnelker.* A slow, leaden, mind-dulling afternoon with the Swiss family Schnelker. And what a miserable pack of greedy hateful bastards they were.

Billy Gaines had given him a quick fifteen-minute summary of the problem and had then gone off about his personal business. Billy Gaines (only Jacob Prinz ever called him William) was the politician of the firm, a glad-hander, a hoo-hawer, a rib-nudger, an elbow-tapper, a very social creature. A Great Guy. A Good Old Boy. He brought in a heavy percentage of the firm's business and carried the lightest load of any of the senior partners.

In purely legal terms *Schnelker* raised no problems that would interest the law reviews, but the case was fiendishly complex. A mess, as Prinz had said. Unless the family agreed to a settlement, Gaines, Prinz and Delancy could look forward to years of endless, repetitive wrangling. And very profitable years they would be.

Gordon yawned suddenly, his mouth gaping so wide his jaws creaked. Even if he had come to it fresh, alert, and interested, *Schnelker* would still have acted on him like a sleeping pill. A soporific to deaden his apprehension about what was happening in the courtroom with Lee Wallis on the stand. Gordon shook his head roughly and stood up to swing his arms, fighting off the drowsiness that felt like a thick blanket in his mind. He sat again and turned to look directly at Nico Kronstadt who was leaning against the open door, arms crossed, nodding approvingly.

"Very athletic," he said. "We like to see our young men keeping fit."

"I'm just trying to stay awake," Gordon said in a surly growl. "You're far from home, aren't you?"

"I walked back with Jake Prinz. Thought I'd look in and see if you were ready for a drink."

So Prinz had gone to court to have a look for himself. Gordon grinned suddenly. "By God, I could use a drink," he said readily. He snatched his jacket from its hook, scooped up his sack of tobacco, and pushed Nico out into the hall.

"You look like the end of a long dreary day."

"Let's not even talk about it," Gordon said.

Nico eyed him thoughtfully as they waited for the elevator. "Prinz was dropping clumsy hints about why you weren't in the courtroom today. I wondered."

Gordon shrugged angrily. "They threw me out of the game."

"I thought it might be something like that." Nico went first into the self-service elevator. "I suppose you're feeling pretty sore about it, but I wouldn't worry too much, in your shoes. Maybe it's just as well. You wouldn't want anyone thinking you had any responsibility for Delancy's defense. He is not doing a good job."

"How much of it have you seen?" Gordon stopped to let a scampering of stenographers beat him to the main entrance. Then he went through and joined Nico on the sweltering sidewalk. "You have any place special in mind for this drink?"

"The Rodeo is nearest." Nico led the way. "No, I haven't seen much of it, but I've gone through the transcripts. Today was my longest session in court. Frankly, I was shocked by Delancy's performance. I think Prinz was, too. That man Wallis was David's key witness and he made some real yardage with him." Nico paused in thoughtful appreciation. "I will say that it's always a pleasure to watch David work. He takes his man through a complicated story in careful little steps, and the jury comes right along with him. And all the time he is building those fences and setting up crafty little traps that make life miserable for a cross-examiner. I don't think anybody can present evidence-in-chief more clearly than David."

"He's good," Gordon agreed. He trailed Nico into a long dim barroom that was so cold it made his soggy shirt feel like an ice pack. They took a narrow booth near the front. "What did Wallis say? That he left Pike and Angela before the El Pinar incident?"

"Of course." Nico seemed surprised at the question. "Scotch on the rocks, Gordon?" He relayed the order. "What would you expect him to say? If he admitted he was there at El Pinar, he'd be on trial with Pike. He says he went with Pike to collect the girl, then drove them back to Cordero's so Pike could pick up his motorbike. That's the last he saw of them."

"He says," Gordon growled. "Does he offer an alibi, anyone willing to say they saw him somewhere else that night?"

"Vague, very vague, but not unconvincing. Wallis is a good witness, polite and helpful. He admits he's been a little too wild, spends all the money he makes, drinks too much now and then. But David shows he's steady on his job, never been in any serious trouble, not very much in debt, just an average young man feeling his oats. And Wallis ducks his head and gives them a sheepish grin and the jury sees a clean-cut all-American kid. David did a fine job with him."

"I know how it works, Nico. But what did he actually have to say? A real alibi or just smoke?"

Nico spread his hands. "Who knows? He'd been drinking a little too much with Pike, he says, and he was driving much too fast on his way home. He spotted a patrol car pulling out to chase him so he whipped around a corner and into a drive-in movie to hide. Since he was there, he just stayed and caught the movie. And what will you bet that David doesn't have a patrol car team ready to testify that they lost a speeder in a white sports car somewhere near that drive-in?"

"No bet. But it doesn't mean much."

"He also says that he saw an old high school friend on the street about one in the morning and waved to him."

"And what does the friend say?"

"We haven't seen him yet, but I should imagine he'll confirm Wallis."

"Thin," Gordon said dubiously.

"Most genuine alibis are thin, you know that, Gordie. I'll bet you couldn't prove where you were last night, could you? Find witnesses to back you up?"

Gordon snorted, remembering how he had spent that long destructive night. "As a matter of fact, I could," he said heavily. "But let it go. You're right. Normally I wouldn't be able to." He took a long pull at his drink and crunched on chipped ice. "Well, it's not as bad as I thought. I was afraid Wallis might have set up a really solid alibi that Delancy would have trouble breaking down. But he should be able to handle this one okay, if that's all Wallis has to offer."

Nico shook his head sadly. "You dreamer. Delancy had plenty of trouble. And he didn't break it down. He didn't get anywhere with Wallis."

Gordon gaped at him, feeling an icy chill that was more than just the overactive air-conditioning. "You mean it's over? Delancy didn't—"

"Delancy didn't do anything," Nico said flatly. "Even old Prinz was a touch dismayed, I thought. He was very carefully not talking about it on the way back to the office. That's why I said you were better off out of it, Gordie. You wouldn't want to be tied in too tightly with Delancy at this point. He took Wallis over his testimony several times, and all he managed to do was to fix the details very firmly in the jury's collective mind. He didn't break him on a single point. Wallis just went on being polite and patient with the old gentleman. And that was the ball game, Gordie. Wallis was key. Unless your side can come up with some very hard evidence, Pike is as good as convicted right now." He drained his glass and held two fingers overhead to signal the waiter. "Do you have the evidence, Gordie?"

Gordon felt numb. He sat in a heavy slump-shouldered crouch.

"What have you got, Gordie? Anything useful?"

Gordon shook himself roughly. "No, we haven't got anything good enough. Just a woman who will say she saw Pike and the girl with Wallis in his car at the crossing where the El Pinar road hits the highway."

"Well, that's something," Nico said, trying to sound reassuring. "Will she make a good witness?"

Gordon stared at him blindly. "She's sixty-two years old, wears thick glasses. She saw them at night, through the window of her car. It was cloudy, some moonlight, but not bright. The only light at the crossing is an arc lamp that stands one hundred and twenty feet from the point where she saw the car."

"Tough."

"David will be very gentle with her. He will point out the problem, ask her to explore it with him, and by the time he's finished with her, she won't be sure if she saw a white car or a pink bunny rabbit. That's how I'd handle it. I don't see David having much trouble with her."

"No, David doesn't miss much. Too bad, Gordie, but you don't have to blame yourself. I don't believe anybody could have done much for Pike. David has a very strong case." He sampled his fresh drink, looking at Gordon over the rim of the glass. "How do you feel about it now? Can you still tell yourself that Pike is innocent?"

"I don't know," Gordon said harshly. "And neither do you. We haven't heard the whole story and we aren't going to. The only thing I am sure about is that Pike is not getting a fair trial. God damn that senile, self-loving old bastard," he said bitterly. "He didn't give Pike a chance. Not one. He didn't even try. And he wouldn't let me try."

"He was trying today, Gordie," Nico said. "When he came back from questioning Wallis, I thought for a minute he was going to faint. He was very pale, sweating heavily, shaking. No, don't think he isn't putting out. That was maximum effort for old Delancy."

"But it wasn't good enough," Gordon said angrily. "It hasn't been good enough for a long time. You don't know half of it, Nico. I've been fighting this for weeks and getting nowhere. I finally got so hot about it I went to Prinz and asked him to get Delancy out of there. You can guess how that turned out. Delancy is still in there, fumbling the trial, and I got sent to the showers."

"Good God." Nico whistled softly. "You went to Jacob Prinz with a request like that? What did he—"

"Let's drop it, Nico," Gordon broke in. "I'll tell you about it sometime but not now. I'm likely to start breaking up the furniture if I keep talking about it. What's new with the wedding? Any changes?"

Nico leaned back, showing the quick, delighted smile of a happy man. "Changes every day." He laughed. "Claudia is going to make it the extravaganza of the season. She and my grandfather invent some nutty new wrinkle every time they get together. I never knew she had so much interest in that big-league social stuff."

"I think it's all the Kronstadt money," Gordon said casually. "It's a new toy for her. She'll get tired of it pretty soon."

"Let's hope. The money doesn't matter. She can have any kind of wedding she wants. But I'm afraid she is thinking of the Kronstadts as fashionable jet-setters, beautiful people, that sort of nonsense. If so, we are going to be an awful disappointment to her."

"She's just goosing you, Nico."

"Hope so." Nico didn't sound worried. "You slipped in a pretty good goose yourself, friend."

"I did?"

"That goddamn helicopter. Whatever gave you *that* idea?"

Gordon rolled a thin careful cigarette. "It wasn't exactly a serious suggestion," he said mildly.

"Well, Claudia took it seriously, I can tell you that. She went running off with it. I've had salesmen on my neck for days. I've got a desk covered with catalogues. There must be three dozen different sizes and shapes of helicopter on the market. Did you know that?"

Gordon laughed quietly.

"Actually it may not be such a bad idea at that. The ranch is sixty miles west of Rincon, and that road can be a beast in rainy weather. Half an hour sailing in a helicopter beats two hours hard driving, especially at night. A chopper might make sense at that."

Gordon smiled, trying to share his friend's good spirits, but he could not shake off his depression. It was all but over, and Jonathan Pike was all but convicted. He finished his drink, turned to signal the barman, then thought better of it. Liquor was not the solution. In his black mood he would probably wind up fighting drunk in a South Rincon saloon taking on half the city police force.

"Why don't you come home with me for dinner, Gordie? Change your luck. The old gentleman would love to see you, and Claudia can tell you all the plans. We are going to have a wild bash, boy."

"Can't," Gordon said quickly, positive. An evening like that would turn out worse than a hard drinking session. "Too much to do, Nico. I should get back right away. Give my best to the family." He pushed away from the table and swung out of the narrow booth. "Thanks for the drinks. Let's have lunch soon, maybe get out and play a little tennis first."

He lifted his hand in a vague salute and left before Nico could answer.

It was nearly midnight before he got back to his office after a brief solitary meal at a barbecue shack a hundred miles north on the El Monte Highway. He had been driving too fast all the way and almost lost the road at the sharp curve around the Agroño Wash. His light car wobbled and lurched, oversprung and almost off-balance, snapping up gravel like machine-gun bullets when the right tires drifted onto the hard-packed berm. And that had been enough for him. He had stopped at the first chance and walked in on shaky legs to order a single drink and a very large sandwich. Then he had driven back at the cautious pace preferred by the state highway police.

He went first to the darkened courthouse, parked in Judge Pontalba's empty slot, and walked through dim hallways to the office of the clerk of the court. Tired dirty-fingered girls were feeding the Xeroxed pages of the day's trial transcript through the collating machine, sandwiching the thick stacks between buff manila covers, and binding them in a dangerous-looking device that looked like a mechanical lion's paw. Gordon waited while a girl gummed a label on the first completed transcript. He signed for one of the copies allotted to Gaines, Prinz and Delancy and took it with him back through the dark streets to his office.

He leafed through it quickly to make sure that Nico's judgment about Delancy had been right. Ten minutes' reading gave him all he needed. Cross-examining Lee Wallis—or any other witness suspected of lying— called for rage and fire, the righteous wrath of a defender sure of himself and his cause. Delancy should have called down mankind's tribal curse on his lying head. Anathema.

Instead Delancy had reasoned gently, almost delicately, probing the obvious points and scoring occasionally when he managed to confuse Wallis enough to stick him with a minor contradiction. But the bulk of the testimony stood firm. And that testimony would convict Jonathan Pike.

Nico was right. The trial had ended with Wallis' appearance on the stand. All that remained now was a bleak formality. Pike was finished. Gordon sat heavily for a long silent time, listening to the quiet night noises of cleaners in the offices, muted traffic from the faraway streets. Listening mostly to the slow movement of conviction in his head. He could put it off, wait till morning or even next week. But sooner or later, he now accepted, he would have to do it. Move right up there to the last crumbling edge of the basic pattern of loyalty. It would be that definite a break with his past and the picture he had always held of himself.

Hell with it, he told himself. Overdramatizing yourself again. There are no irrevocable acts, and a man does not change his essential nature. He said it again, silently in his head, and knew it made sense. But he did not believe it.

He got stiffly to his feet, turned to open his locked file drawer and slowly piled his desk high with his own file on the Pike case. All that hard work. The laborious reports that Delancy had ignored, had probably not even read. His often-revised trial plans. His outlines for cross-examination. His investigators' reports on Wallis and the other prosecution witnesses. His information reports on the jury panel. And the forty-one-page critique of Delancy's trial technique that he had prepared for Jacob Prinz and never had a chance to use. The daily trial transcripts with his lengthy annotations in the margins.

He carried it all down the corridor to the room next to the chief clerk's office and assembled it on the long mail-sorting table. He took his time with it, making a firm package, wrapping the paper smoothly, tucking in the ends and sealing them with strips of paper tape, then twine in double strands.

He signed his name across every piece of paper tape, over every join in the folded wrapper. He used one of the Gaines, Prinz and Delancy stickers as a return address and wrote his own name in the open box, addressing it to himself at the Bench Club. In the lower right corner he printed REGISTERED MAIL.

In the morning he would walk the package down to the main post office himself, fill out a certificate of registration, and watch while the clerk canceled the stamps. He could still change his mind, step back from that crumbling edge while he still had time. But he did not think he would.

Gordon went to lunch very late on the Thursday that he would always afterward think of as Decision Day. He took a copy of the Rincon *Record* with him and spread it open on the table beside his plate of roast beef hash.

The *Record* was focusing full attention on the trial of the "Angel Killer." Local feature writers were crowded off the front page to make room for the out-of-town reporters and the notable columnists who were making a point of stopping off in Rincon for a day or two to file some lively copy on the trial. All of them voted guilty. Some speculated in predigested sociological terms on *why* Jonathan Pike had killed. None asked *if* he had killed.

Gordon abandoned the newspaper—and most of his lunch—on the table, paid at the counter, and went quickly out into the pale hot shadow of the restaurant awning.

Turn right for the office, left for the county courthouse. He was still saying that to himself when he was already half a block to the left, determined now to see the end for himself. The formal end, he said in his mind, correcting himself. The actual conclusive and ruinous end to

Pike's chances had come days before when Delancy had failed to break Lee Wallis on the stand. But the rules of trial demand a solemn progression, and so it was still grinding on. The only surprise had been the unexpected brevity of the defense case. The courtroom yesterday had been jammed, everyone waiting to see Pike take the stand and tell his version of the killing of Angela Morales. The lions of the national press had been up since dawn, standing in line to make sure of a seat, and had left grumbling and nasty-tempered when they finally realized that Delancy was not going to put him on.

Big surprise. Gordon made a rude noise. Surprise, hell! He knew exactly when—and why—Delancy had changed his foolish decision to take testimony from Pike. It could have been the most damaging moment of the whole trial, Gordon believed. But Delancy had not saved himself from that disaster. David Burrell had pulled him off the hook by outsmarting him once again. Anyone reading the transcript carefully could see how he had done it.

Before the trial Burrell had made a generous point of showing Delancy and Gordon a copy of Pike's final statement. He had told them that Pike had made other, contradictory statements during the two-or-three-day questioning period after he had been arrested. But Burrell had never let them see the earlier versions of Pike's statements. Delancy had assumed he did not intend to use them. And Burrell had let him think so. Until he did use them.

Burrell had made carefully sure that a different investigator had been used as the principal witnessing officer for each of the four different statements. He had brought them on one at a time. Each witness set the scene with considerable detail and finished by reading the statement he had taken from Pike at that time. Four different, glaringly different statements were presented to the jury. One after the other. Delancy had objected frantically, uselessly. So the jury had heard all those imaginative, convoluted lies in Pike's own words, and later heard each of those lies repudiated.

If Pike had taken the stand, his testimony would have followed the same general line as his final, unsigned statement. But after all four versions had been read to the jury, Pike was a proven liar, totally destroyed as a credible witness. Only a fool would have allowed him to testify after that. And Delancy was not a fool.

So now, on a hot airless Thursday afternoon, the long-drawn-out formality of the trial was coming to its end. Delancy would finish today and make his final appeal to the jury. Gordon could not stay away.

He came to the side entrance that led into the well of the courtroom.

Through small glass panels he could see the wide blue back of a uniformed attendant blocking the way. Gordon tapped lightly on the glass and nodded when the attendant turned to look. The door swung open. Gordon went through and stood there silently for a moment. The courtroom was stifling, the air still and soggy. Faded strips of dark ribbon at the ventilators fluttered to show that the fans were running, but it was obvious that the air-conditioner was out of action.

James Delancy stood at a tall lectern set directly before the jury box. He was bent over the slanting top, turning a page of notes, sipping from a glass of water. His white collar was pulpy. There were dark sweated patches on the back of his light gray jacket. This was final summation, Gordon realized, and Delancy must be well along with it if he needed a break.

Jonathan Pike sat bleakly alone at the defense table. He was turned slightly toward Delancy and the jury, head up, his shoulders squared, hands folded hard together. His mouth was clamped tight. Lumpy muscle bulged his jawline.

Gordon crossed toward him, moving quickly on the balls of his feet, making no sound. But Judge Pontalba sensed movement from the corner of his eye and turned a swift hard glare at him. Gordon paused to let Pike's armed guard see and identify him, passed along the table to Delancy's chair, blocking Pike's view of the jury. He lightly smacked a hand on Pike's leg. Pike started. He looked quickly at Gordon, a bright, terribly intent gaze. He knows what's happening here, Gordon thought suddenly. He doesn't know law or trial technique, but he has been watching and listening for six miserably lonely days, focusing that hard, flaring intelligence to figure out what it all means. And now he knows.

Pike leaned forward to look at Delancy, and Gordon turned with him. Delancy drew a narrow strip of paper from his clipboard and stepped away from the lectern, approaching the jury box.

"I have nearly finished, members of the jury. I have taken a long time reviewing the evidence with you. I have demonstrated, I hope, that the truth has not yet been established, that the complete story of the death of Angela Morales has not yet been told. But it is now clear to all of us that the case the prosecution has presented here cannot justify a verdict of guilty. The case against Jonathan Pike has been built on inference, in unjustified leaps of a wild imagination. Where we demand direct evidence, there is, as I have shown, no direct evidence. No, it simply will not do. Our sense of decency, of simple propriety, is outraged. You, the members of this jury, are the sole judges of the facts in this trial. You will now realize that the facts presented to you are not sufficient for conviction. I hope I have shown you the areas of doubt that demand a verdict of not guilty. I hope I have done that. If I have not, I have failed my client, and I have failed the cause of justice."

Gordon felt a quick, irrational surge of hope. This was the old, bold Delancy and it was fine to hear him. The thin, too often uncertain voice was steady now, level and earnest, ringing with sincerity and inner conviction.

Delancy stood very straight. "You have heard the various, differing statements made by Jonathan Pike to the sheriff's investigators. When Mr. Burrell sums up for the prosecution, I am sure he will make much of the discrepancies, the downright lies, in those several statements. Let him do so. Jonathan Pike did lie. A frightened young man, completely alone, with no one to counsel him, made a very serious mistake when he tried to mislead the investigators. Mr. Burrell, as I have said, will remind you of those lies. I ask only one thing of you, members of the jury. When Mr. Burrell mentions the lies, I want you to say to yourselves that there is one supremely important point common to all those statements that Mr. Burrell will not be emphasizing. In every one of them, Jonathan Pike steadfastly maintained his innocence. And I believe him. I wholeheartedly believe him. I am confident, members of the jury, that you also believe him." •

Delancy drew a deep slow breath that was clearly audible in the hushed courtroom. He moved along the front of the jury box, his long face melancholy and pale. "In my forty-two years as a practicing attorney I have been associated with twenty-four murder trials, and in every one of them, members of the jury, I have felt the most profound sympathy for those twelve honorable citizens who have been required to decide whether a fellow human is to live or die. What a dreadful responsibility that is! Far greater than my own responsibility, which I sometimes find is almost heavier than I can bear. My time of responsibility is now coming to an end. The moment of truth for each of you, separately and together, is now at hand."

Delancy moved back to the lectern, placed long white hands along the upper edge and inclined slowly forward. "To condemn Jonathan Pike to death, all twelve of you must be in agreement. But you cannot share among you that decision. On each of you the burden rests equally, as an individual. To take Jonathan Pike's life, all of you must act together.

"But any one of you can send him free. Any *one!*"

Delancy slowly straightened. With trembling hands he scraped together a collection of papers and stepped back. He bowed formally to the jury and thanked them. He moved stiffly toward the defense table in a weighty silence.

Judge Pontalba pushed his chair back with a squeak. "Ten minutes, Mr. Clerk."

Gordon slid quickly from his chair, held it for Delancy, and poured a glass of water as soon as the old man had seated himself. Delancy took the glass in both hands, braced his elbows squarely, and bent his head so he could drink without spilling. He put the glass down clumsily, spread wide the fingers of one hand just above the surface of the table and smiled thinly as he watched them dance and flutter uncontrollably.

"It's always the same," he said. "I never get used to it." He pushed himself back in the chair and looked up at Gordon, frowning slightly. "Why are you here?"

Gordon shrugged. "War-horse syndrome, I guess. Run when the bugles blow. I had to see it. I missed the early part, but I caught your ending. Very effective, sir."

Delancy let out a long sighing breath. "Let us hope," he said.

"It really was," Gordon insisted. "The jury was with you. And I could see David making notes. I'll bet he's rewriting his whole summation. I think you gave him a shock."

"Gave me a shock, too," Pike said in a slow harsh voice. "Sounded to me like a plea for mercy, not acquittal." He was facing Delancy squarely, but the weary old man would not look at him.

Gordon was careful not to answer. Pike was right, of course. But what else could Delancy have done at that point? Mercy was all he could hope for. Any chance of acquittal had been thrown away long ago.

Gordon went along the front of the table to the chair on the other side of Pike. "Few minutes longer," he said. "Do you want to go downstairs?"

"I'm okay." He shook his head impatiently. "I didn't mean to sound critical, Mr. Delancy."

Delancy made a vague gesture. He was breathing in quick shallow gulps. He fumbled out a fresh handkerchief and touched it lightly to his forehead. When the judge tapped his gavel, Delancy steadied himself with a visible effort.

David Burrell moved forward to the lectern in measured strides, his wide muscular face somber. He put a single sheet of paper on the desk and looked down at it briefly. He was a skilled and vigorous prosecutor when the moment actually came. Nothing displayed his quality more than his manner with a jury. He had many styles of approach, and all of them seemed to be natural and easy expressions of his own sincere convictions. He had read this jury, Gordon could see, studied them hard enough during the long trial days, and now he knew them and could anticipate their responses. Delancy had touched their emotions, had perhaps shaken them. But Burrell would bring them back to a sober consideration of the facts, remind them that a young girl had been brutally murdered and that all the available evidence clearly pointed to Pike.

His manner was simple, matter of fact. He told them what the evidence was, taking them briefly through the chronology again. One damning detail flooded after another. Blood on Pike's clothes. Angela's blood. Brain tissue forcibly jammed into the welting of Pike's shoes. Angela's brains. The tangled litany of lies in the several statements Pike had given the investigators.

"In all those statements, as Mr. Delancy made a point of telling you, Pike said he was innocent. He said a great many things in those statements. We have shown that most of them were lies. In the last of his four statements, The People believe he came closest to the truth, but we know that even then he did not tell us the whole truth. Even that final statement contained a lie—the most flagrant and dishonorable of all his lies. We were disheartened, shamed in our common humanity when we heard Jonathan Pike attempt to shift the blame for this brutal crime onto the shoulders of a friend, a trusting good friend, the young man who had helped him in a time of need, found him a job, offered him the loyalty of an honorable and good man.

"You saw and heard Lee Wallis here in this courtroom. I feel that there is no need to ask you whose testimony you believe.

"No, there is no comfort for Mr. Delancy in those statements Pike made. Any one of them, or all of them taken together, will only prove more clearly the shocking ugliness that defines the character of this savage murderer."

Burrell kept it short and undramatic. The jury had heard all the facts before. He was now listing them in brief outline. Their meaning would be clear to any reasonable person.

Would he leave it there, Gordon wondered, on that flat even-tempered summary? Too dangerous, he thought. Delancy had stirred them. Burrell would have to shift that emotional focus, and he couldn't do it with cool detachment and level tones.

The prosecutor moved confidently back to his table, picked from it an enlarged color photograph of Angela Morales' battered body, and held it down beside his leg as he walked back toward the jury box.

"Angela Morales was fifteen years old when she died. Fifteen. She had been brutally raped, over and over again, before her murderer finally dispatched her by crushing her skull, crushing it so severely that her brains were totally detached from her skull."

Burrell brought the picture up but still held it facing away from the jury. "For six trying days you have listened to testimony in this courtroom. You have watched while a cold-blooded young man sits opposite you, listening to that same testimony, showing no sign of human sympathy or remorse. He merely shrugs, with no expression on his hard young face. A girl is dead—horribly dead. Just one of those things, Jonathan Pike seems to be saying. So what does it have to do with me?

"It has this to do with Jonathan Pike. That cold, savage young man murdered Angela Morales."

Then the photograph was reversed and held against Burrell's chest as he moved along the front of the jury box. He returned to the lectern, turned the picture so he could see it himself, and studied it for a quiet moment. His face was stern now and saddened. He put the photograph gently down on the lectern and faced the jury again.

"The people of this county have charged you twelve citizens with a heavy responsibility. Will our daughters—however young—walk our streets safely, or will they walk in fear? The people of this county are looking to this jury for an answer.

"We live now in times of violence. Savagery has become commonplace. We are bewildered. We are frightened because we cannot find any answer to the inhumanity. So we must hold hard to what we know to be our best safeguard—the law. The animals among us can be restrained and punished only by the calm and rational force of the law.

"And so the people of this county have put upon your shoulders, you twelve members of this jury, the duty of protecting them against savagery and lawlessness. You have sworn to accept that responsibility. I now ask you to do your sworn duty."

Overkill, Gordon thought bitterly as he watched Burrell return to his seat. A tenth of the scathing emotional force would have been sufficient to ruin Pike. Why all the extra steam?

"That son of a bitch," Pike muttered through clenched teeth. "If I could get my hands on that—"

Gordon clamped a warning hand on his arm. Judge Pontalba scowled briefly at them, then looked up across the courtroom at the clock on the far wall. Ten minutes past four. The judge nodded to the clerk. "We will take five minutes. I will then charge the jury."

Gordon held Pike in place until he was in control again.

"What does that bastard want?" Pike's voice thinned with strain. "I sit quietly, and he says I'm a cold-blooded animal. What am I supposed to do, cry my heart out all day?"

204

"And then he would say you were faking a human response," Gordon said. "No, you can't win that one, Pike. However you play it, David would make you look bad. Of course it's dirty pool. And not exactly ethical. No prosecutor should ever make any statement about his personal belief in the guilt of a defendant. But that won't bother David. He's out for blood in this one. He's charging all the way."

"The son of a bitch is trying to kill me. I—"

"Shut your mouth, Pike!" Delancy whispered, coldly furious. "And you too, Gordon. You at least should know better."

Gordon nodded silently. He signaled Pike to keep quiet.

Judge Pontalba opened a thin black notebook. He cleared his throat softly. His chair swung left to face the jury.

Gordon leaned back, arms folded, listening with only half his attention. A judge's charge to the jury, in its early stages, follows a familiar, well-charted pattern. The meat comes at the end. Gordon tuned in occasionally to make sure he was not missing anything important.

"Murder," the judge said carefully, speaking with unusual clarity in a voice that filled the quiet room, "which shall be perpetrated by means of poison, or by lying in wait, or by any other kind of willful, deliberate, and premeditated killing, or which shall be committed in the perpetration of, or in attempting to perpetrate, any arson, rape, robbery, burglary, or kidnapping, shall be deemed murder in the first degree."

The statutory definition, Gordon thought. Fair enough. The judge went on to review the evidence presented, and Gordon again let his attention drift until an unexpected turn of phrase caught him suddenly.

"You have heard medical evidence in this case, which if you find it credible, tells you that a body, the body of Angela Morales, was found decerebrated, torn, crushed, mutilated, clothing torn away, brains separated from the head, skull crushed, face bashed in—"

What the hell *is* this? Gordon came stiffly alert in his chair. What was he doing, trying to incite a riot?

". . . medical evidence that the victim was killed as a result of severe mortal blows, that the defendant struggled with her, enraged by her resistance. There was evidence, if you find it credible, of hair and clothing found at a distance from the location where the body was found, the blood-stained heavy screwdriver at a distance from her body, blood-drenched rocks and foliage at another point, all sufficient for the jury, if they find the testimony to these facts to be credible, to believe that—"

Gordon leaned across, prodded Delancy with an urgent finger. The old man turned his slender tired face, his mouth slack and indecisive. Wearily, sadly, he shook his head.

Delancy was finished, Gordon realized then. His summation had completely drained him, and now he was merely enduring, waiting for the end. And if I get up and object, the judge will throw me out, and Delancy still won't say a word. But why is Pontalba doing it? A judge's function at the end of every trial is to balance out the evidence so the jury can see it in true perspective. The judge is the last to speak to the jury and his words carry an extra weight that can have critical meaning when the jury goes in to consider its verdict. So we expect him to give a temperate, reasoned, even-handed summary of the evidence. We expect him, in a word, to be judicious. But Pontalba's entire emphasis was on the sickening details of the murder. Underlying it was the unspoken assumption that Jonathan Pike was guilty and deserved to be punished.

From the side of his eye Gordon could see that Pike was watching him, still-faced and silent, stiff with shock. Gordon lifted one hand off the table and slowly turned it over. Nothing to be done. It was Pontalba's courtroom.

". . . and if you find that Jonathan Pike murdered Angela Morales, then you will determine whether the murderous acts, the killing, the bashing and crushing of her head, the braining, were committed with the deliberate intent to take her life. If you find there was no intent to take her life in dealing the mortal blows, in braining her at this lonely dark scene, then your verdict shall be murder in the second degree.

"If you find there was an intent to kill her by bashing in her face and head, with willful, death-dealing blows, and that there was sufficient premeditation in the mind of Jonathan Pike as he pursued his victim who sought to escape his clutches, as he repeatedly struck her down, then your finding shall be murder in the first degree."

Dead. Dead. Dead. The word kept time to a slow pulse in Gordon's head. He could not look at Pike.

"You will now retire, members of the jury, to determine your verdict. You will consider the evidence carefully, as you have sworn to do, and consult among yourselves to reach a fair and honorable decision."

Judge Pontalba swung the cover of his notebook closed with a decisive movement. The clerk rapped a quick tattoo with his gavel, declared the court in adjournment until the jury had found a verdict. The judge's charge had taken twenty minutes.

Reporters made one last try for commentary from Delancy. They surged around his chair, thrusting tape recorder microphones at his face.

The old man merely shook his head in dull, insistent refusal. He turned helplessly to Gordon.

"You'd better jump, boys," Gordon said sharply. "The county attorney is leaving. You'll miss him." He rose and helped them along, leaning toward them with both arms spread wide.

Delancy folded his soggy handkerchief with special care, making a neat square. "I am tired, Gordon. I think I will rest for a time. Can you stay with—" He tilted his narrow head toward Pike.

"Glad to, sir."

"Thank you." He levered himself painfully to his feet. "I'm glad you came back, Gordon," he said, and it cost him something to say it. He nodded once and turned away, going unsteadily out through the side door.

Gordon moved quickly to catch Pike and his guard before they reached the staircase leading down to the cells.

"Went mighty fast today, didn't it?" the deputy said cheerfully. "How long you think they'll be out?"

"No way to tell." Gordon followed Pike inside and let the deputy lock them in.

Pike looked at him, clear-eyed and calm, the flare of panic submerged now. Without speaking, he turned away, pulling at his necktie. He stripped off his cashmere jacket, draped it carefully over a hanger, and slowly brushed down the sleeves and back with his hands. His shirt was solidly wet, as if he'd held it under a shower. He unbuttoned it, wadded it, and used it to swab across his chest and under his arms. Then he threw it soggily in a corner of the cell.

"Timed it just right," he said quietly. "I've got one fresh shirt left in the bundle." He opened a cardboard laundry box, took out a folded shirt and shook it out before he draped it over his jacket. "Might as well save it till the last minute." He sat then, elbows on his knees, hands dangling, head low. He did not look at Gordon. "It was bad up there, wasn't it?"

"Yes," Gordon said simply. They were very close to the end now and there was no point in lying. "I've never heard a worse charge to a jury." Gordon sat on the edge of the bunk, slumped down, and braced his feet high on the opposite wall.

"Is there anything you can do about it, or do we just have to take it?"

"Nothing to be done just now. If we should appeal, the judge's charge would be a strong element in our case." But not strong enough, he knew. If Delancy had objected as Gordon had urged, if he had persisted and taken an exception, then the record for appeal would have been protected. As it was, they had nothing.

"Appeal," Pike said. "That's what comes after a conviction. Right?"

"Sure," Gordon said easily. "If they clear you, you wouldn't want to appeal, would you?"

Pike laughed, a short barking laugh that surprised him. "No, I sure wouldn't." He settled back, stuffing a pillow behind his head. "Is it going to be a long wait?"

"Couldn't guess." Gordon rolled up on one hip to get at his tobacco. "They can take all the time they want."

"It's supposed to be better if they take a long time, isn't it?"

He was just making casual conversation, Gordon thought. There didn't seem to be any edge of nervousness in his voice, merely the curiosity of an active mind exploring a new field of interest.

"Everybody has theories about juries," he said. "Some of them seem to make sense. A prosecutor, now, will not want to send a jury out to deliberate just before mealtime. So we score there. It's almost five o'clock and I'd guess this jury is going to stick the county for at least one more free meal before they quit. Then the prosecutor wouldn't want a jury deliberating over a holiday, especially not one of the family holidays like Christmas. And weekends are supposed to be bad for the prosecution too. So are late nights. A sleepy juror is likely to say the hell with it, let the guy go, not guilty, let's all get some sleep. You see how it goes?" He snapped a match on his thumbnail and looked at Pike through a haze of cigarette smoke.

"So it about cancels out, I suppose."

"These bright notions tend to work out that way, I've noticed. Something for you, something for me. You let yourself worry about that sort of crap too long, and you are likely to fret yourself into a nervous tizzy. Let it go. How about something to eat? You hungry?"

"Not right now." Pike shook his head, but he managed a quick slanting smile. "Gut's in a knot."

"Let's have a drink then. Coke or coffee?"

"Yeah, a Coke would be fine."

Gordon called the deputy, gave him coins for the machine. He asked him to send out for steak sandwiches and a large container of coffee. It might be a long wait and Pike would probably be hungry after he'd had a chance to relax.

"What happens if they want to take all night?"

"Never happens." Gordon dropped the cigarette butt and stepped on it. "The judge will blow the whistle on them about ten or eleven o'clock and send them to a hotel. Then he'll have them hauled out of bed and back at work about nine tomorrow morning."

"You want to make a bet on this one?"

"Sure, but there's no way to set the odds. I'd just as soon match coins. Nobody knows anything about juries. Nobody."

The Cokes came and the empties went back. The steak sandwiches were hot, smelled marvelous, and came with a rich and mysterious sauce. Gordon wolfed his share before Pike started, but Pike finally ate. They settled back comfortably with paper cups of coffee scalding their fingers.

They could hear footsteps hurrying down the circular iron staircase from the courtroom, ringing against the metal plates. Gordon sat up quickly, apprehensive. Too soon, he thought, this is much too soon. He flicked a glance at his watch. Six thirty-two. And we adjourned—when? A little before five o'clock. An hour and a half? How the hell could they have reached a verdict in an hour and a half? They couldn't even have reviewed the evidence in that time.

Pike was watching him steadily, his pale eyes like ice. He did not seem to be breathing.

The sheriff's deputy rattled the cell door. "Everybody up! We've got a verdict!"

The well of the courtroom was a bustle of sudden movement. The public section was almost empty. Only a few people in the first row. Two men were seated at the press table that had room for ten. Uniformed attendants moved quickly, buttoning jackets, smoothing hair, swallowing hastily, as if they'd just been pulled away from dinner. The second door guard went loping up the aisle to take his post.

Two extra deputies were assigned to Pike now. One stayed back halfway toward the side door, the other two close enough to grab if he made a move. This could be a critical moment, as they knew. A man on trial, hearing himself judged guilty, will often make a last desperate charge for freedom. In a wilder time of the southwestern tradition, this would be the moment when you guarded carefully against attempts at rescue. The guards waited until Pike was seated before they brought their chairs up close behind him.

Gordon stayed where he was in front of the table, surveying the courtroom. Judge's bench vacant. Jury box empty. Only one junior assistant at the prosecution table. So why the urgency?

He saw David Burrell burst through the side door in a flurry, jacket unbuttoned, one hand checking the knot of his tie. He slowed abruptly when he saw Gordon and stopped when he was close.

"Hell of a surprise," he said, still gasping to control his breathing. "Judge isn't here yet, eh?"

"Don't know."

Burrell went briskly toward the clerk who was seated at his table in front of the bench. Gordon drifted along behind him.

"Judge is waiting in his chambers," the clerk said stiffly. "It's not him holding things up; it's Mr. Delancy. Seems he went home, silly old bugger—" He glanced warily at Gordon and forced a small apologetic smile. "Well, I guess nobody expected the jury to find a verdict this fast."

"But it is a verdict?" Burrell said sharply. "You're sure?"

"Absolutely, Mr. Burrell. The judge sent me to make sure it wasn't just they wanted to ask a question or something like that. No, it's all over. Nothing left but the cheering."

Gordon fixed him with a hard angry stare, saw him flush and turn away. "Is that the way you feel too, David? Are you cheering?"

"Relax, Gordon. Take a slow breath. We haven't heard the verdict yet." Burrell smacked a hand lightly on Gordon's shoulder. "I go all out to win, you know that. But I've never found anything to cheer about in a murder trial."

Gordon eyed him closely, believing none of it. "Didn't you cheer just a little bit when you heard that shitty charge Pontalba made to the jury?"

Burrell swung around quickly to see who could have overheard him. Then he seized Gordon's arm and pushed him across to the jury box where they could be alone.

"Don't ever talk like that to me again," he said in a fast hard undertone. "That charge shocked me as much as it did you. I don't know what got into old Pontalba."

Gordon nodded soberly, unconvinced. "You dropped a little poison in the well yourself, David."

"No," Burrell said flatly. "Don't splash those hot tears on me, sonny. What I did was convict a murderer. I hope I convicted him. I sure as hell tried."

"More than that."

"I did everything I could. The bastard is guilty. I suspect you know that as well as I do. Jimmy Delancy made my job a little easier, but God and Clarence Darrow couldn't have got Pike off." He studied Gordon with a slow movement of narrowed eyes. "You couldn't have got him off either, sonny."

"I could have made you sweat."

"I always sweat. That's why I win."

"But there's something more this time, isn't there, David? Something just for you. A personal sting. What is it?"

Burrell leaned back against the railing of the jury box. He looked angry, but he shook his head. "No, I don't think so. I don't do things that way. I felt this one, sure. The books call it 'atrocious' crime, and that's just what this one was. An atrocity. Who wouldn't respond?"

"You don't worry about convicting the wrong man? Wouldn't you like to take a good solid crack at Wallis, just to see if he fits better?"

"No. Maybe he was in on it with Pike, maybe not. Pike lied so hard and so long that Wallis got away from us. We'll never be able to touch him. So maybe Pike's good old buddy did get away with something. But that doesn't mean Pike is innocent. I'll never believe that."

"You'll never even consider the possibility."

"There isn't any possibility," Burrell said flatly, positive. "The man is guilty. Even if that jury comes back in here and says not guilty, I'll still know Pike is one guilty son of a bitch."

Gordon stared at him for a long moment. "Don't you ever give anyone a break, David? This kid—"

"This kid." Burrell almost spat the words. "He's a full-grown man and a full-grown murderer. But to answer your question. Yes, I give people breaks. A lot of them. You talk like a damn fool. Pike had two trials before he even came into this courtroom. First, the police investigators checked all the evidence and suspects before they decided Pike was the guilty man. They could have set him free, but they didn't. Then the file came to my office, and my people went over the whole thing again. We could have set him free, but we didn't. On the average, I throw out at least a third of the cases that come to me. Various reasons: Because I think we may have the wrong man. Because I don't think the evidence is solid enough for conviction. And once in a while because I give somebody a break."

Gordon nodded silently. The quality of sincerity was unmistakable in David's voice, in his bearing. But sincerity, he warned himself, merely meant that David believed what he was saying. It did not necessarily mean it was true.

"I have to make distinctions. Every prosecutor does." Burrell went on, speaking quietly but with a remarkable intensity of feeling. "So I concentrate on the people who seem to be salvageable. Nobody wants to send a man to prison if he's worth saving. Nobody wants to see him convicted of murder if he is innocent. But the trouble is the bleeding hearts these days want to save *everybody*. 'He's young, don't ruin him for a foolish mistake, give him a chance.' Or they say, 'What a bright young man. Don't stunt his development at this stage.' Kids know all about that stuff. They trade on it. Not one of them ever believes he is really going to be punished for what he has done. They count on warmhearted people

211

rushing in to save them. But in the long run that's no good. You have to make distinctions. Human behavior in a civilized society has to be based on right and wrong. The day you quit enforcing the law is the day you license crime. And don't you forget it!"

"I won't forget," Gordon said. "There isn't any ground in between, then? It's either black or white, in or out, right or wrong?"

"It's a grown-up world, Gordon, and that's the way it runs. We've seen hundreds of young men like Jonathan Pike come through my office. I could write his history without even talking to him. Lonely, repressed kid, right? Brighter than anyone around him but not enough self-discipline to channel his mind in any useful way. A runaway, a drifter, a drop-out.

"People like that can be very engaging. They are good company. When it suits them. But they are also dangerous. They are shrewd enough to spot human weaknesses, cunning enough to capitalize on them, charming enough to get away with it if they are caught. So when people like that come to a prosecutor's office, they are never first offenders. They have been offending all their lives. It's just that this time they got caught. And not a single damn one of them ever believes that he is going to have to pay for what he's done."

Gordon smiled, but it was not because he was amused. "You are full of lectures today, David."

"It's always like that after a summation," Burrell admitted with a small answering smile. "I probably won't stop talking for two days." He turned away, then stopped to look at Gordon over his shoulder. "But I noticed you were listening. I hope you learned something."

I hope I did, Gordon thought. But what? Something about Pike? Or something about David Burrell? He saw Delancy hurrying down the long aisle from the main entrance, and he moved forward to meet him.

The jury filed in awkwardly. They kicked the legs of their chairs, made minute adjustments of clothing, cleared throats and seated themselves stiffly, aware of a solemn formality. None of them looked at Pike.

Delancy came through the door from the judge's chambers, where he had gone to make his apologies in decent privacy. He did not trouble to take his seat. Gordon nudged Pike and rose with him as the judge entered.

Judge Pontalba nodded brusquely to the clerk. "Let the record show that the defendant is present with counsel. Very well, Mr. Clerk. Take the verdict."

The clerk came slowly to his feet, as if savoring his moment of importance and prolonging it. He pulled at his sleeves surreptitiously and turned to face the defense table, bracing himself with military precision. "Jonathan Pike, you will please face the jury."

Delancy shifted back so that Pike would not have to move. Pike stood erectly but not stiffly, and Gordon wondered again at the control he could exercise over himself.

"Members of the jury, have you reached a unanimous verdict in the case before you?"

Juror Number One rose hesitantly. "We have, sir."

"How say you?" the clerk intoned. "Do you find the defendant Jonathan Pike guilty or not guilty?"

The foreman of the jury swung to look directly up at Judge Pontalba. "Guilty of murder in the first degree."

A low approving murmur droned through the courtroom. The armed guards behind Pike leaned forward, watching him, then relaxed when he sat down again and folded his arms. Judge Pontalba rapped his gavel sharply twice.

"The court will be in order. Mr. Delancy, do you wish the jury polled?"

"No, your honor."

The judge turned his complete attention to the jury. He regarded them with a small pleased smile, running his benign gaze slowly along both rows.

"In discharging you, members of the jury, I first want to commend you on your verdict. You have fulfilled your heavy responsibility as citizens of this county and state. I know it has not been easy for you. I want you to know that I would have found as you have found, and I say that for whatever satisfaction it may be to you as jurors in this difficult case. With the thanks of this court, you are now discharged." He nodded at the clerk. "We will stand adjourned, Mr. Clerk, until nine thirty tomorrow morning."

"Now what?" Pike asked quietly.

A hell of a question, Gordon thought. He looked at Delancy for an answer. Delancy squared himself. He had changed his rumpled clothes, even had a long cool bath, Gordon suspected. He was wearing a stark black suit with a stiff-collared white shirt and a narrow dark necktie. Funeral clothes.

"We will appeal," he said, slow and tired, with a strained heaviness in his throat. "That is mandatory. I will be talking with you soon. Tomorrow or the next day." He looked at Pike then, for the first time since he had returned to the courtroom. His wide thin mouth pursed in a bleak, *V*-shaped smile. "There is no reason for despair, young man. This is only what a prizefighter would call the first round. The fight is still before us."

Gordon said nothing. He came to his feet when Delancy rose and stayed there, nodding as the old man said good-bye and went away up the aisle. He reached under the table for his heavy briefcase and balanced it on the back of a chair.

"The first round," Pike said thinly. "The fight is still before us." His tone mocked Delancy's brittle voice. His eyes were bright and hard. "That's bullshit, isn't it?"

"Not entirely," Gordon said. He took Pike's arm and led him toward the staircase. "Let's wait till we get downstairs. I don't want anyone overhearing me."

"Why not? What's so important about anything you could say now?"

"You'll see."

Gordon kept him moving so that he had no time to talk. When they were alone in Pike's cell, he gestured for Pike to sit. He swung his briefcase up on the bunk, unstrapped it, and took out a fresh yellow legal pad and two ballpoint pens. He dropped them beside Pike on the blanket. He sat on the edge of the uncovered toilet so that his head was only inches from Pike's.

"What happens now is a cut-and-dried routine. In a week or ten days Judge Pontalba will call you in for sentencing. After that you will be taken to the state prison at Yucca. We will file an appeal. Every convicted defendant in a capital case is automatically allowed one appeal. It will take quite a time. The trial record has to be printed. There's a lot of research to be done before briefs can be written. Then they have to be printed. We don't have a separate court of appeals in this state, so our appeal goes directly to the State Supreme Court. The calendar is always crowded, so there will be a long wait. I'd say it will be at least a year before the appeal can be heard."

"Jesus!" Pike groaned. "That long?"

"At least that long. And there isn't a single damn thing you or anyone else can do about it." Gordon leaned urgently forward. "But there is something you can do to help yourself right now. And you are the only one who can do it."

Pike smiled grimly. His eyes narrowed in wary appraisal. Slowly he nodded. "Okay."

Gordon pointed to the legal pad and waited until Pike had it braced on his knee, pen ready. "Write exactly what I say. I'll go along slowly enough for you to follow."

214

So here we go, he thought with an edge of excitement. You still have time to step back. Until you actually say the words, you are still a loyal and well-regarded associate of Gaines, Prinz and Delancy. But afterward what are you going to be?

"Write this," he said in a voice that was unexpectedly rough, "and make sure it's legible.

"Chairman, Grievance Committee, Rincon County Bar Association . . .

"Dear Mr. Chairman—"

He waited a week.

For all of that time Rincon lay under a steaming blanket of searing, oppressive heat. Dense unmoving clouds hung low, trapping moisture and bringing a sharp rise in humidity that made the air lifeless. In the arid world of the high desert, ten percent humidity can be stifling. People moved, short-tempered and sluggish, from one air-conditioned haven to another. Men had given up talking about the heat. They merely made ritual gestures, a finger thrust inside a soggy collar, a hand flicking as if to shake off a torrent of sweat, and then dismissed the subject.

Jonathan Pike's cell in the basement of the old county courthouse was probably as comfortable as any place in town, Gordon thought.

At the moment he was experimenting with a new adjustment in which his single narrow window was cracked only an inch and heavily shielded. The fan over his door was directed straight down on his head. It was hard to keep papers on his desk, but he felt he was a little cooler this way. The steady breeze on his damp shirt gave him an illusion of coolness.

He was still chewing his way slowly, methodically, through the dull complexities of *Schnelker v. Schnelker*. He felt completely sure that he would never have anything to do with the actual trial, but he went through his assigned work with a dogged thoroughness, concentrating completely and trying not to think of Jonathan Pike.

The summons was relayed down the chain of command on the seventh day. Gordon buttoned his collar, slid his necktie into place, rolled down his sleeves. He carried his jacket with him until he was in the air-conditioned corridor outside Jacob Prinz's office. He put it on before he knocked and went in.

They were ready for him. Stern, cold-eyed, speculative. Jacob Prinz. James Oliver Delancy. Heavy with years and dignity. And suspicion.

"Sit there, Gordon, if you please." Prinz said, indicating a chair directly in front of the massive carved desk. "We have a serious problem, Gordon. Very serious. One which concerns all of us." Prinz opened a thin folder. "First, I want to know whether you have been approached by anyone from the County Bar Association in the past few days?"

"No, sir," Gordon said easily. Make them come to you, he reminded himself. He had rehearsed this meeting a dozen times in his mind. They have to come to you. Wait for it.

"Have you been in communication with the association in any way?" Gordon shook his head.

"Do you know the chairman of the Grievance Committee?"

"I'm not sure," Gordon said thoughtfully. "Is it still Kleinschmidt?"

"It is."

"Well, I know him, of course. But I haven't seen him for a couple of months."

Prinz eyed him for a quiet moment. "Aren't you curious why I am asking you these questions, Gordon?"

"Get on with it, Jacob, for heaven's sake." Delancy stirred impatiently. He looked drawn and pale, but tension had clearly overridden weariness.

"We agreed that I would handle this, James," Prinz said. "Please allow me to proceed. Well, Gordon?"

"I assume you are laying the groundwork for something definite, sir," Gordon said. "What is it?"

Prinz lifted the top sheet from the file open on his desk. "What can you tell me about this?"

"This" was a letter on heavy legal bond bearing the insignia of the Rincon County Bar Association. It was signed by Juan Elias Kleinschmidt, chairman of the Grievance Committee, and addressed to James Oliver Delancy, Esq.

In it Mr. Kleinschmidt stated that he had received a letter from one Jonathan R. Pike, a prisoner at the state prison at Yucca, where he was held under sentence of death. "Said prisoner alleged that he had not received a fair trial. A photocopy of prisoner's letter is enclosed herewith."

The grave allegations contained in the prisoner's letter, Mr. Kleinschmidt went on, seriously reflected upon the integrity of the two defense attorneys and the trial judge. Mr. Kleinschmidt, aware of his responsibility as chairman of the Grievance Committee, had himself appointed a member of the bar to interview Jonathan R. Pike and determine whether any formal action was indicated.

Regrettably, Mr. Kleinschmidt announced, action was necessary. Mr. Kleinschmidt had this day challenged the validity of Pike's conviction by filing a petition for *habeas corpus* with the State Supreme Court. The

216

president judge of the Supreme Court had appointed the Honorable Wesley J. Richardson to conduct the hearing. Messrs. Delancy and Guthrie would be informed by Mr. Justice Richardson when a date was fixed for the hearing. Mr. Kleinschmidt signed off with "cordial fraternal salutations."

Gordon whistled softly. He reached forward to return the letter. "I never heard of such a proceeding before. Is it something new?"

"Completely unprecedented," Delancy said in a thin harsh voice. "And totally unjustified."

"Please, James. Let me continue. Well, Gordon, what do you have to say?"

"I don't know what to say, Mr. Prinz. What are the specific allegations Mr. Kleinschmidt refers to? What charges are we supposed to answer?"

Prinz smiled sourly. "Pike offered a complete list, masterfully organized, well-written: Hostile atmosphere. Inflammatory publicity. Prejudiced jury. Inadequate preparation by counsel. Counsel's refusal to object to prejudicial acts and statements by the trial judge. Counsel's inept challenge of prosecutor's flimsy evidence. Trial judge's viciously hostile charge to the jury. Pike didn't miss a thing, Gordon. An excellent brief. One might almost think he had legal training."

"Or legal assistance." Delancy's expression was as tightly strained as his voice.

"Pike is a very intelligent young man," Gordon said soberly. "And bitter."

"And what about you, Gordon?" Prinz demanded. "Are you also a bitter young man?"

Gordon lifted one hand, half-shrugging. "I'm not bitter, sir. But I won't pretend I was pleased with the way the trial went. You know my opinion. I made a point of telling you."

Prinz stopped Delancy before he could speak. "No, James, recriminations will not help. You must let me handle this."

"But what about Kleinschmidt?" Delancy insisted.

"Yes," Prinz said slowly. "Kleinschmidt. You do know him, don't you, Gordon?"

"Yes, sir."

"And you remember Jackie Kleinschmidt, I assume?"

"Of course. We worked together here in the office."

"Until he resigned."

Under pressure, Gordon said to himself. Under one hell of a lot of pressure, gentlemen. Applied by both of you. Yes, I remember Jackie Kleinschmidt.

"Another bitter young man. With an embittered father who would welcome any opportunity to strike at Gaines, Prinz and Delancy. Another chairman might have ignored Pike's letter. At the very least, another chairman would have come to us first before taking such drastic action. Do you think Pike could have known that Juan Elias Kleinschmidt held a strong animosity against this firm?"

"I don't see how," Gordon said. "But he's a very intelligent young man, as I said. Maybe somebody told him."

"Exactly!" Delancy exploded. "Exactly what I—"

"James, if you interrupt once more, I will wash my hands of this whole affair. You agreed that I should conduct this—meeting. I insist that you keep to that agreement."

After a moment Delancy nodded grudgingly.

"We are drifting from the central issue," Prinz said briskly. "The letter has been written and delivered. The action has been taken. It is now for us to decide how we shall reply to the charges filed by Mr. Kleinschmidt. I have a proposal to suggest which simplifies matters by narrowing the area of challenge to James Delancy alone." He glanced sharply at Gordon, clearly waiting for a response.

"Yes, sir." Give them nothing, Gordon told himself again. Make them come to you.

"I have prepared a deposition for your signature. In it you state that your contribution as Mr. Delancy's assistant was limited to certain minor areas of pretrial preparation, that you had no part in deciding the trial plan, and no responsibility for its outcome." Prinz pushed three stapled pages toward Gordon. "I am sure that Mr. Justice Richardson will then excuse you from the hearing."

The first and most obvious move, Gordon thought, and one he had been anticipating. He looked carefully at Prinz, then at Delancy, feeling the tension build as he delayed his reply. "I can't do that, sir," he said.

Delancy slapped both hands sharply down on his knees. He turned to Prinz, mouth open, and then subsided when Prinz scowled and shook his head.

"Please explain, Gordon."

"I did have a great deal to do with the pretrial preparation, Mr. Prinz. In fact, what preparation was done was entirely my work. I did offer detailed proposals for every stage of the trial itself. I made to Mr. Delancy, and to you, sir, the same objections that Pike has now filed with the Grievance Committee. How can I possibly deny that? Or," he said, letting his voice drop to a weighty quietness, "to put it another way, why should I?"

218

"Ah," Prinz murmured, "I think I am beginning to see."

"I told you, Jacob! From the first, I told you."

"Be still, James. Try to listen. Mr. Guthrie is coming to the critical point now, I suspect. Let us assume for the moment, Mr. Guthrie, that you and Mr. Delancy attend the *habeas corpus* hearing together. What will your position be? How will you defend yourself?"

Now it comes. Gordon held his face in cold still lines, showing nothing of what he was feeling. He shifted to get at his wallet, opened a compartment, and took out a folded slip of paper. He put his wallet away then and stretched across the desk to drop the paper near Prinz's hand. "When Mr. Delancy dismissed me as his assistant in the Pike case, I collected my entire file, the file I told you about, Mr. Prinz. I packaged everything, including my exhibits, and mailed the package to myself. What you have in your hand, Mr. Prinz, is a certificate of registration that says I sent such a package to myself at the Bench Club exactly nine days ago."

Prinz nodded. He understood exactly the point Gordon was making, but he wanted to make sure it was equally clear to Delancy.

"And when—if—you present that sealed package at the hearing, you will be able to establish that on every point of objection raised by Jonathan Pike, you, Gordon Guthrie, sat on the side of the angels. Am I right, Mr. Guthrie? You do not feel that the hearing presents any danger to you, either in a personal or professional sense, do you?"

"None whatever, sir."

Prinz swung his chair to face Delancy. "James, please come out into the hall for a moment with me. I want a private word."

"And I want a word with this—"

"Not now!" Prinz seized Delancy's arm in a quick hard grasp and pulled him to his feet. "You must listen to me." He hustled his furiously protesting partner toward the door, and there was no gentleness in his urging.

Gordon had time to roll a cigarette before Prinz returned. He had it in his mouth and was searching for a match. He took the cigarette out and placed it carefully on the edge of the desk.

Prinz walked around behind Gordon, studying him with slow deliberation. He went back to his chair, seated himself heavily and rocked back and forth several times, watching Gordon with a faint half-smile. "I suppose it is the size," he said, as if he were explaining something to himself. "We never suspect that tall, raw-boned, good-natured young men will develop into sly, crafty schemers. So we look at you, Gordon, and see a young man as big and awkward as Abe Lincoln, and we tend to think he must be just as honest and loyal. A sort of visual deceit, you might call it."

Gordon struck his match, watched the initial spurt of flame ignite the wood. He took up his cigarette, lit it without taking his eyes from Prinz's, and blew out the match with the first breath of smoke. He understood the baiting. He would not rise to it. Not yet.

"I could say that I underestimated you, Mr. Guthrie, but it would not be true. The fact is that I didn't estimate you at all. And that was a serious mistake, wasn't it? You are a young man who must be considered at all times with extreme caution. My mistake. So let us get to the core, Mr. Guthrie. What is your price?"

Gordon's face darkened.

"You have planned very carefully, Mr. Guthrie. Now that I can see the design clearly, I realize how much serious effort you have devoted to destroying Mr. Delancy."

Gordon started to answer, then checked himself. Prinz wanted no answer, merely an audience.

"I told you before, when you wanted him removed from the trial, that James Delancy is my very good friend. An injury to him is equally an injury to me and this firm. You are in a position to hurt him and I intend to stop you. So I repeat, Mr. Guthrie. What is your price?"

"Price for what?" Gordon's voice was unsteady, and that angered him but not as much as Jacob Prinz's words had angered him.

"I will spell it out, Mr. Guthrie," Prinz went on. "If you sign that deposition, I can persuade Wes Richardson to excuse you from the hearing. Alone, Mr. Delancy can explain that the objections Jonathan Pike has raised are essentially areas of judgment that must be left to the discretion of the defense counsel. Anyone can seem wise after the event, but that is merely second-guessing and may be disregarded. Possibly mistakes were made. If so, they were honest mistakes and do not in any way reflect on the integrity of the defense effort. Such an approach would be successful, I believe. Provided you were not present to contradict him at every step." He paused. "This is what I want from you, Mr. Guthrie. Your absence. Your silence. Your continuing silence. And, of course, that registered package."

Prinz was speaking calmly, deliberately, but his voice was going thin and strained. Only then did Gordon realize that Prinz was almost shaking with a barely contained rage. Prinz was as furious as Gordon himself.

He finished his cigarette and dropped the butt in an ashtray on Prinz's desk, taking his time. All right, he thought, so we play it ugly. You chose it. He settled back and folded his arms. "You are asking me to commit perjury, Mr. Prinz. Why? Not just to protect your good friend. You're more interested in covering for yourself and the firm. That's understandable, but Mr. Delancy did not give Pike an adequate defense. You know that and so does Pike. The trial transcript will show that Mr. Delancy ignored every useful suggestion I made. And my file will prove I made them. That is the evidence, and the *habeas corpus* hearing will make it a matter of public knowledge."

He paused, but Prinz said nothing. "You refused to remove Mr. Delancy even when I warned you that his mistakes were damaging the firm's reputation. You were in court yourself. You saw what was going on. You did nothing about it, and Jonathan Pike was convicted. So don't try your tired old venom on me, Mr. Prinz. I won't have it. And don't sneer at me and say, 'What is your price?' I am tired of that, Mr. Prinz. What I want to hear from you first is a decent expression of regret, maybe even sorrow. You are just as responsible for what happened to Jonathan Pike as your good friend is, because you let him do it."

"We are drifting again," Prinz said coldly. "What is it you really want, Mr. Guthrie? Beyond my expression of regret and sorrow?"

"You still don't understand the situation, do you?" Gordon said in a voice full of amazement. "Tell me this, Mr. Prinz. If I attend that hearing and offer all my evidence, what do you think the outcome will be?"

Prinz shrugged, a thin flush of anger touching his face. "No one can be sure, but it is possible that James Delancy will be reprimanded, even censured. And Gaines, Prinz and Delancy will be disgraced. Is that what you wanted me to say?"

"That's part of it. But you are still missing the point. What is the hearing about, anyway? Not Delancy, Mr. Prinz. Not even this firm. The subject is Jonathan Pike. And what do you think will happen to Pike after the hearing?"

"Very well." Prinz waved an impatient hand. "So Pike may get a new trial. Is that what you want? Is that why you have developed this elaborate scheme? Just to make sure that Pike gets a new trial?"

"You are being insulting, Mr. Prinz. Stupidly insulting. I have developed no schemes. Pike began this himself. And James Delancy made it possible. All I've done is make very sure that I am protected. I'm not going down the drain with Mr. Delancy."

"Delancy is not going down the drain." Prinz coughed at the sudden harshness in his throat. "I can't understand what you want, Mr. Guthrie. Suppose Pike does get a new trial? You don't by any wild stretch of your imagination hope that you will have anything to do with conducting it, do you?"

"I really haven't gone that far with it, Mr. Prinz."

"Put it out of your mind," Prinz said bluntly. "I think I can make very sure that, if there should be such a trial, you will have nothing whatever to do with it."

"Yes, I imagine you could," Gordon said, almost mildly. He was beyond anger now. "If that's what you decided to do. But suppose I signed that deposition you have there and cooperated all the way. What then? No reprimand for Delancy. No embarrassment for Gaines, Prinz and Delancy. No new trial for Jonathan Pike. But what"—he let his voice soften to a whisper—"what for Gordon Guthrie?"

"I began this discussion by asking you to name your price, Mr. Guthrie. Please do so."

Gordon slid down comfortably in the deep chair and brought one leg up over the other. He wasn't beyond anger, he found. He *was* anger. Possessed by such a demon of anger that he was not Gordon Guthrie just then, but someone totally new, someone who was going to beat this controlled, icy man at his own game and enjoy doing it.

"I don't imagine," he said in a quiet, musing tone, "that you would want me to stay on at Gaines, Prinz and Delancy?" He cocked an eyebrow at Prinz, gave him a moment to answer, then went on. "And I don't suppose I would be very happy here now. So let's assume I am going to leave, set up my own office, lease a suitable space, buy books and furniture, employ a professional staff and at least one assistant. A very expensive undertaking. I would estimate that I would need something in the neighborhood of fifty thousand dollars. Don't you think that's about right, Mr. Prinz?"

"Are you finished?" Prinz held himself stiffly. His mouth barely opened as he spoke.

"I have hardly begun," Gordon said cheerfully. "An interest-free loan of fifty thousand dollars would set up an office and furnish a little backlog of security. But we would have to understand that I was leaving here with the most cordial possible approval of all the senior partners of Gaines, Prinz and Delancy. Bright young associate spins off on his own. Chip off the old block. A boy we are all proud of." Gordon smiled into Prinz's furious glare. "A boy we are going to help. Now and in the future. A discreet announcement in the *Bar Association News*. Interviews in the local press. A small friendly party at the Bench Club when I open my new office. What do you think of that program, Mr. Prinz?"

"Have you finished?"

"Almost. While we are talking of friendly gestures, there is one very generous gesture I think you will want to make. A new office sometimes has to wait quite a time before the volume of business builds up. I think it would be a nice generous gesture if you gentlemen at Gaines, Prinz and Delancy picked one of the more challenging cases on Mr. Delancy's list and referred it to me. Something that carried a good fat fee. You could explain that Mr. Delancy is cutting his workload and that you can wholeheartedly recommend Mr. Gordon Guthrie, formerly Mr. Delancy's assistant and one of the most brilliant young attorneys you have ever known. Something along that line would do very well, Mr. Prinz."

Gordon stared impassively at Prinz's angry, suffused face, watching the obvious effort toward self-mastery, sensing the torrent of furious diatribe that was forming in his mind and being strangled to death in his throat.

"So now we discover," Prinz said thinly, "that it is not Jonathan Pike who is the prime factor in this equation, but Gordon Guthrie. You will sell him out for a fifty-thousand-dollar loan, will you? Perjure yourself for an office of your own?"

"You made the offer, Mr. Prinz," Gordon said evenly. "It originated in your mind, not mine. You made it to protect yourself. Delancy goes along to protect himself. But what protection does your brilliant young pupil, Gordon Guthrie, have unless he learns the lesson from you?"

Prinz turned away abruptly. He pitched the three stapled sheets of the deposition he had prepared for Gordon and threw it across the desk. Gordon caught it, folded it in thirds, and slipped it in his breast pocket.

"I'll redraft it, Mr. Prinz. I'm sure I can do a better job." He waited until Prinz faced him again. "So now you know the price, Mr. Prinz, and you'll have to move fast. You'll get your deposition and my file after I have what I want. If I were you, I'd start with a phone call to your bank. You will probably want to set up some devious roundabout structure for my interest-free loan so that it doesn't obviously come from Gaines, Prinz and Delancy. Any way you like it is all right with me. Have Miss Dorelli bring in Delancy's list of pending cases, and I'll pick the one I want. We'll have to get that settled right away. I don't suppose you will want me to resign until after the hearing?"

"No." Prinz's voice was a hollow croak.

"Vacation then," Gordon said agreeably. "I haven't taken any time off this year, so it will seem legitimate enough if I go away for a while. That will give me time to see what office space is available."

"You intend staying in Rincon, then?"

"Oh yes, Mr. Prinz. We are going to be very close friends, all of us. Gaines, Prinz and Delancy. Gordon Guthrie and Associates. The best of good friends."

Gordon swung his foot down and pushed up out of his chair. "One last suggestion, Mr. Prinz." He waited for Prinz to look up at him. "If I were you, Mr. Prinz, I really would do something about retiring Mr. James Oliver Delancy. I don't think you can afford him any longer."

IV

———❖———

JONATHAN Pike sat slumped, hunch-shouldered, on the far corner of his narrow bunk. On his lap he held a thick cardboard box-file. His thumb snapped the cheap latch open, then closed again. He was staring absently at the gray-painted wall, his eyes turned away from the glare-spot thrown by the bare overhead bulb. For the moment, a very brief moment, he was caught by memory and speculation. The latch clicked up and down in a steady quiet rhythm.

He could hear the guard coming toward him along the steel corridor. An open hand swept lightly across the bars of his cell, making a barely audible *thrup*. Pike turned with the sound. The skinny sandy-haired one. Johnson. He liked to wear cowboy boots with his uniform.

"Your visitor just checked in."

Pike nodded. He watched the guard roll a fine-meshed screen across the barred wall of his cell and reach up to clamp it tightly in place. Then the corridor was murkily dim, vague as the bottom of the sea. With the shielding of the screen, his cell seemed brighter, the light more concentrated. The familiar eight-by-seven oblong. Fixed bunk. Chipped cement floor. Thick uncounted layers of lumpy gray paint on walls and ceiling. Stained washstand jammed too close to the open toilet bowl. Stacks of newspapers and magazines in the corner. High thin bookshelf crammed full. Narrow flap of a writing table with its bench seat that had to be stored underneath if he was going to move toward the door. Home, he thought sourly, but now the thought no longer troubled him as it had in the beginning.

He turned up the lid of the file box and searched down through the layers of roughly trimmed newspaper clippings, looking for last year's collection. He spotted it easily enough because it was the fattest in the stack and the only one that carried his picture. The story filled all of page three of the Rincon *Record* Sunday supplement. Almost half the space was taken up by bold dramatic headlines.

STILL GETTING AWAY WITH MURDER!
Five Years Later!
Five years after Judge Manuel Pontalba sentenced him to death for the brutal rape-mutilation murder of fifteen-year-old Angela Morales, South Rincon schoolgirl, Jonathan Pike, convicted murderer, today quietly celebrated his fifth anniversary in Cell Number Twelve on Death Row in the State Prison at Yucca.

"Celebrated," Pike repeated to himself. His mouth pulled back in a hard bitter line.

Nine appeals for a new trial have been decisively rejected, but Pike and his lawyers have shifted from county to state to federal courts, playing one set of judicial rules against the other, desperately staving off each new execution date.

"Desperate" was exactly the right word, Pike thought, and still is.

Even before Judge Pontalba pronounced sentence, on the morning after a Rincon jury had found him guilty of first-degree murder, Jonathan Pike himself fired the first shot in his campaign to thwart justice. In a letter to the Rincon County Bar Association, Pike accused his own defense attorney, noted lawyer James Oliver Delancy, of gross incompetence and inadequacy in presenting his case. He went on to suggest the man who had defended him was guilty of collusion with the prosecutor to insure Pike's conviction.

Readers of the Rincon *Record* will recall that that effort was rejected. After a careful review of the evidence, Mr. Justice Richardson declared that Attorney Delancy had done his best with an impossible case. Justice Richardson then set a new date of execution, the first of many which Pike was to evade.

Pike snorted quietly. A careful review of all the evidence! Balls. What it amounted to was three long days of dreary legalistic bullshit in that cramped little hearing room in the Supreme Court building at El Monte. Nobody had talked about evidence. They were all too busy covering up for James Oliver Delancy. Even the Bar Association man, Kleinschmidt. He was supposed to be presenting Pike's side of the argument, and clearly he had been no friend to Delancy. But he was very damned careful to say nothing to trouble the judge or Delancy—who looked even thinner and more tired than Pike remembered. Professional courtesy, they called it. Pike could think of better words.

Kleinschmidt had done well enough when he was questioning Delancy about the venue of the trial. "Would Mr. Delancy please explain to the court why he had not asked for the trial to be moved out of the prejudicial atmosphere created in Rincon by the local newspapers and television?" Good question.

But even on that one Delancy slipped the hook. The publicity had been damaging to Pike, Delancy conceded, but that publicity was not limited to Rincon County alone; it was substantially the same all over the state. A change of venue would not have improved Pike's chances. Furthermore, Delancy had been confident that the good sense and human compassion of the residents of Rincon would be sufficient to offset any prejudicial publicity.

Balls to that too, Pike thought. They'd have lynched me on Main Street if they'd been able to get their hands on me.

But Kleinschmidt had let Delancy get away with it, probably, Pike suspected, because he wasn't any better prepared than Delancy had been in the original trial. Or any more interested in the fate of Jonathan Pike.

The issue of the inflammatory pictures of Angel's mutilated body was dismissed as irrelevant. No defense attorney could have kept them out if the trial judge accepted them.

And Delancy's very brief and ineffective cross-examination of witnesses was presented as a skillful display of forensic strategy. He had, he insisted, prepared well and carefully and given his best effort. When it came to the point of decision, Mr. Justice Richardson agreed with him. He also recalled

"We must not lose sight of the many problems which confronted Attorney Delancy when he undertook the defense of the petitioner, Jonathan Pike. At that time Mr. Pike had already made a statement which in many of its details was tantamount to confession. Mr. Pike did not take the stand to testify that his statement was not entirely voluntary, as he later claimed. Therefore the jury was justified in accepting that statement as true. Further, the physical evidence offered by the prosecution strongly indicated petitioner's guilt. In the opinion of this court, Attorney Delancy would have been justified in pleading his client guilty and asking for the mercy of the court. This court finds no merit in petitioner's plea for a writ of *habeas corpus* setting aside the verdict. The writ is therefore denied."

And where was Gordon Guthrie all this time? Off somewhere by himself in the high lonesome, and he had taken with him all the files he had told Pike he had ready for the hearing. It was a long time before Pike knew, or could even guess, what had kept him away.

"Attorney Guthrie had a subordinate role in pretrial preparation and took no active part in presenting the defense case. He is therefore excused from attending this hearing."

That was the first official statement from the bench, and Pike had known right then that he was cooked. He had pulled back into a hard protective shell, hiding behind a chill contemptuous half-smile. But the ice was deep in his guts. He listened to it all with no change of expression, and he came away from the hearing walking well and straight, his mind numb with the cold awareness of death.

He had been brought straight to the state prison. Legendary, notorious old Yucca with its sprawl of squat gray buildings sweltering under the desert sun. Probably the oldest and least functional state prison in the country. Pike was stripped, showered; his head was shaved; he was dressed in stiff new gray denims and heelless slippers, and locked into Cell Number Twelve on the second tier of a small separate maximum security block inside the walls of the maximum security prison. He had been introduced to the other occupants of Death Row, but it was a week before he registered their names. The daily prison routine was explained and promptly forgotten.

That mental numbness had persisted for months. The sleep period. A guard had shown him how to fashion an eye-shield from his hand towel to block the constant glare of lights. At seven and eleven and four Pike would struggle up out of a soggy stupor, take his meal tray and scrape it clean, shove it outside and collapse again in that drifting daze. It had been a sort of hibernation, he suspected now. The mind retreating from unacceptable reality as a bear hides from the freezing world that would kill him.

The sleepiness eased off gradually, but the physical lassitude stayed with him for a long time. In those days he had no writing table or bench-stool in his cell, so the bunk was his headquarters, awake and sleeping.

He was jolted only briefly when the warden's secretary came to his cell with an impressive file of legal papers that required his signature. If he wished to sign them. The secretary made it clear that it was up to him. Nobody was forcing him. In the case of *Pike v. Pike*, Mrs. Jonathan Pike had filed for divorce, charging desertion. Clark County, Nevada, Pike noted as he signed his name above the blank spaces. You won't like that country up there, Katie-kiddy. Too bleak and dry for a river-town girl. The secretary banged his notary seal, and it was over that easily. Bye-bye, Katie. Better luck with the next one.

He was beginning to stir around, walking a few short laps after meals, trying some bunk-side exercises to ease cramped muscles. He sampled the radio outlets, plugging his earphones in at odd times but never staying with any program more than a few minutes. The television he ignored totally after one try. The tier set was wheeled into the corridor, programs determined by majority vote of the inmates, and anyone who wanted to join in could pitch his earphones out through his cell door and the guard would hook him in. Pike had unplugged himself after ten minutes of *The Defenders*. He had seen enough courtroom drama to last him for a while.

He had discovered the prison library then, read aimlessly at first, then began to focus on one writer at a time, racing through four or five books a day. A scattering of the Waverley novels. Everything of Rudyard Kipling. Especially the *Barrack-Room Ballads*, which he read aloud to himself in a slow hypnotic undertone. From there to Rex Beach and Jack London and the poems of Robert W. Service. Then he came across the complete works of C. S. Forester and, in reading them, discovered he was getting fat.

He could still remember that. In one of the Hornblower novels, where the now-mature hero strips for his bath and is disgusted to see the small belly-lump pushing out below his ribs. And Pike had fingered his own belly, which he had always thought of as flat, and had pinched up a handful of loose blubber. The prison denims came in small, medium, and large sizes. Because of his height, Pike had drawn the largest, which meant a plentiful series of tucks in the waistband. But the tucks now, he noticed, were not nearly so plentiful or as deep. Have to start dieting, he told himself, go slow on those good Mexican beans which were a daily prison staple.

He went through the Foresters at a four-a-day clip, and when he had finished them, he forgot about the dieting.

The librarian sent him a mixed bag of modern realists and he sampled a little Mailer and Bourjaily, some Baldwin and Jones, a late Hemingway, an early Faulkner. All of them went back half-read. Too much of the current scene for his taste. He hadn't consciously thought of it before, but he was carefully avoiding anything that touched on the contemporary world. He wanted nothing more to do with it. Other

Death Row prisoners subscribed to newspapers and magazines and always passed them along. Pike had been politely grateful, but he did not look at them.

He was still wallowing in elderly historical novels, sailing to unknown islands, fighting old lost battles, when he lucked onto a stack of books by Frank Dobie, and from then on his reading had a sense of direction. He gobbled all the easier books, first, the wild spooky stories of lost gold mines and savage scalping Apaches, the heroic sagas of cattle drives, the dreary ones about life in a sod shanty, the wholesome morality plays starring the good guys and the bad guys. He enjoyed them all and read without criticism and because of them wanted to move on to more solid information that would re-activate and exercise that good mind that had been lying unused for too long, half-drugged with fear.

From Joseph Wood Krutch he learned something of the desert he was living in but was never able to see. Krutch led him on to other naturalists. It was then that he began the first of the notebooks that now filled half the space under his bunk. Through easy translations he backtracked to get the feel of the Spanish experience in the area and then, with the journals of Lewis and Clark, of Pike and Fremont, returned with the early American discoverers.

But it was the southwestern pocket of the country that held his attention most of all, and he began to organize his research in a systematic way. The librarian at Rincon State University drew up a reading list and allowed him to draw the books. And so eventually Pike could feel that he really knew the high desert. He had come here with the first of the renegade mountain men, had been with them to meet the wild tribes of the rocky highlands and the civilized farming Indians in the watered valleys. And stayed to meet the early prospectors and settlers, the miners and cattlemen, and their back-shooting hired gunmen. And fought to subdue the Indians, and later to preserve the Union, and then still later, against the Indians again in those last murderous, conclusive campaigns. Had watched the rawhide towns blossom when the railroads came. Sweated to make a living out of cattle or copper or long-staple cotton. Worrying always about how to pay for the schools and churches and roads. Worrying, most of all, about how to raise a healthy family and live a sane godly life in that blast-furnace heat of the desert, under the constant scorching wind, with never enough water and always too much sun.

There was no end to it. The notebooks seemed to write themselves. Solid facts, historical progressions, sober speculations, wild guesses, bitter arguments.

Pike shook his head roughly, shoved himself back against the cool steel wall, and laughed silently at himself. You are just as bad as that feature writer from the Rincon *Record.* He jumped all around the story and lost the thread of what he was saying because he didn't know the facts and was too dog-lazy to find out. So what is your excuse, friend?

The notebooks had been empty, still unwritten, the systematic reading not yet begun when Pike had received the heavy package from Gaines, Prinz and Delancy some ten months after he had been locked in his cell. Abruptly, it had yanked him out of his pointless, mind-drugging reading back into the real world, like a larva plucked from its protective cocoon before it is ready to fly.

The printed trial transcript was six-hundred-and-ninety-two bound pages in three volumes. The appeals brief that came with it ran one-hundred-and-sixty-one pages. Pike read all of it straight through without a break in one all-night session. And read it again the next night. And twice more that same week.

He told himself, and he tried his best to be persuasive, that these people had finally done a job for him. So they stank up the trial. Okay, no argument. But they really put some muscle into it when they organized that brief for appeal. Look how they picked up real yardage with that business of the shoes. I guess that finally registered with Delancy. The cops searched my place, located a very well-hidden sack of marijuana in a matter of minutes, but somehow didn't spot those shoes that had been tossed casually and very visibly into an old dried shrub. It took them two days to find them. So maybe somebody dumped them there *after* the first search? Anyway the possibility is there, and it makes the evidence look just a little fakey, right? Those shoes were the only physical evidence linking him with the killing. The blood on his clothing and body was not important. It was proven to be his own blood type, and its presence was easily explained by the events of the night in question.

It had, Pike suspected, been a serious error to let Delancy keep him off the stand. Even if the jury had not believed a word he said, the trial record would have shown that he flatly denied having killed Angela Morales and that he had sworn that the damaging parts of his statement had been forced from him by police intimidation. As it was the brief merely claimed that the statement was tainted evidence and should not have been admitted, but there was nothing in the record to show that the claim had been made during the trial, as it should have been.

Too late now. Pike read the brief closely again and again and each time managed to believe in it a little more. Repetition is what does it, he told himself. If you want to generate a sincere belief in salvation or Communism or man's damnation, you just keep reciting the appropriate litany over and over and never let anyone interrupt you. Above all, don't ask questions, and never listen to anyone who wants to ask them.

He had four months more to wait. Busy court. Crowded calendar. They were four long quiet months without a word from anyone. He didn't read much then, couldn't concentrate. The three-station radio was a help. He ignored the news and entertainment channel, plugged his earphone into either the music or sports slot, snapping it in and out like a kid playing Lucky Dip at a carnival, taking whatever he found. Sports was either early football or end-of-season baseball. And who cared? Except that Willie Mays was off on an autumn fence-busting spree and Pike worked to catch him on his good days. The rest of the time he just drifted with whatever came along. Until a day in early October when young Mr. Randolph came to bring him the news.

Barrett E. Randolph was thin, intense, very stern.

Guards placed folding chairs in the corridor. One of them, three feet away, faced Pike's cell door behind the fine-screen mesh. The other was off to one side. That was for the guard captain who watched Randolph to make sure he didn't pass anything to Pike through the screen. What, Pike wondered, did he think could be passed? A very thin pencil, perhaps. Maybe one of Gordon Guthrie's skinny cigarettes. Or he might smuggle in an atomizer and spray Pike's cell with a shot of bourbon. But none of that would suit young Mr. Randolph's style.

He sat on the edge of his chair, upright, hands cupped on his bony knees. Chin high. Dark reddish hair well-brushed and glossy. Pink translucent skin dotted with orange freckles. The thin lipless mouth of a good hater.

"Mr. Pike," he said in a flat, clear, official-sounding voice. "I am Barrett E. Randolph from the firm of Gaines, Prinz and Delancy."

Pike knew all that. Visitors were always announced well in advance. He wondered why Randolph thought it worth repeating.

"Randolph, you said? What happened to Delancy?"

Randolph's chin pulled in sharply. His pale skin darkened in the folds around his mouth. "Mr. Delancy retired last year," he said stiffly. "He died a few months later."

"He had the smell," Pike said softly, as if to himself.

Young Mr. Randolph glared in outraged silence.

Pike sighed. "Sorry," he said perfunctorily. He had hoped for something a little better than this stiff little man. "Well, what about the other guy? Delancy's assistant. Gordon Guthrie? What about him?"

Randolph let out a strained sound through his nose. "Mr. Guthrie is no longer with Gaines, Prinz and Delancy. He left to open his own office. Now then, may we attend to business?"

Pike shrugged.

"Gaines, Prinz and Delancy," Mr. Randolph said, "at the court's request, agreed to undertake your defense and to represent you in the later appeal, which is mandatory in the event of a conviction for a capital crime." Randolph delivered the stilted phrases with a slow, official clarity. No personal intonation whatever. "I have been sent here by the firm to inform you that we have now discharged the responsibility we accepted. The court has been advised and has relieved us of any further responsibility."

"Wait a minute." Pike shook his head quickly. "I'm not following you. What about my appeal?"

Randolph blinked. "You don't know? Haven't you seen the newspapers? The Appellate Division of the State Supreme Court returned its decision at the end of yesterday's session."

"Nobody said a word to me," Pike said tightly. "Well, what was it? What did they say?"

"The judgment of conviction was affirmed. A copy of the decision was sent to you by registered mail." Young Mr. Randolph edged forward in his chair, ready to rise.

"Affirmed," Pike said. He scrubbed a hand across his chin. "Well —" He cleared his throat roughly. "Where does that leave me? What happens now?"

"That is no longer in our hands," Randolph said with careful detachment. "A new date of execution has been set for December twelfth, some ten weeks from now. During that time you will probably wish to consult with another attorney to determine your best course of action."

"And you are just pulling out? Dropping me with no warning at all?"

Randolph stiffened. "I explained that, Mr. Pike. Gaines, Prinz and Delancy have nothing further to do with your problems. Speaking for myself, I can tell you that I was greatly surprised when Mr. Prinz decided to go forward with your appeal. After what you tried to do to Mr. Delancy, I expected the firm would wash its hands of you once and for all."

Pike slowly straightened. He pulled his gut in hard and braced his shoulders. He stared at Randolph's stern young face, held his eyes for a long moment, then smiled nastily. "Just suppose the court had reversed the decision? That would have made old Delancy look foolish, right? So maybe Prinz wanted to make sure that wouldn't happen."

233

Randolph's hands clenched. Dull red patches mottled his face. But he held himself silent and unmoving until he could trust himself to speak. Young Mr. Randolph did some growing up in those moments. He turned stiffly toward the guard captain. "I think that concludes my business here this morning, captain."

"And what am I supposed to do about a new lawyer?" Pike's voice was tightly challenging. "Put in a Help-Wanted ad? Send up a smoke signal?"

Randolph came to his feet.

"If you write to the Legal Aid Committee of the Bar Association," he said thinly, "they should be able to help you."

"I don't want one of their out-of-work hacks." Pike drew a slow breath, holding Randolph with that cold, pale-eyed stare that had disconcerted far more experienced men. Then he said, "What was it you said about Guthrie? That he's in business for himself?"

"Mr. Guthrie has his own office, yes."

"So take him a message for me."

"What message?"

"What message would it be? Tell him I want to throw a little business his way."

He gave himself a week. Just to be safe, he drafted a careful letter to the Legal Aid Committee, rewrote it twice and made a clean copy. Then he waited.

It took three days. A bad three days. He couldn't retreat again into the shocked stupor of his early time in prison. That was used up, the door closed. He had to stay with the chill reality now.

He had put on a good act for Randolph, he reminded himself. Cool. Imperturbable. Like Walter Mitty, inscrutable to the last, and just as big a fake. You held it in while Randolph was watching. That pinch-faced, righteous little shit never guessed that your guts were falling out. Now you can put on the act for yourself.

The three other prisoners on his tier tried to help. All of them had been through the same thing. They sent cheerfully obscene notes, odd-ball magazines, newspapers, crossword puzzles, books of double-crostics. The intellectual wife-murderer in the end cell challenged him to a long-distance game of chess. The young black cop-killer sent *TV Guide* and offered to let Pike choose all the programs for the next week.

It helped. He'd never been the sort of person who drew—or much wanted—any outgoing compassion from people around him. It surprised him. And it helped. He kept aimlessly busy. He caught himself occasionally on the ragged verge of wild uncontrollable panic, and then he quickly soaked his head under the cold tap, damn near drowning himself, until he was sure he was back in control again.

Best of all was finding a short piece on a case of Gordon Guthrie's in *True Detective* magazine. The story concerned a Mrs. Mary-Anabel MacKinnon who had been charged with murdering her husband. Mary-Anabel told the sheriff that she had been startled by an intruder on a dark stormy night when she was alone at home. Fearfully she had left her bed to investigate, taking her husband's double-barreled Churchill twelve-gauge as protection. The prowler came at her from the dark hallway. Mary-Anabel fell back, half fainting with terror. As she struck the floor, both barrels of the shotgun went off accidentally. She was horrified to discover that the dead intruder was her husband, unexpectedly back from an out-of-state business trip.

The sheriff arrested Mary-Anabel. The husband's return, he told the press, could not have been unexpected. He had sent a telegram in the afternoon of that day telling Mary-Anabel to expect him home sometime after midnight. The husband had been a moderately successful businessman. Also he carried a quarter million dollars in life insurance.

Investigation of Mary-Anabel turned up a number of lovers. Mary-Anabel was a restless, attractive young woman. Most recently she had been involved with a handsome widowed rancher who very much needed outside capital to expand his operation. Another "Ragged Stranger" case, the magazine said. (Whatever *that* was, Pike thought.) The magazine praised the sheriff for his speedy efficient investigation.

For some reason the story had been delayed, and when it was finally published, two extra columns had been added to let the reader know how it all came out. Mrs. Mary-Anabel MacKinnon had been acquitted. A young Rincon defense attorney in his first major trial had destroyed the sheriff's perfect case. There was a small blurred picture of Gordon Guthrie inset at that point. Guthrie had, the reporter said, "man-handled" the deputies' testifying, had called their interrogation of the sensitive young widow "callous and inhuman." He had even suggested that it may have been less than legal. The judge had interrupted then, demanding that Mr. Guthrie lower his voice and moderate his tone or face a citation for contempt of court.

Mr. Guthrie was equally offensive when he cross-examined the telephone operator who said she had read the text of Mr. MacKinnon's telegram to Mary-Anabel over the phone on the afternoon of the killing. After a day of what the magazine called "savage, relentless" questioning, the harried operator admitted that she had no independent recollection of the call. The sheriff's investigators had checked her records, found the telegram in her working file, and reminded her that she must have placed the call to Mary-Anabel. The original telegram, however, did not carry the time and date signal that should have been stamped on it when the call was concluded. "A technicality," the sheriff said. "Proof that the phone call was never made," Guthrie maintained. "My client had no reason to suspect her husband might be returning earlier than expected. She was alone in an empty house. She was terrified when she heard an intruder. She grasped the unfamiliar shotgun, hoping to frighten the prowler away. She fired it accidentally. A tragic mistake."

The jury agreed. But the trial judge spoke harshly to young Mr. Guthrie before discharging his client.

Pike read the story several times, quietly delighted. "Savage, relentless," he repeated in his mind. Man, I could have used some of that savage, relentless shit in *my* trial. I just hope Mr. Savage-Relentless got enough of Mary-Anabel's quarter million so he can afford to take on a free client.

He tore the page carefully from the binding and stored it with the papers he considered important.

Pike could hear him as soon as they swung open the big steel door. A normal conversation, making some easy comment about a bet on the World Series, but the big resonant voice echoed along the corridor, bouncing off the metal walls.

A tier guard padded up quickly, slid folding chairs into position, checked the screen clamps and went away again. Then Pike could see him coming along with the captain of guards. But the moment he was in sight, Gordon Guthrie swung around, making the captain veer away sharply to keep from running into him.

"What the hell is *this!*" An edge of anger made the voice even bigger. Gordon pointed at the screened cell door. "I'm supposed to talk to my client through that thing?"

"Warden's orders." The captain moved past, shifted his chair a little closer, and waited for Gordon to sit.

"You take away my briefcase. You don't even leave me a pencil to make notes. Now you expect me to sit out here and yell through that screen?"

The captain wasn't listening. He had heard it all often before.

"The lawyer-client relationship is sacred. Do you realize that, captain?" The harsh rumbling voice was softer now, a menacing sort of purr. He plays it like a goddamn minstrel, Pike was thinking.

"You're making me sit out here where you can hear every word I say.

You're keeping three guards within hearing distance. What's worse, you're letting two convicted criminals listen to a privileged conversation."

The captain nodded, untroubled. "Warden's orders, Mr. Guthrie. It's the way we do things. Standard procedure, you might say."

"I'll say a lot more than that, captain. I want you to move back at least ten feet more. I'll keep my hands where you can see them, but I want you back there out of earshot."

"I'm ready to cooperate the best I can, Mr. Guthrie. But I have to do my job. Now don't you pay any mind to me. I'm not here to listen. I'm just watching." The captain skidded his chair back out of Pike's line of vision.

Gordon lifted his light chair and put it down with the back facing Pike's cell. He straddled it like a saddle, held both hands high and opened for the captain, then deliberately placed them together on the backrest. He grinned suddenly at Pike.

He hasn't changed much, Pike thought. Still as large and rough as ever. Wind-reddened face. Hair a little less shaggy now, shaped closer to his big head. Lightweight pale tweeds that were better cut and more expensive than anything Pike had been able to afford even in his best days. He was not sleekly massaged or manicured, wore no spectacular jewelry or frenchified neckwear, but there was that in his manner that warned you that just walking through his office door would probably cost you a thousand dollars.

Gordon had been inspecting Pike, too, but nothing he saw pleased him. Where was that air of cocky self-assurance that had been so offensively noticeable during the trial? There might be a trace of the old insolence in that slanted smile, those slightly hooded eyes. But only a trace.

"You're getting fat," he said abruptly and watched Pike's face darken slowly. "Just a little over a year in this place and I'll bet you've put on twenty pounds."

Pike made a small embarrassed movement of one hand.

"They serve up an extra couple thousand starch-calories every day. That's supposed to keep you fat and quiet. Like feeding you saltpeter to make sure you've got a limp dick."

Pike laughed softly. He saw it now. And very effective it was, too. It had worked easily with the guard captain and it had almost scored with him. Guthrie was a sly one, no question about it. Catch them off-balance. Give them a few unexpected clouts in unprotected areas, and very likely the rest of the session will go exactly the way you want it to go.

"Mr. Savage-Relentless," he said in a tone that made Gordon strain to

237

hear. "I can see why you're such a monster in the courtroom. I was just reading about the MacKinnon trial. I wondered how you managed to crack that telephone operator. But now I can see how it works."

Gordon glared briefly. There was still a deep vertical scowl line between his eyes, but he managed a smile to match Pike's. "I just wanted to find out if your brains have gone fat, too," he said. "Little Mary-Anabel. What a lucky girl she was."

"You mean she was guilty?"

"I don't know," Gordon said. "I didn't ask her. No, her real lucky break was that lazy sheriff. He was so sure he had her sewed up tight that he called off his investigation too early."

Pike cocked an eyebrow.

"Little Mary-Anabel shot up ten boxes of shells the week before her husband came home. Just practicing. She'd never touched that shotgun before. Plenty of people heard the shots, some of them saw her plinking away at bottles. But the sheriff never got around to them."

"Suppose he had?" Pike wondered aloud. "You could have explained it. What really counted was that telephone girl. She was your big score."

Gordon shook his head. "That's the way it turned out in the end, but I went to trial with nothing. It was coming on for showdown time, and I still had a bust hand. Then I got one of the deputies so tangled up with his testimony that he had to get out his notebook and duty reports to explain what he meant. There was one little item that sent me chasing after the telephone girl. I barely spotted it. Christ, it was like a TV trial where Perry Mason gets the word just before his time runs out."

Pike waited.

"Little item. You'd hardly notice it. The notebook entry showed the deputy had questioned the girl. It summarized the evidence and the general line of testimony she could offer. But when the deputy came to fill out his duty report, he put down three hours and twenty minutes for the interview. Three hours and twenty minutes."

"Too long," Pike said promptly.

Gordon nodded approval. "Exactly. The girl's records were the simplest kind of time reports. You could have checked back through a year's file in half an hour. So what was the deputy doing the rest of the time?"

"Neat." Pike smiled, full of admiration. "And the moral of today's story is: 'Yell for Gordon Guthrie if you're ever in trouble.' Which is exactly what I'm doing."

Gordon eyed him speculatively. After a moment he nodded as if to himself. "Okay. I think we might have got you off if we'd run the trial

238

right. So maybe you've got something coming. We'll see how it works out. How much money have you got stashed away?"

Pike drew in a long breath, let it out slowly, watching Gordon closely. Guthrie had a big-featured, candid face. You would have said it was not the sort of face that was capable of hiding anything. But it was hiding plenty right now. "Say something more," Pike suggested.

"Nobody listened when you were talking about those fat envelopes with five hundred dollars in twenties that used to come in every month. Nobody asked you for money because the court was supplying a free lawyer. Nobody remembered those envelopes. Except me. So how much have you got?"

Pike considered it carefully, then shrugged. "Eighteen hundred, maybe. It might be a little less."

"Where?"

"In Puerta del Lago. Banco Sonora del Crédito."

"That's about what I figured. Okay. I'll leave an unlimited power-of-attorney form with the warden. You sign it and send it to me, and I'll cash you in. I'll take half. I'll deposit the rest in your prison account and you can draw against it."

"And what will I be paying for?"

"What every other Gordon Guthrie client gets." Gordon grinned at him. "Total defense. As long as your money lasts."

Pike snorted lightly. "And how long would that be? Two days?"

"Don't worry about it. I'm not expecting you to buy your own ticket. Not yet."

"And what does that mean?"

"I'll bill you for all the expenses. And one of these days I'll charge you a fee that will choke you. But first I'll show you how to get the money."

"Any time." Pike grinned. "Show me now."

"I haven't organized my schedule yet. I'll let you know. First, I have to start building up a little journalistic interest. Then I'll get some of the good magazine writers thinking about you. When the time comes we'll go public. *The True Story of Jonathan Pike, His Ordeal.* An autobiography. All your own words. Don't worry about that, I'll find the right man to do the book for you, and when it hits the best-seller list, they'll all be praising the sensitive quality of the writing. But actually they'll be weeping for this poor lonely young man caught up in death's evil coils."

"Jesus." Pike groaned.

"We'll give them the real truth about Angela Morales. We'll show them the mysterious Lee Wallis and let them wonder about him." Gordon was warming up now. "The brutal questioning, the warped and damning publicity. The shocking, incredible story of that mishandled trial. And now, one young man, valiant and unafraid, challenging from his prison cell the system that would send an innocent man to his death. One man alone defying the entrenched forces of inhumanity. Heartbreak on every page." Gordon chuckled, a little cynically. Then he looked at Pike's strained face. He grinned to relax the tension. "So you see you don't have to worry about the money. It's there to be collected when the time is ripe. Right now we'll have to see about that stay of execution. I'll handle that. Then—"

"How?"

"That's what you're paying me for. Leave it to me. I can't say just where we'll go from there. We'll request a stay to allow time to appeal for a new trial. Our next move depends on which court grants the stay."

"You just lost me there. I thought the appeal was denied. Can we just go back and start all over again?"

"If you've got grounds, you can always appeal."

"Do we have grounds?"

"That's my job," Gordon said with an edge of impatience. "Why not just leave it to me?"

Pike leaned forward. His pale eyes narrowed in a penetrating stare. "I have to leave it to you. I have no choice. Do I have to like it?"

Gordon smiled. "Who cares whether you like it or not? You're just the poor goddamned client. Clients never get a choice."

Pike let out a breath. "So what is the timing? How do you see it?"

"Boy." Gordon shook his head sadly. "Just put all thought of time out of your head. When you came in here, you moved into lawyer's time. That has absolutely no reference to civilized human time. Let's see how it stands. You've been in here fifteen months, about. In that time one appeal has been filed and rejected. How long do you think it will take for the next one?"

Pike lifted an open hand and rocked it gently.

"So just forget about time. Ride with it. I'm scheduled to try a case in Arizona next week. It shouldn't take me more than a month. I'll pick up the stay before I leave and start organizing the appeals brief when I get back. So if you want a very rough guess, I'd say you might see some kind of decision around this time next year."

Pike just grunted, but it sounded as if someone had kicked him hard and unexpectedly.

"What did I tell you? Lawyer's time. Forget about it. You can't do a thing to speed it up. Maybe one thing. Do you want a tip?"

Pike nodded.

"I just hired an investigator. A tough old ex-cop. Joe B. Texer. He did six hard years for manslaughter. He wasn't in Death Row, but it was almost as bad because you can't let an ex-cop out in the exercise yard with a lot of cons who'd just love to stick a knife in him. So Joe B lived about the way you're living. He figured out a pretty sound routine to get him through it."

He looked to see if Pike was interested. "Joe B played a kind of game. Up in time for some light calisthenics before breakfast. Then a mile walk to the office, up and down the cell. His work schedule followed a definite, fixed pattern. Reading, some writing. Half an hour walk before lunch, half a mile back to the office afterward. And an afternoon work program as different from the morning routine as he could figure it. Stop off at the club for a fast game of handball on the way home after work. Strip down to shorts, bare feet. Hard game, swinging both hands hard and fast as they would go. Sluice down then with the best shower possible; get dressed and walk home in time for dinner. Rest and recreation in the evening. Early to bed and early up. And never let the routine drift away from you. Stick with it, no matter what. Except for genuine emergencies. Doctor, dentist, something like that, but never anything less. Take half a day off on Saturday. All day on Sunday. Lie around the house like any other slob, watch the ball games, eat a little too much. Get ready for the big week coming up. Joe B said it worked for him. He was a bum when he went in, a know-nothing lout. He had the beginnings of an education when he came out. Took every correspondence course he could afford. But most of all, it kept him sane." Gordon smiled faintly, half in apology, knowing he'd been overselling. "Does any of that sound useful to you?"

"Of course," Pike said politely. "Please thank Joe B for me. Tell him I'm going to buy a flute and I'll ask him to show me how to stick it up my ass and play 'Yankee Doodle.' "

Gordon's watchful face exploded in a huge grin of delight. "That's better. Had me worried for a minute there. Just a little bit too much the nice-boy for the guy I remembered. Okay, Pike, you do your own time. Just remember I want you in good shape when I get you out of here. I'll be booking you around the country on a big lecture tour, and we want to give the ladies something worth looking at. Well, I'll leave it to you. I've got to get moving."

Pike's head came up with a jerk. "Can you stick around a minute longer, Mr. Guthrie? I had a—"

"Name's Gordon. Most people call me Gordie." He overrode Pike's voice with a burst of power. "I'll call you, Jon. Okay?"

Pike swallowed painfully. "Okay. Thanks." He stared, scowling over

241

Gordon's head, planning what he wanted to say. "I sit here by myself, and I get ideas. Some of them are crap, and I let them move on out. But lately I've been wondering a lot about Lee and Nacho Cordero. You were saying that you had an investigator in your office. How about sending him out to—"

Gordon rocked his chair back on two legs. "Just hold it right there," he said. "You've got some notion that the truth is going to help you? Forget it." To help Pike understand, he made a dismissive gesture with a big hand. "We are way past that point. The jury decided the facts when they brought in a verdict. The facts in this case are settled because the jury said so. If the jury was wrong, there's nothing we can do about it on the basis of fact. I'm talking now about the old facts, the facts brought out in the trial. New facts might be something different. New evidence the jury did not have a chance to consider"—Gordon paused thoughtfully—"could be useful maybe. But our best approach is to attack the verdict on procedure. Legal rules. Due process. Do you understand what I'm talking about?"

Pike looked at him patiently. "I understand the words," he said. "I'm not stupid. But I don't understand what you mean in a legal sense."

Gordon smiled. "You're not exactly as big a pain in the ass as most of my clients." He laughed to take the edge off. "Let's go back. You were asking about Wallis and Cordero. Okay. The day after the trial I had a private talk with the head honcho at the local Narcotics office. I laid it all out for him, the way you told it to me, especially the guesses you made about how Cordero was running his racket. A couple of months later we had another talk. The Narcs had been taping Cordero's every move, and they finally figured that you had it about right, that Cordero was using that reefer truck as a stalking goat, letting it hang out there in plain sight to attract all the attention while he was really bringing the stuff across some other way. Probably walking it over the border. But the Narcs came up with very little. Just enough to be reasonably sure Cordero actually is running stuff up from Mexico. They'll hang it on him sooner or later. But so far he's still in the clear. And that goes for Wallis, too. A couple of the Cordero cousins are making the Puerto del Lago run these days. Wallis is on the Denver route. And sometime when he least expects it, the Narcs are going to haul him in and strip his truck right down to the bare metal. And probably won't find a thing. And that is exactly all we know of Wallis and Cordero as of this moment."

Gordon brought his chair down on all four legs. "It doesn't matter one minor damn what we find out about either one of them. The jury said, 'Jonathan Pike is guilty.' The jury did *not* say, 'Take another look at Lee

Wallis.' The jury did *not* ask anyone to investigate Nacho Cordero and find out if he set up Jonathan Pike for an easy fall. The jury decided the facts. And from now on, for the rest of your life, those are the facts. What we are concerned with now is a question of law."

He could see Pike shaking his head in bewilderment, and he showed him a quick confident smile. "Don't let it bother you if you don't understand it. There's more than one lawyer practicing right now who can't appreciate the difference between facts and law. Well, this isn't a classroom, and I don't have time to explain."

"I'd appreciate a general statement," Pike said stubbornly. "I see the distinction you're making, Mr.—Gordon. Okay, so the jury has frozen the facts and we can't argue them any more. But what is it we *can* argue? What is the law here?"

Gordon flicked a glance at his wristwatch. "I'm pushed for time, so this will have to be fast. Just off the top of my head. If you really want to dig into it, I'll send you some books. Now here is about the way it will go.

"I will tell the court that you were convicted because, and only because, you were deprived of certain rights guaranteed to you by the Constitution of the United States of America. That is our basic contention, and we will stay with it all the way.

"I haven't read the trial transcript for a long time, but I can remember most of the major points. First, we will show that you were interrogated without being advised of your right to have an attorney present.

"Second, we will show how that interrogation went, every grisly detail. Stripped naked. No food. No rest. Whip-sawed by the good guy–bad guy routine. The whole ugly picture.

"Then we will show that the Rincon *Record* and the radio and television stations controlled by that paper, deliberately and with malice, named you a confessed murderer weeks before the trial began and continued to poison the judicial atmosphere all through the trial. We will show that a fair trial would not have been possible in Rincon County.

"We will show, and this may be news to you, that one juror has publicly admitted that he was allowed to make an outside telephone call after the jury had been sequestered to consider its verdict."

"What about?" Pike asked eagerly. "Who did he call?"

"Doesn't matter," Gordon told him. "Only the fact of the call matters.

"Then we'll go into the trial errors. Negative evidence, most of it, but useful. The trial judge allowed the county attorney to express his personal belief in defendant's guilt, and did not correct or admonish him."

"That bastard Burrell!" Pike said with the strongest feeling he had displayed so far. "He was really out to gut me. At the appeal, he—"

"Not now," Gordon interrupted. "We'll get to *him* later. You'll see. Right now, let me finish. I told you I was in a hurry."

Pike nodded silently.

"We'll go into the matter of those pictures of the dead girl's body. They should never have been admitted. Judge Pontalba vomited when he saw them. But still he let Burrell put them in. We aren't on firm ground here because the trial record doesn't show what happened. But the people who were there are still available. Plenty of them saw Judge Pontalba desert the bench, actually run out to be sick. He didn't even take time to call a recess. So I'll get affidavits from a couple dozen witnesses and see if I can't get them accepted as an amendment to the record.

"Our major effort is going to be directed at that prejudicial charge Pontalba delivered to the jury. Pontalba is an old man, and he keeps talking about retiring. But on the bench or off, I'm going to nail him. He's going to be a very sorry man. He's going to wish he'd cut out his tongue first. And that is a promise you can hold me to any time."

Gordon pushed up from his chair and stretched. "Well. Long speech. Generally, that will be the basis of our appeal. We'll take it to every court in the appellate structure if we have to. Until we find the right judge. It may take some time. It may take a hell of a lot of time. But eventually we'll wear them down. You see how it's going to shape up?"

Pike smiled. He nodded with slow pleasurable anticipation. "I won't push you again, Gordon. Thanks. I'd like to follow the way you develop the brief."

"I'll put you on the distribution list," Gordon said. "Okay, Jon. Hang tough, boy. This is only the beginning."

Gordon came out of the small wicket inset in the high prison gate and went quickly across the graveled parking space toward the small nondescript rental car he had left in the farthest corner. Until he moved back into the shadow of the prison wall, he kept his head low, squinting against the afternoon sun.

Claudia had the seat slanted back and was comfortably slumped against it. Probably the radio would be going softly and a magazine would be open on her lap, but Claudia would be just coiled with her knees on the seat, comfortable as a dozing cat, allowing the time to drift along. She needed no outside entertainment.

Gordon rattled his knuckles on the window as he came forward to open the door. Claudia looked up at him with a lazy smile.

244

"Sorry I took so long. It's quite a process, getting in there. They've got a Frisker device set so sensitive that I thought they were going to pull the fillings out of my teeth just to make sure I wasn't packing a gun."

"And now that you are out, let us please go somewhere else. This must be the bleakest section of this very bleak desert."

"They don't put prisons in the high-rent district." Gordon turned the switch, gave the motor a moment to warm, then backed quickly into the sunlight and swung forward in a long arc toward the highway.

"Do we have to arrange an alibi for you this evening?"

"No," Claudia said. "I've already made my clever little excuses. As long as I appear sometime before lunch tomorrow, everything will be all right. Nico won't even think about me before then."

Gordon looked at her in surprise. This was something new. Usually she was elaborately careful never to mention Nico's name when they were together.

It had been so ever since he had found her waiting for him in his darkened outer office after everyone else had gone. He hadn't quite believed her voice saying, "You're working too hard, Gordie, love. You need a little healthy distraction." Afterward he had come to believe it, but even now he didn't do much thinking about it. If Nico was fool enough to bore or ignore Claudia, whatever followed was obviously his own fault.

"Keeping busy, is he?" Gordon said now.

"Day and night." Claudia put her head back. "It's like living with a law student preparing for exams. I think he's planning to read through the official account of every trial ever held in this part of the country. He even has one of the law professors from Rincon State come in to quiz him every evening. Sort of catechism, I suppose."

"Well, Nico's the conscientious type. He'll make a good judge. It's what he was born for, I suspect."

Claudia blew out a brisk, exasperated breath. "All those times when he was talking about 'public service' I always thought he meant something like the Senate or running for governor, or even one of the big Washington agencies. Who would ever have believed he'd be satisfied with an appointment to the Superior Court?"

"It's not exactly Siberia," Gordon said uncomfortably. "It's the first court in the trial structure and in a lot of ways the most important. Hell, it's quite a compliment being appointed by the governor."

Claudia glanced at him skeptically, then closed her eyes and let out another sighing breath. "The Honorable Nicanor Kronstadt could have any appointment in this governor's power. I know that as well as you do, so please let's not talk about it anymore. What are you going to do about Jonathan Pike? Are you taking on another free client?"

"Yes, I'll take him on. But he won't be on the free list all his life. Sooner or later, he'll pay his way. He's showing pretty good style, I would say. Fifteen months in that stinking hole, and he's still hanging in there pretty good. I think he probably has guts enough to go all the way."

"Does he need guts just to be your client?"

"For what I've got in mind, Pike is going to need guts by the mile. I think he'll make it. At least he's got enough confidence in me to stand still and let me get the job done. I've got a lot of plans for young Mr. Pike."

The good sure sense of confidence stayed with Pike for quite a time. Guthrie, he suspected, had much the same effect on all his clients, and perhaps that was why he had so many of them now.

Pike was beginning to move around a little more. He did not bother himself with the rigid program recommended by Gordon's prison-wise investigator, but he noticed that now he was getting out of bed with some real interest in the prospects of a new day and taking enough exercise so that his muscle tone was slowly improving. He was still carrying too much weight, but from time to time he would remember Gordon scowling at him, and then he would pass up the good Mexican beans and the thick slabs of bread that came with every meal.

He was still reading but no longer as a narcotic. Every book now seemed to spark a new chain of thought, and he began developing some of his thoughts in the first of his notebooks. Anything now could spark a speculative response. An unexpected turn of phrase in a magazine article. An overblown opinion in a radio lecture. Even television, especially the late-night talk shows.

A month later he shook himself out of it. Five weeks of his remaining time had already gone by. It was nearly a month since Guthrie had come to see him. And now Pike was beginning to measure his time from the other end. Four and a half weeks to go. Thirty-three days more before the day set for his execution.

With Guthrie on his side he wasn't really worried. But he *was* getting a little twitchy, and he wasn't sleeping well. As long as that December twelfth execution date was on the books, he was not going to feel easy. Where the hell was that stay? What are you doing for me, Gordon? Get out there and earn your money, man.

He wrote a letter saying all that. Then the next morning he tore it up and tried again. He rather admired the casual tone of his last paragraph. He hated to break in on the Great Mouthpiece, but there was this matter of Christmas cards. He'd been offered a very good buy. What did Mr. Guthrie recommend?

The reply came in four days. An unsigned letter written by Gordon's secretary, dictated by phone from Phoenix, Arizona, where Mr. Guthrie was still involved with a long difficult trial.

"Dear Jon," it ran. "Not to worry. Haven't written before because all reports so far are negative. After I left you I had only three days in Rincon, so I didn't get beyond a preliminary session with the attorney general. As a courtesy, he had to come first. I wanted to let him know what I was planning and to give him a chance to spare everybody all that trouble by granting a stay himself. He thanked me for the opportunity but declined.

"One of my assistants applied to Judge Pontalba as a matter of pure routine and went immediately to the Appellate Division of the State Supreme Court when Pontalba turned him down without a hearing. Pontalba himself came to the Supreme Court to oppose our application. Slightly unusual for a trial judge to take such a continuing interest. We expected Burrell to be there, and he was, firing all his guns. Between him and Pontalba, the court was brain-washed. Score: 3–0.

"I am now going after the judges of the Supreme Court separately. Any one of them can grant the stay if he wishes to. And I think I know the one who will wish to.

"I am still hooked into this trial that just won't get itself finished. We'll take another week, and then I'll be back to handle your problem myself. It's just a matter, as I told you before, of finding the right judge. That's my job.

"Order your Christmas cards. Relax. See you soon."

Pike rolled back on his bunk, grinning. It was almost as good as hearing Gordon blaring away impatiently out in the corridor. You heard the man. Relax. Twenty-eight days.

And then it was suddenly five days to go and Pike stopped relaxing. Thursday. So there was something to do. The guards liked to say that this was the day they had to work for their money. It was supposed to be a joke. Death Row guards had the easiest job in the prison, and they knew it. They were senior in service, easy in manner. And all of them were determined to let nothing ruffle the quiet drift of their days.

On Thursday the Death Row inmates were taken one by one to the narrow shower cubicle on the first tier. Shower, shave, fresh shorts, clean denims. The day of luxury. Pike took his thin cake of lemon soap with him when the guard unlocked his door. He hung his towel around his neck and remembered to go slowly down the tight steel staircase. Very much like the stairs in the Rincon County courthouse, he thought, but not quite as worn. The Death Row block at Yucca was almost a hundred years old, but it had not seen much wear in that time.

The shower was tepid, sun-warmed water hosing down from an open pipe in the ceiling. Pike soaped himself from scalp to feet and pranced a little, as always. He dried on the newly issued towel that was supposed to last him for a week—if he had another week. He drew a comfortable pair of shorts. The worn clean denims were a reasonable fit here and there, and soft as watered silk.

Then he moved out to the corridor where the prison barber was stropping a double-edged blade around the inside of a water glass. One blade was the issue for all six inmates, and Pike was number five today. Pike handed him the small sliver that was left of his good smelling soap.

The barber gave it an extravagant sniff. "Live it up, sport." His brush was worn to stubbles, but it was still soft enough to work up a thick lather. The barber was not intentionally clumsy; he just didn't know much about his job. He nicked Pike several times along the jawline, but the rest went well enough. A nice feeling. Pike stroked his smooth cheek with the back of his hand.

"A dollar tip for this good man," he said and laughed with the barber. Thursday was a fine day. But then the barber ran his hand over Pike's soft bristly hair and turned to look at the guard. "Four weeks?" Every fourth Thursday was haircut day, which meant a quick close zipping of hand-powered clippers over the whole head.

"Let it go," the guard said quickly. He shifted uneasily toward the back of the barber's straight chair.

The barber stayed like that for a time, moving his hand lightly over Pike's thick short hair. "Oh," he said then in a strange voice. He patted Pike's head gently. "Okay. Well, good luck, sport."

Pike did not stiffen. He got up from the chair and walked down the corridor to the stairs and up to his tier, staying carefully ahead of the shuffling steps of his guard. And he could feel the ice form inside him. No haircut on Thursday. Why not?

Because next Monday is execution day, and Jonathan Pike will get a haircut then. And a close shave that goes straight up over his head. Shiny as Yul Brynner. Not as pretty, maybe, but just as cleanly shorn. Monday. Four more days.

He moved far back inside himself then. He came out for a quick moment when he read a telegram from Gordon Guthrie: NO LUCK YET. BUT NOTHING TO WORRY ABOUT. BEST. GORDON.

Then he closed in and went blank. Anyone can learn to do it. You go inside where the spirit lives. And say good-bye. After that it is easy. No more talking. A few shrugs, an occasional nod, once in a while a slow half-smile. Just so no one gets the notion you are looking for company.

One prison chaplain made a cautious effort, accepted no as meaning no, and went away without arguing. By order of the legislature, he would be back Monday night, unobtrusively available, formally somber, Bible in his tightly clenched hands. But silent and that was all Pike asked of anyone now.

The blankness grew out of a small secret core. It spread in slow concentric circles that he could almost measure, like the tiny movement of water when a leaf drops in a pond. He was inside the circle now. When the blankness spread wide enough, it would fill the universe he knew.

The captain of the guards came himself to explain about Monday's dinner. That last dinner was strictly movie stuff. They didn't go in for it at Yucca, but there was some shrimp in the kitchen and a chicken. How about that, okay? Shrimp salad, fried chicken. The cooks could whip up a cake. Chocolate. They just didn't have the allowance in the budget for anything fancier.

"Fine," Pike said from deep inside the blankness. Before the captain left, he remembered to say "Thank you." That was for himself, because he was still the same man and held to the same standards even if he was now concerned only with the growing blankness.

On Monday the shower was almost hot. Pike was number one this time. The clean denims were short-legged. Bermudas, you might have said, if they had been trimmed more neatly. Saved the trouble of slitting the legs at the last minute to allow room to clamp the electrodes.

The barber had a new blade. Pike had brought a fresh bar of lemon soap. He presented it to the barber after he had run an approving hand over his silky Yul Brynner skull.

"Lots of luck, sport."

Pike shook hands through the cell doors on his way back down the corridor.

Dinner was chicken, as promised. Four lightly fried pieces. Cold, of course, and soggy with oil. The shrimp salad was a moist lump that Pike could not bring himself to touch. He ate most of a drumstick, then sent the rest of the chicken along the tier for sharing. He spooned up half the plate of rich plump beans, marveling that even now he could feel a mild twinge of guilt about them. Fuck you, Captain Hornblower. And you too, Gordon Guthrie.

Gordon Guthrie. I made a big mistake about him. And an even bigger one about Jonathan Pike.

He was on his feet well before time, standing easily balanced, hands locked behind his back. Parade-rest they called it when they were teaching us to march. Ready for parade. Then he waited—and let the blankness grow at its own pace until it almost filled him.

Two of them rolled the fine-meshed screen in front of the cell door, hurrying, too busy to explain. Pike looked at it vacantly, without interest. Visitors? At this time of night? On this night?

One visitor. Gordon Guthrie, big and quick-moving, his rich pale topcoat giving off little ripples of wintery night air. He stripped the coat, dropped it on a chair that a guard had provided, and stepped back close to Pike's cell before the captain of the guards caught his arm to warn him. He stepped away a pace then, braced fists on his hipbones and gave Pike a triumphant smile.

Pike stared at him. The blankness receded. Only a little, but enough so that he could look out around the edges.

Gordon smacked his hands exuberantly together. "By God," he said in a trumpeting voice that rattled the old walls. "By God, we showed them. Didn't we, Jon? Didn't we, boy?" He sat down abruptly on the mound of his topcoat, beaming, red-faced. The scent of good whiskey was not very noticeable.

"Did we?" It was his own voice, Pike knew. But it came thinly out of the blankness. He brought his hands from behind his back, folded his arms loosely, and leaned against the steel wall.

"Captain," Gordon boomed. "This is a rare moment, you agree? Once in a lifetime. Do you think you could shift down the hall a little way? A few extra feet, captain?"

The captain said something that Pike could not hear, but he saw Gordon move closer to the door.

"Got 'em!" Gordon whispered, hoarsely confident. The whiskey scent was stronger now. "I hooked all of them! AP. UPI. The *Time* stringer from El Monte. Newsmen from NBC. CBS. Best of all, I got the chief hatchetman from the Rincon *Record*. Every damn one of them!"

Pike nodded from the blankness. It was thinning now. The slow circles were fading away into the texture of the water. He could see Gordon clearly now.

"Hairbreadth Harry!" Gordon said in a rapid, excited mutter. "They came to watch an execution and what they got was great third-act drama. And every one of the silly bastards is bitching because he'll have to junk the story he's already written and do a new one. But the new one is ten times better. They'll see that when they think about it. I've been down there for an hour, letting them pump me about Jonathan Pike, taking their mealy-mouthed sympathy and shaking my head. Too bad. I did the best I could for the boy. Damned shame. Travesty of justice. An innocent man dies tonight, gentlemen. The whole tear-jerking bit. You should have seen them lapping it up."

Pike shook his head roughly. The blankness was going.

"Then Joe B came rushing in with the stay, and you have never in your life seen anything like *that* scene! Joe played it just right. God knows I rehearsed him often enough. Charging in, out of breath, waving the stay over his head like Old Glory. 'Stop the execution!' " Gordon reared back, bellowing with delight. It was a long moment before he could catch his breath, and then something in Pike's face stopped him.

"You 'rehearsed' him?" Pike asked. This time he recognized the voice and heard the anger in it.

"Hell, yes, I rehearsed him. This kind of thing needs split-second timing, or you don't get the effect. We got the effect all right. You should have—"

"I got the effect, too, you know."

Gordon stared at him. "I told you I was taking care of everything, didn't I? I couldn't tell you more than that. It had to come as a surprise to all those reporters. And it worked! Just the way I set it up."

"You planned it this way? You had the stay in your pocket, but you kept it secret—even from me—until you could spring it tonight?"

"I got it last week. And saved it to use when it would do you the most good."

"When it would do *you* the most good."

"What's wrong with that?" Gordon's eyes took on a bright glint. "We're in this together. If I look good, you look even better. I told you I was going to start building up some journalistic interest, didn't I? How the hell do you think it's done? You need showmanship, the old razzmatazz. Jonathan Pike is going to be front-page news tomorrow morning. Because I gave it the right build-up. I've been working on nothing else for two weeks, making sure the right people would be here for the big final scene. You think that was easy? Do you have the least idea how hard it is to set up something like that?"

"No," Pike said stiffly. "I was just sitting here waiting."

Gordon rocked back in his light chair. "I had to go all the way to the

Federal District Court to get that stay, and it was hard slugging. I couldn't get the right answers from any of the state courts. I finally convinced Judge Bannerman that the Constitutional issues I put to him were the kind that had to be considered. He thought the state courts should have handled it, but if they wouldn't, then he said he would. So I asked him to leave the date blank, and I would make another try with the state courts. He let me have it on that basis, as long as I made sure that a stay of execution reached the warden here before midnight.

"I sat on it and waited. If I'd released it then, you'd have seen a little nothing story back with the classified ads. Just another piece of legal in-fighting. A routine stay of execution. Who cares? But a last-minute stay! Stop the executioner with his finger on the button! Pure movie-land, Jon-boy. The whole world is going to know about it tomorrow. And from now on everybody is going to know who Jonathan Pike is and worry about him. That's why I organized it like this. Now do you understand, you silly bastard?"

Pike could feel the cold anger tightening his face. "If I could get my hands on you," he said levelly, "I would be in this cell for a murder I *did* commit."

Gordon straightened quickly at the menace in those words. Then, suddenly, he grinned. "Don't think about it, boy. You kill me and who will get you off?"

"You don't know what you did to me tonight, do you? They were going to kill me." Just perceptibly he had begun to shake.

"No they weren't," Gordon told him. "I had the stay in my pocket."

"I didn't know that. You let me think—"

"I let you make a contribution." Gordon's voice was quieter now. "The only contribution you could make. I put your name in headlines all over the country. Sympathetic headlines. They won't be saying 'Jonathan Pike, convicted killer.' They'll be saying, 'That poor boy. What a terrible thing to do to him!' What more do you want? So you had a few bad days. You'll probably have a few more before we're finished. Just keep your eye on the target, boy. I'm going to get you a new trial. And then I'm going to get you off. You just keep thinking about that. Then maybe you won't be feeling so sorry for yourself."

He got up abruptly and snatched at his wadded coat. "Okay. I'll be in touch. Make sure you order all the papers tomorrow. See how it feels to be a hero. And remember who did it for you."

Pike remembered. And so did a lot of other people. Pike was not a hero, of course, but he was national news for several weeks, and Gordon Guthrie's name rode with his in all the front-page stories.

252

Valuable publicity, Gordon found. New business did not come with a sudden flood; it never works like that. But the inquiries were more frequent and much more serious. Referrals more than doubled, and feelers from out-of-state law firms were now almost routine. Best of all, everyone seemed to understand that if you called Gordon Guthrie these days, you'd better be ready to talk about large sums of money. All in all, that dramatic play with Pike's stay of execution had worked out very profitably. Even for Pike.

Gordon was whistling cheerfully as he crossed the street and turned into the lobby of Nico's Rincon apartment house and pushed the button for the elevator. It was just a modest little place, Claudia liked to say with a mocking glint, handy for those evenings when the long trip out to the ranch was a little too much to face. The whole twelfth floor of a new building. Wrap-around terraces. Seventy feet of glass sitting room wall that looked out onto a grassy spur of San Xavier Park. Home away from home for the young Kronstadts.

The elevator delivered him to a circular foyer, and from there cocktail party sounds led him the rest of the way. This was not Gordon's idea of a useful way to spend the early evening, but the engraved invitation had promised the Chief Justice as guest of honor, and Gordon had not wanted to miss his chance.

The Chief Justice would be addressing the State Bar Association's annual dinner later on, but this was an opportunity for a select few to meet him in a quieter setting.

He was too late for the formal receiving line but he collared an elderly lawyer and asked him to lead him up for an introduction. He looked almost eye-to-eye with the Chief Justice and felt his big hand surrounded by long hard fingers. The Chief Justice smiled easily and well, but all the while his eyes were level and measuring. He must have met a couple of hundred new people that day, but Gordon had the idea that he would be remembered if they ever met again. A man of parts, the Chief Justice, just as he should be. Gordon turned away to look for a drink.

Nico took his arm before he moved a step. "Glad you came, Gordie. I didn't really expect you to show up."

"Couldn't resist. The Chief Justice. Wow. Boyhood ambition."

Nico laughed infectiously. "Yours and everybody else's. I never thought half these people would come. I just sent the invitations as a courtesy."

"You've got a big drawing card, boy. You should have sold tickets." Gordon shook his head when a waiter offered a tray of champagne glasses.

253

"Whiskey in my study," Nico said. "I want a word with you anyway. There's a small problem."

He moved in a slow unobtrusive drift toward a distant hallway, speaking to people as he went but never quite stopping. Gordon trailed him closely down the hall and went in through the door he was holding open.

The room was soundproofed, well lighted, and nicely designed as a working area. There was a long narrow *L*-shaped table against two walls with a padded swivel chair in the open angle, two low crowded bookcases with cabinets below, a pair of soft leather chairs around a circular table that held a tray of bottles and glasses.

The swivel chair was occupied, propped well back, supporting a slender dark-suited man who had his feet crossed on Nico's work table, head tilted up, staring at the ceiling through a pale haze of cigar smoke. It took Gordon a moment before he recognized him. Nico's grandfather, of course. He knew him as soon as he turned his head. But the old gentleman had gone completely white since the last time Gordon had seen him. Now his long shapely head seemed to be structured in fine-textured stone that took a high gloss from the overhead lights.

"Evening, Don Francisco. Nice to see you again."

"Evening, Gordie." The old man took his cigar from his mouth and smiled absently. "And don't you start grumbling, Nico. I'm just giving myself a peaceful moment. I'll be out again before the guests leave."

"No hurry, Grandfather. Don't move." Nico pawed among the papers heaped on his table. "This is what I'm looking for. Make us some drinks, Gordie."

Nico sat in one of the chairs at the low table and spread a manila folder open over his knees. "I've been drawing up the criminal calendar for next session, Gordie. I'd planned to assign myself to it, but then I heard you might be going to take the Williston case. I tried to reach you at your office to make sure, but you seem to be an elusive fellow these days. Are you going to take it?"

"Haven't made up my mind." Gordon dropped ice cubes in two glasses, poured Scotch liberally, and pried the cap off a bottle of soda. "John Williston came to me yesterday. I said I'd think about it. Not much money and not my sort of case, but I don't like to say no to old John."

"Well, I have to get these calendars set this week," Nico said impatiently. "Can't you be more definite than that? I said I'd take the criminal list this session, but if you're going to appear for Williston, I'll have to pull out and move over to the civil side."

254

"What's all this?" Don Francisco demanded. He wheeled his chair around to face Nico directly. "You can't try Gordie's case? Why not? Are you two boys feuding again?"

Nico laughed easily. He took the glass Gordon handed him and sat back. "Nothing like that, Grandfather. It's just one of the rules of the game. A judge shouldn't try a case when the defending attorney is a close friend. Tends to cast a little doubt on his impartiality, and we can't have that."

The old man snorted. "Nonsense. You're good friends with half the lawyers in town. How are you going to do your job if you pull out every time one of them has a case in your court?"

"It's a problem," Nico sighed. "I suppose every judge worries about it. You spend your early years on good friendly terms with all your colleagues, and then when you go on the bench you are suddenly expected to push back and keep a very frosty distance. Can't be done, of course, but you are expected to try. Nobody tells me when I should withdraw from a given case; it's entirely in my own discretion, which just makes it harder sometimes." He took a long thirsty pull at his glass. "Well, let me know about Williston as soon as you can, Gordie. My colleagues are beginning to think I've been ducking the criminal side lately. I'd like to pull my own weight, if I can."

"Hell, go right ahead and—" The old man stopped in midsentence when the door opened suddenly and swung against the wall.

"I might have known." Claudia stood in the doorway, trying hard to smile for them and not quite making it. "Nico, some of your guests are leaving, and I still don't know who they are. It's a little awkward."

She was slightly flushed, very much the dutiful hostess coping with her husband's professional associates and trying to hold to a stern line, but the old man's blandly amused smile and Nico's quick darting grin were too much for her.

"You are looking rarely beautiful today, my dear," Don Francisco said with complete admiration. "Parties bring out the best in you."

Claudia let out a long slow breath and shook her head hopelessly. She took Gordon's glass from his hand and drank it empty in one pull. "Now please, Grandfather. Nico. You too, Gordie. On your feet, men. Everybody out."

The old man regarded his cigar, blew on it gently, and put it down with a sigh. He swung his feet to the floor and pushed himself up out of the deep chair. He kissed Claudia's cheek lightly as he moved past her toward the door. "Beautiful," he said again before he left.

And it was true, Gordon thought. The only possible word. A knot

255

tightened hotly in him and he knew it would not be safe for him to say anything just then. He could feel it closing his throat as he looked at her.

He kissed her, too, trying for Don Francisco's affectionate lightness of manner, but it didn't go exactly as he had intended. Claudia moved away quickly, going away down the hall in a blaze of golden silk. And Nico stared at him curiously, speculatively, for a long moment before he came out to join him.

"You'll be at the dinner tonight, Gordie?"

Gordon shook his head. "Not a chance." It came out more roughly than he had meant.

"Should be a good speech," Nico said, reminding him that the Chief Justice would be on the platform. "There'll be room at our table, if you change your mind."

"I'll read it later."

"Think about it, Gordie. You'd have a chance for a quiet word with old Judge Bannerman. Wouldn't do you any harm to mend a few fences. I understand the old boy is a little sore. He didn't like the way you presented that stay of execution he gave you." Nico studied him openly, curious to see how he would respond. "You were unusually melodramatic about it, Gordie."

"I was unusually effective, you mean," Gordon said with an edge of anger. "Because I handled it the way I did, I put Jonathan Pike on half the front pages of the country. I created a new and sympathetic atmosphere for him. If I'd just walked in there with the stay, you wouldn't have seen any newspaper attention at all. My way, it made news. So the hell with Judge Bannerman and anybody else who doesn't like it."

Nico walked beside him to the elevator and waited as Gordon went into the small cage. "And what about Pike," he asked in a wondering tone. "I can't imagine he enjoyed it very much."

Nico, too, Gordon thought angrily, and that anger was reflected in his voice. "Goddamn it, Nico. I'm trying to save his neck. And when I get him out of there he won't care any longer how I did it. All he'll remember is that I put him through a few jumps to dramatize his case."

"Yes," Nico said quietly. "I imagine he'll remember it very clearly."

Pike remembered. There was never a day of his life that he was completely free of the blankness he knew was still inside him, waiting. It turned him quieter, less restless physically. The long solitary hours were almost welcome now. He began to ration them, shaping them in small meaningful parcels, making them work for him. His daily program gradually came to be as rigidly organized as Gordon had recommended, though it was designed to suit Pike's requirements and not merely to pass the time.

He added a subscription to the New York *Times* air edition to the other newspapers available on the tier, and every morning he read all six of them completely. His *Atlantic Monthly* and *Harper's* beefed up the magazine supply and later, when he became more curious about the world, *Foreign Policy Review* and the English *Economist.* He joined the historical societies of five southwestern states and took all their publications for his small growing library.

His reading was more and more aimed at regional history, but it was not until the first visit of the prison education officer that it took on a disciplined shape. The prison education officer was a local volunteer, a middle-aged widower, retired principal of the Yucca High School. He came to Death Row in answer to a call from Timmy Anderson, the teen-ager in the last cell.

The aging volunteer was just as surprised as Pike when he heard what Timmy wanted. The kid had killed one of a pair of cops who had surprised him when he was looting a television shop. Timmy just sprayed shots blindly while he was running for the door. One slug bounced off a display case and went neatly, perfectly, through the left eye of a cop who was diving for cover. The miraculous accuracy of pure chance. Timmy's trial lasted two days. His mandatory appeal was still pending. But there was little chance that the verdict would be reversed. The governor had already let it be known that he would not consider commuting the death sentence. He spoke of "examples" and "deterrence" and "society's responsibilities." Timmy didn't stand a chance.

But still he wanted to get his high school diploma. He was only a few months away from certain death, a nineteen-year-old who had not graduated because he just couldn't get the hang of algebra and plane geometry. But he had a lot of free time now, and if he really buckled down to it and got some good hard coaching, why he'd just take another crack at those exams. Breeze right through them. Get that old diploma. He'd be all set then, right? Pike thought it might have carried a certain magical meaning for him. All his life Timmy had been told that a bright young high school graduate has the whole world open to him. Everything to live for. He's ready to charge right into the great battle of Life. He's the Future. The world depends on people like him. Isn't that right? So how could anything bad happen to him if he had that diploma?

The volunteer shook the dazed stare from his eyes and went away, promising books and instruction time. And he did his part, sitting hunched outside Timmy's cell door with his lapboard, going patiently through the ritual drills. And getting nowhere. Timmy just was not getting the hang of it, and each day just added another layer of confusion.

Pike got into it out of sheer boredom. He stopped the volunteer after the second week's session. He discussed Timmy's problem and offered a solution. So Timmy was moved to the cell next to Pike's, and every afternoon Pike took him through his assignment. He gave Timmy the secret. Memorize. The world is full of people who can't understand mathematics. Pike was one of them, he said, though it was not exactly true. So forget about trying to understand. Just memorize the goddamn book, pass the exam and forget it.

It worked. Timmy droned through the set examples. Pike held the book on him. They sat side by side with the blind steel wall between them and talked into the empty corridor. One of the guards looked in occasionally to make sure Timmy wasn't cheating. An intensely concentrated month wore Timmy to fretful impatience and a barely passing grade in algebra. The volunteer was astonished and unbelieving until Pike explained the system.

Another trying six weeks for plane geometry. And Pike was beginning to enjoy himself. Geometry went easier because Timmy saw no sense to it whatever, which made it easier for him to memorize the incomprehensible lessons. A big fat 73 on the final exam and Timmy had his diploma, a specially-issued, stamped and ribboned document from the State Board of Education. Timmy stuck it on his cell wall with paper tape provided by a sympathetic guard, and then he danced. He thanked Pike and the volunteer. He sent each visiting member of his family to stop at Pike's cell to add their thanks for helping their boy.

Timmy had another eleven weeks to live, but they were not fearful weeks. He expected something good to happen any moment.

The volunteer suggested that Pike himself should go on with his formal education, and he made out a good case. He sent for Pike's freshman transcript from the skyscraper office of the University of Pittsburgh and paid the small fee himself. But the prison could offer no help with college-level work, and when Pike investigated the cost of correspondence courses in subjects that interested him, he decided to save his money. The volunteer arranged an informal association with Rincon State University, got the required course reading lists from the history department and showed Pike how to borrow the books from the university library.

And that was how it had started.

258

Timmy was gone soon after. They had come for him shortly before midnight, and for Timmy there had been no Gordon Guthrie waiting in the wings with a dramatic last-minute reprieve. Timmy's freshly shaved head glistened in the overhead lights of the corridor when he stopped outside Pike's cell to shake hands. He was sweating hard, and he kept clearing his throat nervously, but he was holding himself in good control. Pike gave him an approving nod and gripped his hand firmly.

"Send it to my ma, huh, Pike?" Timmy pushed his rolled-up diploma through the bars. "I'm just afraid they'll forget, and I want to make sure she gets it."

"Sure. Count on it, Timmy. Good luck."

Timmy almost laughed. "Guess I already used up all my good luck. Hope you make it better, Pike. Thanks a lot for—" He made a slow vague gesture toward the diploma, then smiled and moved away with the guards.

And then a few days later the volunteer did not show up for his usual visit. He had died in his sleep, they told Pike, that queer, kind little man still full of curiosity and hope. He and Timmy had given Pike something valuable, and Pike hoped he could remember them just as they were. If he could, there was no chance that he would ever feel bitter or sorry for himself.

So his days were organized now, and he could pretend they were useful. At least he wasn't letting time dribble away.

His first writing came straight out of the prison records, a wild, sad, and sometimes funny story about the first man to be executed at the state prison at Yucca. It had been a territorial prison then, part of the federal structure, and had been built to house the incorrigible hard-cases who couldn't be held in local jails. It also had had a primitive adobe Death Row and the only gibbet in the territory.

Ansel Goree had been its first victim. The year was 1889. Ansel was a Civil War veteran, badly wounded. Gimpy leg. A furiously scarred face that would grow a beard only in freakish clumps. Sometimes he had worked as a sheepherder, but mostly he lived alone in a cabin he had built in the Sangre mountains. He owned a rifle, a Bible, a copy of *Pilgrim's Progress*, and four different editions of *Robinson Crusoe*, one of them a presentation piece bound in Florentine leather. He had brought the books with him to Yucca. They were still in the prison library.

Ansel had picked the site for his cabin very well, setting it below the snow line where it was shielded from the winds. Lodgepole pines gave him timber for the cabin and a small corral. He had a good spring close by, a mountain meadow full of wild hay, and a plot of loamy earth where he sometimes grew vegetables. He had been the first man up in those parts, and he had picked well. The trouble was he didn't bother doing anything about homesteading or buying the land, and, of course, somebody else got around to it a few years later.

Things went along all right for quite a time. Nobody cared much about that crazy man living up there. But after a while the rancher who had proved up the land wanted to tap the spring and put in a tank for his stock. And he liked the look of that meadow full of sweet hay, too. So the harassment started.

It went on for years. Ranchhands would come up with a wagonload of supplies, camp nearby, and stay while they cut that big stand of hay. And old Ansel would watch them rake the rows and turn them to dry evenly, and when it was just right, he would pick a dark night and slip down there with some pitch-pine splinters and fire the whole lot. The rancher never did make a crop off Ansel's meadow.

The tapped spring ran sweet and never failed, but somehow the tank the rancher had dug down in the flat of the valley was always springing leaks. You just never knew if it would be full to running over or just a five-foot-deep mud sink. But Ansel always had all the water he needed.

Probably nothing would ever have happened except for some very bad luck. The rancher went broke after the rough winter of 1888 and had to sell his spread. The new owner was up on all the latest efficiency dodges including barbed-wire fencing to keep the stock from straying. When his fencing crew reached Ansel's place and got out their poles and wire-stretchers, Ansel laid up in the rocks with a canteen of water and a sack of jerky and fired some carefully aimed warning shots every time someone lifted a post-hole digger. After four days of it the crew got tired and went away.

And then some natural-born fool sent a deputy sheriff up to chase Ansel off. The deputy must have been a born fool, too, because he went. Ansel would never explain just what happened up there, but a few days later the deputy's horse came wandering in to town and the sheriff sent a man to backtrack him. He found a fresh grave with a deputy's star nailed to a whittled cross. So the sheriff blew his whistle and waved his arms and came up leading a twenty-one-man posse to collect Ansel Goree.

It was quite a scandal. Four possemen were lightly wounded and went home. The sheriff had the pommel of his silver-mounted saddle shot clean off. It took them three days, and they got Ansel finally only because a lucky bullet had creased his skull. They found he had been wounded six times. One shot had carried away three fingers from his right hand, but he had still been firing accurately up to the end.

After all that commotion they had to take strong action. Everyone agreed. But first they had to let Ansel heal up. While they were waiting, the good people cleaned out his cabin and burned it. The local editor was downright angry about the law's delay. He wrote thunderbolt editorials, warned against "mollycoddling," and demanded "action now!" The minute the doctor said Ansel was strong enough to hang, he went to trial, and eight days later he was in Yucca prison. That day happened to be opening day for the new prison. The territorial governor, a defeated ex-Senator from Tennessee, had a lot of trouble with his speech. He never did quite get it clear who Ansel Goree was or what he was doing there.

The hangman didn't do much better. He couldn't get the neck-snapping knot set right, and Ansel had to show him how it went. Then, while the distinguished guests and officials were standing around wondering what came next, Ansel beckoned to the newly appointed warden, told him how to get down and around to the back of the platform where he would find the long wooden trigger that released the trap door.

"On my signal," Ansel ordered. He saluted the governor, one ex-soldier to another. He turned his lumpy scarred face up toward the new flag over the prison and slowly raised his right arm.

"On My Signal," Pike thought, had to be the title. He liked the story after he had rewritten it a few times. Ansel Goree was very real to him, that solitary scarred man who never did find a Man Friday to share his loneliness. He paid a lifer-prisoner in the main cellblock twenty-five cents a page to type the sixteen pages of the manuscript for him.

And then what? Most of the magazines he read seemed to draw on staff writers for most of their pieces. Maybe they didn't want outside contributions. So what should he do with the damn thing? Of course it might not be good enough for publication. But he wanted to know.

In the end he sent it off to the editor of the Rincon Historical Society's quarterly. Perhaps they would not be too demanding. And what a joke that was. He couldn't have chosen worse. Or better, as it actually turned out. The editor's answering letter was still one of his buried treasures.

"The staff is delighted, Mr. Pike," he wrote, "and so am I. The sharp criminous whiff of 'On My Signal' is very stimulating.

"You will understand when I tell you that I was careful to make a thorough check of your references. I had always assumed that Governor Brainerd had given the territory a reasonably fruitful term of office. The sources, however, give no sustenance to that assumption as you have sharply pointed out.

"Mr. John Ellerton, the university librarian, is an old friend, and it was he who explained to me the depth and range of your recent studies. I congratulate you. It is most impressive.

"And now to the heart of the matter. The *Quarterly* would be pleased to publish 'On My Signal.' However, you must know that we serve largely as an outlet for academic writing. Our contributors may well find that certain professional considerations greatly increase the value of publishing with us. Certainly they cannot be strongly attracted by the twenty-five dollars which is the maximum honorarium our budget will allow.

"So, without consulting you, but anticipating your approval, I have taken the liberty of sending 'On My Signal' to the executive editor of *National Heritage*, a magazine directed toward a wider general audience than the *Quarterly* can hope to reach. The executive editor, I mention in passing, is my son, so I feel fairly sure that I understand his publishing policy and his needs. If I am mistaken, be assured that the *Quarterly* will welcome 'On My Signal' if it should again become available to us.

"And now may I offer a word of unsolicited advice? You write well and clearly, your research is sound and imaginative, your feeling for place and time is remarkable and most enjoyable. However, you are addressing yourself to an area which is overpopulated by professional historians eager for publication credits. Let me put a word in your ear for your consideration: Fiction. I think your talents, and I have no hesitation in saying that I consider you very talented indeed, might find greater play in the broader and more competitive world of fiction. My very best regards—"

And my very best regards to you, Mr. R. W. Emerson Graves, and to your sympathetic and helpful son, Mr. H. D. T. (for Thoreau?) Graves. One hundred dollars for "On My Signal" after he had given it one last rewrite following young Mr. Graves' suggestions. And on up the money ladder with the pieces that followed until the last long piece on the five-man jailbreak from Yucca in 1921 and the six-month chase that resulted finally in the death of all five had brought him six hundred dollars.

In those days fiction was still something for the future. Pike had found a comfortable spot for himself with *National Heritage.* He did not have many competitors in the western-badman sort of piece he was specializing in, and he could see and appreciate the advantage he had with young Mr. Graves. When *National Heritage* ran one of his stories, Pike was always identified as a youthful condemned murderer waiting in Death Row for the day of his execution. They always ran the same retouched photograph that made him look as sorrowful and sensitive as young

Werther. Gave them all a grisly little thrill, Pike suspected. But if being on Death Row gave him an extra edge with the magazine, Pike was not fool enough to object or to resent it.

Maybe his stories weren't actually anything to be proud of. But they were all Pike had. He needed the small stiffening of self-respect they brought him. The money came in handy, too. The latest story had taken almost a week to shape. He was writing more carefully. The long quiet time was ending now—the time of waiting for some court—any court—to consider his appeal for a new trial.

After the federal court had granted Pike's stay of execution, Gordon Guthrie started along the slow plodding road of appeals. He began with the lowest rung, back at Judge Manuel Pontalba's Superior Court in Rincon County.

"Any court can grant a new trial," he explained to Pike. "And we might as well give the state courts another chance to think about it. For one thing it's cheaper. And it just might work. It still all depends on finding the right judge."

Judge Pontalba had again not been the right one. Pike did not believe that Gordon had wasted much time or effort on him. Pike had read the brief, gnawing his way through the tangled legalisms to find the nub of argument. Overly complex, he felt, though it was clear enough when you puzzled it out. But Pontalba had not troubled with it. And again David Burrell had himself appeared to defend his record in the Pike case. There was no chance that either of them would reconsider old decisions. The trial record, Burrell insisted, was the basic document. No other evidence could be offered in this court. And, anyway, the evidence Mr. Guthrie wanted to introduce was "inherently incredible." The testimony of the telephoning juror, even if accepted, would "not be sufficient to establish prejudice."

A month later the State Supreme Court upheld Pontalba after a brief session. The evidence was insufficient to warrant a new trial. Affidavits referring to trial judge's prejudicial behavior were not admissible. The trial record spoke for itself. Appeal denied.

Then Gordon abruptly moved all the way to the United States Supreme Court.

"Gives us time to think," he told Pike. "We have to go federal now anyway. So we reorganize our case to emphasize the Constitutional grounds. I don't expect the Supreme Court will give us a hearing on the basis of the brief I'm submitting. Too many good reasons to throw us out. But it will be the best part of a year before they get around to saying so."

It was actually eight months. The order read: 890 Misc. *Pike v. Cochran. Petition for writ of certiorari is denied.*

No explanation for the decision was forthcoming. The Supreme Court does not have to explain to anyone.

"Who the hell is Cochran?" Pike wondered.

"Head of the state prison system," Gordon said. "He's the gentleman who is holding you under lock and key. So officially he's the one we go for. Just a matter of form."

"Now what happens?"

"Same thing, except now we're federal. We start at the lowest court and work our way up as far as we have to go."

The beginning point was the United States District Court in El Monte. Gordon applied for a writ of *habeas corpus,* filed his brief and waited. The waiting lasted eighteen months, during which Pike wrote the first of his imaginative replays of western history, got permission to install a writing table and bench, and made the beginning of a library.

Judge Odell Bannerman had accepted the Pike appeal as part of his workload, but after his acceptance, he sent no messages whatever.

"Not unusual," Gordon wrote. "He knows you're safe, and he probably figures this is a complex problem that is going to take him a lot of time, so he's waiting for a good clear stretch so he can concentrate on it. Relax. Lawyer's time, remember?"

The main thrust of Gordon's federal appeal went to the point of Pike's unsigned statement, which Gordon maintained had been involuntary, and that Pike's defense lawyer had failed to ask the questions during trial which would have established the facts. Okay, Pike thought. It was a Constitutional question so the federal court would have to consider it, but that goddamn trial transcript didn't show a thing to help us. So how was Gordon going to make it stick?

"My job." Gordon grinned reassuringly, waved a big weathered hand, and went hurrying off to another trial.

Pike followed all his cases very closely, subscribing to local newspapers wherever Gordon was appearing. Gordon was piling up trial experience, testing himself against wily veteran prosecutors, and getting better all the time. Pike cheered him on.

And he was a fine dirty fighter. It was not always easy to keep up with all the details; most newspaper reporters were weak on facts and seldom caught the meaning of an extended cross-examination. But the squeals of outraged opponents often came through clearly.

They complained about his rudely aggressive trial tactics, his constant and critical comments to the press. They particularly resented his frequent appearances on local television talk shows. "Poisoning the judicial atmosphere," the prosecutors said. "Correcting the prejudice that already exists," Gordon had answered solemnly and laughed. "Look, these guys have already tried my client in the papers. Why can't I do the same thing? They say he's another Jack the Ripper. I say he's an innocent man, a credit to the community, a churchgoer, a family man, wouldn't swat a mosquito if it was about to bite him. He shouldn't even be on trial."

Pike caught him twice on late TV shows, both times from Los Angeles during the course of a widely publicized trial. Gordon was defending a movie producer who had somehow managed to lose a young girl off his yacht during a calm cruise to Catalina.

"Accident. One of the mysteries of the sea," the movieman said.

"Murder," the cops claimed. "The girl was four months pregnant. The movieman was married, up to his ass in debt, and the girl was pushing him. He killed her all right."

The prosecutor was a local favorite, a bluff, burly, no-nonsense man who did very good Will Rogers' imitations but patterned his slam-bang courtroom behavior on the more flamboyant Earl Rogers.

The TV host admired him. "He's a man who will tell you to go to hell," he said to Gordon.

"He's a man who will tell you to go to hell," Gordon agreed soberly. "And if you give him half a chance, he'll help you get started."

That broke up the show and got Gordon reprimanded in court the next day. Gordon apologized profusely, tongue clearly poking a dome in his cheek. On behalf of the TV host he offered the enraged prosecutor equal time, and when the DA refused, he took it himself.

"Very difficult gentleman," he explained sadly on the next program. "Doesn't want to be friendly. An ugly duckling who grew up to be an ugly duck. But a very able prosecutor, as you were saying. He'll tell you so himself."

The judge pretended not to notice. The prosecutor lost his temper— and his case. The jury disagreed, nine to three for acquittal. The prosecutor promised a speedy retrial.

"No possibility," Gordon said flatly, rocking back on two chair legs, grinning at Pike through the fine-mesh screen. "My man is still out on bail. He'll be discharged as soon as things quiet down a bit more. I'm letting him stay on in the Malibu house until then. I've already sold his Brentwood Hills place, and I'll put the Malibu house on the market as soon as he's off the hook."

"Happy to see you're turning a buck. Was it a big score? What does a case like that mean to you in terms of money?"

"Money?" Gordon pretended astonishment. "You aren't seeing the problem, Jon. Here was this man on trial for his life. Those people were trying to kill him. Naturally he's going to want the best defense possible, isn't he? Who thinks about money at a time like that? It's one of the facts of life that the best costs the most. Everybody knows that. The old Apache saying you know: Maybe you don't always get what you pay for, but you are sure as hell going to pay for what you get." And he chuckled quietly, studying Pike. "I hear you've been doing pretty well for yourself, too." It was a question.

"Not too bad," Pike admitted. "They seem to like my stuff."

"I like it myself," Gordon said quickly. "Read them all. Liked them very much. I think one of those hard guys you wrote about was an ancestor of mine. When you get enough of those stories together, you might have a pretty good book."

Pike cocked a wary eyebrow.

"Forget it." Gordon waved a hand carelessly. "I'll let you know if I want something. I never bother dropping hints when it comes to money. No, you hang on to what you've got. You'll need all of it, and plenty more when I move you into the next phase."

And it was left that way for the rest of the eighteen-month period that Judge Odell Bannerman held Pike's appeal on his desk.

Then, on a shadowy cool morning in El Monte, Judge Bannerman fitted a small yellow rosebud in his coat, came in from the garden for breakfast and fell abruptly dead. His workload was parceled out among his colleagues. Two weeks later Judge Ransom Pierce denied Jonathan Pike's appeal, basing his decision entirely on the trial record which, he declared, gave no reason to believe the disputed statement had not been entirely voluntary.

Pike was not shocked or even greatly surprised. He had been through it too often. But what now, he wondered dully. Another court, I suppose. Another appeal, another rejection without any consideration of the issues raised in the brief. How long was it going to drag on like this?

He could still not guess how long it was going to drag on; the end even now was no closer than it had been then. But it did not drag on "like this" much longer after Judge Pierce's decision was handed down.

"Time to move on to Phase Two," Gordon announced briskly. He leaned forward, shot a warning glance to make sure the captain of guards was keeping his distance, and spoke very quietly. "Get your notebook. I want you to write down what I'm going to tell you. It's not complicated, but you've got to keep it absolutely straight."

Pike flipped to a fresh page in his current notebook and poised a

266

ballpoint. But it was a long wait before Gordon spoke. He seemed troubled about something, Pike thought. Not worried or uncertain, just hesitant and a little cautious.

"I'll tell you how I've got it shaped," he said. "You don't have to write this. I'm just talking about the schedule. Tomorrow morning I'm going to call a press conference. I've got a lot of ground to cover. I'll end up by telling them that I am pulling out as Jonathan Pike's lawyer."

He held up a hand the moment Pike jerked his head in surprise. "Listen to the rest of it. I'll tell them that I can't afford the time. And that is the truth. I'm preparing four cases for trial right now. I'll be in court with one of them next week and overlapping the work on the other three. So I can't very well pull out and run over to the United States Court of Appeals whenever the judges decide they want to hear your case. Time is the one thing I haven't got right now."

He winked slowly, slyly. "You see the message, do you? Gordon Guthrie is a dirty, unfeeling bastard. He's making so much money now he won't touch a case unless it's worth half a million to him. I want them to get that message. Anybody cares to shake hands with me has got to know it's going to cost him real money. Softens them up from the beginning. The other side is that you are going to look like poor little Ragged Dick tossed out into the cruel cold snow. And that is good too. You haven't been getting enough press attention lately. So here is how we go." He gestured toward Pike's ready notebook. "Now is the time to write."

Pike eyed him suspiciously. He stroked his penpoint in tight angry circles along the top margin of the page.

"In the next day or so you will be getting a package from my office. There will be a brief for the United States Court of Appeals, marked 'For Your Information.' There will be another separate piece headed 'Motion To Proceed *In Forma Pauperis.*' Do you know what that means?"

Pike shook his head without looking up.

"It's Rule Fifty-three. You state that you are unable to pay the usual costs of appeal in federal court and ask for special consideration. What it amounts to is that one copy of your brief will be enough for the court, and it doesn't have to be printed. Quite a saving there, boy."

"I see," Pike muttered.

"Before I forget," Gordon said abruptly, interrupting himself. "How much money have you got in the bank—a couple of thousand?"

"Maybe a little more," Pike said cautiously.

"Leave fifty dollars in the account and send me your check for the rest." He waved an impatient hand. "I'll give it back later. The point is that you don't have enough to cover costs and attorneys' fees, but some nosy clerk of courts might decide that you should make a partial payment if he finds you've got something socked away. So don't forget that check."

"Okay."

"I'm sending you an appeals brief that will knock their learned heads off. I want you to rewrite it a little bit, juggle the language around to make it more casual, not so legalistic. You'll know how to handle that. But don't touch a single word that is underlined. Make a very special note of that. Don't change any underlined words or phrases because they are all procedural stuff and they have to be in there. Are you still with me?"

Miles ahead of you, Pike thought. "Go ahead," he said.

"Use the prison-issued paper. Copy the brief and the motion in longhand. You've got ninety days to file, so there's no hurry. All the details will be in the same package."

"Right."

"The court will appoint an attorney to represent you at the hearing. It won't be me, but that doesn't matter. The key point is the brief. Whoever your new lawyer is, make sure he understands that he can make any additions he likes, but he can't cut out anything or change the basic structure of the brief. The chances are he'll like the idea of having all his work done for him and won't object. But if he does, you may have to lean on him. Can you manage that?"

"No sweat."

"Okay, then we're on our way. I won't be seeing you for quite a while, but I'll be watching everything. As far as the public is concerned, you are going to be running the whole show all on your own. You understand me?"

Pike laughed silently.

"All right, all right," Gordon said, grumbling. "So it sounds corny when you say it straight out all in one lump. But it's going to develop slowly in little bits over a long period of time, and when the whole thing is pieced together, it's going to look like a goddamn miracle. That's what we're aiming at."

"Why?"

"Because for the first time we may be coming close to a final decision, and I want to shift the public focus onto Jonathan Pike. No Gordon Guthrie in sight. After my press conference tomorrow, you'll be back in the news. I'll use that to get the magazine people interested in you. My press agent is already working on it. In a very little while you are going to be a celebrated young man."

"I am?"

Gordon chuckled quietly. "Don't give me any of that 'innocent bewilderment' crap, Jon-boy. I can see the wheels spinning around in your head. You know where I'm aiming. We want to get the public interested and involved. I'll plan to peak our campaign in about eight months, around October–November, so we'll have one hell of a big audience holding its breath, waiting to see what the appeals court is going to do with you."

"And what are they going to do?"

Gordon shrugged. "Couldn't guess. But they may give it to us. You'll be going in with a very good brief. You are saying that when the state courts violated your constitutional rights, they lost jurisdiction, therefore the federal court should grant a writ of *habeas corpus,* tell the state to set you free, or bring you to trial again. You might score with that one. It will be a three-judge panel this time and those guys on the U.S. Appeals bench are wise old heads. So this could be the end of the road. And that is just the point. We have to be ready for it. By the time we get a new trial I want everybody in the country rooting for you. We'll get a fund-raiser in to run a national subscription for money to pay the trial costs. Might even turn a little profit on it. But, best of all, the publicity will help us get exactly the kind of jury I want the next time around."

"You are going to handle the new trial if we get one?"

"Hell, yes. All I'm talking about now is just a tactical sidestep. Officially I'm pulling out, but I'm not going very far. For this stage we are simply going to change the picture. You'll be the front man. Jonathan Pike, alone against the Fates. The brilliant young self-made lawyer who writes better appeals briefs than the law professors. We'll talk up your high IQ and tell them how the history department at Rincon State thinks you're a minor genius. We'll reprint all those stories you sold to *National Heritage* and see that copies get to the right people. I'll get the warden in on it, too. He's pretty sold on you, you know. He thinks those stories of yours are making him famous. I'll get somebody down to interview him, and I'll make damn sure the story swings on Jonathan Pike. You see how it all interplays? Everything adds one more little touch to the final picture. But first we have to get you out in front all by yourself so there won't be anything to distract from your public image."

Pike blew out a long whistling breath. "You make me sound like a candidate for governor."

"Just how do you think candidates are born?" Gordon demanded, riding his heavy voice over Pike's. "They aren't hatched out of special eggs, you know. There is always somebody out there in the shadows making things happen. So don't worry about it. As Harry Golden says,

'Enjoy.' It's going to take time and a lot of work, but you'll see it shape up about the way I said." He nodded slowly, half smiling. "Makes a pretty picture, doesn't it?"

He slapped both hands briskly on his legs and pushed up from the chair. "Give it some hard thinking. You might come up with a new wrinkle. I won't be seeing you for a while, but I'll be in touch. You write me if you've got any problems, but you be damn careful what you say. Everything you write is censored, and we don't want the warden or any of his people to get the notion that you aren't handling all this yourself. If there is anything really tricky coming up, I'll send one of my assistants down to brief you. That all clear? Any questions?"

"Not yet. I'll probably have a million tomorrow when I've had time to think."

"By that time you should be able to answer them yourself. Just keep both eyes on the target. That's what counts. Make up the details as you go along." He flipped a big hand and turned away. "Good luck."

Pike stayed where he was, hunched on the forward edge of his fixed bunk, watching Gordon Guthrie swing down the corridor and out of sight.

Big confident man in a hurry—rough, boisterous, self-admiring. And why shouldn't he be? He had come a hell of a distance from those poor-boy days when he had been junior to James Oliver Delancy. The big cases, the big money, the front-page notoriety, he had it all. And savored it with a sardonic, half-mocking amusement. A good man to have on your side.

If he was.

The appeals brief from Gordon's office was a thick eighty-two-page document. Pike stacked it on his writing table and unfastened the corner clips.

More than half the text was underlined in blue pencil. Untouchable, those parts. But after he had read it through once, Pike was not so sure. When the tier guards changed shift he sent a note by one of them to the prison librarian, asking to borrow the big unabridged *Webster's* for an overnight session.

By breakfast-time, when the overweight dictionary had to go back, he was reasonably sure of his ground. Current legal vocabulary must at one time, the eighteenth century perhaps, have been the shared and accepted language of educated men. But English is the most protean and muscular of tongues. It accepts new words from any source, alters meaning and emphasis, demands constant revision. So when a professional group

270

willfully freezes an archaic form of English as the only acceptable version, it is possible to suspect that those professional gentlemen are more interested in protecting a private preserve than they are in clarity of expression.

From the very beginning, Pike had been irritated by the ornately decorated style of language in the briefs he had read. Even when the words themselves were understandable, the sentence structure tended to be so elaborate that you needed a diagram to locate the governing verb. But Gordon Guthrie had told him to simplify this one, and a long sleepless night with *Webster's* had shown him where he could move freely.

He was extremely careful to alter nothing that referred even slightly to legal procedure, but he rewrote completely when it was clear that the problem was a matter of logical exposition. One paragraph that began on page 22 and ran almost to the bottom of page 27 he particularly disliked. In it the brief-writer had tried to cover the entire chronology of Pike's interrogation by the sheriff's investigators. He had all the facts, but he had so obscured them by extra words that it was hard to tell whether the writer was objecting or merely reporting.

David Calder Burrell, Rincon's county attorney, was mentioned only once. He had been present during the questioning, the writer said. Pike grinned mirthlessly over that. Later in the brief the writer mentioned that the questioning had lasted for seventy unbroken hours in four different offices of the courthouse. The writer forgot to add that Burrell had been present during almost all of that grueling interrogation, and that he had conducted much of it himself. He had been there almost all the time and had been in nominal control. That, Pike felt, needed emphasizing.

After several false starts he finally broke that long, complexly coiled sentence into thirty-two separate statements of fact and wrote each in a two-or-three-line sentence. When he was finished, he thought that anyone reading the brief now could move through that experience with him, feel his bewilderment, humiliation, exhaustion, and the growing panic as relays of fresh questioners came at him relentlessly, never giving him a moment to rest. The progression was clear now: from the first clumsy mauling in the patrol car on the way to the courthouse to the final despairing session with himself naked and cold under a thin army blanket, by then half-starved, mentally numb and shaken, physically so exhausted that he could not have signed that last damning statement even if he had been willing to.

He put the draft aside then. He would come back to it later.

He followed Gordon's instructions faithfully, putting the rest of the brief into the kind of language a reasonably intelligent nonlawyer might be expected to use, but not altering any of the purely legal references. But, as he worked over the brief, he came gradually to sense that Gordon might have overlooked a useful possibility.

"I am not yet the complete jailhouse lawyer," he wrote Gordon in a carefully phrased letter that took him half a day to organize. "In shaping my brief for the United States Court of Appeals, I have been reading through all the source material we have in the prison library. In my notes I have two briefly outlined citations to recent Supreme Court decisions. Neither is detailed enough to tell me if the ruling might have some application in my case. I would very much appreciate your professional opinion.

"The cases are *Mapp v. Ohio* (1961) and *Massiah v. United States* (1964). From what little I have read about them, it seems that *Mapp* might support an objection to the search of my apartment and the grounds outside. The Rincon County sheriff collected evidence which was later used against me in my trial, but he did not have a proper search warrant. As I translate the *Mapp* ruling, that evidence was obtained illegally and therefore should not have been admitted. Right? Wrong?

"In *Massiah,* the judgment was that postindictment interrogations are specifically barred by the Constitution. I am snatching at straws with this one. I don't know if it applies to my case or not. When was I indicted? Was that seventy-hour interrogation still going on?

"I read a discussion of *Escobedo v. Illinois* in the *Yale Law Review* last week. At first I thought the *Escobedo* ruling had no value to me, but now that I see how disturbed prosecutors and police departments are about 'the breakdown of law enforcement,' I am wondering if I missed some deeper significance in the ruling. How do you see it?

"I have a lot of other problems, too, but I think I have a toe-hold on them now. The brief is coming along fairly well. But these possibilities I have asked you about keep rattling around in my mind, and I have no way of checking them here.

"Any guidance would be gratefully received."

That should take care of the warden and the censors, Pike thought. Reading the letter, they would assume that he was just another penniless do-it-yourself lawyer trying to suck up some free legal advice.

It was a pleasant thought that he might have caught Gordon Guthrie napping. He enjoyed it for the three days it took for an answer to reach him from Gordon's Rincon office.

"Dear Jon Pike," wrote a man who signed himself David Simon. "The Great Man got himself married last week and is off on his honeymoon."

Married? How did he ever find time for *that?*

"He phoned from Nassau last night," Simon went on, "and said it was okay to answer your letter, provided I first make it clear that this firm is not acting as your legal adviser and that this letter is merely a friendly gesture. Do I make it clear, friend?

"Toward the points you raise, let's take *Mapp* first. Miss Dollree Mapp ran a boardinghouse in Cleveland, Ohio. The local police suspected that one of her boarders was operating a gambling den in the house. They entered without a warrant, found no evidence of gambling, but did turn up a trunk full of pornography. Miss Mapp said she was holding the trunk for a former tenant and knew nothing about its contents. She was convicted for possession of obscene materials. She appealed, claiming the illegal search had violated her Constitutional rights. The State Supreme Court upheld the conviction. The United States Supreme Court knocked it down.

"I am oversimplifying a complex decision, but I think you can see in this short outline why *Mapp* is not useful in your case. Too bad. At first glance it looks pretty good, but the special circumstances of *Mapp* don't work for you. The Rincon County sheriff did search without a warrant. But at that time you were already under arrest. The critical point of *Mapp* is that the Cleveland police had no reason to suspect the presence of pornographic material in Miss Mapp's house when they searched it. In your case, the Rincon sheriff had good reason to believe he might find something that could establish your connection with the murder of Angela Morales. He could easily have picked up a search warrant, and should have, but I don't think any court would reverse just because he was a little bit careless. So let's forget *Mapp*.

"And *Massiah* is no help either, although not for the same reasons. In Rincon County—in most southwestern states, for that matter—grand juries have disappeared, and indictments have gone with them. These days an 'information' filed by the county attorney serves the same purpose. The only way we know when the information was filed is to look at the records of the clerk of courts. In your case the record shows that Mr. Burrell's information is dated the day after your interrogation had ended. That's the record, and we have to live with it.

"About *Escobedo,* I'm going to be a little shifty, in the grand old pettifogging tradition. Basically, I would say no, forget it. But as you said in your letter, the ruling is upsetting a great many people, and its rather ambiguous language may be interpreted in strange ways by other courts.

"Danny Escobedo was suspected of being an accomplice to murder. The police mouse-trapped him by telling him one of his friends had

273

named Escobedo as the killer. Danny panicked and told the whole story. He had been present, he admitted, but the death shot had been fired by the same friend who had tried to push the blame onto Danny. During all of that interrogation Danny Escobedo's lawyer was downstairs in the stationhouse. He had demanded to see his client but was barred until after the police had taken the confession.

"A five–four majority of the Supreme Court ruled that Escobedo's confession was tainted evidence. The point to remember here, as Mr. Justice Goldberg wrote, is that the decision in *Escobedo* rests entirely on the Sixth Amendment guarantee of right to counsel and not—repeat not—on the Fourteenth Amendment guarantee of due process or the Fifth Amendment privilege against self-incrimination. Referring specifically to Jonathan Pike, we have to say that you did have a lawyer available during your interrogation. You actually spoke to him several times. The fact that he did not advise you to keep your mouth shut says something important about his qualifications as a lawyer, but it does not change your situation. If ever you can get to a full *habeas corpus* hearing in federal court, the behavior of your first attorney could be a key element in establishing the complete picture of that coercive interrogation. But it is not useful in appeal. Your lawyer was there, you were represented, and *Escobedo* is not for you.

"Sorry to be so negative on all counts. But don't get discouraged. Keep scratching around. You might spot a winner.

"Write if you turn up anything I can help you with on a 'friendly' basis.

"Best of luck. David Simon."

Two days later Pike's copy of the Rincon *Record* carried a honeymoon picture of Gordon Guthrie and his bride on a Nassau beach. Nice-looking girl he'd picked. Pike admired the slim, long-boned body that wore its bikini with easy grace. Hair and eyes looked to be dark. Face finely featured. Smile radiant.

NOTED TRIAL LAWYER MARRIES DETROIT REPORTER, the caption read. Under it, a brief story.

Gordon Guthrie, Rincon's most famous trial lawyer was married Sunday to Miss Ellen Chalmers of Grosse Pointe, Illinois. The couple met when the twenty-three-year-old bride interviewed Mr. Guthrie following the successful conclusion of his most recent case, the trial of Henry Johannsen, who was acquitted Saturday of the murder of Detroit auto magnate William O'Donohue. Married after a whirlwind courtship, Mr. and Mrs. Guthrie are honeymooning in Nassau. The couple will make their home in Rincon.

Pike took another careful look at the girl's face. Pretty. Gentle. He wondered if she would be tough enough to handle old Savage-Relentless. Maybe she could. He'd never seen Gordon Guthrie looking so fatuously happy before—or so young.

David Simon's letter went in a fresh manila folder. It was the first entry in a file that was three inches thick before Pike had finished drafting the lengthy brief for his appeal.

He questioned every citation in the original brief, suggested additional sources, and asked for explanations. David Simon sent books, newspaper clippings, tearsheets from legal journals, marked copies of the *Pacific Reporter*, and an endless series of cheerfully goading letters that pushed Pike into a serious program of legal research. He had to pull himself sharply away from the books and work twenty-hour days for the last week to get his brief in the mail before the court's deadline.

He was now tuned to what Gordon called "lawyer's time," and the nine months delay before the Court of Appeals reached a decision did not weigh too heavily. He had his basic routine well set, and after filling two notebooks with all the legal nuggets he had mined from David Simon's course of instruction, he went back to his slow, meticulous search through the prison records for other material he could use for stories in the *National Heritage* magazine.

He was working well and regularly again when his new court-appointed attorney came for a conference. For a moment he was so irritated by the interruption that he almost told him to come back some other day. The guard stared when he saw Pike's hesitation, then smiled when Pike grinned at him.

"Forgot where I was for a minute," Pike said, shaking his head. "Please ask the Honorable William Redpath Wellmann to step into the office."

The Honorable William Redpath Wellmann was a retired municipal judge from El Monte, a large fleshy man, white-haired, short of breath, and very tired. He was pleased with the brief Pike had filed, thought he might have a few additional points but probably would not. He was sure the court would be favorably impressed, as he was. He wished Pike well and went away, and after a few days Pike could not remember what he looked like.

The publicity program that Gordon had planned began slowly but built momentum like a stone rolling downhill. In the local newspapers the stories were much the same as before. STILL GETTING AWAY WITH MURDER was the keynote for most of them. But then a clever young staff writer from the Los Angeles *Times* came to see for himself and later wrote a three-parter that closely followed the line Gordon had decreed. Pike tried not to laugh when he read of himself as the "sharp-minded, imperturbable self-made lawyer," who was, with no help, directing a brilliant series of appeals. The title of the series was A NEW AND FAIR TRIAL—WHEN?

A newspaper syndicate bought second serial rights to Pike's *National Heritage* stories and led off each one with a capsulized biography that repeated the message.

During the same week three magazine writers applied for interviews, and the warden had to set up a formal schedule. A photographer from a picture magazine tried to force his way in when the guards told him he couldn't bring his camera into Death Row. Then the warden banned everybody for a couple of weeks. But eventually they all got in, and their pieces were everything Gordon could have hoped for. Pike was always pictured as "alone." But if the writers liked to call him "sardonic" and "coldly confident" and spoke of his stories as if he had suddenly become a respectable historian, at least the best of them paid some serious attention to the major Constitutional issues that gave weight and merit to his appeals. So maybe it was worth the trouble.

Gordon Guthrie kept himself completely in the background. Even the Honorable William Redpath Wellmann was largely ignored because his presence tended to distract from the image of the "lone, almost lost, but indomitable young man on Death Row."

But Gordon was in the news in his own right often enough for Pike to follow his fortunes. CBS television scheduled a Special Events program called "The Quality of Justice," and there was Gordon Guthrie talking for ten dramatic minutes on the sadly mishandled case of Jonathan Pike. He predicted that the United States Court of Appeals would find for Pike. Eleven days later the three-man tribunal handed down its decision.

The score was 2-1 against Pike, but the split decision delighted the Honorable William Redpath Wellmann, and he came bustling down from El Monte to explain to Pike that you might almost call it a victory.

"A young man like you may not be able to appreciate what this means," he said, spraying a fine enthusiastic mist toward the mesh screen. "Did you read what Judge Galen said in his dissent?"

"Yes," Pike said, but Wellmann went on to tell him anyway.

"Remarkable," he insisted. "Even if you had read it you would probably not understand the force of judicial disapproval Judge Galen was expressing. 'The evidence before us is sufficient to show that the interrogation of this unlearned youth was unconscionably long and arduous. It is a shabby and revolting exercise of police power in a situation in which the police alone were powerful and Jonathan Pike was unaided and powerless.' "

Wellmann rattled the stapled pages in his excitement. "And here! Listen to this! 'Jonathan Pike has a right to have this court consider all the aspects of that interrogation, not merely those few selected facts that are available in the trial record. His contention that a consideration of all the facts would prove that his unsigned statement was the product of coercive treatment cannot be ignored by this court.' Now!" Wellmann smacked the wadded pages against his knee and sat back beaming at Pike.

"Yes," Pike said.

"Well, don't you see, young man? Judge Galen has challenged his colleagues to reconsider their hasty judgment. The other two members who ruled against you refused to look into anything other than the trial record. Now that we have Judge Galen's forceful statement to buttress our position, I feel much more hopeful."

"About what?"

"I have petitioned for a rehearing *en banc!* All seven of the judges together instead of a three-man panel." Wellmann scowled at Pike's lack of interest, but his high good spirits could not keep him from patting himself appreciatively on the knees. "Marvelous opportunity to see if Judge Galen can influence his colleagues when they meet as a unit. I am absolutely sure he can. I have instructed the clerk of courts that I will continue to represent you without filing for an additional fee."

"Thank you," Pike said politely. He tried to rouse himself enough to share some of the old man's enthusiasm. "You've done very well, sir. I'm grateful."

"Well, you're disappointed, of course. Who wouldn't be? But we're on our way now, young man. Mark my words. You'll see."

Pike saw six weeks later. The United States Court of Appeals rejected the Honorable William Redpath Wellmann's petition and refused to reconsider its decision.

Mr. Wellmann wrote Pike a lengthy, all but incoherent letter. Deepest regrets. Heartfelt sympathy. Must, however, withdraw due to press of business and precarious state of health. Farewell, Mr. Wellmann. Pike never heard from him again.

Pike blinked to bring his mind back into focus. He had been drifting off into past miseries, reliving the bad old days. You are probably enjoying it, too, you delicate, sensitive shit. He got up quickly and bent low to get his head under the single tap of his washstand. A little cold water for all those hot memories.

He picked up the yellowing page of the Rincon *Record*'s Sunday supplement and folded again along its deep creases.

"Pike." The captain of guards waited until he turned to face the screened doorway. "Mr. Earl Coker." He put his chair close against the cell bars and sat there with his arms folded.

Pike stared at the man in the facing chair, sensing something familiar about him. Mr. Coker was short and wide and round-faced. He wore a lot of loose pale hair and a lumpy dark suit with a vest loaded with protruding pencils and tag-ends of paper. A thick woolen necktie was knotted a good inch below his open collar button. He cocked a merry cynical eye at Pike and slowly smiled. Pike caught the similarity then. Coker would have been just right to play the lazy half-drunken reporter who is the hero's best friend in a 1930's gangster movie.

"Coker?" Pike said, still wondering. Then he got it. He flipped open the folded sheet in his hand and looked again at the headline. STILL GETTING AWAY WITH MURDER! And under it, a name that Pike was surprised he had almost forgotten. "Earl G. Coker, Staff Writer, Rincon *Record* Services, Inc."

"You son of a bitch," he said quietly. "I've just been reading this piece of shit."

Coker leaned forward to see what he meant, then sat back and lifted a pudgy hand. "Peace, friend. That was last year's stuff. I'll do it better this time."

"There won't be any 'this time.'" Pike choked down a surge of bitterness in his throat. "What makes you think I'll talk to you?"

"Why not?" Coker spread his hands wide in a gesture of innocence. "Why did you let me in if you don't want to talk? You can turn down visitors you don't want to see, can't you?"

Pike held himself hard. He wasn't going to give this bastard anything, not even an explosion of anger. When he was sure he was in control again, he folded the newspaper page and dropped it in the box file. He leaned casually against the gray steel wall. He folded his arms loosely, forced himself into an easy posture, and spoke very slowly, almost drawling. "Well, Mr. Coker, there is a rule here on Death Row that you may not know about. Whenever an authorized visitor is scheduled, I get an extra session down in the shower room. An extra shave. An extra change of clothes. If you ever had to live with just one shower a week, Mr. Coker, you'd understand what that means. Why I wouldn't dream of turning down any visitor the warden approved. Even if Mr. David

278

Calder Burrell asked to see me, I'd say yes. At least until I got my extra shower."

Coker chuckled. His fleshy face went rosy with pleasure. He fished out a wad of dingy gray copy paper and plucked a pencil from his vest pocket. "Okay, so I got in. Let's get on with the story now."

"What story?" Pike said blandly. "I've had my shower."

"Come on, come on. You're not a baby. So I wrote a hatchet job last year. The *Record* policy is, 'Jonathan Pike is guilty.' You expect me to change policy? That's for the front office. I'm just a hired hand. They point me at it, and I write about it. So let's get at it. The Court of Appeals already turned you down. That's the end of the line for you. Right?"

"End of the line?" Pike stared at him. "Did somebody abolish the Supreme Court when I wasn't looking?"

"Huh?" Coker scratched his head with the butt of his pencil. "Supreme Court? You already went to the Supreme Court. They turned you down. You can't go back again. Or can you?"

"Jesus," Pike groaned. "You are a very stupid man, Mr. Coker. Your paper must have a lawyer. Go ask him. I'm not giving free lessons in the law."

"Okay, you're the legal expert." Coker shrugged it off. "God knows we've been reading enough about what a hotshot lawyer you are turning out to be. Okay, so you can go back to the Supreme Court for another round. 'It's not the end yet,' Pike says. 'Next stop, Supreme Court.' So what are you going to say to them? You figured out a new snow job you think will work?"

"Oh, fuck off, you idiot," Pike said sharply, caught in a sudden burst of impatience. "You wouldn't understand if I told you." He tapped the bars to signal the captain of guards.

"Now wait a minute. You don't have to be so feisty. I don't give a damn about the legal stuff. I'm looking for a human-interest story. Something for the home folks. A day in the life of Jonathan Pike. How about that?"

"Fuck off."

"I'm going to write something, boy," Coker said, trying to sound a note of menace. "I didn't drive ninety miles down to this sandpile Devil's Island to go home empty. You just better believe it. So let's work out some sort of handle. Show me how to angle a good story, and I'll give you a break. Something for me, something for you."

Pike stared at him with open contempt, but his silence seemed to encourage Coker.

279

"Every one of those big-league magazine pieces had something to say about how bad it is for you on Death Row, inhuman conditions, all that crap. Horror stuff. Maybe it's not such a bad idea. How about if we slant the story that way? Six years of life on Death Row. A pig lives better. But Jonathan Pike comes smiling through." Coker nodded approvingly. "I'll take a couple of wallops at the warden, too. No chance for exercise. Lights on all the time. Lousy food. Once a week bath. All the grisly details. Give me the real dope, and I'll handle the story right."

"You really are a fool," Pike said softly. "What do you want to blast the warden for? He's a decent man doing a miserable thankless job."

"You *like* it here?"

"I'd do anything in the world to get out of here," Pike said with a sincerity that surprised him. "It's a hell of a life for a human being. But that's not the warden's fault. The state legislature sets the rules. Why don't you go up to El Monte and tell those bastards we need some new thinking about state prisons? This cellblock was built a hundred years ago for just one purpose: To hold condemned prisoners for a short time until they were executed. And to make sure they didn't get a chance to kill themselves before the state decided it was time for them to die. In those days the average stay here was less than a week. They never planned for anybody to stay here any longer."

"It's different these days," Coker said with a flash of genuine interest.

"Here and in every other state it's different," Pike agreed. "But everywhere the rules on Death Row are still just the same."

Coker considered it, scowling thoughtfully. Then, regretfully, he shook his head. "No, there's no story in that. Not for me, anyway. Let's think of another slant."

"I've got a much better idea," Pike said.

Coker smiled hopefully.

"Suppose you just get the hell out of here."

"Now goddamit, Pike! I told you I have to take back some kind of story. Just give me a good lead, something to hang my piece on. Okay? For instance, what's the very worst part about living so long on Death Row? The very worst."

"The very worst?" Pike glanced at the captain of the guards who was now standing beside Coker's chair, ready to escort him outside. "The very worst? Well, I guess I would have to say that the worst thing for a modest man like me is having to learn to masturbate with the lights on."

V

A STINGING cold wind was booming down from the everlasting snows of the Rockies, slashing along the deserted dark Denver streets, scouring dirt and rumpled papers from the roadways and flinging them halfway to Texas. When Gordon Guthrie came out of the lee of the darkened building, an icy gust flipped under the tail of his unbuttoned overcoat, making it snap like a storm flag. He loped diagonally across a complex intersection and ducked into the dimly lighted entrance of the Brown Palace Hotel.

They had redecorated the place recently, subduing the opulence of the old boom days, but even so the Brown could still give Gordon the feeling that he was a young bucko just down-mountain from the silver mines, poke weighing heavy in his pocket, thirst raging, horny as a mountain ram. A great old place, full of memories. He noticed he was swaggering a little as he went up to the desk.

"Late tonight, Mr. Guthrie." The night manager slid along behind the desk counter with a sheaf of messages in his hand.

Gordon grunted amiably. He riffled the sheets to make sure there was nothing of special importance in them.

"Lonnie Wetherill has been phoning you about every hour since eleven o'clock. He'd like to come over if you're not too tired. He's waiting at the Press Club. He asked me to call him if—" He lifted one eyebrow and waited for Gordon to decide.

Gordon peeled back a wilted cuff to see his watch. Two twenty. "Was he drunk?" he asked.

The manager grinned. "At this time of night? Probably. But he sounded okay."

"Well, give him a call. If he's still tracking, tell him to come along." Gordon picked up his key and went toward the bank of elevators.

The softly lighted carpeted hallway was quiet. Gordon slipped his key in and tried to turn the lock silently, got it to the critical point and felt it slip away again. The heavy brass bolt snapped back like a pistol shot. He could hear Jumbo growling as he opened the door.

"Why can't you learn how to work that lock?"

Gordon closed the door and came into the sitting room. He threw his coat on the couch. Jumbo had one of the big chairs pulled up to a card table piled high with books and papers. He had all the lights burning. There was a bound stack of daily trial transcripts handy on the floor and one on the card table, braced open with a large square-cornered reading glass.

"Up late, Jumbo." Gordon moved past him and into his bedroom, peeling off jacket and shirt as he went. He unloaded the pockets of his jacket and folded it for the valet. He hung his necktie on the closet rack and stuffed his shirt in a laundry bag. Then he went into the bathroom, ran a bowl of warm water and stuck his head under. He toweled his head roughly, picked up his pajama top from the bed and buttoned it on his way back to the sitting room. He stood there ruffling his damp hair, looking down at his father, half-smiling.

"Is it okay for you to be reading, Jumbo? What did the doctor say?"

"Hell with him," Jumbo muttered. He touched fingers delicately to the black piratical patch over his left eye and winced slightly. "He says I'll get used to them goddamn glasses. In time, he says. Two weeks and I still can't see anything. What I need is a spyglass."

"A cataract operation is always a shock, Jumbo. You have to give it time."

"Easy for you to say. You're not the one who has to go around fumbling like a blind jackass. It's like living under water. Everybody is just a different-sized fish floating around." Jumbo scowled at him. "In dirty water," he added, and then grinned reluctantly when Gordon laughed at him.

"Hell with it. Make a drink, Gordie. I could use one."

Gordon mixed rum and limes and soda for Jumbo, poured himself a thin whiskey and water and filled both glasses with chips of ice. He put one glass on the table and took his over to the couch. He pushed his coat to the floor and stretched out full length.

"What have you been doing all day, Jumbo? Anything interesting?"

"Took a walk, by God." Jumbo glared at him defiantly. "Hired a bellboy to play Boy Scout for an hour. First time I been on the streets in a long while. Still can't tell a red light from a Budweiser sign, but I can keep from bumping into people. Spent most of the afternoon down in that steam bath. Everybody's half-blind down there."

Gordon chuckled. "Sounds like you're coming along fine. What does the doctor say?"

"Hell with it," Jumbo growled. "I'm going to be stumbling around in the half-dark all my days. I'm tired of talking about it. What are you doing over there in that courtroom? I been trying to figure it out, reading them reports. Far as I can see, you just keep hammering away at everybody with the same old questions, day after living day."

"Conditioning the jury, Jumbo. We took eight days and questioned almost two hundred people to get the jury we wanted. You can't hurry that. Or shouldn't. The wrong jury can kill you."

"Well, I'm damned if I can figure out what you're up to. There's that doctor was on the stand for a long, long time, telling about what happened to the man who was killed. And when it comes your turn, you don't ask him a single question. Then you get a cop who didn't do a thing but pick up the murder gun and put it in a bag, and you keep after him for a whole damn day. What kind of sense is that?"

Gordon sighed. He was touched that the old boy was interested and trying hard to understand. He was also tired.

"Do you really want to know, Jumbo? I'll hire a couple of senior law students to come in and give you some quick instruction. You might like that."

"Don't try to push me off, damn you." Jumbo's single yellow eye glared with the old habitual truculence. "I just asked a simple question. So give me a simple answer."

Gordon drained his glass and put it down on the floor. "Jumbo, I really wish I knew a simple answer. The doctor you were talking about. He was testifying to the physical condition of the body. It took a long time because the changing state of the man's health during the month before he died is an important factor in fixing the time of death. But we aren't disputing any of the medical facts. So why ask questions? The cop is another matter entirely. He says he found the gun just outside the back door in a flower bed. We are contending that the gun was actually dropped inside the house, in the hallway, and that some one of the investigators must have kicked it out accidentally when there were ten or twelve people milling around in the house after the killing. Now that is an important point for us. I couldn't break the cop and didn't expect to, but I did get a chance to let the jury know what our position is. The man I'm really laying for is the ballistics expert from the state crime lab. The rest is just preparation for him. He is one guy I *am* going to break."

"Hoo-whee," Jumbo whistled. "Rough tough Gordie Guthrie. A real hard man, huh?"

"I'm just as tough as I have to be," Gordon said wearily. "Just like rough tough Jumbo Guthrie."

Jumbo's mouth twitched. He closed the trial transcript, leaving the magnifier to mark his place, picked up his glass and moved his chair back away from the table. "Ain't it time for bed? You been up since daybreak."

"I get all the sleep I need. I'm waiting for someone." And the light tapping at the door came as if Lonnie Wetherill had been standing out in the hall waiting for his cue.

Gordon rolled to his feet and went to the door.

Lonnie bustled in, bear-thick in a fur-lined coat, a dark Astrakhan cap pulled low across his forehead. He was using both hands to support a pair of bright plastic boxes. He headed directly for the card table and dumped his load. "I saw Cozy's was still open when I came by so I stopped off for a couple of orders of ribs. I'll trade for a drink." He pulled off his cap and nodded at Jumbo. "Evening, sir. Don't believe we've met. I'm Lonnie Wetherill."

"My father, Lonnie," Gordon said from the bar corner. "Jumbo, this gentleman with the Care package is Lonnie Wetherill, of the Rocky Mountain *Bugle*, or *Trumpet*, or whatever."

"*Clarion*, sir. *Clarion*." He leaned across the table to shake Jumbo's hand. "Pleasure, sir. Real pleasure. I'm sorry I didn't know you'd be here, Mr. Guthrie, or I'd have brought more ribs. But maybe we can piece out." He peeled foil lids from the plastic containers and pulled a thick wad of paper napkins from one roomy pocket.

"None for me, thank you." Jumbo levered himself up from the deep chair. "I'll just leave you two young fellows to get along by yourselves. Past my bedtime." He felt along the wall for the molding of his bedroom door. "You wake me before you go, Gordie. We'll have breakfast together. You'll excuse me, Mr. Wetherill. Glad to have met you."

"Take your coat off and sit down, Lonnie." Gordon gave him a full glass and indicated a chair. He picked up a container of ribs and put it on a handy table. Then he fished a twinned section from the sauce, tore it apart, and stripped off the strands of barbecued meat with his teeth. "Good," he said with a full mouth. He dropped the bones in an ashtray and reached for more.

"Cozy is a master. The Gordon Guthrie of the sauce pots."

Gordon cocked an eyebrow. He was too busy eating to answer.

"I've been trying to get you all evening," Lonnie complained. "Don't you take calls from the press anymore?"

"I'm always available," Gordon said easily. "Tonight was a work session. Big day coming up tomorrow, and I had a problem with my colleagues. It took longer than I thought."

"But you prevailed?"

Gordon nodded. He took another rib.

"Elkins, Root and Kantor." Lonnie chanted the names with obvious distaste. "Pack of dusty old farts. How did you ever get tied up with them?"

Gordon shrugged. "They were attorneys for my client. And I have to work through a local firm. I'm not licensed to practice in Colorado."

"Ah." Lonnie nodded wisely. "All is now clear. I had assumed that you big-league defense boys just went raiding over the country whenever you took the notion. Well now I've got it straight. And the hell with it. What I really came to talk about is a brilliant idea that came to me while I was playing backgammon at the Press Club. I have been trying to get to you ever since."

Gordon balanced his peeled bone on the loaded ashtray. "Okay, you got to me. What is this brilliant idea?"

"I just received an advance copy of Jonathan Pike's biography. *Autobiography*, I should say." Lonnie hesitated. He scowled at Gordon. "I suppose there is no reason to suspect he *didn't* write it himself?"

"Shouldn't think so," Gordon said cautiously. "He's written a lot of other stuff." He knew beyond any doubt that Pike had written every word of the book, but he did not want to explain why he was so sure.

Five thousand dollars down the drain, he reminded himself with some bitterness. That was the fee Gordon had paid a talented free-lance writer to do a draft of Jonathan Pike's autobiography. The man had done a good, careful job, particularly in his handling of the trial and the shifting elements of all the subsequent appeals. Then Gordon had sent the manuscript to Pike, suggesting he make some changes to reflect his own style of writing. Pike had done more than that. He had rewritten the whole thing. The book was Pike's, all right, every expensive word of it. The title was the publisher's, and Gordon didn't think much of it. *Shadow of Death*. But the publisher's salesmen had liked it, so perhaps it had some value. A twenty-five-thousand-dollar advance against a straight fifteen percent royalty. Thirty-thousand-dollar advertising budget to start off. Initial printing, thirty thousand copies. A built-in promotional campaign that should push the book onto the best-seller list a week after publication. And it was all Pike's. Every word of it. The boy could still surprise him.

"What were you saying?" He had not been listening and Lonnie had been going on without slowing for breath.

"Goddammit, Gordie! I just told you. Wait till you read it. *Shadow of Death*. It's a brilliant book. A great crime thriller. An honest, sensitive autobiography. A savage indictment of the life-in-death a condemned man leads in prison. And it's well written, Gordie. Sharp, simple, and logical. Even I could understand what all those various appeals were about. Pike himself comes through as a real and sympathetic person. Well, you know him, of course. You've known him from the start. But wait till you read his book."

"I have read it," Gordon said.

"Oh, you have? Yes, I suppose the publisher would send you an advance copy. Well then, you know what I'm talking about. So now we get to my great idea. I want you to review it for me, Gordie."

"Sorry, Lonnie," Gordon said, shaking his head. "I can't. The Chicago *Tribune* sent me a set of galley proofs, and I agreed to review the book for them. I think they plan to syndicate it though, so you can probably buy the local rights if you want that."

"Shit," Lonnie said heavily. "Me and my great ideas. Only a month late."

"I'm the obvious one to review it," Gordon said, feeling apologetic for no reason. "I was involved in his first trial you know. And I did a little work for him later on."

"Yeah." Lonnie took a morose gulp. "Do you see him much these days?"

"No time," Gordon said carefully. "He writes my office once in a while. We give him a little research help, chase citations for him, that sort of thing. But basically he's been on his own for a long time."

"He's been toughing it out in that hole a hell of a lot longer than I could have." Lonnie waggled his bushy head. "How long is it now, eight years?"

"About that."

"Eight years not knowing when he's going to get chopped. It's a goddamn wonder he's still sane. How does he stand now? Where is he? Up to the Supreme Court again?"

"Yes, he's filed for a writ of *certiorari*."

"And what's likely to happen?"

"Good question. The Court could grant the writ and give him a full hearing. Or they could reject the application again."

"Suppose they grant it. What happens?"

"They listen to what his lawyer has to say. They listen to an attorney for the state, probably the attorney general, argue against him. Then they decide."

286

"And if they decide for Pike? What happens then?"

"They would probably send it back to the Federal District Court and order a *habeas corpus* hearing."

"Jesus," Lonnie muttered. "I do keep asking for it. Okay, we've gone this far, let's go all the way. *Then* what?"

"The District Court holds the hearing, listens to Pike and the opposition and decides. If they find for Pike, the chances are they would order the state to retry him or set him free."

Lonnie's interest quickened. "So the District Court sends the order down to the state. And then what?"

"The state would have a lot of problems with a brand-new trial after all this time. Witnesses die off or move out of reach. The value of the physical evidence deteriorates. Later Supreme Court decisions change the ground rules. For instance, if the Federal District Court orders a new trial, they might bar any use of the unsigned statement that was used against Pike in his first trial. Maybe the state will just say the hell with it and turn him loose."

Lonnie drew a deep breath. His eyes met Gordon's, and he almost grinned. "I catch. Now the target looks clearer." He paused. "If you hadn't told me different," he went on innocently, "I just might think you were handling the case yourself. It's got your style. All the Gordie Guthrie trademarks. Tricky and devious."

Gordon laughed.

"Are you pretty sure the Court will rule for Pike?"

"Nobody can ever be sure."

"I get tired just thinking about it," Lonnie complained. "And here is this guy Pike handling all this complex maneuvering all by himself? It's hard to believe, Gordie."

It sure as hell is, Gordon agreed to himself. But that's the way we set it up, and an awful lot of people do believe it.

"As you were saying, Pike is a remarkable young man." And now for Christ's sake, leave it at that, he shouted in his head. This is one time when I am heartily sick of Jonathan Pike and his endless problems. "But Pike isn't my client now, Lonnie. Charity Mitchen is. I have to focus on her."

Gordon made Lonnie a fresh drink, gave himself a glass of ice water, and came back to the couch.

"Well, maybe I can retrieve something out of this long evening," Lonnie said. "Would you stand still for a feature piece, Gordie? I know we did a couple of columns on you earlier, but I was thinking of something with more depth this time. I'd like to trail you around, get the feel of how it is when a hotshot lawyer comes barreling into a strange town and takes on the local cock of the walk. We had Percy Foreman here last year and Lee Bailey a few months back. I'd like to do a piece that contrasted your different styles in the courtroom, a little something about philosophies of justice, and a spoonful of gossip-column dirt about those enormous fees you fellows charge. Get right inside the Charity Mitchen case with you and see how it is when somebody's life is hanging in the balance. Just Gordon Guthrie between you and the noose. Could be a fine piece. Will you do it, Gordie?"

Gordon got up slowly and put his glass down on the small bar. He dumped the bone-loaded ashtrays in the empty plastic boxes and stacked them on a side table where the maid could see them. He went into the bedroom, found his limp sack of tobacco on the dresser and brought it back with him. He took a long careful time rolling a toothpick cigarette.

"What is it, Gordie? Are you trying to tell me you won't do it?"

Gordon smoked his cigarette in two puffs and put it out. "We've got a pretty good thing going here, Lonnie," he said awkwardly. "Between us, I mean."

"Are you turning me down, Gordie?"

"Maybe not. I'm not sure. If I tell you something in confidence, can I be sure you'll keep it in your hat?"

"I hate off-the-record crap, Gordie. I usually refuse to listen."

"But that's the way it would have to be."

After a moment Lonnie sighed. "Okay then. Newspaperman's word of honor. You might not believe it, but I know quite a few gamy secrets I don't talk about." He lifted his glass and squinted through it at Gordon. "I may be the least bit drunk tonight, but I am still a functioning newspaperman."

"All right." Gordon sat in a chair close to Lonnie's. "I told you earlier that I had a long session with my local colleagues tonight planning our moves in court tomorrow. I don't want to say any more about it now, Lonnie. You come and see for yourself tomorrow. You'll understand then why I can't give you any answer about the feature piece. Not tonight."

Lonnie squinted both eyes. "Is that all you can say, Gordie?"

"For the moment."

"I'm beginning to see a little glint of light. I will now go home and sleep for a few hours and get myself down to the courthouse bright and early this morning." He drained his glass and placed it ceremoniously on the bar. "Please say good night to your father for me. I hope we'll meet again."

"Good night, Lonnie."

In the quiet courtroom Gordon sat hunched over yesterday's trial transcript, quickly scanning the marked passages. Beside him Ellsworth Penn, senior partner of Elkins, Root and Kantor, and counsel for the co-defendant, fiddled restlessly with a mechanical pencil, snapping the point in and out in a slow mindless rhythm.

"I don't like it, Gordon," he said in a whisper. "Let's take another look at it. I don't approve of—"

"Nobody asked you to approve," Gordon said sharply. "You agreed that I was to run the trial for both defendants. So just sit back and let me run it."

He rose and offered a courtly bow when his client was escorted through the side door into the well of the court. Mrs. Charity Mitchen. In pink, as always. "The Pink Widow," the reporters called her sometimes, when they were running out of other things to say about her.

The State charged that Charity Mitchen, together with Carl J. Bowne, had entered a conspiracy to murder Roy Ewell Mitchen, husband of Charity, remote cousin of Carl. Bowne alone was charged with firing the fatal shots. Mr. Mitchen had been a lucky and very rich real estate speculator. Mrs. Mitchen stood to inherit everything. Unless she was executed for murder.

"Gordie, dear, please talk to that awful matron. This is the second time this week she's brought me the wrong shade of lipstick. This one just isn't *right* with this shade of pink."

Gordon patted her absently, not listening. He nodded briefly to Carl Bowne, the shambling oxlike boy who trailed behind her.

Before he sat in his chair at the far end of the defense table he closed the bound transcript and slipped it under his briefcase. He would not need to refer to it again; he could recite the pertinent parts verbatim if he should ever want to. If he should ever need to. That was the hook he was hanging on. It all depended on the actions of the district attorney for Denver County.

With his last witness yesterday, the DA had blundered. Probably he had been tired after a long day. But that lack of attention could ruin him unless he managed to retrieve his mistake the moment court opened this morning. Gordon would have to wait and see. And be ready to jump.

The DA's witness was a man who swore his name was John Smith and had a long prison record to prove it. Smith had worked as handyman at one of the Mitchen housing developments where Carl Bowne had been employed as a salesman. Smith testified that on January 15, Bowne had come to him with a proposal that they join together and kidnap Roy Mitchen and hold him for a million-dollar ransom. Later, Smith claimed, the proposal had shifted from kidnapping to murder. Smith to do the actual killing, Bowne to give him money enough for "a couple of new Cadillacs."

Q. And what did you answer?
A. I told him I was interested.
Q. Were you serious in that answer?
A. I was just kidding him along. He had a bottle with him. As long as I was agreeing with him, he was pouring like rain. I didn't figure he had money enough to hire a killing, but he had that bottle.
Q. Very well, Mr. Smith. Now tell the court what, if anything, Carl Bowne said to you in regard to Roy Mitchen's wife.
A. He said she was in love with him. She'd do anything he said to do. If we kidnapped Mitchen, she was going to get the money fast and quiet and pay it over and not say a word to the cops till it was all over, so there wasn't going to be any risk at all.
Q. And just how did it happen that Bowne's proposal turned from kidnapping to murder?
A. He got impatient, I guess. He'd been drinking a little along with me. Anyway, he said, hell, it takes too long that way. Let's just kill old Mitch and get it over with.
Q. Did you see Carl Bowne again after this occasion on January 15 when you more or less agreed to help him murder Roy Mitchen?
A. Never did. As a matter of fact, I didn't see him again until right here in this courtroom.
Q. Why was that?
A. Federal police arrested me the very next morning. On a fugitive warrant from Wyoming. So I never did see Carl after that.

The district attorney handed Gordon the file on John Smith and turned the witness over to him for cross-examination. Gordon waited for a moment, remembering. His investigating team had given him a complete report on Bowne's movements for the past several years. He could place the man exactly for just about any day during that period. And he knew that John Smith could not possibly have had his conference with Bowne in Denver on January 15. During the middle two weeks of January, Bowne had been hospitalized in Colorado Springs with viral pneumonia. For most of January 15 he had been in an oxygen tent. And the district attorney knew that. He had backtracked every move of Carl Bowne and Charity Mitchen. So why didn't he correct Smith's fraudulent testimony immediately?

No answer. An honest oversight? Or a dirty try with a perjured witness?

Gordon went ahead with his questioning, expecting to be interrupted at any moment. He paced himself carefully to make sure that when he dismissed Smith, there would be no time for the DA to call another witness before adjournment. He traced Smith's active and unsuccessful criminal career step by step, establishing from his admissions that Smith was a habitual liar and that he had more than once perjured himself during his many trials. Still no response from the district attorney's side of the court.

Shortly before the end of the day's session, Gordon took Smith once again through his account of the meeting with Carl Bowne.

Q. What day did you say this was?
A. I saw him on January 15.
Q. You are completely certain of the date? It couldn't have been the fourteenth, for instance? Or the sixteenth?
A. No, sir. I can definitely swear I saw him on the fifteenth.

Gordon had dismissed the witness. The district attorney was collecting his papers. He had made no effort to address the court before adjournment.

And now, at the beginning of the new court day, the district attorney was still silent. He sat in a close huddle with two assistants and had to be nudged when the judge entered.

"Very well, sir." The judge nodded and tapped his gavel.

"The People will call Police Lieutenant William Fifer," the district attorney announced.

Gordon rose slowly. He stood in an easy slouch, hands in his pockets, bulky shoulders hunched, waiting for the judge to recognize him. It took a moment. The jury noticed him first and the double row of heads turned to look at him. The district attorney stopped halfway to the witness stand. The judge swung his chair around.

"Yes, Mr. Guthrie?"

Gordon swept one hand through his hair. He bowed his head thoughtfully, then looked at the judge. His big-featured face was lined, sober, almost sorrowful.

"Your honor, it is my painful duty to inform the court that my learned opponent, the district attorney for Denver County, has knowingly introduced perjured evidence into this trial and has willfully suppressed vital evidence now in his possession."

The judge rocked slowly back. Very deliberately he reached forward to place his pencil in its rack. Then he turned to the district attorney.

The district attorney was a solid, robust man, full-fleshed, healthily colored. His face went suddenly white. Small beads of sweat popped into view on his forehead. He stared at Gordon incredulously. He shook his head slowly, unable to speak.

"Your honor, the district attorney yesterday put a convicted criminal, an admitted perjurer, on the stand and allowed him to give false testimony in this trial. The district attorney has in his files an investigator's report that proves that on January 15 Carl Bowne could not possibly have met with John Smith in Denver, as Smith was allowed to testify. The district attorney—" Gordon turned to look at him for the first time. When he spoke again, he abandoned the note of cool sobriety. His voice soared in the quiet courtroom with a blood-chilling ferocity.

"The district attorney *knows,* your honor, that Carl Bowne was hospitalized in the Colorado Springs Hospital on January 15. The district attorney *knows* that Smith's testimony is false. The district attorney knew it at the time Smith was testifying, yet he did nothing to set the record straight. The district attorney came into this courtroom this morning, still aware of that perjured testimony, knowing his trial record was polluted by falsehood, yet when the court instructed him to proceed with the trial, he did not seize his opportunity to repair the damage. Instead he called a new witness, planning to go on as if nothing had happened. If the defense had not brought this ugly situation to the court's attention, the district attorney would have allowed the jury to accept perjured testimony."

"No, your honor. No, that isn't true. I was—"

Gordon's voice overrode the district attorney's, submerging his thin, outraged denial in a surging roar.

"Is this man so lost to honor that even now he will try to excuse what he has done? Caught red-handed, yet he still squeaks denials." Gordon swung his massive head toward the judge again. "Well, your honor," he said more quietly. "It does not matter what the district attorney says now. My client's case—and the co-defendant's case—have been prejudiced beyond repair. The defense, your honor, moves for a mistrial."

Before the district attorney could respond, Gordon let his voice rise in a last angry explosion. "The defense, your honor, *demands* a mistrial."

The judge hardly seemed to breathe. His face showed no expression. Slowly he took off his gold-rimmed reading glasses. He was too experienced, too wily, to rule on Gordon's motion immediately. His narrowed speculative eyes swung toward the district attorney.

"It is true, your honor," the district attorney said in a hasty flood of words, "that we now know that John Smith's testimony is worthless and very likely perjured. I apologize to this court. Most sincerely, your honor. And I apologize wholeheartedly to Mr. Guthrie and his colleagues for the defense. May I explain, your honor?"

"I was about to invite you to explain, sir," the judge said dryly.

"When I arrived in my office this morning, one of my assistants was waiting for me. He showed me the report to which Mr. Guthrie has referred, a report that does indeed place the co-defendant, Carl Bowne, in the Colorado Springs Hospital on January 15. It was then time for me to leave for court. I instructed my assistant to telephone the state prison immediately and have John Smith brought directly to this courtroom under guard. It was my intention, sir, to ask the court's permission to put him on the stand again for the express purpose of correcting the false testimony he gave here yesterday. That is the complete truth of the matter, your honor. I have never—" The district attorney swallowed painfully, twisting his neck awkwardly to ease the tension. "Your honor. Mr. Guthrie. I have been a member of the bar for thirty-nine years. I respect the law above all. Every time I present a case for trial, I hope to do justice. I can say that with complete sincerity, and I believe that my record will bear me out."

After a long moment the judge looked down somberly at Gordon. "Do you accept that apology, Mr. Guthrie?"

"I accept it, your honor. But the damage has been done."

"You will persist in your motion for mistrial?"

"I have no option, your honor."

"Come forward, please. Both of you. Mr. Clerk, the jury will withdraw."

The side-bar conference, the recess while the judge considered his decision, and the later full-court session when the judge read his formal statement, took up most of the morning and gave the television cameramen time to assemble their equipment on the long icy steps outside the courthouse.

The district attorney had no comment for them. He bustled past the standing microphone, head down, almost buried in the high fur collar of his overcoat. Gordon waited until he was well away and then came carefully down the slippery steps.

"Mr. Gordon Guthrie, the noted defense lawyer who set in motion the series of events this morning that resulted in the court declaring a mistrial in the Mitchen Murder Case. Mr. Guthrie, can you tell us why the trial was halted?"

"You heard the judge's decision, sir. He agreed with me that the prejudicial effect of Smith's perjured testimony could not be completely erased from the minds of the jury. In that case, it could no longer be a fair trial."

"Is that all?" The reporter glared at Gordon.

"All?" Gordon held his voice low, but the anger was clear in his tone. "All? A fair trial is guaranteed to every American citizen. Charity Mitchen's right to a fair trial was placed in danger when Smith was allowed to offer his perjured testimony."

"It was a mistake, I understand," the reporter insisted. "The district attorney apologized and had Smith right there in court ready to admit that he had lied. Why wasn't that good enough?"

"You'll have to ask the trial judge," Gordon said easily. "It was his decision."

"You don't believe it was a mistake?"

"The district attorney told the court it was a mistake, an unfortunate oversight. I accept that. We all make mistakes. And every time we do, we have to pay the price. I think that is why the judge declared a mistrial today."

"Will there be a new trial? If so, when?"

Gordon shook his head, smiling. "That's a question for the district attorney. If he still thinks he can win his case, I suppose he will schedule a new trial. The timing is also a matter for him to determine."

"Will you make a guess, Mr. Guthrie?"

Gordon shook his head. "No guesses." He moved across the sidewalk toward a clump of waiting reporters and slowed to let them surround him. He kept walking, answering the same questions with a word or a laugh. After a few blocks they dropped back, content with the story they had, knowing Gordon was not going to enlarge it for them.

"Now I know the answer," a sharp voice said behind him.

Lonnie Wetherill's rakish fur cap came almost to Gordon's shoulder. He tilted his head back, scowling red-eyed up at Gordon.

"No feature story. You're not going to be around town anymore, are you?"

"I'll have to clean up a few odds and ends, Lonnie. A couple of days, I imagine."

Lonnie sighed noisily. "This very definitely is not a good season for me. Nothing seems to work out."

294

Gordon shook his head. "I had no choice, Lonnie."

"You bastard, you set it up. Don't tell me you didn't have any choice. You mouse-trapped that old boy. You made him look like a goddamn thief. He was almost crying. You could have accepted his apology and gone along. Why didn't you?"

"I didn't trap anyone, Lonnie," Gordon said patiently. "He did it all himself. And he'll have to live with it. All I'm doing is protecting my client. That's my job."

"Well, how does a mistrial protect her? You'll just have to go through the whole thing over again, won't you?"

"There will probably be a new trial. But that's for the future. Near future, distant future, whenever. I can't plan that far ahead."

"I don't understand what you're talking about. I doubt if you do. And something else I don't understand is how you ever persuaded that judge to declare a mistrial. Your objection just wasn't that serious."

Gordon looked at him amiably. He was willing to explain but not to Lonnie Wetherill. He could trust a newsman to keep certain kinds of secrets, but this generalized sort of secret would make too good a story. Even if Lonnie didn't write it in his column, it was bound to dribble out. Denver newspapermen were a cheerful, gregarious lot, and sooner or later Lonnie would let it slip. He wouldn't be able to resist the temptation.

"The judge decided for himself, Lonnie," he said quietly. "Go ask him why he did it." He stopped across the street from his hotel. "Will you come up for a drink?"

"No thanks. Hell, you make me get up this early, I might as well get some work done while I'm at it. I'll call you later."

"Any time."

When he opened the sitting room door, Jumbo raised a hand imperiously, commanding silence. He was crouched behind his card table again, bald head shining under the light, his big veined nose less than ten inches from a portable television set. Gordon waved at him, dropped his loaded briefcase and signaled to call room service before he stripped off his overcoat. He stretched out on the long couch, waiting for Jumbo to finish.

". . . this surprising decision in the Mitchen Murder Case." The television reporter's voice crackled in the quiet room. "No date has yet been set for another trial, but the district attorney's office indicates that an announcement will come shortly. I return you now to our studio."

Jumbo snapped the volume button and pushed back in his chair.

"Hoo-boy," he said softly. "I wouldn't plan on running for anything in this town, was I you, Gordie. They just plain don't like you in Denver. Not today."

Gordon grinned lazily. Without getting up he reached back to pick up the telephone. He balanced it on his chest, dialed the Rincon area code and then his office number. He put the phone base on the floor and laid the receiver over his shoulder.

"They'll get over it, Jumbo."

"Not soon, they won't. They are speaking real mean about you, boy. What did you do to that judge anyway? From what this fellow was saying, you must have put the evil eye on him."

"The judge is a fine, compassionate gentleman, full of human understanding," Gordon said amiably. "Also I promised him a reversal if he should make me go on with the trial, and we should lose. He saw the light."

"You just plain scared him?"

"You're making it sound illegal, Jumbo." Gordon unbuttoned his collar and eased the knot of his tie. "It is really a matter of simple understanding. There is a new phenomenon abroad in the land. I didn't invent it, but I recognize it when I see it."

"You're talking smart again," Jumbo growled. "What the hell does that mean—a new phenomenon?"

"Here and there, from time to time," Gordon said, "you run into a new kind of judge. He is defense-oriented. Usually out of a sense of self-protection. He has conditioned himself to give the defense every inch of leeway possible. Do you know why?"

"You're going to tell me, I guess."

"Judges don't like it when appeals courts reverse their decisions. It makes them look bad. Their colleagues at the Bar Association make little jokes about them. But if they lean over backward for the defense, they're safe. Even if the trial ends in a conviction, there is very little chance that an appeals court would reverse because the trial judge has already made sure that there isn't any solid basis for an appeal. Acquittals, of course, are never reversed. So if a judge makes a habit of going with the defense, he is going to come out smelling like a rose. The word is getting around. When you find a judge who's caught the message, the job gets a little easier."

"And you found one—?"

The phone came alive and Gordon cut him off. "Just a minute, Jumbo." He tilted the speaker toward his mouth. "This is Guthrie. Get me David Simon, please." He swung his feet to the floor and sat up.

"David? It went about the way I expected. Mistrial. So I've got an empty month with nothing scheduled. Have you figured out what I'm going to do with it?"

"I heard," Simon said. "Answer to your question is no. San Francisco won't move us up on the calendar, won't even discuss it. Seattle is too jammed for any possible adjustment. Dallas is a possible, but Joe B says he'll need another week or ten days to finish checking the jury list. Do you want a suggestion from the ranks, boss?"

"Let's hear it."

"How about a vacation? Let us wage slaves get caught up with the routine for a change?"

Gordon grunted. "First, tell me what's happening with Jon Pike. Anything new?"

"Not exactly. But it looks promising. The Supreme Court has asked for a response from the Attorney General, so some one of the Justices must be interested. Guess who wrote the Attorney General's opposing brief? Want three guesses?"

"David Burrell?"

"He really has a sort of permanent hard-on for Pike, doesn't he?"

"I wouldn't exactly put it that way. But it is something more than a normal response. Okay, David. Is that all we've got in the works?"

"Three or four new referrals you may want to follow up. But none of them looks very exciting. If you are really hot about getting to work, do you want me to call Roger Farrall and—"

"No." Gordon said flatly. "Forget it. I don't even want to talk about it again. I'll be back in Rincon in a day or two. I'll call again before I leave here."

He cradled the phone, lifted the set back on its side table. The waiter tapped on the door.

"Yes, come in," Gordon called. "Fill the ice bucket, please. Better bring us some bottles of soda, too, and some fresh limes. And a couple of menus. You want to eat lunch up here with me, Jumbo?"

"Up here? You hiding out, boy?"

Gordon grinned. "Might be a good idea, at that. No, I've got some things to read. Thought I'd give myself a quiet afternoon."

"Damn right it might be a good idea. Those television people are ready to whip up a lynching party. Is it right about Mrs. Mitchen's jewels? They say you made her give you a million dollars' worth of diamonds."

"Jesus," Gordon muttered. "It gets bigger all the time. But to answer your question, no. I didn't make Mrs. Mitchen do a damned thing. She

297

wanted to hire me, and the only money she had in her own name was a few thousand in her household account. So she put up her diamonds and her new car as security for my fee. And the diamonds are not worth anything like a million dollars or even half of that. Now have you got that straight?"

"You shout at me one more time, boy, and I'll be over there pounding your head. You hear me?" Jumbo looked ready to clear the card table away with one sweep.

Gordon spread both hands in a peaceful gesture. "I hear you. Everybody on three floors can hear you. Quiet down, Jumbo. It's just that I get a painful gripe in the ass when I hear that stuff. You'd think no other lawyer in the world ever protected his fee. When he's in trouble, a client will promise the moon, but afterward it is often very hard to collect anything more than heartfelt gratitude. Charity Mitchen hired me because she needed me. She agreed to my fee without any argument. When I get her off, she'll have all of Mitchen's money. She'll pay me my fee, and I'll give her back the diamonds. The car I'm keeping for myself. Now what in hell is so bad about that?"

"I don't know," Jumbo said heavily. "I can't exactly say why I don't like it. I listen to those television fellows, and you come out like some kind of monster, all full of tricks to defeat the law. They say you like to ruined that district attorney. They say you didn't need to break off the trial, cost the state all that money for a new one—"

"They say a lot of shit," Gordon broke in roughly. "My Christ, Jumbo, do you think I'm an idiot? Would I chew up the DA and bully the judge if I didn't *need* that mistrial? I'm not in there enjoying myself, trying to score off the opposition. I'm trying to win a case. I'm trying to save my client."

Jumbo glared with his single yellowish eye. "I notice you put yourself first on that list."

"If I don't win my case and save my client, I'm not in business any longer. So who cares which one I put first? We sink or swim together. And today I struck a damn useful blow for my client. Maybe I saved her life. I don't much care what anyone says about it. I know what I did, and I know how valuable it was." Gordon hesitated.

"This is just between us, okay? I'll probably have to come back here for another trial, so I can't risk any loose chatter. Solemn promise, Jumbo?"

Jumbo nodded silently.

"The value of a mistrial coming at the right moment is that the prosecution has revealed its case, and the defense can take steps to counteract it. That's clear, isn't it? Every prosecutor tries to save a few surprises for the last minute. The Denver DA had one for me. You read my trial outline. Do you remember that Charity Mitchen had an alibi for the time of the killing? Do you remember what it was?"

"Not exactly."

"One o'clock in the morning," Gordon said, speaking precisely, with the sureness of perfect memory. "Charity Mitchen stopped at an all-night drugstore. She had turned her ankle earlier that night when she was out with friends. The ankle was paining her, so on her way home she stopped to buy an elastic bandage. The clerk was an elderly woman, alone in the store. She showed Charity how to adjust the bandage and put in the holding clips. They had a couple of rehearsals before Charity got it just right. At one twenty that night Roy Mitchen was murdered ten miles away on the other side of Denver. So my client can't be involved directly in the murder if she was in that drugstore. Are you with me so far?"

"I think so," Jumbo said uncertainly.

"Yesterday the DA gave me an amended list of witnesses he meant to call. All but two checked out easily. No trouble about them. The two we couldn't find were a couple of boys who graduated from high school last year. They worked together on the night shift at a garage in the area of the drugstore where Charity stopped that night. They lived five or six blocks away. They always drove home together. People they worked with said they liked to stop for a chocolate malt on the way home. Young boys, remember, nondrinkers. So where did they stop that night?"

"At the same drugstore?"

"Who knows?" Gordon said easily. "It was on their direct route home."

"Why don't you ask them?"

"I would like to," Gordon said with a choked laugh. "God, how I would like to. But I can't find them. The DA has them hidden out somewhere. The first sight I would ever have had of either of them would have been in that courtroom. If the trial had gone on a few days more."

"Is that why you made all this mess? Just so those two boys couldn't come to court?"

"Haven't you understood anything I've said, Jumbo? Think about it this way. The woman clerk in the drugstore was a middle-aged widow. The job paid her less than sixty dollars a week, and she has a young daughter to take care of. Charity Mitchen is going to be a rich woman if I win her case. The clerk's alibi is an important part of that case. My investigators checked her out carefully and finally said okay, so I was

299

counting on her. And now I have to wonder if little Charity didn't slip down to that drugstore and buy herself a witness. That's what I thought of the moment the DA showed me that amended list."

"You think the lady is lying to you?"

Gordon shrugged. "They all try it, Jumbo. They think their counsel is bound to do a better job for them if he actually *believes* they are innocent. It really doesn't make a damn bit of difference, but they can't see that. I am committed completely to Charity Mitchen, innocent or guilty. I can't afford to take a case on a faked alibi. If those two boys just happened to be in that drugstore and can testify that Charity never came in that night, then she will hang, Jumbo. I won't take that chance. I have to *know* before I go into that courtroom again."

"And you don't think you can trust her story?"

"I can't afford to trust anybody. In a few days the DA will have to let those boys go back to their normal life, and I'll get an investigator on them as soon as they show up. And if there is a new trial, I'll be ready for them when they testify."

"Why don't you just ask Mrs. Mitchen about it? Tell her you're worried and ask her to help out."

"Because I couldn't afford to believe a word she said. That sly, giggly little bitch has been lying to me from the beginning. I thought I had her straightened out by now. But maybe not. I am sure as hell not going to go back into that courtroom until I know of my own knowledge exactly what she was doing every minute of that night. I'm not going to ask her. I'll put my own people on it."

Jumbo ruffled the sparse gray fringe of hair around the back of his neck. He adjusted his glasses with both hands. "You keep talking about that lady like she was some kind of worm you wouldn't even want to step on. What's the matter with you? Whose side are you on anyway?"

Gordon caught himself, bit off an angry response, and shrugged helplessly. "I'm on my client's side. Charity Mitchen's side, Jumbo. Don't make any mistake about that."

"You sure make it easy for a fellow to make a mistake," Jumbo said with a truculent yellow glare. "Seems to me like you're strictly on Gordie Guthrie's side."

Gordon looked at him soberly, silently. Jumbo had been growing crankier by the day and the demands on Gordon's patience were sometimes more than he could take. Of course it was hard on Jumbo, the serious trouble with his sight coming on with no warning, and then dragging on for almost three years before the developing cataracts matured to the point where they could be removed. A bad time for old

Jumbo, very bad. He wasn't suited to a quiet sedentary life, and he had few inner resources to call on. He stormed against the Fates like a Grecian king raging against the thunder. Gordon tried to remember that and not rise to Jumbo's challenges. The trouble is, he told himself, you just aren't used to being criticized. The only rough arguments you get these days are in the courtroom. Except when Jumbo whips out that knife and goes straight for your gizzard.

"Let's just say we're both on the same side, Jumbo. And leave it at that. What do you want to eat for lunch?"

Jumbo rose and stood looking at him from under heavy gray eyebrows, his face red in angry blotches and clenched like a fist. "I don't want to eat with you. Sometimes you get to be somebody I don't even know."

He turned away and moved cautiously toward his bedroom. The door closed solidly behind him.

Gordon's quiet afternoon stretched into the early evening. An odd, disquieting feeling hung in his mind, as if he had forgotten something, lost track of an important train of thought. Jumbo's unseen presence, he realized, drifting around like an errant ghost in a mystery story, nibbling away at his concentration.

Old Jumbo had tried to be a good and dutiful guest, but he had been master of his own house too long to adjust to another setting and different schedules. It was a wonder, Gordon thought, that he had lasted this long without exploding. But you didn't have to be such an impatient shitheel about it. You know how cantankerous Jumbo can be. Just try to ride with it.

In another day or so I'll finish up here, and then I'll load Jumbo and all our gear in that elegant new Continental I took as part of my fee, that dull-silver beauty upholstered in pearly rawhide and strips of solid silver. We'll cruise down through the Rockies, take our time and see something of that great wild country and blow the city stink out of our lungs. Should do us both a world of good.

Okay, decision made. After that Gordon could get back to work. Quietly in the background he could sometimes hear the low rumble of Jumbo's radio or the cassette player he was using to sample "Books for the Blind." Gordon read diligently through the accumulated stack of investigators' reports, drafts of briefs and petitions he had to approve, and then skimmed a thick backlog of legal reporters to see what his colleagues were up to in other jurisdictions. He quit when the bellboy came up with his daily delivery of newspapers.

He had the air editions from New York and Washington and the afternoon final of the local paper. Gordon dug out money for the boy and stopped at the bar cabinet to make his first drink of the day before he spread the Denver paper out on Jumbo's card table to read what it had to say about his morning in court.

The stories were cautious. Except for Lonnie Wetherill.

GUILTY? GET GORDIE GUTHRIE! The editor had boxed Lonnie's column below the fold and given him an italicized banner to set it off. Gordon read the story quickly.

Today in Superior Court, Part III, we were shown a lively example of the cynical skill that brings Mr. Gordon Guthrie at least half a million dollars in legal fees every year from clients who fear for their lives.

Half a million, Gordon repeated silently. Don't I wish that was the solid truth. There had been half-a-million years and one that was even better, finally. But that was not a dependable average. And nobody ever seemed to mention the mountainous expenses. As far as Lonnie Wetherill was concerned, it was all profit.

. . . the bumbling hick lawyer, the earnest hayseed waylaid in the wicked big city. He plays the part beautifully. The casual lock of sandy hair flops forward on signal when Mr. Guthrie is expressing bewilderment. And why wouldn't it? Mr. Guthrie's hairdresser charges fifty dollars a session and is worth it to Mr. Guthrie. We admit he is impressive, that tall bulky figure looming in the courtroom, his hands distorting the pockets of his three-hundred-dollar suit, his splendid necktie subtly twisted to show us that Mr. Guthrie never did quite catch onto city ways of dressing. Just a plainspoken country boy. And if you don't believe it, just watch while he rolls a skinny little cowboy cigarette, twirls it up in his mouth and pops a kitchen match alight with his thumbnail. A simple man of simple homely virtues, content with simple pleasures. Isn't that right?

Believe it at your peril.

Gordon laughed silently. Lonnie had been striking a blow in support of the local lawmen, but underlying the sarcasm and the high-minded disapproval ran the unstated conviction that he believed Gordon Guthrie to be a new and dangerous kind of legal magician. That was great stuff for pulling in new clients. Maybe he should put Lonnie on the payroll.

And that headline—GUILTY? GET GORDIE GUTHRIE!—might be very

302

useful one day. If the Denver papers both adopted the same tone for their follow-up stories, they would be presenting Gordon with a nifty little gift package. After the firm rulings in the Sheppard case, all courts were especially sensitive to press reports that could create prejudice within the community. When it came time for Charity Mitchen's new trial, Gordon just might want to move it out of Denver. And Lonnie Wetherill's small drop of poison would make a change of venue almost a certainty. Thanks again, Lonnie. Gordon tore off the bottom half of the page, folded it, and crammed it in his overloaded briefcase.

He took the air editions with him and stopped to freshen his drink at the bar. Then he remembered Jumbo and put together rum and limes and soda in a glass full of ice and walked over to Jumbo's closed door. He tapped the glass lightly against the wood. "Drinks time, Jumbo," he called. "You want yours in there?"

The door opened promptly, as if Jumbo had been waiting just inside. He glowered at Gordon, accepted the drink with a quick nod, and lifted it in salute. He was oddly subdued and formal this evening in a heavy winter suit complete with buttoned vest and Christmas-gift necktie that was a little too jaunty for his somber expression. His weathered face was shinily clean, still moist. Probably put in a couple of hours in the steam room, Gordon guessed. Got a haircut, too, and a barbershop shave.

"You're looking very elegant, Jumbo." Gordon went back to the bar for his drink. He picked up the Washington *Post* and left the others on the card table for Jumbo. He stretched on the couch, snapped the paper open, and groaned when the doorbell rang.

"You expecting company, Jumbo?"

Jumbo was at his card table, magnifying glass poised over an open newspaper. "Won't be anybody for me," he said without looking up.

Gordon got to his feet. He took a hasty gulp of his drink and carried it with him to the door.

She could still surprise him. They weren't supposed to keep that flawless total beauty on tap forever. Of course a few mythical magical dames managed it. Madame Farrall Kronstadt, for one. She glowed in the dim hallway like a pearl just slipped from the oyster. In a long suede coat that almost touched the floor, she stood waiting, a little hesitant. The coat was a snug-waisted affair with the fur inside except where it frothed out at the collar and cuffs and the long front opening.

"Claudia? What are you doing here?"

She slipped past him quickly, crossed the room, and shrugged out of her coat. She threw it over a chair and turned to face him, not noticing Jumbo rising at the far end of the room. She stood very straight, almost defiantly. Her long pale hair was held close to her face by a knitted skier's headband. It was the same bright shade of red as her tight stretch pants. The scoop-necked after-ski sweater was all the shifting tones of red there are or could be. Snow-bunny clothes. Fun clothes for the funsy ski resort.

Jumbo put his half-finished drink on the bar with a small click. Claudia swung around swiftly.

"Didn't mean to startle you." Jumbo stuffed his reading glass in his side pocket. He stared briefly at Gordon, nodded to Claudia, and moved forward. "How you this evening, Miz Kronstadt?"

"Oh, Mr. Guthrie. I'm sorry. I didn't see you. I was so eager to see Gordie, I just didn't think anyone else might be here."

"Well, I'll just leave you to it." Jumbo crossed to his bedroom door and swung it noisily shut behind him.

Claudia looked just a little startled.

"And you are the girl who was always so hot for discretion," Gordon said sourly. He closed the hall door and stood with his back to it.

"There is nothing indiscreet about my visit, Gordie," Claudia said firmly. "I have come as an emissary." ·

Gordon looked at her. After a long moment he grunted. "Daddy?" he asked, knowing the answer before he spoke.

"He phoned me just after he saw the one o'clock news. I chartered a plane and came as quickly as I could."

"Chartered a plane," Gordon said, unbelieving. "What for?"

Claudia flashed a quick mocking smile. "Gordie, Gordie," she said softly, shaking her head. "I don't have to tell you why."

"Guilty? Get Gordie Guthrie!" It was drawing flies already.

Gordon moved past Claudia to the bar cabinet and busied himself with bottles and glasses, giving himself a minute to think.

Announcing herself as an emissary could only mean that Claudia had come to plead for her father. And Gordon did not want to hear what she had to say. The answer was no. Now and for any reasonable future—no.

Roger Farrall had involved himself in a complicated criminal mess and Gordon wanted no part of it, no matter what fee was offered. Farrall and six others had pooled their resources, bribed a surprisingly wide range of Interior Department officials and had nearly walked off with the mineral rights to thousands of protected acres of federal grazing land. It was a sort of miniature Teapot Dome, not quite as much potential profit, but much the same idea, and one that was going to end just as disastrously for Roger Farrall and his clumsy colleagues. A federal grand jury had indicted the conspirators and trial was already scheduled.

He mixed a careful eight-to-one martini, swirled it in ice, and strained it into a stemmed glass. He sprayed the surface with oil from a strip of lemon peel and carried the glass across to Claudia.

"I turned the case down, you know." He sat in a deep chair facing her. "Sometime last year."

"I know that, Gordie. You said you had no time. And it was true then. We checked." She shifted down to the end of the couch closer to Gordon and touched his knee lightly with one finger. "But it's different now. You've got a mistrial here. So you do have free time. I called your office while I was waiting at the airport, and David Simon told me you had nothing definite on your schedule for the rest of the month."

"You may just have got the man fired."

"Don't grumble, Gordie-dear. You're caught, and you know it."

She is just as arrogant and insensitive as ever, Gordon thought, looking somberly at her, wondering how he could break through that childish self-assurance without hurting her too much.

He shook his head slowly, obstinately. "I'm sorry, Claudia. Really sorry." He reached for his tobacco on the low table between them and slipped a sheet of rice paper from the folder, watching very closely what he was doing so he would not have to look at her. "When your father and his friends came to me last year, I was glad I could just show them my schedule and send them away without any bad feeling. I didn't want to explain why I wouldn't touch their case for a million dollars. I don't want to explain now."

Claudia sipped at her drink, made an appreciative murmur, and put the drink down. "All right, don't explain, Gordie. Just fix it. Get my father out of that mess he was foolish enough to blunder into."

Foolish? Blunder? She couldn't believe that, could she?

"Nobody can get him out of it, Claudia," he said heavily. "That's just one of the reasons why I won't touch it. They've got him on at least eight counts, and the evidence is solid. Eyewitnesses, filmstrips, tape recordings, numbers of the currency he got from his bank and passed on to people he bribed, and a raft of supporting documents. Your daddy and his friends were really very stupid. And they are all going to prison, no matter who appears for them."

"Are you afraid of the case, Gordie? You?"

Gordon shrugged irritably. "I'm not Don Quixote, kid. I don't go in for hopeless causes. I'm in this game to win, and I have to keep winning all the time. So far I've only dropped one big one. You remember it, the Van Dulken trial in Philadelphia. You were there part of the time."

She smiled at him slowly. "I remember. It was a lovely time."

What Gordon remembered was disaster. And not only the trial. Ellen had later had the same idea as Claudia—surprise Gordon and spend a quiet, warm weekend. It would be good for Gordie to relax for a while during the trial. So Ellen had arrived and found Claudia already there. She left immediately, bleak-faced and silent, and waited at the airport for the first plane back to Rincon. For days he hadn't known what she intended to do, and Claudia was also worried. Would she tell Nico, sue Gordon for divorce, what? Then Jumbo had telephoned, blistering the wires and Gordon's eardrums. Ellen had come to him, and he had quieted things somehow. So it could have been worse.

Claudia was still watching him, lazy-eyed.

"Maybe you jinxed me in Philadelphia," he said, only half-joking. "Anyway I lost the case. I don't need any more like that one on my record. Van Dulken was a gamble, and I took it knowing that. But your daddy is a loser all the way. I won't touch his case."

"You are afraid." But she was not sure. The confusion in her voice and manner made her seem suddenly young and shaken.

"Call it what you like," Gordon said impatiently. "Five years ago I was snatching at any case that came near me. Now I can pick and choose. But even if I couldn't, I wouldn't touch your daddy's case. He is going to trial with six co-defendants. There will be seven defense attorneys at the same table. Any defense run by a seven-man committee is bound for disaster."

"But you could take over the whole thing, couldn't you, Gordie?"

"Sure. I could make them move over and let me run it. But I'd have to lean an awful lot of weight on six well-connected local attorneys who already have good reason to hate my guts. Just think how I'd come out of that one."

"But, Gordie, you could—" She broke off abruptly as Jumbo's bedroom door swung open and smacked back against the wall. He stood heavy and hunch-shouldered in the doorway, wearing hat and overcoat, small overnight bag in one hand. He took off the hat and nodded in Claudia's direction.

"Didn't mean to interrupt," he said stiffly. "Gordie, I'm going to check back in the hospital. See if those doctors can't hurry up those tests and let me go on home. I'll send for the rest of my gear tomorrow."

He was moving forward as he spoke, heading toward the front door and being careful not to bump into any of the furniture. He was almost out of the room before Gordon reacted.

"Jumbo! For Christ's sake!" He untangled his legs, dropped the unlit cigarette and jumped toward Jumbo before he could get away. The powerful old man swung his shoulders at him in an awkward lunge and got clearance enough to reach the corridor. Then Gordon caught him and held him against the far wall. "What the hell is this?"

Jumbo glared at him with fierce hooded eyes. "You think nobody remembers about you and that woman in there? You got a wife, you know, a better wife than you deserve. And that woman's got a husband. Man who used to be your best friend. Man you grew up with. What kind of shit are you, anyway?"

"Good God, Jumbo, she just came to see if I'd take on a case for her father. He's in serious trouble."

"I know all about Roger Farrall. Why don't you take his case? You're two of a kind. You both think nothing counts but money, and it don't matter a damn how you get it." He shrugged away from Gordon and turned toward the elevators.

"Jumbo, you can't go out by yourself without—"

"I can do whatever I have to do," Jumbo said in a ferocious undertone. "I'm not staying here with you and that blond whore."

"You are one hell of a man to be talking about women, Jumbo. Who put you in the judgment business? You think you set a great example?"

"You got a mean mouth, boy," Jumbo said more quietly. "No, I never thought I was any great shakes as a husband, but I always worked at it. You act like being married is some kind of boy's game, and you can just forget it any time that Farrall woman whistles you up. I don't know why her husband puts up with it. I don't know why Ellen does either. I don't think she will this time."

"Do you plan to tell her, Jumbo?"

Jumbo looked at him with fierce scorn. "I wanted a *man* for a son," he said in a terrible voice. "For a while I thought I had one. Even thought there might be some grandbabies growing up by now."

Gordon tried to speak, but Jumbo wouldn't allow it.

"A man," he said again. "Not a fast-talking, tricky dollar-chaser who doesn't give a dribbling fart for anyone or anything on earth except himself."

"For Christ's sake, Jumbo!"

"You know what I'm saying," Jumbo said stubbornly. "I'm not quick with the words like you, but you know what I mean, all right."

Jumbo stood facing him, almost trembling. For a wild moment Gordon thought he was going to hit him.

"I'm going to get out of this place," he said slowly, tired now. "I'm going back to the hospital and wait till that doctor turns me loose. I don't want to be around you anymore."

307

"Suit yourself," Gordon said hopelessly. "How long do you think it will be?"

Jumbo shook his head. "Can't say. Week, maybe. They still got to run some tests." He moved away along the corridor, fumbled for the elevator call button. He looked back. "Hell, Gordie, I didn't mean all that about—"

"I know, Jumbo," Gordon said hastily, wanting an end to it. "Don't let it worry you. Maybe the hospital is a good idea for a while. I'll call tomorrow and see how you're getting along."

Jumbo nodded heavily. "Take care, boy."

He moved silently across the carpeted hallway of his suite and stood just inside the door looking at her. She was leaning back against the brocaded couch, her ruby suede ankle boots crossed on the low table. She seemed completely relaxed, but Gordon could sense that she was not.

"I could hear all of that, Gordie."

Gordon lifted one hand and let it drop.

"Is he going to make trouble?"

"No." He moved back to his chair. "Would it matter?"

"Yes," she said. "It would make a mess if it happened now."

"Don't worry about Jumbo. He isn't out to make trouble. He wasn't even talking about you, actually. I was the target. It was just an expression of fatherly grief at the way a son has turned out. He wasn't even thinking about you."

"He was concerned about your wife. Is that what you mean?"

"Don't play bitchy little games with me, Claudia. But yes, I guess he was worried about her. Mostly."

Claudia looked at him, gravely quiet. "You aren't much of a homebody, are you, Gordie? You seem to be about the least married man I ever knew."

"Let's drop it, shall we? It really isn't worth talking about. Ellen doesn't like living in hotels, and it seems I spend half my life in hotels in strange cities. And I work a twenty-hour day when I'm in court, and that doesn't make for much of a family life."

"Your father seems to like her just fine."

Gordon shifted restlessly. "They like a lot of the same things. She spent a lot of time with him out there in the desert. She planted a garden for him and organized an irrigation system. Made a damn showpiece out of that piece of scrub land that Jumbo loves. He thinks she is about the greatest thing that ever came into my life."

"And what do you think?"

"I think she is back in Grosse Pointe visiting her family just now, and that it is about an even-money bet that she will never want to live with me again. And now can we please, for Christ's sake, change the subject?" He was a little surprised at the depth of his anger.

"Don't roar, Gordie-dear. Be my sweet cowboy-lover. Whisper to me."

Gordon grunted. He drained his almost empty glass. He reached forward to pick up the cigarette he had abandoned and watched it promptly unroll in his hand, shedding bright flakes of tobacco over the table.

"Poor Gordie." She laughed softly. "Things are coming apart, aren't they? Neither of us have done very well in the marriage department, have we?"

"We don't even do very well in the father department."

"I'm still hoping I can do a little better. With your help."

"Why did your father send you anyway? Why didn't he come himself?"

"I was at Vail with a skiing party. Much closer to you than he was in Rincon. So he phoned and asked me to come."

"Why didn't he go to Nico for help?"

"Nico doesn't know anything about this kind of problem, Gordie. And, anyway, no judge could let himself be involved with anything like this. Nico will do what he can, of course, but it can't be much."

Gordon stopped halfway to the bar cabinet and looked back at her. "Are you sneering?"

"You know I wouldn't sneer at Nico!"

But he didn't know, he realized. In fact, he really didn't know much of anything about Claudia. Perhaps it was because he didn't want to. He wondered if Nico did. .

She was watching him closely, wide blue eyes darkly troubled as if she knew what he was thinking and hated it.

"Nico really is trying to help," she said firmly, as if she needed to convince herself. "In fact, there is something just a little inhumanly noble about him these days. I wish he would break down, spray around a few heartfelt cowboy curses and relieve the tension. His father-in-law is a crook about to go to jail, and some of that mud is bound to hit Nico sooner or later. He must hate it. But he never lets me know that it troubles him."

"He doesn't have anything to worry about." Gordon made a long drink and came back to his chair. "He never has had."

"You don't know, Gordie. Nico is more complex than you think. And

309

a lot more serious about his work." She studied him carefully, her fine eyebrows pulled into a tight flat line. "You don't know how serious he is. If he should ever have to make a choice between his wife and his work, I don't think I would stand a chance."

She might very well be right, Gordon thought. The only surprise was that she knew it.

"That isn't what I was talking about. I know how Nico feels about the law. What I meant was that Nico's future won't be affected one way or the other by your father's troubles. As far as Rincon is concerned, Nicanor Kronstadt is as near to untouchable as you can come. He is our man of probity and good conscience. We depend on him. I suppose every community has someone like Nico. We need people who seem a bit better than the common run. We need exceptional men to look up to. Nico is ours and as long as he is, nothing can ever touch him."

"Oh my," Claudia breathed quietly.

"Okay, an overstatement," Gordon said impatiently. "The hell with it. Just don't try to tell me Nico is going to be hurt when your daddy goes up for a stretch in the pen. It simply isn't so."

"You're a hard man, Gordie-love." Claudia swung both feet up and around and eased them down in Gordon's lap. "Pull the laces, please. These boots are too tight."

The boots were glove-soft, cinched with woven silk laces. Gordon stripped them off and dropped them to the floor. Her feet felt cold, and he held them both in one large hand, warming them.

"How did your father get mixed up with those hoods anyway?"

"I don't know. I never heard of any of them before."

"Why did he do it?"

"Money, of course. I always thought he had enough for any sort of reasonable life, but I suppose Nico's sort of money made him feel inferior. He wanted to compete, so he needed more money, and he started cutting corners to get it. The sad part is that money doesn't actually mean anything to Nico. But it was always very important to Daddy, and I think that is a big part of what happened to him."

"Good Christ," Gordon said in quiet disgust.

"Don't be superior, Gordie. You are just a little bit greedy yourself."

"I suppose." Gordon accepted that with no argument. "I like the idea of making the top dollar. But mostly it's just a game. After a certain point, money doesn't mean much, except that it shows I am winning cases. Don't ever get me confused with your daddy."

"No fear." Claudia finished her drink and sat back, holding the glass in both hands. She curled her toes lightly around Gordon's warming hand. "I wonder if he knows about us? I don't think so, but he might."

"So?"

"So he might have thought that if I came and asked you, you would take his case just to please me."

Gordon snorted. "Fat chance."

"Perhaps he thought I could coax you. Offer my fair white body, something like that."

Gordon looked at her evenly for a long moment. "You get very good ideas sometimes. You think this one is worth trying?"

"Well, nothing else seems to work." Claudia's eyes widened, blandly innocent. "I'd hate to think I hadn't done my very best for my father."

Gordon swung her feet quickly aside, stood and caught her when she leaned forward. He brought her up lightly against him. She came even closer and lifted her chin high.

"My very best," she said in a warm private whisper. Her arms closed hard around his neck.

He came awake suddenly and completely as he always did. The easterly bedroom windows were bright with sunlight that hurt his eyes. He licked his dry lips and tried to swallow. He stretched cautiously, trying not to disturb Claudia. She slept quietly, making soft burbling sounds, with her face pressed against his arm. Very slowly, inch by inch, he pulled it free. He stroked bright silky hair back from her forehead and kissed her softly before he rolled out of bed. She moved once, then murmured and settled deeper into sleep.

Gordon crossed the icy floor quickly, his big naked body goose-bumped with the cold. He eased the open window down to the sill, pulled his robe from the back of a chair, and went quietly out into the darkened sitting room. He piled ice in a tall glass, filled it with soda from an open bottle, and drained it in one long pull. He poured more water and drank again. Then he went quickly through into Jumbo's bathroom.

He ran a basin of cold water and looked at himself in the too-bright mirror. You are a piss-poor specimen this morning, friend, he told himself. A red-eyed crack-lipped rummy. You got yourself drunk, didn't you? Wallowing cross-eyed drunk like a drill sergeant on an overnight pass. Whiskey, oh whiskey, I know you of old. Enjoy the hangover, pally, you earned it.

He stuck his head under the cold water for as long as he could and came up shuddering. He scrubbed vigorously with a towel until he could feel his skin begin to tingle. He brushed his hair roughly with the damp towel and went more steadily back to the sitting room.

311

He swept the long heavy draperies back from the tall windows, and then, with the light bouncing off the fresh fall of snow on the Denver rooftops, he could see well enough to find his limp sack of tobacco on a side table. He rolled his first cigarette of the day with unusual care, lit it, and drew the smoke deep into his lungs and held it there, warm and solid, until he felt slightly dizzy. Then he let it out in a long coiling plume that danced in the morning light. He laughed at himself.

It was always like that after the tension of a trial had suddenly eased. Gordon always wound himself to a peak of total concentration and the letdown was almost a physical shock. Liquor helped. And women. And wild uninhibited talk with good friends.

But last night was something rare even for you, wasn't it? You hit that Jack Daniels bottle a very severe blow. Those Jack Daniels bottles, he thought, correcting himself when he saw the second one standing in the light with an inch missing from the neck. Whatever happened to dinner? He could remember eating some of the good smoked salmon. But when the waiter came back to collect his rollaway table, the big T-bone went with it almost undamaged. Claudia had stayed pretty much with a bottle of wine and an enormous salad, so perhaps she wouldn't be suffering this morning. Good for her. But he needed food and right-damn now.

He made himself a light therapeutic bourbon and water and took it with him to the chair closest to the telephone. He sipped cautiously, put the glass down, made another skimpy cigarette and smoked it completely. One more sip and he would be ready to talk to someone.

Anyone. Let's hear some wild singing laments for dead lovers, and I'll come in on the chorus with you, Chloe. Tell me sad tales of overly ambitious kings and their shamed and loving daughters. Speak to me of friendship and how it is when friends don't mean as much to you as that monster in your crotch poking up like a long-distance flashlight to see you on your way to— And let that be enough. Wallow tomorrow. Let's get some food.

He reached for the phone and jerked away as if he had been stung when it rang under his hand. Nerves like a butterfly. He shrugged at himself. He took one more medicinal sip and then picked up the phone.

"I won't apologize. I knew you'd be awake by this time of day."

David Simon calling him from Rincon, Gordon thought sourly. Brisk, quick, and, as always, a little too eager. "I'm awake. Barely."

"Lots of news. Which will you have first? Good, bad? Sad or funny?"

"However it comes."

He listened with the forepart of his mind, storing away information to think about later, as he might listen to a witness on the stand while he was planning another step in his trial strategy. The facts would be there when he wanted them.

"Okay," he said flatly when Simon wound down his lengthy recital.

"You got all that, boss?"

"You want me to repeat it back to you?" Gordon said, ominously quiet.

"Sorry. Anything for me to do?"

"Nothing. I'll leave here sometime today. See you tomorrow. Let's make it an early day."

He hung up then, tapped the phone bar for the operator, got room service, and ordered an enormous breakfast. "A pot of coffee and a quart of orange juice right away, on the double. Breakfast half an hour later."

No problem. Gordon allowed himself one more thin cigarette and finished his watery drink in tiny sips, making it last until the coffee arrived. He drank half the orange juice in a thirsty swig, poured a scalding cup of coffee, and held it as he walked to the windows and looked down at the snow-shiny streets of Denver.

It was a much brighter day than it had been before David had called with the morning's news. Gordon was off the hook now. No need to devil himself with vague guilts about Claudia's father. Not that he would have, he assured himself, but this way it was easier for all of them.

He poured coffee in the other cup and took it with him into the bedroom. Claudia seemed to be sleeping soundly, but now she was on Gordon's side of the bed, as if she had shifted to find him. Gordon sat on the floor, crossed his legs, and held the cup high. He blew fragrant steam across her face, making her hair riffle. Her breathing rhythm changed, but she kept her eyes closed until she had given herself time to consider the idea of a new day.

"What a lovely morning smell." She smiled lazily and brushed hair up and away with a long bare arm. "I could hear you on the phone. How busy you are, Gordie."

"It was David." Gordon held the cup so she could sip from it without moving. "Things are happening fast, he says. It seems I couldn't take your daddy's case now even if I wanted to. It's a little complicated, but you'll see what I mean when I tell you—"

Claudia pushed the cup aside impatiently. "Explain later, Gordie. Come up here now." She held the blankets back and then Gordon could smell the warm loving-animal's perfume of her in the cool bright room.

He explained later.

Two days later he was using almost the same words to explain to

Jonathan Pike. The windowless Death Row block was overly warm and steamy, and Gordon was sweating lightly in his winter clothes.

Pike, comfortable in T-shirt and denims, listened with a quizzical half-smile, head slightly cocked, eyes hooded with his usual hint of sardonic suspicion.

He seemed much the same, Gordon thought, but he was beginning to show the marks of his years of confinement, the dry waxy skin, the slower movements, the enforced calmness of manner. He had lost weight. There were dark permanent shadows under his eyes, eyes that were now lusterless and enduring, only occasionally brightened by a sharp amusement. As they were now.

"Are you telling me the Great Man outsmarted himself?"

"You could say it that way." Gordon shrugged amiably. "So go ahead and laugh. Don't mind me."

Pike waggled his head, pretending amazement. He let out a long audible breath. "Hard to believe."

"It took me a while to take it in, too. Have you got it all straight now?"

"Let's go through it slowly once more."

Gordon rocked back in his flimsy folding chair and crossed his arms. "What started it all is that your book took off a little earlier than I expected. I knew we were going to make some money with it, but I didn't expect it so fast. But apparently that's the way things happen with books. If it's going anywhere, it zooms like a rocket, and usually it all happens before publication day."

"Exactly what has happened?"

"First we collected the advance when we signed the contract. Twenty-five-thousand dollars against a fifteen-percent royalty. Then last week the Book-of-the-Month Club decided to take it for the January selection. I'm not exactly sure what that will come to, about seventy thousand, I think. We split it evenly with the publisher. So call it thirty-five thousand more. A total of sixty thousand so far. Are you with me?"

Pike nodded.

"You remember how our agreement goes?"

"You take ninety percent of the first hundred thousand and we share fifty-fifty on anything over that."

"And I'll bet you never expected to see any profit for yourself out of it, did you?"

"I was just hoping to make enough to pay my own way, maybe clear enough to buy some books I'd like to have."

"You can buy yourself a library if you want one. A few days ago

Bantam Books offered two hundred and fifty thousand dollars for the reprint rights. We have to split that evenly with the publisher, too, so we net a hundred and twenty-five. That means the book as of today has already earned over one hundred and eighty thousand dollars. I take ninety out of the first hundred, and forty out of the next eighty. That's about one hundred and thirty thousand to me. Which leaves a little over fifty thousand for you. All that before a single book has been sold anywhere. Are you beginning to feel rich?"

"The word is numb. I can't take it in that fast."

"The publisher is willing to bet the book will sell at least one hundred thousand hard-cover copies. I'll let you figure out for yourself what that means in hard cash."

Pike whistled softly. "We've done damn well, haven't we?"

Gordon raised one eyebrow and smiled at him. "And you are now beginning to wonder just what in hell I did to deserve the big cut. Aren't you, Brother Jonathan?"

Pike thought about it. "Maybe. But I don't think so, Gordon. I'm not stupid. I know what you've done for me. And I know you collect bigger fees from other clients. No, I think I'm happy with our deal."

"Good. Because now you can start laughing. You are going to see me earn that fee. There really ain't going to be a lot of profit by the time I'm finished."

"I didn't quite follow what you said about that. I gather the Supreme Court is going to take another look at my petition and decide I should furnish my own lawyer. Is that it?"

"No, you're jumping too fast. The Supreme Court doesn't require any appellant to spend his last dollar on his own defense. The Court realizes that every man has other obligations that have to take precedence. The Court has already accepted you as a pauper. They won't change the rules on you now."

"So what are we worrying about?"

"Think about it for a minute. Look at that big fat fee you are paying me. One hundred and thirty thousand dollars, and that's only the beginning. What did you buy with it?"

Pike studied him thoughtfully.

"Or to put it another way," Gordon went on, "what did I do to earn that fee? I could explain that most of it goes to pay for work done over the past seven or eight years. But we have been building you up as the brilliant young self-made lawyer who has been handling his own case from his prison cell. So I better not push that one too hard or people might begin wondering about you. Anyway, it is right now, today, that we have to think about. The Supreme Court has given you a full hearing. They will appoint a free lawyer, if you ask, but what about that lawyer you just paid a hundred and thirty thousand dollars? Why isn't he appearing for you?"

"Why isn't he?" Pike asked soberly, his pale translucent eyes glittering.

"So you see." Gordon spread his hands wide. "It's a question I couldn't answer. Except to say that I am appearing for you. Which is what I have to say. And it's going to be a hell of a lot of work getting ready, I can tell you that, you rich young wastrel. Teach you to throw your money around, hiring the most expensive lawyer in the country."

Pike chuckled then. He cut it off short and forced himself to speak in a brisk, businesslike voice. "I'm glad you'll appear for me, Gordon. For some reason, I didn't think you could. I always thought Supreme Court lawyers were a different kind."

"Well, there are lawyers who specialize in the big federal cases, but the Supreme Court will admit any lawyer in good standing. All I have to do is pay a twenty-five-dollar fee and ask to be admitted *pro hac vice*—for this time only. They'll let me appear, all right. They'll even give me an elegant parchment certificate suitable for framing."

"Good," Pike said almost absently. Then he apologized quickly. "It's just that too many things are coming in at me all at once. I can't take them in so fast. The good news about the book. And then the Supreme Court. I could hardly believe it when your office sent me the word. Why do you think they granted the petition?"

Gordon shook his head. "You'll never know. The Supreme Court doesn't say, and there has never in history been a leak about their decisions. Those nine gentlemen sit in a room all by themselves without even a clerk or stenographer. They do their own work, and they keep their mouths shut afterward. But if you want to guess, you could figure that some one Justice read that good brief we submitted and saw a Constitutional question that needed an answer. If you've been reading their recent decisions, you can see a definite pattern developing. There is such a thing as a current of legal history, and this time it's on our side."

"You hope," Pike said a bit skeptically.

"I see it clearly. That's why I think we are close to a final decision now. I know I said the same thing when we went to Federal Appeals a couple of years ago. I was wrong then, but I'm right this time. Even if I hadn't been pushed back into the case, I'd want to come back and see it through to the end. It's just possible we may make legal history."

"Why do you say that?"

"Just part of the developing pattern I mentioned before. The Court is giving very serious thought to the rights of an individual charged with a crime. What it amounts to in essence is that the Court thinks it is time that the cops began doing their own investigation and stopped trying to beat confessions out of the nearest suspect. Have you read the decision in *Miranda v. Arizona*?"

"I read it. I'm not sure what it means."

"You're not supposed to know. No one is. *Miranda* was one of those five-to-four decisions, and there is still a lot of opposition in the Court. So Chief Justice Warren wrote it in very ambiguous language to soften the blow. I'm certain that he meant it as a general guideline for pretrial procedure rather than a set of hard and fast rules. Even so, *Miranda* did clear the air. The earlier decision in *Escobedo* was a shock. Justice Goldberg made it too definite, too much a formal charge on the lower courts. The Supreme Court stepped back a little with *Miranda*, but the meaning is the same, and for our purposes the basic tone is even better. Chief Justice Warren called confessions or any information taken from interrogation the fruit of the poisoned tree. So we will go to them and show them the poisoned fruit used in your trial and ask them to do something about it. And they will."

"You sound awfully damned confident."

Gordon laughed. "Confidence is my professional manner, Jon. Even when I don't feel it. But I feel it this time. I'm confident. Those nine gentlemen are going to decide in our favor. I'm sure of that."

The sureness never left him. He paid his taxi, got out, and slowly turned to look up at the white marble block of the Supreme Court building glowing against a sleety winter sky. He checked to make sure it was still with him, as a man will search himself for the key to his house before he approaches the door. No fumbling, no doubts. He had it.

But he went warily up the marble steps that were slippery with cold February rain. Cold lofty marble halls. Bronze doors to shield the nine honorable gentlemen of the Court. An attendant to guide the visiting attorney to a seat in the first row behind the railing. Attorneys to the right of him, attorneys to the left of him, silent and brooding. Struck with the majesty of the place and the moment. And why shouldn't they be? This was not merely the big leagues, but the World Series, the Test Match, the World Cup.

As always in any courtroom Gordon could feel his pulse rising in preparation for challenge. And he smiled easily for himself. This was what he did. Sometimes he said he did it for a living. And sometimes he admitted that it was the meaning of his life. He sat straight in the hard chair and willed his body to relax. Just another day in another courtroom.

Except that it wasn't. Of the twelve million cases tried each year in the country's courts, only some four hundred thousand are appealed. Of that number less than four thousand reach the Supreme Court. And the court gives less than two hundred a full hearing. The odds of getting here are appalling. And how many of those two hundred cases does the Court decide in favor of the appellant, Gordon asked himself. He refused to remember the answer.

The Court Crier rose with no warning, smacked his gavel twice, and stilled the high-ceilinged room. Gordon stood and watched the nine Justices file in through the long red draperies behind the bench and wait in front of their chairs as the crier droned the traditional opening.

"The honorable, the Chief Justice and the Associate Justices of the Supreme Court of the United States of America. Oyez. Oyez. Oyez. All persons having business before the honorable, the Supreme Court of the United States of America, are admonished to draw near and give their attention, for the Court is now sitting. God save the United States of America and this honorable Court."

The nine Justices seated themselves, the Chief Justice in the tall center chair, the Associates to his right and left according to seniority, the most recently appointed being on the wings. The Chief Justice turned open his leather folder, leaned forward, and with no further preliminaries, looked up and said, "Number 156, Jonathan Pike, petitioner, *versus* J. G. Cochran, director, Division of Corrections."

Without rising, the Clerk of the Court said promptly, "Counsels are present." Gordon got up, walked sideways to the narrow aisle and was led forward to a table at the left of the bench. He turned, waited, then nodded as a brisk young man came through the gate. Peter Pelletier, Assistant Attorney General in charge of criminal appeals, was surprisingly young for his job and almost offensively sure of himself. Gordon had met him yesterday morning when they had both been admitted to the Supreme Court bar in a brief ceremony at the beginning of the day's session. He nodded again as he saw David Burrell come striding in behind Pelletier. Burrell returned his nod silently and turned away toward his own table.

Well, why shouldn't he be here, Gordon thought. Why are you surprised? You know Burrell volunteered to prepare the answering brief filed by the state, and he still has that continuing and all-but-unexplainable determination to see Jonathan Pike convicted once and for all. So he probably had himself appointed a special assistant to the Attorney

General just to make sure the Supreme Court hearing was contested with all-out vigor. Then Gordon put such thoughts out of his mind.

"Mr. Guthrie." The Chief Justice looked toward him.

He went quickly, a little too quickly, toward the tall rostrum set between the two tables. His hands wanted to tremble with excitement and he gripped them hard on the tilted edge of the rostrum and forced himself to take in a slow breath. He stood there empty-handed—no briefcase today, no documents, no slips of paper with key words to jog his memory. He was prepared to discuss any phase of Jonathan Pike's case; and he knew that the Supreme Court wanted to hear oral argument. All the Justices had read the opposing briefs. They knew all the facts. But they had questions and now was the time for asking them.

Each side would be allowed an hour for presentation, but answers to questions from the bench might consume much of that time. Gordon was anticipating this. He was ready to talk for the entire hour, but he packed the meat of his statement into the first few minutes. And it was meat. You did not try dramatics here.

He began with a short review of the disputed facts in Pike's case. Of course he knew that these honorable gentlemen had read the briefs, but even so, he felt better when he was completely sure they were all thinking about the same problem at the same time.

After a few minutes Gordon was well in his stride. His voice was steady and firm, controlled but clearly audible. He moved a step back from the rostrum and let his arms hang easily, standing slightly hunched in his usual courtroom posture. The Chief Justice seemed to be watching him with special interest, he thought, that big white-maned head tracking him as he shifted. Most of the Associate Justices were equally intent, except for a pair toward the left side who were leaning in toward each other, heads lowered. One was stabbing a pencil at a pad in front of him, talking quickly and quietly.

Not now, gents, Gordon wanted to shout. Forget the golf game or the fishing or whatever the hell it is. Let's have a little close attention here. Without realizing it, he raised his heavy voice.

"Jonathan Pike did have a lawyer during that grueling and exhausting seventy-hour period of interrogation," he said. "We admit that. But that lawyer arrived almost twenty-four hours after Jonathan Pike's arrest. His first consultation with his client lasted for less than ten minutes. At no time did he advise Pike of his right to refuse to answer questions, nor was he ever present during any of the interrogation. I submit that, in such circumstances, Jonathan Pike might have been better off with no lawyer at all."

Gordon paused. He knew he had to budget his time, but he also knew that a few minutes could be wisely spent to put the clear emphasis exactly where he wanted it.

"Jonathan Pike knew nothing of the law," he went on. "He knew nothing of his rights. Knowing that he had been furnished a lawyer by his employer, he assumed that he was receiving every possible legal protection. And he therefore assumed that the coercive and illegal conduct of the county police was the normal and legally sanctioned procedure for questioning a suspect in a murder case. But even so, he protested. Alone, he withstood that savage, incessant questioning for seventy long hours. Until finally his strength was exhausted and the relentless interrogators forced a statement from him. That statement came from a mind weary and distraught after hours of questioning for the sole purpose of convicting him. And his lawyer, his silent, absent lawyer, offered him no support, no advice until after that statement had been obtained."

Gordon moved up to the rostrum again and leaned over it. "I suggest to this honorable court," he said sharply in a tone that demanded attention, "that Jonathan Pike was not represented by legal counsel during the critical period of his interrogation." He straightened then and looked along the row of intent faces above the bench. There it is, gentlemen, he said to himself. That's the nub of the argument. Any questions?

The first came briskly, almost irritably, from one of the conversational Justices on the left wing who had been talking before. He kept stabbing his pencil at his pad and spoke without looking at Gordon.

"Mr. Guthrie, are you asking this court to regulate the *quality* of a lawyer's assistance to his client?" His thin hard voice seemed to express shock at the thought.

Gordon fought hard to keep his face straight. "No, Mr. Justice," he said soberly. "I don't think we can safely go much further than the American Bar Association regulations governing an attorney's conduct. It was not quality I was stressing here, sir. I was limiting myself entirely to the question of that lawyer's physical presence."

He took a moment then, hoping for other questions that would allow him to expand on that idea, but none of the other Justices took the opportunity. Possibly, he thought with a wild surge of hope, because they saw his point and agreed with him.

Try another approach.

"In its decision in *Escobedo v. Illinois*, this Court questioned the value of a lawyer who is not allowed to be present during interrogation. I would suggest that—"

320

"One moment, Mr. Guthrie." A tall stooped Justice two seats down from the Chief Justice straightened quickly. "Are you incorporating in your argument the Sixth Amendment guarantee of counsel?"

Gordon drew a silent breath of relief. That's better, he thought. Let's get a little debate going here, gentlemen. "No, Mr. Justice," he said promptly. He looked along the bench and briefly poked a tongue into his cheek. "But you tempt me, sir. The decision in *Miranda* tells me to leave the Sixth Amendment out of this argument. But if you are inviting me—"

"No, no," the Associate Justice said hastily, and then joined in the general murmur of quiet laughter.

Gordon tried again to tempt the Justices into an extended discussion of the theme of the present-but-nonfunctioning lawyer, but none of them rose to his bait. He went on to touch the other bases, not sure just which approach would be most effective with the members of the Court.

He quoted from the Court's decision in *Irvin v. Dowd* to show how closely the prejudicial quality of pretrial publicity in Pike's case paralleled the facts in that classic case. He used *Rideau v. Louisiana* to emphasize the meaning of unfair and distorted television reports on the final outcome of Pike's trial. He suggested that the Court's decision in *Lynumm v. Illinois* gave adequate reason to throw out all the statements forced from Pike by relentless police interrogation.

The white light on the top of the rostrum came on as he was speaking of *Brown v. Mississippi*, and he wound up that portion of his presentation with another brief sentence. Only five minutes more remaining of his allotted hour. Back once again to the central theme. Time for one more try.

"The core of my argument is that a lawyer who is available but not physically present is no lawyer at all. The mere existence of legal counsel in some other place does not meet the requirements of legal representation. Only legal counsel actually on hand during the critical moment of interrogation can do that. If Jonathan Pike's first lawyer had been present during any part of that interminable seventy-hour questioning period, it might be said that we would have no proper argument to present to this Court. But if a competent lawyer had been present during that interrogation, we may be very sure that it would not have lasted seventy hours, nor would its outcome have been the same."

The Court was aware that time was running out for Gordon, but none of the Justices cared to break in when it was obvious that he had not yet finished.

Gordon stood straight and stern, head up, his voice somber.

"Jonathan Pike was not given a fair trial. His case was irreparably damaged during pretrial interrogation. His rights were ignored or flagrantly violated. His attorney did not furnish the protection and advice to which Jonathan Pike was entitled.

"Further, it is important to emphasize that Jonathan Pike has never received a fair hearing in any of the lower appellate courts. No consideration has ever been given to the merits of his allegations of unjust, even illegal, conduct on the part of the police investigators. The prosecuting attorney of Rincon County has pursued Jonathan Pike through the appellate courts with unusual vigor and tenacity. His contention has been that Pike's allegations merited no answer. And court after court has seized upon the prosecuting attorney's assertion as the easiest way out of a difficult situation. No court has yet honestly faced the unpalatable facts of this tragic miscarriage of justice. The undeniable merits of Pike's case have never been considered seriously. So, finally, Jonathan Pike has brought his case, and his life itself, to this Court, because this Court alone is empowered to correct the errors and abuses of the past."

The red light flickered. His time was up. Gordon bowed to the Chief Justice, stepped away and returned to his chair.

Then he could hear the roaring surf-beat of excitement in his head. For the moment it was almost deafening. He watched Pelletier approach the rostrum, but he heard no single word of what he said. Pelletier was visibly nervous. And now that his own ordeal was over, Gordon could spare a shred of sympathy for his opponent. He locked his hands together below the surface of the table, feeling the tremor in his fingers. After his long experience in trial courts, he hadn't expected a response like that, but perhaps it was fitting. Perhaps every lawyer appearing before the Supreme Court should come away with a heightened sensitivity.

An earlier Chief Justice had once tried to define the special meaning and purpose of the Supreme Court. The words seemed to echo with a special solemnity in Gordon's head today. "No litigant is entitled to more than two chances, namely to the original trial and to a review, and the intermediate courts of review are provided for that purpose. When a case goes beyond that, it is not primarily to preserve the rights of the litigant. The Supreme Court's function is for the purpose of expounding and stabilizing principles of law for the benefit of the people of the country, passing upon Constitutional questions and other important questions of law for the public benefit." William Howard Taft. Probably all of his successors would have put it much the same way.

Today Jonathan Pike was the appellant in the courtroom, and the Supreme Court was considering only the narrow details of his specific case. But the Court had agreed to hear him only because his problem raised a question of broad national importance. If Jonathan Pike were to benefit ultimately from the Court's decision, he would benefit no more than any other citizen of the country, though Pike would be more sharply aware of the meaning of the Court's action.

Gordon came alert to his surroundings when one of the Associate Justices interrupted Pelletier with a brusque, disapproving shake of his head.

"You have referred to the trial record three times. Why do you bother with that?"

"Very well, Mr. Justice. I won't press it."

"I want you to press it. The trial record shows this court that Mr. Pike's attorney failed to challenge the validity of his unsigned statement. Yet you object to the trial record being admitted as an exhibit in this Court. Why is that? Do you feel it is information that should be withheld from this Court?"

"Certainly not, sir." Pelletier flushed. "We felt, Mr. Justice," he said in a shaken voice, "that the trial record would be irrelevant to any issue being determined in this Court."

"Did you?" The Associate Justice sat back with an air suggesting polite disbelief. "Did you indeed. Very well. Please go on, Mr. Pelletier."

Gordon exulted silently. Got it! he shouted in his mind. One of them is hooked and right now I'm willing to bet they all are. If this was an ordinary trial court, I'd be ready to set up champagne for the house.

And there it is, he thought more soberly. That's what the Supreme Court is all about, and why most attorneys are scared to death to come here. In this country we don't have the tradition of oral argument that is common in British courts. We rely too much on written briefs. But a brief can't talk; it can't give immediate answers to exploratory questions. The Justices of the Supreme Court want to hear those answers. The measured hour allowed by the Court is for oral argument, not for expanding the brief or delivering set speeches.

Being caught out with that specious answer about the trial record, Pelletier was rattled and off stride. In the course of his allotted hour he never did quite regain his composure.

Gordon stopped briefly in the huge vaulted hallway outside the courtroom to shake hands formally with Pelletier and David Burrell. He even waggled his head in sympathy when the youthful Attorney General spoke in wondering complaint about the cavalier way the Court had treated him.

"I didn't expect anything like that, did you, Mr. Guthrie? It wasn't like any courtroom I've ever been in. The Justices seemed to be having a fine time in there, talking to one another and joking while you're trying to make an argument. It's hard to adjust to such—such informality."

David Burrell pushed roughly between them. "Let's get on, Peter. We've got things to do."

Gordon stepped aside politely, not smiling. David knows, he thought. David sensed the attitude of the bench when Pelletier flubbed that question about the trial record.

"It's all so different from our State Supreme Court," Pelletier went on, talking too much now that the tension of the courtroom was behind him. "Here they don't even care about precedents or existing law. They don't ask you about cases the way our judges do. They just kept hitting me with those hypothetical questions, trying to carry every idea to its extreme. What kind of law is that? I've been preparing this case for months, but some of those questions took me by complete surprise."

Gordon winked solemnly at Burrell. "What did you think of it, David?"

"Quite a show," David said, and there was no humor in his voice. "Hotshot Gordie Guthrie tells them a lawyer ain't a lawyer unless you can actually see him in the flesh. The idea is so crazy the Justices all want to play with it. But it doesn't mean a thing. Peter falls on his face when one of the Justices throws him a tight curve. And that doesn't mean anything either. Facts are what they'll decide on. And the facts are all in the briefs. The facts say that Jonathan Pike was convicted in a fair trial, and by God, after eight years of fiddling it's high time we sent him to the chair and got it over with. You listen to me, Gordon—"

He moved closer, tanned muscular face tight with restraint. He tapped Gordon's chest with a finger like an iron rod. "I was there during that interrogation. I talked to that murdering son of a bitch myself. I heard him. You didn't. I *know.* And you don't. He's guilty. Write that down on your bleeding heart. He killed that girl. He confessed—he as good as confessed. He came damn close to admitting the whole thing. He did it, Gordon. Just remember that when you're parading your smart-ass tricks and trying to stop the course of justice. You're defending a guilty man. A murderer."

He took in a quick ragged breath. "Now, goddammit, Peter, let's get the hell *out* of here." He took his colleague by the arm, and Gordon stood back to let them go.

Trust Little David to find the vulnerable gap in the armor and slip the knife in deep. A born killer, David was. And he might have the right idea

324

about the Court's response, Gordon realized. Maybe the Justices had been amusing themselves on a dull Court day. But he did not believe it. The sureness was still with him. And now it was bolstered by the memory of that Associate Justice sinking back in his chair and watching Peter Pelletier with a dubious eye.

They'd won. He knew it. But it was going to be hell to wait through the long months until the Court announced its decision.

Gordon got Pike's letter when he was on his way to dinner. He put it away to read later and did not notice it again until he was undressing for bed. He gave it priority over the stack of papers he had kept for his night-time reading.

"DEAR GORDON—

"Caught you on a late-nite talk show yesterday and I am writing to thank you for the confidence, sympathy, kind words, all that. But I wish to hell you would stop calling me 'cool, calm, unperturbed.' What am I supposed to be? Is there some special virtue in wailing? Not my style. Not yours either, I suspect. You didn't do much wailing when your TV host tried to equate you with a hired gunman brought in to shoot down the innocent nesters, did you?"

Gordon chuckled. No, he had not. He had responded to the harsh metallic voice of the talk-show man with a purposefully slow drawling tone, patiently amiable, a son of the Old West, hard to arouse but hell on wheels once his dander was up. He was finding the pose increasingly useful these days.

"I would like to suggest that you are looking at only one side of the picture, sir," he had said with a dignified reserve. "I do move around the country quite a lot in answer to calls for my services. From your question, I gather you find that unhealthy for the course of justice?"

He had allowed the talker to nod and open his mouth and then used his enormous voice to overwhelm him in a sort of absentminded eagerness. "Let's draw another picture for your audience here in the studio and see if they agree with you. I'll give you the case of our former Chief Justice of the Supreme Court, Earl Warren. In his early days, Mr. Chief Justice Warren was, for a period of twenty years, a county attorney, which means that he was the legal officer responsible for prosecuting crimes committed in his county. Twenty years, think of that. A full lifetime career for many people. The average lawyer in Mr. Prosecutor Warren's county might try one or two criminal cases a year.

Mr. Prosecutor Warren was practicing criminal law every day of those twenty years.

"I will now invite you, sir, and every member of the audience, to tell me what you would do if you found yourself unjustly accused of a crime in Mr. Prosecutor Warren's county? Would you willingly trust yourself to a local attorney with little or no training in criminal courts? Or would you look elsewhere to find an attorney who also specialized in criminal cases and was prepared to meet this endlessly experienced prosecutor on his own ground with some reasonable chance of success? I leave it to you."

The audience response had been gratifying, Gordon remembered. A gale of applause had told the TV host to lay off. And he had. He had even tried to change sides.

"Would you say then, Mr. Guthrie, that the highly successful defense attorneys such as yourself and Mr. Bailey and Mr. Foreman and the others, are a useful, even necessary counterweight to the exceptional training and experience of professional prosecutors?"

Gordon was tempted to poke at the overly elaborate language but managed to hold himself in. "Couldn't have put it better myself, sir," he said with his heartiest good humor.

"The plug for the book was very effective, I thought," Jonathan Pike wrote. "Our publisher is very grateful for your continuing support. I have seen no reason to tell him why you want to help."

Bitter, Brother Jonathan? Probably it was about time for that response. The gratitude of clients diminishes rapidly as they consider the bill.

"We are still Number Two on the New York *Times* Best-Seller List. Total copies to date for *Shadow of Death*: 140,000. I am told another printing is scheduled if sales hold as they have been.

"I don't even try figuring what that means in terms of money to spend. I never would have thought that anything could make this place more intolerable than it is, but I was wrong. A poor man in prison can manage a resigned tranquillity. A rich man gets full of twitches, thinking of the things he could have if he were free. No tranquillity for him."

Not bitter then, Gordon realized. And not grumbling. He was beginning to admire Jonathan Pike, though he was not sure that his feeling was justified.

"I have been trying to work, but it comes slowly these days. I have been putting together a collection of the best of the short Yucca pieces and I've added a new one called "Escape from Yucca," which will also be the title of the book. The publisher says he plans to bring it out when sales of *Shadow of Death* begin tapering off.

"David Simon wrote me a detailed report about the Supreme Court hearing. Your basic argument and the answering brief from the state (a poor piece of work, wasn't it?) should give the justices a lot to think about. David Simon was so optimistic, almost euphoric, that I keep looking around this cell and wondering how it is I'm still here.

"What I am trying to say is that my days now are largely spent in trying to prepare myself for a life in the outside world. The prospect is slightly terrifying. I have been away for so long and so conclusively. I have had only one window for looking out at the world from Yucca. It's small and I don't know how good the view is, but I am genuinely grateful for television. Because of it my eight years have not been totally isolated. I have heard and *seen* most of the happenings that other people have experienced in normal day-to-day living. The emotional response is second-hand (how could it be anything else?), but you'll hear no more snide cracks about TV from me. I am beginning to think it may be the only genuine marvel of our time. I'll certainly put its value a million light-years above that cock-simple competition with the Russians to see who could put a man on the moon.

"With TV I watched the war in Vietnam grow from a minor exercise to a major effort, and then begin to dwindle. It looks like it will be over soon, along with the American dream.

"I saw the blacks explode from their ghettos and shake up the lily-white world. I saw the pot-happy hippies bring the Third Consciousness to the point of suicidal silliness.

"But I wasn't actually a part of any of these experiences. I watched them all through the wrong end of the telescope. So I can't feel identified with any of the highly charged movements of the recent past. And now I am beginning to wonder if I will want to be involved after I leave here. I believe I can live as a reasonably useful citizen, but the sense of identity and involvement that is needed for participation in great events has probably been withering since the day they locked me in here. I can see now that I am not quite the person I thought I was. A voyage of self-discovery will be the first item of business when I leave here.

"Now I can hear the rattling of pans in the corridor that means another breakfast is on the way. It's time for me to get out of this place, Gordie. I'm ready and eager. Anyway I'm too rich and pretty to waste any more time here. I want to share the wealth with some of those willing, love-minded girls I keep hearing about, before they change their minds about love being the answer to everything."

* * *

327

Gordon laughed silently. He put the letter back in its prison envelope and bounced it in his hand, staring up at the shadowed ceiling. Because of what he had been through, but even more because of what he had not been allowed to experience, Jonathan Pike would know himself to be different—and vulnerable because of that difference. Now it was possible for him to speculate about the meaning of freedom. He was scared. Naturally. What's so strange about that?

But it was a long time before Gordon slept, and when he did, he was restless.

Jonathan Pike rolled heavily out of the bunk. The movement forced a thin whisper of air from his dry throat. He braced a bare foot against the cement floor and leaned to the right, stripping a worn towel from its rack. Without getting up, he soaked the towel under the cold tap and scrubbed it roughly over his face. Soft four-week-long hair bent pliantly under the towel and sprang up again, but the three-day stubble on his chin clutched at the soft old fabric and plucked away tiny flecks of lint that dotted his face like a sporadic snowfall.

He watched with a drowsy lack of interest as they rolled the mesh screen in place across the front of his cell and latched it firmly. The folding chair came skidding along the floor, and Gordon Guthrie followed closely behind.

Pike got up slowly and stared out at him, morosely, silently. A big healthy, virile, exuberant bastard, giving off waves of fresh warm desert air. A living advertisement for the Good Life. Wide warm winner's smile. Fuck you, Mr. Guthrie. Pike covered his eyes with the cool damp towel and tried to come alert.

"What the hell has happened to you?" Gordon unbuttoned his lightweight jacket and sat on the forward edge of the chair, leaning closer toward Pike's door. "Are you sick?"

Pike shook his head. He braced his arms on his knees, towel dangling to the floor. "You didn't give me any warning," he said in a slow, sleep-thickened voice.

"My fault," Gordon said readily. "I left in a hurry. I did try to get the prison on the phone from my car, but there's something wrong with the pickup down here. It kept sliding off before I could make contact. But why are you looking so drag-ass? You just get out of bed?"

Pike moved one hand in a vague circle. "Haven't been sleeping well lately. My schedule is all screwed up. Too many things to think about." He drew in a long cautious breath and looked directly at Gordon for the first time. "So why are you here? What's the great rush? Got some bad news for me, have you? How bad did we lose this time?"

Laughter exploded from Gordon. The joyous sound flooded Pike's cell and brought him erect, eyes glittering. "Don't ever go into the fortune-telling business, Brother Jonathan. You'd lose your shirt."

"We won?"

"All the way. The Supreme Court has ordered a full hearing in the Federal District Court."

Pike sat heavily on the edge of the bunk. His hands twisted the worn towel, tightening slowly until it quivered with tension. A single drop of water was squeezed out of the damp cloth and fell with an audible sound on the floor. Pike was trying to smile. His mouth pulled back against his teeth. His eyes were closed. Tears were streaming steadily down his face.

Gordon turned away, making it seem a casual movement to let him cross his legs and sit more comfortably. He looked off toward the far end of the cellblock.

"It was a seven-to-two decision," he said quietly, holding his voice to a soothing rumble, all in the same uninflected tone. "But that doesn't mean two of the Justices were against us. All I've got is the bulletin from the UPI wire and it didn't give any details, but the word is that the two dissenting Justices didn't even want to remand your case for a hearing. They were ready to settle it themselves, right then and there."

Pike made a quick, strangled sound. He brought the towel up and scrubbed his face hard.

"In a way," Gordon went on easily, "I think we can thank David Burrell for a part of the Supreme Court response. I don't believe they would have been so forceful about it if they hadn't known that David has been blocking every try we made to get the lower courts to consider the merits of the case. Burrell never bothered to deny our charges. He just concentrated his whole effort on avoiding any court test. So by the time we got to the Supreme Court, it was obvious that we had never had a fair hearing in any of the lower courts. In the long run, that hurt Burrell. I think it may have been the decisive factor."

Pike pulled in a long shuddering breath. "So," he said, fighting for control. "So what happens now?"

"Everything happens now." Gordon spread his arms in a huge expansive gesture. "Call it a new ball game, Jon-boy. And best of all, a new referee. The order will come down to the Federal District Court in El Monte sometime this week. It won't be a request or an advisory opinion; it will be a peremptory order. The District Court will schedule a *habeas corpus* hearing on the first open date. There are six or seven weeks left of the current term, so we can expect action sometime during that period."

"What does the hearing mean—" Pike's throat closed suddenly and he tried to cough it free.

"It will be a limited hearing, if that's what you're asking. It won't go into details about the death of Angela Morales or any of the questions of guilt or innocence. The hearing will be restricted to one subject only: Did the sheriff's investigators behave illegally when they forced that statement out of you during a seventy-hour questioning period? The court will hear witnesses and review the evidence, but only toward that one question. Both sides will be represented." Gordon paused, waited for Pike to look up again, then flashed his widest grin.

"Would you like to take a little trip, Jon? Drive up to El Monte and take a look at the big city? Get a little sun? Buy yourself some new clothes and a civilized haircut?"

Pike froze. His thin face tightened. Pale eyes shone with naked, raw desire.

Gordon nodded forcefully. "You'll have to be a witness, you know. And you could hardly expect the court to come down here. So you'll have to come to the court."

Pike, he realized, could not speak, so he went on quickly with an enthusiastic flood of words, feeling slightly foolish, but knowing it was easier for Pike this way.

"I stopped to see the warden on my way in, to let him know what was happening, what it meant. He has called off that monthly head-shave routine, so you'll be able to grow a ducktail if that's what you like. He's agreed to let a man come down here from one of the good shops in Rincon and show you his catalogue so you can pick out some court clothes."

Pike was nodding numbly, incessantly, staring wide-eyed at Gordon. Christ, Gordon thought, this place almost got him. After all these years, it almost broke him. We were damn near too late.

"Sedate clothes, I'd say," he went on, talking in that calm, chatty tone. "Nothing gaudy. Dark suit. Plain necktie. A little color in the shirt, maybe, but don't overdo it. We want to look like a couple of respectable gents when we walk into that courtroom."

But none of it was working, it seemed. Pike was breathing in quick shallow gulps. His hands were working at that towel so hard that tendons creaked. Gordon pushed back his chair and rose.

"Well, lots of work to do between now and then. I'll send David Simon down with the Supreme Court decision as soon as it comes in. Or I'll come myself, if I can make it. It should be something worth reading. Thirty-seven pages, they tell me, and that may be some sort of record for the Supreme Court. Anyway, it's not the usual thing."

330

Pike stared at him blindly.

Gordon smacked his hand explosively against the steel wall. "So brighten up, Jon-boy!" he roared. "We're on the homestretch, with a clear track and the sun shining. Let's see that smile, boy."

He saw it. A bone-tight death's-head smile distorting the thin waxy face. Tears flowing again. But it was a smile, and Pike held his chin high and proud.

"That's more like it. We'll lick 'em this time. Just you wait and see. I told you it was coming, didn't I? Now it's our turn at bat and we are going to knock the goddamn ball clear out of the park."

Pike nodded. And now the smile seemed more natural, almost easy.

It was only a few minutes after eight in the morning, but now Gordon was standing alone at the top of the long low incline of marble steps in front of the Federal Building in El Monte.

One cameraman with a tripod-mounted Leica was sited several steps to the right where he could command a long view of the approach to the Capitol esplanade. The other photographer, a burly man who could support the backpack, was setting up a portable TV camera down on the street beside seven bored reporters from local papers and wire services who were sitting on the lowest step, waiting for something to happen.

Gordon had been put through a rough fifteen minutes when he first arrived. The worst moment came when he told them there would be no statement from Jonathan Pike, that no questions would be considered or answered.

"What the hell, Guthrie!" a voice shouted. "You suck up all the space you can get when you've got something to sell. Now give us a break, goddammit!"

The chorus approved, and Gordon had to wait a minute before anyone was willing to hear him.

"Ease off, gents," he said calmly. "Ease off. There will be no comment. That's final."

"Wait till you want—"

"Now damn you!" Gordon roared. His voice shook the budding acacias in the park. "Just remember where this man has been for eight years. Eight years in a cell on Death Row. Think about it. He is Dreyfus coming back from Devil's Island. He is in no shape to handle tough questions from tough reporters. You know that. He can do himself a lot of harm and absolutely no good. Now fuck off. Maybe after the hearing I'll have a statement. As of now, nothing."

And after a few minutes of grumbling to establish a grievance, they gave up and went down to the street level where they had a better chance of finding a hook for their early stories.

That reference to Dreyfus was pretty good, Gordon told himself approvingly. I'll bet half of them use it somewhere. And it is just the tone I'd like them to strike.

He stretched in the sunlight, eyes shielded by dark glasses, staring east over the plantings of the long esplanade toward the dome of the state capitol outlined against the jagged mass of volcanic mountain from which El Monte took its name. The Capitol was wide and low and graceful, an almost-Monticello design in pale yellow stone with pickings of white at the roofline and windows and the narrow entrance. The "Yellow Dinosaur," they had called it when it was abuilding just after the turn of the century. It had then seemed grotesquely large for a newly formed, sparsely populated state. They were proud of it now. Its picture decorated the publicity brochures they issued to attract new business. People now spoke of it with the modestly casual sort of reference that Philadelphians use in pointing out Independence Hall.

The eight-lane roads on either side of the esplanade were almost deserted. A few cars drifted slowly past but none stopped, and the waiting line of reporters did not bother to watch them. But they jumped as one man when a black official limousine swung quickly toward the inner channel and stopped.

First, Peter Pelletier, briefcased, dark-suited, bareheaded. He shifted to let David Burrell climb out after him, and stopped, smiling affably, willing to answer any questions. But Burrell put a hand on his shoulder and urged him forward impatiently, throwing brief unhelpful comments over his shoulder as he went toward the steps.

By most men's standards Burrell should be an old man, Gordon thought, wondering at his tireless vitality. David must be nearly sixty by now, but he showed no sign of aging. He came bounding up the broad steps like a tennis star loping toward the net. His hair was speckled with gray over the ears, but he was tanned, his skin glossy with health, tight-stretched over solid lumps of muscle. He stared at Gordon when Pelletier waved a sketchy salute, but he gave no sign of recognition, his flat, measuring eyes flicking warily from side to side. No fraternizing with the enemy for David. Gordon nodded casually, not moving from his patch of morning sun. He watched them go inside and disappear down the wide marble hall.

The reporters collected in murmuring knots, sharing their complaints. None of them turned when a yellow-striped city taxi slid to a halt close to them.

A slim man in dark gray came smoothly out of the front seat beside the driver before the cab had completely stopped. He moved with no apparent haste, but he climbed the long steps like a mountain goat. He shot one quick look at Gordon, went inside, scanned the vaulted lobby, and came outside again. All that time his right hand had been cupped out of sight under the edge of his dark jacket.

Gordon had his wallet ready in his hand, turned open to one of the cards that carried his picture. He held it up in plain sight.

"That's all right, Mr. Guthrie," the man said. "I know who you are. Just stand completely still, please."

He did not look at Gordon. His sharply angular nose seemed to sniff the breeze, right and left, then back again. Gordon watched him intently, and slowly he understood what was happening.

"This is the critical moment, is it?" he asked quietly.

The man nodded, a barely perceptible movement up and down. His eyes moved constantly along the streets below him. "Usually it is," he said in a casual tone, as if he were just passing the time of day. "You let them think this is their big chance and then you give them a dead space, no movement at all. Most of them can't stand it. The nerves go jumpy, and they have to do something."

Gordon nodded appreciatively. He could see how that would work. And he could think of several ways he could use it in a courtroom. "What do you look for? What's the tip-off?"

"Hands, Mr. Guthrie. Always hands. You can't shoot a man with your feet, and a mean look never hurt anybody. So you watch for hands doing something out of the way."

He raised his left arm and swung it overhead in a slow circle. With almost the same movement he dipped into a pocket and brought out a small gold badge. Deputy Marshal, United States of America. Gordon had time to read the lettering as the man slipped the point of the clasp through his buttonhole and let the badge dangle.

Then the back door of the taxi came open, and the reporters surged forward. One beefy marshal, obviously assigned to the job, came out first and blocked them away, scooping with both arms like a defensive tackle. Jonathan Pike followed, ducking carefully through the low door, followed by another marshal.

"No handcuffs?" Gordon said, almost to himself.

The marshal beside him chuckled easily. "Are you kidding, Mr. Guthrie? This poor devil has been trying for eight years to get right where he is today. You think he's going to run off now?"

"Not a chance," Gordon agreed.

333

"I'm responsible for him," the marshal said soberly. "My name's on the receipt. If I thought there was any chance that he might be running, I'd have him in leg irons. But from what I hear, you've practically got him free already. Why would he want to run?"

"I wish it was that certain," Gordon muttered. "How is he taking it?"

"Bad. Shaky. You'll see."

Gordon could see when Pike came slowly up the shallow steps shielded by a marshal on each side. His paper-white waxy face was damp with sweat. He was holding one hand up over his eyes and squinting hard. His legs moved unsteadily, and for a moment Gordon thought he might fall. He went quickly down two steps and caught his arm.

"Jesus, Gordon. I never expected anything like this." He peered at Gordon under the shade of his hand. "It's so *bright*."

Gordon pulled off his sunglasses and opened the temple bars wide. He slid them up over Pike's nose and hooked the wires over his ears. "Is that better?"

"Much better. Thanks." Pike shook his head slowly. He brought a folded handkerchief from an inner pocket and touched it lightly to his forehead. "I've been living like a mole, I guess. I've been half-blind all morning." He ran a dry tongue along his pale dry mouth. "And the noise," he said in a half-whisper. "I'd forgotten about the noise."

There were no more than a dozen cars in sight. It was not yet rush hour, and the Federal Building was well off the main truck route. Gordon would have said it was a pleasantly quiet moment in a quiet pocket of El Monte. But trying to listen with the unusual sensitivity of Pike, he could hear the horns and whistles and screeching of brakes and the shouting of reporters blocked away down at the street level. It was nothing like the deathly stillness of Death Row.

"This is the Great Outside, Jon. You'll get used to it. Let's go in, shall we?"

"Could we stand here for a minute, Gordon? Just a minute?"

Gordon glanced at the nearest marshal, caught a glimpse of a shrug, and said, "Sure. The court won't be sitting before ten. We've got plenty of time."

But a few minutes more was enough for Pike. He studied the long vista toward the Capitol, measured a thick pale cloud tearing itself to shreds on the mountain spires, and then suddenly shivered. Sweat beaded on his forehead again, and Gordon turned him quickly toward the entrance.

"A little bit at a time is the way to go," he said easily. "It won't be long before you're used to it."

Pike shook his head. He walked silently beside Gordon to the elevators

334

and went with him to the eighth floor and along the corridor to the small room that had been assigned to them as a temporary office.

At the door Gordon dropped back for a word with the marshals. "Can you leave us alone in here?"

"Sure. That's all right, Mr. Guthrie. The windows are barred. Just the same, please leave the door open. But don't worry, we won't be listening."

"Okay. That's fine. I wonder if there's any chance of some coffee? Maybe a few doughnuts, something like that?"

The marshal checked his watch and then nodded agreeably. "There's a staff canteen in the basement. It should be open by now. I don't suppose Beef would mind going down, would you, Beef?" He grinned slyly at the wide heavy-set marshal. "Beef is always ready for another meal, any time."

"Uh, Gordon?" Pike spoke hesitantly from the doorway. "You think there might be some orange juice?"

"Sure thing." Gordon separated a twenty-dollar bill from the pad in his money clip and handed it to the marshal. "On me. Let's have enough of everything for all five of us."

Pike retreated into the small room. Gordon led him around the side of the narrow conference table and pulled out a chair facing the bright windows where Pike would not be aware of the watching marshals outside.

Gordon didn't like the slowness, the uncertainty he could sense in Pike. Shock, probably, he told himself. Sudden unexpected changes. No wonder he was unsteady. But all the same, it disturbed Gordon. He perched on the windowsill and pulled one leg up over his knee.

"How are you for coincidences?" he said with a slow smile.

Pike blinked. "I'm in favor. I guess I'm in favor. What have you got in mind?"

"I thought you'd like to know what's going on this morning in Part Two, just next door to our courtroom. The federal district attorney will be bringing a man in for arraignment on a charge of smuggling narcotics from Mexico. An old friend of yours."

Pike hooded his eyes but not before Gordon caught the bright flash of wicked joy.

"Nacho?" he asked in a whisper.

"Ignacio Cordero, the indictment says," Gordon told him, grinning hugely. "There are three others involved, too, but Cordero is the big cheese."

"What about Lee? Did they get him, too?"

Gordon snorted lightly. "It was the other way around, as a matter of fact. Mr. Wallis is probably as tricky a bastard as you said he was. He is scheduled as the chief government witness against Cordero. It seems your good old buddy finked on his boss."

Pike sat back in a comfortable slouch, laughing softly, arms loosely folded, head cocked. Gordon studied him carefully, liking what he saw now. A little more like it, he thought. He reached out toward Pike's arm, took the cuff of Pike's new suit between two fingers and pinched it up. "Nice suit. Good goods."

It was a silky pewter-gray flannel, shaped well to Pike's lean body in a conservative, unobtrusive way. With it he wore a shirt striped in black and white hairlines and a big knotted tie in dark-gray knitted silk.

"Just right," Gordon said.

"Christ, it ought to be," Pike said sharply. "I nearly fell over when I got the bill. Two hundred and fifty dollars. For a goddamn ready-made suit. Eight years ago I could have got it for a hundred."

"Maybe so. Lots of things have changed in eight years. That's just one of them. Eight years ago that book of yours would probably have gone for four bucks a copy. Today you are getting seven fifty for it. They call it inflation, Brother Jonathan. You'll be learning more about it as you go along."

Pike twitched one side of his mouth. "I'm willing. Let's start right now."

Gordon nodded soberly. "We're on the way. Are you ready for it? Do you understand what I want from you?"

"I think so. You want me to stick to that outline you sent me. Volunteer nothing."

"That's it. The actual words don't matter. Say it however you like. But don't go off on any tangents. I don't know which of them will be handling the cross-examination. Burrell or Pelletier. Whoever it is will be trying to open doors to expand the scope of this hearing, and we don't want that. So when you are asked a question, don't be in any hurry to answer. Give me time to object. I may have to teach them a few lessons, so don't get in my way."

"You're all primed for a fight, are you?" Pike grinned. "I've been waiting to see it, the Great Guthrie strutting his stuff."

"Too bad, you'll have to wait some more," Gordon said shortly. "The watchword for today is dignity. Sober dignity. Don't you forget it. We've already got the court with us. The Supreme Court ruling was damn near to being an order to give us a new trial. Burrell and Pelletier are running under the handicap this time. They have to prove that the interrogation Burrell put you through was completely legal and aboveboard. We don't have to prove a thing. The facts are all we need. And we know what the facts are. So don't look for any fireworks from me. Not today. We'll save them all for the new trial."

"You're that sure, are you?"

"I'm sure," Gordon said flatly. "How about you? Can you take a couple of rough hours on the stand? You're not feeling too shaky?"

Pike looked at him with narrowed insolent eyes. He did not smile, but an edge of his lip tilted for a brief moment. "It's just physical, Gordon," he said with elaborate patience, as if it were something he had to explain to a child. "The sun, the wind, the noise, all the people, the traffic. Of course it's a shock. But my mind didn't go numb. So don't worry about me, friend. Nobody's going to run me off the stand."

"Let's leave it like that." Gordon fought back the old wild urge to slash a knuckly backhander straight across that lightly contemptuous smile. Let it go, he told himself. It's just Pike's device for holding confidence in a situation he can't dominate. But it is useful to him, so let it go.

He got up and turned to the window and braced his hands on the high sill. He thought of warning Pike about his attitude and then let that one go, too. A jury might be irritated by it and might turn ugly, but there was no jury involved in today's hearing. It would be conducted by a single-judge court. Pike's manner would not be an issue.

Gordon swung around when the short thick-bodied marshal came in with paper cups and plates packed inside a cut-down carton. He saw Pike snatch greedily at a slopping cup of orange juice and gulp it down. No lack of confidence there, he thought. And maybe it's just as well. Pike might be in for a bad session today.

It all seemed to go very slowly, and a lot of it Pike did not understand.

The state, represented by Assistant Attorney General Peter Pelletier, introduced an imposing series of depositions, and the small, shrunken monkey-faced judge had very sharp questions to ask about them.

A deposition was a written statement signed under oath and meant to be used in court in place of oral testimony. But why didn't the state bring the witnesses instead?

"Eight years have passed, your honor," Pelletier explained. "Four senior officers of the Rincon County sheriff's department have retired in that time. One has since died. Two are resident outside the state and are reluctant to return. The sheriff's senior deputy, upon whom we had depended for much of the state's evidence-in-chief, is recuperating from abdominal surgery and cannot appear at this hearing."

It must have been an earthshaking eight years, Pike thought, not for the first time. Had *everything* changed in those years or was it merely that it all seemed completely new to him after being away so long?

Gordon was consulted about the depositions. Apparently it was important that one of his assistants had been present when some of the depositions had been taken, but not for all of them. The discussion took place at side-bar with both attorneys talking quietly to the judge. Probably the court stenographer could hear what they were saying, but Pike could catch only an occasional word, usually when Gordon's huge voice rose briefly in emphasis.

The lunchbreak came finally after long hours in which Pike fought against an almost irresistible urge to yawn. The most important day of his life, and all he could think about was the dreary dullness of what was going on. But when he saw the waiters unloading insulated carriers on the conference table in their room, he became eagerly alert. Who said it was dull? Let's stretch this hearing out for days. Hell, weeks!

The marshals joined them at the table, one sitting nearest the door and trying to pretend he was standing rigidly on guard while he dug in with both hands.

An avocado stuffed with lumps of crabmeat, a salad made of six different lettuces, small spring onions and radishes, sliced tomatoes, dead-ripe and glistening, a rare New York cut of Angus beef that literally made Pike salivate, a baked potato with sour cream and chives, a towering strawberry shortcake, quarts of milk, iced tea, and scalding coffee.

"I should have asked you what you wanted for lunch," Gordon said, half-apologetically. "Just take whatever looks good. Anything missing you can order for dinner."

It was only the thought of dinner to come that kept Pike from clearing the table single-handed. Gordon was content with steak and salad and then sat nibbling at the long spiky onions, watching with awe as Pike worked his way through the complete menu.

"If you fall asleep in there this afternoon, you'll be lucky if you get bread and water for dinner."

Pike grinned with a full mouth and reached for another hot roll. "Don't worry about me," he said after he had swallowed a huge lump. "What were you guys doing up there all morning? Did anything important happen?"

"It's all important," Gordon said absently. He dipped a stumpy radish in a pool of salt and bit off the tip. "But Pelletier isn't showing much early foot. I can't figure what he's up to."

"Explain, please." Pike speared a strip of steak and held it poised on his fork.

"I don't know how to explain it," Gordon said with a laugh. "It's mostly a feeling I have. Pelletier should be making a better case. Those depositions aren't going to do him much good. He must know that."

"So if he's booting it, why are you unhappy?"

"I am always suspicious when the other side starts doing me favors. That's when I begin looking over my shoulder for the big surprise that is supposed to knock me on my ass."

"Any ideas?"

"Not yet."

The big surprise came an hour later. Pelletier opened the afternoon session with two witnesses, both now senior deputies who had been present during some part of Pike's interrogation but not all of it. Gordon questioned them amiably, challenged their too-clear memories by probing for other information they could not supply and then waved them away with no interest.

Then the Assistant Attorney General called the honorable David Calder Burrell as his next witness, and Gordon stiffened like a gun-dog sniffing a fresh warm trail. David Burrell took the oath, sat on the front edge of the witness chair, and identified himself as county attorney for Rincon County at the time of Pike's arrest.

"And you are still, at this moment, county attorney, Mr. Burrell?"

"I am."

"Were you present during the interrogation of Jonathan Pike?"

"For most of it, yes. The record my secretary kept at the time shows I was in the sheriff's office for at least fifty of the seventy hours in question."

"Please tell the court, to the best of your recollection, exactly what you observed during that period."

Burrell looked briefly at Gordon, then settled himself well back in the chair, and spoke directly to the court stenographer.

Gordon had heard it all before in almost the same words. The questioning had been scrupulously fair, said David Burrell. It had been conducted in accordance with the accepted rules of the time. Certain psychological pressures had been applied, that was granted. No criminal is likely to confess if he is treated daintily. But at no time was Pike physically mistreated. At no time were his legal rights violated. The rules were observed. The rules that were then in current practice in all police investigations.

That was the one harmful element in Burrell's testimony. And when it was Gordon's turn with the witness, he went directly to the heart of the problem. "You told us often about the rules then in practice, Mr. Burrell. Are those rules still in practice?"

"Not after we were—"

"Yes or no, please," Gordon broke in. "We will have the explanations later. For the moment tell me yes or no."

"No." Burrell squared his shoulders and hunched forward in a belligerent crouch.

"These rules you speak of are not actually rules at all in a formal sense, are they, Mr. Burrell? What you refer to as rules are merely loose formulations based upon practices that have been condoned by trial courts in the past."

"They are the traditions of legal conduct, if that is what you are asking me."

"It isn't," Gordon said mildly, "but let it pass for the moment. Did the rules then in effect require you to advise a suspect that he did not have to answer your questions?"

"Yes."

"Was Jonathan Pike advised of that right?"

"That should have been—"

"No, Mr. Burrell, that won't do," Gordon said sharply. "If you can't answer the question, say so. Don't tell me what should have been done."

"I cannot answer that question," Burrell said through clenched teeth.

"Did the rules then in effect require you to tell a suspect that he had a right to a lawyer?"

"Yes."

"Was Jonathan Pike advised of that right?"

"He must have been," Burrell said. "He had a lawyer."

Gordon stepped back, lifted both arms and let them drop. He looked to the heavens as if praying for patience.

"Now that you have managed to get that off your chest, Mr. Burrell, please answer my question."

"I cannot answer the question."

"I thought not. Since you have made a point of telling us that Jonathan Pike did indeed have a lawyer, suppose you tell us how long a period passed before that lawyer appeared on the scene?"

"I cannot answer that question."

"I think you can do better than that, Mr. Burrell." Gordon smiled gently. "You told the court of the record kept by your secretary. Is that record available to you?"

"I have some notes in my pocket."

"Please refer to them and tell the court when it was that you first saw Jonathan Pike after his arrest?"

Burrell turned the cover of a new slim notebook. "At three thirty on Sunday afternoon."

"He was arrested shortly after noon on Sunday. I suppose you had to be notified and then change into city clothes and drive back to your office. Does that account for the delay?"

"Yes."

"The interrogation was already under way?"

"Yes."

"Without a lawyer to represent Pike?"

"Yes."

"That was in accordance with the rules then in practice?"

"Yes."

"At that time you could not say, of your own knowledge, whether Pike had been warned of his right to remain silent or of his right to have his attorney present?"

"No, not of my knowledge."

"Did you ask the sheriff if he had been advised of his rights?"

"Not at that time, no."

"Did you ask anyone?"

"Not at that time, no."

Gordon smiled again. Burrell was inviting another question. He was hoping Gordon would ask when he *had* asked, and he had a good answer ready. So let him choke on it. Gordon shifted ground slightly.

"At three thirty on Sunday afternoon when you first saw Jonathan Pike, how was he dressed?"

"His clothes had been—"

"Can't you answer a direct question, Mr. Burrell?" Gordon's voice burst over the quiet room. "You are an experienced trial lawyer. You know the meaning of questions, and you know how they should be answered. Do I have to ask the court to give you instructions?"

The judge tapped his gavel lightly. "A little less vehemence if you please, Mr. Guthrie. And you, Mr. Burrell, will please answer the questions as they are put to you. Let's move along, Mr. Guthrie."

"Do I have to repeat the question, Mr. Burrell?"

"When I first saw him, Jonathan Pike was wearing an Army blanket."

"Nothing more?"

"Not that I noticed."

"His clothes, even his underwear, had been taken to the laboratory for analysis, I believe. Is that correct?"

"So I was told."

"And when were his clothes returned to him?"

"I cannot answer that question."

Gordon lowered his head. He stared for a long silent moment at the floor between his feet. He spoke without looking up. "Mr. Burrell, I am going to ask you to reconsider that answer. You have told us that you were present for fifty of the seventy hours of Pike's interrogation. If necessary, I will divide those fifty hours into fifteen-minute segments and ask you about each of them. Two hundred questions, Mr. Burrell. Until we arrive at the time when Jonathan Pike's clothes were returned to him. Let us start with the fifteen minutes between three thirty and three forty-five on Sunday afternoon. How was Jonathan Pike then dressed?"

"This is ridiculous," Burrell muttered.

The judge's gavel rapped sharply in warning.

"My apologies, your honor," Burrell said quickly. "Mr. Guthrie, I answered your question as well as I could. During the questioning period I never saw Jonathan Pike wearing anything but the Army blanket I mentioned before."

"Very well," Gordon said easily. "Now tell the court whether stripping a suspect naked constituted mistreatment, according to those rules you have been quoting."

"No, it did not."

Gordon sighed heavily. "Let us return for a moment to the question of legal representation. What was the name of the lawyer who first appeared for Pike?"

"Eugenio Salazar."

"And when did you first see him in the sheriff's office?"

Burrell consulted his notebook. "On Monday morning about eleven o'clock. He told me he had been retained to represent Jonathan Pike and asked for a consultation with his client. Which was promptly granted."

"And how long did that consultation last?"

"A short time. Not more than ten minutes."

"Was Mr. Salazar alone with his client?"

"I cannot say. I was not present."

"Afterward did the interrogation proceed as before?"

"Yes."

"When did Mr. Salazar next appear on the scene?"

"Later that same day, about six o'clock. And then each morning until Jonathan Pike was charged and transferred to the county jail."

"Did Mr. Salazar have any other consultations with his client?"

"Not that I know of."

"Mr. Salazar had no complaints about the way his client was being treated?"

"Not to me."

342

"He did not ask permission to stay with his client during the questioning?"

"He did not ask me."

"Didn't you find that unusual, Mr. Burrell?"

David Burrell looked at him and seemed to hesitate before he said, "No." And Gordon was completely sure of what he was thinking, as sure as if he had lifted off the top of his skull and seen it written there. Burrell wanted Gordon to ask him why he did not think Salazar's behavior unusual. And then he would reply that he had assumed that Pike had confessed to his attorney, and that Salazar had realized that there was nothing to be done for him. And wouldn't Burrell relish the opportunity to say that? Too bad, David, old friend. No more questions about Salazar just now. He gave Burrell his best smile and stepped back a few feet.

"You have told us that Mr. Pike was not advised of his legal rights. You have told us that he was stripped naked and forced to remain naked during all of the interrogation. You have told us that his lawyer was unable—or unwilling—to help him in any way. Now please tell us how much sleep Pike was allowed during that seventy-hour period?"

"I cannot answer that question."

"Let's try it once more, Mr. Burrell," Gordon said with an exaggerated patience. "Please tell the court if during any of the fifty hours you were present you saw Pike asleep?"

"No."

"If I told you that he had not been allowed to sleep for more than ten minutes at a stretch, would you want to dispute that statement?"

"I cannot answer that question."

"Possibly not. Try this one, Mr. Burrell. How much food did Jonathan Pike consume during that seventy-hour questioning period?"

"I don't know exactly," Burrell said with a show of cooperation. "There was always coffee available. The men sent out for sandwiches and soup from time to time. How much of it Pike ate, I couldn't say."

"Did you ever inquire?"

A mistake, Gordon realized immediately when he saw Burrell's eyes brighten.

"I asked the sheriff," he said. "He told me that Pike was too nervous to eat. He said Pike had turned down all their offers to get food for him."

"Too nervous, Mr. Burrell?" Gordon asked sharply. "Or too exhausted?"

"Nervous," Burrell insisted.

Gordon shoved both hands in his side pockets, hunched his shoulders and stared up at Burrell through his heavy eyebrows.

"I do not think," he said with slow deliberation, "that we need to inquire very far to determine the reasons for the nervous exhaustion that made it impossible for Pike to eat. You know the reasons yourself, don't you, Mr. Burrell? You saw that bewildered young man stripped naked in the sheriff's office. You saw his lawyer come and go, offering no assistance, not even a word of comfort. You saw him subjected to the cruel, sly psychological pressures recommended in all the police manuals. You were there when he was bullied and badgered by eight members of the sheriff's department working in relays.

"You never saw Pike asleep during that seventy-hour period, but you know that the sheriff's men went home at their usual times each day, slept in their own beds, ate well, changed into fresh warm clothing, and returned again, refreshed and eager to resume their unremitting effort to break that young man's will and spirit, to force a confession from an innocent man.

"You saw all that, Mr. Burrell. What is even worse, you were a part of it and approved of it. No, I do not think it will be difficult for this court to understand the reasons for Jonathan Pike's nervous exhaustion."

Burrell's face darkened. His voice was thin with choked-back rage. "Were those questions, sir?"

Gordon shook his head. "No," he said. "No, they were not questions, were they, Mr. Burrell? I am afraid I was making a speech. I could rephrase what I said so that it would form questions, but I do not believe that this court requires your answers."

He moved away and stood with his back to Burrell. After a moment the judge stirred in his high-backed chair. He leaned forward.

"Have you finished with this witness, Mr. Guthrie?"

Gordon shook himself as if he had been caught in a dream. "My apologies, your honor. No, I have not quite finished. I think there is one more point Mr. Burrell can help with."

He came back and stood squarely in front of the witness stand.

"Those rules you spoke of, Mr. Burrell. The rules that were then in practice. They have since been changed, have they not?"

"Yes."

"So that if Jonathan Pike had been arrested yesterday, you would not have dared to ask him a single question before making sure he had been warned that it was his right to refuse to answer. Is that correct?"

"I would make sure that he was informed as to his rights."

"But that is not what I asked you, is it, Mr. Burrell? Do you need the question repeated?"

"The answer is that I would not question him without making sure he had been informed."

344

"Thank you. You would also be careful to make sure he understood that it was his right to have his attorney present whenever you questioned him. Correct, Mr. Burrell?"

"Yes."

"So we are progressing." Gordon smiled with no warmth. "You would also, if Pike had been arrested yesterday, make sure that he was properly fed, allowed adequate rest periods, and was decently clothed at all times. Correct, Mr. Burrell?"

"Yes," Burrell spit the word out as if it choked him.

"So we see," Gordon said softly, "that the rules have been changed, bringing a human note of decency and fairness to the conduct of your office these days. Tell the court, Mr. Burrell, if those changes in the rules came about as a result of any action on your part."

"I cannot answer that question as it is phrased."

Gordon glared at Burrell until the prosecutor was forced to look away.

"I think you could answer it. But I will make it easier for you. Tell us this, Mr. Burrell: Is it not true that all of those changes in your rules of behavior have been established by outside authority? Yes, Mr. Burrell, or no?"

"Yes."

Gordon nodded approvingly. "And I am sure that you, as a compassionate man, eager to do justice without coercion or intimidation, have been heartened by these changes that protect the rights of all decent human beings. I am sure that you approve of all of this, Mr. Burrell."

Gordon took one step back. He saw Burrell ready to reply and cut him off. "Never mind, Mr. Burrell. Your answer will not be needed. I am sure the court understands."

He turned toward the judge and said, "No more questions, your honor. I have finished with this honorable witness."

There was no unusual emphasis in what he said, but David Burrell flushed dangerously. He tensed in his chair and glared toward Peter Pelletier, as if ordering the Assistant Attorney General to come to his rescue. Pelletier nodded without understanding.

"You may step down, Mr. Burrell," the judge said. "We will take ten minutes, Mr. Clerk." He tapped his gavel once and swung his chair around quickly.

"You really stung that fellow, Mr. Guthrie," the tall marshal said as he led Gordon and Pike back to their small waiting room. "He looked like it would give him the greatest pleasure to eat both your ears right off your head."

Gordon grunted. He put a hand on Pike's shoulder and pushed him inside, leaving the door open.

"It gave me the greatest pleasure, too," Pike said, mimicking the marshal's easy southwestern drawl. "I was remembering it all. Remembering, hell, I was living it again. It was a pleasure to watch you claw him, Gordon. I wish I could have done it myself."

"Let's have no more of that," Gordon said roughly. "It's exactly the wrong tone now. When we go back in there, I want you to be cool. Calm. Unperturbed. We're practically home free right now. David gave us everything we needed. I never thought he could be such a fool, but I'm grateful for it. So don't you go thinking about personal vengeance. We don't need anything like that."

"You're sure we've got it made?"

"Dead certain," Gordon said flatly. He pulled a chair away from the table and sat. He swung both legs up on the polished tabletop and crossed them at the ankles. "So certain, in fact, that I have been wondering about putting you on the stand. The court doesn't need any more information about what happened during that interrogation. Anything you could say would just be repetition. There isn't any real need for you to take the stand." He studied Pike with a clear cold eye.

"Yes there is," Pike said promptly. "I don't want anyone saying I ran away. That little Attorney General doesn't scare me the least bit."

And looking at him, Gordon could believe it. Pike was relaxed now, confident, very much in command of himself. He should do well on the stand unless Pelletier could find some way to make him lose control, and that was not likely.

"I'll think about it," he said easily. "Now let's have a quiet few minutes for reflection." He locked his hands behind his head and closed his eyes. "There's a washroom behind that door if you need it," he told Pike.

The marshals came in noisily, one at a time, to use the washroom with lusty splashings of water and loud complaints about the nonabsorbent, impermeable paper towels.

Pike was standing before the open window, staring through the close-set bars at the play of birds over the dark mountain. When he spoke, his voice was almost inaudible, but something in his tone made Gordon strain to hear.

"Listening to Burrell on the stand brought it all back to me, that bad time when they were pounding at me. And in here, looking out this window, I'm still remembering. But this time I've been thinking about the last time I came up to El Monte. Remember, Gordon? It was for the

346

Delancy hearing, when I was trying to get a new trial by showing that my lawyer was an inept old bumbler who wasn't capable of giving me a proper defense. I've been meaning to ask you about that, why you never showed up to help me. But there never seemed to be a good time to bring it up. Until now. And then I got caught up watching those birds, remembering it was just about the same view I had out the window during that first hearing. And then it came to me, without even thinking about it. Just suddenly, I knew." He turned slowly as if someone moved him with a puppet's rusty control wires. "You sold me out, didn't you, Gordon?"

Gordon opened one eye. Pike was a hazy outline against the brightness. "You could put it that way," he said lazily. "If you wanted to put it the ugliest possible way."

"No," Pike said. He sat on the sill and held both hands locked hard between his knees. "No, I don't want to be ugly, Gordon. I just want to know. You told me what to write to the Bar Association so they would set up the hearing for me. You were going to appear with all your files and cinch the case for me. But at the last moment you were excused. You never did show. Why not, Gordon?"

Gordon held his voice too low for the marshals to overhear. "It seemed the best for all concerned at the time."

"Even for me?"

Gordon swung his feet to the floor and brought his arms down. Pike seemed very young just then, crouched on the sill, forehead knotted earnestly, eyes steadily on Gordon.

"Even for you," Gordon told him. "Can't you put it together for yourself?"

Pike waggled his head. "Jesus," he said softly. "Some of the reviewers say I'm a pretty inventive fellow with fiction, but I'm really not that good. No, I can't put it together so it comes out your way, Gordon. Can you?"

Gordon scowled irritably. Then his expression cleared, and he smiled thinly.

"You've developed considerably in your time down at Yucca. Surprised a lot of people, including me. We invented this pose about you making yourself into a sharp-nosed jailhouse lawyer, and, by God, you go right out and turn yourself into one of the best brief men I know. You start out scribbling stories to keep yourself occupied, and you wind up writing a best seller that any professional would be proud of. You're a source of endless delights, Brother Jonathan, but when it comes down to the grubby details, you are still just a little bit green."

Pike stared at him intently. "Tell me, Gordon," he said patiently. "Don't bother buttering me up, just tell me."

"All right," Gordon said, blandly agreeable. "Let's suppose I had made my dramatic appearance at that hearing and sunk old Delancy with my big guns. What then? Have you ever thought about it?"

"Then I'd have had a new trial."

"You would indeed. And your good and helpful friend Gordon Guthrie would have been kicked out of Gaines, Prinz and Delancy. So what would have happened at that new trial?" Gordon waited to see if Pike wanted to guess, then went on.

"You would still have had David Burrell against you, just as hellishly determined as ever. You'd have had a new lawyer, some unpaid, court-appointed lawyer who wouldn't give a damn about you and who probably wouldn't do any better for you than Delancy did. So you would have been convicted again." He gave Pike time to consider that one. "And probably," he said, heavily slow, "you would have been executed, because I would have been in no position to help you."

"So that's the way you justify it," Pike said wonderingly.

"Justify, hell!" Gordon said in disgust. "Why should I justify myself? Did I owe you anything? By agreeing to stay away from that hearing, I got the start I needed to get where I am now. And I made damn sure you didn't suffer by it. So what in hell have you got to yell about?"

"My God," Pike muttered. "Five minutes more of this and you'll have me apologizing. You are a prime bastard, aren't you, Gordon? Doesn't it even bother you?"

"Not for a minute," Gordon said, bluntly confident. "I do what needs doing in the best way I can. If anybody gets in my way, I roll over them. And I give every client the same all-out effort. As you should know damn well."

Pike stared silently at the floor.

Gordon shifted closer, tapped his knee, and waited for him to look up. "We'll finish in here this afternoon," he said slowly. "I'm completely confident that the judge will find for us. He'll send an order down through the state courts to Rincon County. He'll say, 'Free Jonathan Pike, or try him again under the new rules.' You saw Burrell on the stand today. He's eight years older, but he hasn't slowed down much, has he? Just thinking about you going free is enough to make his blood come to the boil. He'll never give up, you can count on that. So you'd better be thinking about that new trial. You've got plenty of money now. You can hire any lawyer you want. So make up your mind. When Burrell comes charging at you again, who do you want standing beside you?"

Pike strained back, tensing his shoulders. He pulled his hands free from their knee-lock and spread them in a wide, expressive gesture. "Okay," he said in a thin voice. "But I still say you're a bastard."

Gordon sighed wearily. "A nice guy would just get you hanged."

Peter Pelletier remained standing as the judge seated himself and nodded to the clerk. "The state, your honor," he announced, "will have no further witnesses."

The judge made a scribbled note on his pad. Without lifting his head, he aimed the tip of his pencil at Gordon.

"Your honor, when I left here at the break, I was totally convinced that the state had failed to make its case. The issues on which the state has the burden of proof have not yet even been considered. All direct evidence points to a refutation of the state's position. I was, your honor, prepared to come back into court and say that we had heard no evidence that required an answer and would therefore rest our case."

Gordon put his hand on Pike's shoulder and shifted to stand behind him. "That, your honor, was my decision as an advocate. But a lawyer is also a human being. A court proceeding is sometimes a very human exercise, and the stringent rules of legal economy do not always apply.

"I would remind the court that Jonathan Pike, following the advice of his attorney, did not testify at his first trial eight long years ago. He had no opportunity to deny publicly the charges made against him. I realize, your honor, that this is not the time or the place for protestations of innocence. However, Jonathan Pike is present in this courtroom. I promised Mr. Pelletier that he would be made available to him, and for that reason Jonathan Pike was brought here from the state prison at Yucca.

"So, with the court's permission, I shall call Jonathan Pike to the stand. I shall ask him one question. And then turn him over to Mr. Pelletier."

The judge nodded grumpily, already suspecting that Gordon might be talking more for the newspaper reporters than the court record.

Pike went slowly toward the clerk. His hand was steady on the Bible, and his voice sounded clear enough when he took the oath. But his knees wobbled when he climbed the three low steps to the witness chair, and he was clearly happy to sit before he displayed any obvious weakness. He watched Gordon come slowly toward him.

"I will ask you, Jonathan Pike," Gordon said in a harsh voice, "to tell this court whether at any time during the seventy-hour interrogation period we have heard so much about you ever confessed to the murder of Angela Morales."

Gordon stood with his hands behind his back, waiting for the answer.

349

Pike's voice held firm as he answered. "No, I did not."

Gordon nodded several times, then slowly turned and gestured to Pelletier. "Your witness, Mr. Attorney General."

Pelletier rose and with both hands gripped the lapels of his jacket. He tilted his chin high and smiled thinly up at the judge.

He's been seeing those movies about the genially sarcastic British barristers, Gordon thought sourly. He's clutching his silk with the elegant angularity of an eminent QC preparing to address the Lord Chief Justice. And, sure enough, when Pelletier spoke, his voice was unusually light and crisp, amused but respectful.

"The state, your honor, cannot subscribe to Mr. Guthrie's characterization of the evidence that has been presented here today. In fact the state will soon be asking the court to take a diametrically opposite view. However, your honor, we do agree that any testimony here elicited from Jonathan Pike would be repetitious and self-serving and therefore without value to this court. The witness is excused."

Pike waited to make sure that was all. When Gordon nodded, he swung down from the stand and came slowly back to his seat. He held his open hand an inch above the tabletop and smiled with cheerful self-mockery as he watched the fingers shake.

Gordon poured a glass of water from the thermos carafe and pushed it toward him. "Don't let it bother you," he said quietly. "Only lawyers are comfortable in courtrooms and even they have some bad moments."

The judge busied himself with his notebook, pretending not to notice as the press table had speedily emptied. As far as the reporters were concerned, the show was over. There remained the final statements by both sides, but in this hearing they would be formal documents, carefully prepared long ago and already supplied to the press.

Pike tried to listen attentively, but he could not keep his mind from drifting. It was important, even critical, he knew, but this sort of legal commentary was dull. And Gordon seemed to be doing his best to keep it on a scholarly level that drained the emotional value from his most powerful arguments. Pike let out an audible breath when it was finally over and the judge rose.

"How long is he going to take to make up his mind?"

Gordon shrugged. "Judge's time is even slower than lawyer's time," he said. "It won't be soon, you can be sure of that. This will be one of the earliest federal decisions balancing out the *Escobedo* and *Miranda* opinions. Every judge in the country is going to be studying it to see if it has some useful guidelines. And they'll be picking plenty of holes in it if this judge gives them a chance. So he'll be careful. He'll take plenty of time to think about it. My guess is a month, at least."

Pike whistled thinly.

Gordon grinned at him. He latched his briefcase and pushed back his chair, almost tripping Peter Pelletier who was coming around the table behind him.

"I just wanted to tell you how much I enjoyed listening to your presentation, Mr. Guthrie," Pelletier said, putting out a long thin hand. "Too bad the case wasn't challenging enough to generate some of your famous fireworks."

Gordon stared at him, shaking his hand mechanically. What's this, he wondered. Pelletier isn't any beginner. Why the gush?

"I suspect this is just the first of a long series of problems we'll be facing because of the *Miranda* decision," Pelletier said soberly. "I think it is extremely important that we handle them so that they will cause the least possible bad feeling among the legal community."

Ah, Gordon thought. Now I see. Young Mr. Pelletier is telling me that he could have done a hell of a lot better job if he'd been willing to get down in the gutter and fight dirty. And he could have, too. He didn't get where he is by running away from back-alley brawls. Also, I suspect he is warning me that he'll give me fits if he ever gets me in a courtroom where he can come at me with both hands working.

Gordon put a little more pressure in his handshake and smiled. "I'm glad you feel that way, Mr. Pelletier. It's always better if we can keep this kind of argument on the highest level. It's dragged on far too long as it is. High time we got it settled."

"Yes," Pelletier said. "I agree." He nodded pleasantly, including Pike in the gesture. "Good luck."

"What was that all about?" Pike asked. He waited for the marshals to form their protective circle and then moved toward the door.

"Mr. Pelletier was just telling me that his heart wasn't in this case. That's why he went so gently with us."

"Sour grapes?"

"No, I think it's the real thing. And I am beginning to think Mr. Pelletier is the real thing, too. I like his style. He would make a good—" He stopped suddenly as a hand hooked inside his elbow and pulled him sharply around. His eyes were then only inches away from David Burrell's, and he could see the flush of angry blood that mottled Burrell's face.

"You son of a bitch," Burrell said in a harsh abrupt voice. "What were you trying to do to me in there? Haven't you ever heard of professional courtesy?"

The marshals herded Pike further along the hallway but not so far that they could not hear.

Gordon shook his head, blandly astonished. "Why, I thought I was brimming over with courtesy, David. How did I offend you?"

"Courtesy!" Burrell almost spat. "You came at me like a gutter rat. A hoodlum!"

"I came at you, David," Gordon said, painfully polite, "just the way I come at any witness for the opposition. The trouble is you've been on the other side so long, asking the questions, that you've forgotten what it's like on the stand. Nobody asked you to come here, you know. You volunteered. And you got it just where all volunteers get it."

"You are nothing but a loud-shouting trickster, Guthrie. I—"

Gordon slammed one hand flat against Burrell's chest and shoved him hard against the wall. He held him there, using his height and his extra fifty pounds to keep him from moving. When he saw that the prosecutor was standing still, he tapped him once on the chest with a jarring forefinger.

He smiled brightly at Burrell. The smile was all teeth, no eyes. "I let you off easy, David," he said. "Be grateful. If you had offered any evidence that was likely to hurt my client's case, I would have taken David Burrell apart on the stand. I would have ripped your reputation and your character into small dirty scraps."

"You—you're mad!" Burrell gulped air through an open, straining mouth. "You've gone far beyond even *your* courtroom tactics this time! I—"

"Would you like to know how I would have destroyed you, David?" Gordon went on, ignoring Burrell's protests. "I'll tell you. Somehow you have the idea that you are untouchable, don't you? You don't know how very lucky you were today."

Burrell straightened against the wall, standing squarely braced. "You could not possibly harm me in any way," he said, stiffly dignified and completely sure of what he was saying.

Gordon laughed. "A series of half a dozen linked questions, David. That's all it would have taken. I would have begun by asking you to tell the court the name of the man who supplied Pike's first lawyer. Who was it who paid the fee for Gene Salazar?"

"Why, the man Pike worked for paid it. Cordero." Burrell blinked rapidly as if the act might help him to understand.

"Ignacio Cordero, right," Gordon said, still smiling. "I would then have asked you if you knew that Ignacio Cordero was today arraigned in Part Two of this court for a long series of narcotics offenses dating back many years. Many years, David. A period of time, in fact, that spans your total tenure as county attorney."

Burrell stared at him in bewilderment.

"I would then have asked you if you knew that Gene Salazar was, and is, Ignacio Cordero's attorney of record."

"But what connection—"

"That would have been the next question, David. I would have asked you how many times you consulted privately with Gene Salazar during the period of Pike's interrogation."

"I never talked to him privately during that time!"

"Possibly not," Gordon said casually. "You will notice, David, that I haven't waited to hear your answers to any of these questions. In this situation, the answers don't matter. The questions are the point. Especially the last one. Are you ready for it, David?"

Burrell stared at him, stony-faced now and silent.

"I would have asked you if you came to a private agreement with Gene Salazar. An agreement that allowed you a free hand in questioning Pike, provided you did not ask him any questions whatever about his association with Ignacio Cordero who, according to the Narcotics Bureau, at that very time was actively engaged in smuggling drugs across the border from Mexico." Gordon lifted an eyebrow, waited briefly and then went on. "A long-winded question, David, but I'm sure you wouldn't have had any trouble answering, would you?"

"You are mad, Guthrie," Burrell repeated in a thin, barely controlled voice. "Nothing like that ever happened, and you know it."

"No, I don't know it, David, but I would have allowed you to explain to the court. Salazar did behave very strangely, didn't he? And so did you, David. I would have given you all the time you needed to explain. But somehow, I don't think you would have been very convincing. Do you, David?"

"No one would ever believe such vicious and irresponsible nonsense," Burrell said firmly.

Gordon smiled with his teeth. "Our friends, David," he said, "are always willing to believe the worst of us. But let's say that in your case, it would be different. Then all you would have to worry about would be the swarms of newspapermen flocking around ten-deep, all wanting the real inside story. And they would have been after you all the rest of your professional life, David. So, as I said before, be grateful. You really had a very easy time today."

"Everything they say about you is true," Burrell said harshly. "You have no regard for truth or justice, have you? Anything goes with you, any lies, any character assassination, just so you win. Winning is all that matters to you."

353

Gordon stepped back, showing no sign of anger. "If I wanted to debate, David," he said, "I might say that I learned courtroom tactics from watching you operate."

"You'll have another chance to watch me!" Burrell said through clenched teeth. "You'll get this decision, there's no doubt about that. It was practically ordered by the Supreme Court. But then you come back to my county, Guthrie. You'll get a new trial, all right. And I'll string your guts from the flagpole before I'm finished with you. And this time we'll make damn sure that Mr. Jonathan Pike goes to the chair. Remember that, Guthrie."

Burrell swung away abruptly, walking quickly down the hall with lunging strides, his arm movements awkwardly out of rhythm.

The marshals looked at Gordon silently, startled by the ferocity they had witnessed.

Pike grinned crookedly. "You might have made an enemy for yourself there, Mr. Guthrie," he said, and his tone was almost mocking.

"David's a self-made enemy," Gordon said. "He doesn't need any help from me."

Pike shook his head. The pale gray eyes were full of pure joy. "You scared him with that Salazar stuff. Do you think that's what actually happened?"

Gordon shrugged. "I don't know."

"You really are a bastard," Pike said. "I'm just glad you're my bastard. I'd hate to have you on the other side."

VI

SHROUDED in his black silk robe, Judge Nicanor Kronstadt waited out of sight behind the open doorway that led from his chambers to the courtroom. Going around the long way, Gordon Guthrie would need a few more minutes to reach the side entrance.

From where he stood Nico could see a long wedge-shaped section of the court, the short flight of steps leading up to the bench, and his high-backed well-padded leather chair. One of the perquisites of being the judge: He gets the only comfortable seat in the courtroom. And by God, he thought, there are times when he needs it. The high narrow windows lining one side of the vaulted room seemed brighter now. Each framed a different but similar view, like a linked series of Japanese scroll paintings, slaty blue sky with thin patterns of white cloud, and a delicate tracing of bare shrubbery along the lower edge. Bleak but serene. About the way I feel.

He shifted back so he could see the corner of the defense table where Jonathan Pike should be waiting with his guards. And as he turned, he saw the massive quick-moving bulk of Gordon Guthrie come lunging hurriedly from the doorway. Nico put a finger firmly on the button that would light a small lamp on the clerk's desk. The brisk rapping of the gavel came almost immediately. He waited a moment for the murmurs to die away, then went in.

Gordon had been watching Pike as he crossed the well of the courtroom, wondering what it was that made him seem so different today. Clothes, of course, but he had seen that good flannel suit before. And now Pike's hair was longer, with flourishing sideburns down to the bottom of his ears. So of course he looked different. But Gordon was struck by another distinction that came to him as he slid into the seat next to Pike. He's grown up, he thought, and wondered why the thought surprised him. Because you've been thinking of him as a boy all these years, he told himself. And now that he's thirty years old or thereabouts and a mature man, maybe it's time you stopped calling him a boy, even in your mind. He probably never was a boy anyway. People like Pike are born all grown up.

And he looked very much at ease this morning, too, sitting erect and balanced, chin up, hands relaxed on the tabletop. He smiled for Gordon and rose as the clerk's gavel called for attention.

The judge stood quietly, surveying the courtroom. It was crowded today, even a few standees back near the main entrance. Mostly they would be the newspaper and magazine people who had been plaguing his clerk for weeks to make sure of reserved seats. Of course they would want to witness the final act in the long dramatic story of Jonathan Pike. In a very real sense Pike was their creation. They had taken his desperate, perilous situation as the bare threads of their stories and woven a glittering pattern of legend around them. So here we are, gentlemen, Nico thought. Without your help, I do not believe that Jonathan Pike would be in this courtroom today. So I suppose it is fitting that you should be here when the story ends. I wonder how you'll like it.

He nodded to the clerk, swung the loose fabric of his robe to one side, and sat well back in his deep chair. He waited until the courtroom was completely still, then leaned slowly forward, linking his hands together.

"Eight years and three months ago," he said in a clear, steady voice, "Jonathan Pike was convicted in this courtroom for the murder of Angela Morales. He was sentenced to death. That death sentence was delayed to allow him an opportunity to appeal. On eleven other occasions, subsequent death sentences were also delayed because one or another of the courts in the appellate structure had agreed to consider still another appeal by Jonathan Pike.

"Those appeals incorporated a wide range of serious allegations. Mr. Pike claimed that he had been denied a fair trial. It was his contention that inflammatory and prejudicial publicity had poisoned the judicial atmosphere. He claimed that his defense counsel had been inactive to the point of negligence. He claimed that gruesome photographs of the body of Angela Morales had been admitted improperly. He claimed that the trial judge had shown prejudice against him. He claimed that the several statements obtained from him by the sheriff's investigators during questioning were the product of coercion and inhuman treatment.

"Running through the varied list of allegations was the unstated, though strongly implied, claim that Jonathan Pike was innocent.

"For eight years, those appeals, imaginatively prepared and presented with great skill, were rejected by the courts which considered them." He paused. He poured half a glass of water and drank it slowly. "Six months ago the Supreme Court of the United States granted Jonathan Pike a full hearing. His case was then remanded to the Federal District Court at El Monte for a further hearing on the sole question of the statements in dispute, and the manner in which they were obtained. The decision of the District Court was that the statements *had* been obtained improperly.

"The state was then ordered to retry Mr. Pike for the murder of Angela Morales. In this new trial they were denied the use of any information or evidence based on those earlier improper interrogations. The state was given a period of ninety days in which to bring Mr. Pike once again to trial or to set him free.

"The ultimate decision—a new trial or prompt release—rested with the county attorney of Rincon County. The gentleman holding the office at that time was Mr. David Calder Burrell, who had also been county attorney during Jonathan Pike's first trial. Mr. Burrell ordered his assistants to begin preparations for a new trial. But within one week of that ninety-day period of decision, Mr. Burrell died suddenly of a heart attack at the conclusion of a long and arduous trial in this courtroom.

"His successor as county attorney reconsidered Mr. Burrell's decision. It was his right to do so and his duty. He initiated a series of discussions with attorneys for Jonathan Pike. Those discussions developed into negotiations. And negotiations resulted in agreement.

"It is not the intention of this court to comment on that agreement." The cold tone of voice, the stern lines of his face showed clearly what that comment would have been if he had allowed himself to make it. He pointedly did not look at the county attorney. "Exercising the discretion of his office, the present county attorney decided not to bring Jonathan Pike to trial again. Instead of a second trial, the agreement calls for Jonathan Pike to come into this courtroom today and offer a plea of 'no defense' to the charge of murder. In return he is then to be sentenced to a term of imprisonment equal to the time he has already served, and is to remain under the control of this court for an additional probationary period of five years.

"This agreement was reached through a process of negotiation commonly called 'plea bargaining.' It is a fully recognized legal device allowing defense and prosecution to make a deal that saves the time and expense of trial. It spares the defendant the chance of a more drastic sentence and spares the prosecution the chance of an acquittal.

"A plea of *non vult,* or 'no defense,' is the same as a plea of guilty. It is used in capital cases where a plea of guilty is not allowed." The judge paused to take another slow sip of water. He swung his chair to face Jonathan Pike. "It now remains for this court to ratify that agreement by taking Jonathan Pike's plea and then passing sentence. However, before we proceed, I wish Jonathan Pike to understand exactly what is entailed in his plea. I will not accept the simple statement of 'no defense.' I will require Mr. Pike to take the stand under oath and answer a detailed series of questions relating to the murder of Angela Morales and his subsequent behavior."

He paused then, watching Gordon Guthrie climbing to his feet, kicking back his chair, and waiting to be recognized. Guthrie's eyes were bright and hard.

"Mr. Guthrie?"

"I respectfully remind the court, your honor," Gordon said in a low growling voice, "that an agreement between Jonathan Pike and the county attorney for Rincon County has already been ratified by the president judge. Any expansion or modification at this late date cannot be accepted."

Nico stared at him for a long moment. "*I* am the president judge, Mr. Guthrie. I have not forgotten any of the details of this agreement. But you are mistaken in thinking that it has already been ratified. The agreement was accepted by the court, subject to its ratification at this proceeding. The offer made to Mr. Pike cannot, in honor, be rescinded and will not be. However, this court will require a full confession before ratifying the agreement."

He lifted a hand before Gordon could respond. "No, Mr. Guthrie. We will not debate. I am now going to call a recess, and you may have as much time as you need to discuss this matter with your client. If he wishes to withdraw from the agreement, he is free to do so at any time. Mr. Clerk, we will stand in recess." He was down the steps and through the door to his chambers before the clerk could pick up his gavel.

The door to Nico's office swung open more easily than Gordon had expected. It crashed against the wall before Gordon could catch it. He let it close noisily behind him.

"What the *hell* do you think you're doing, Nico?" Gordon's face was tight and angry. He did not bother modulating his heavy voice. "You are crucifying my client. What for?"

Nico was standing at the side of his desk holding a slender-spouted silver coffee pot in his hand. He looked silently at Gordon, deliberately put the pot on its tray, and went around to his chair. He sat and folded his hands on his desk folder.

"Are you talking to me, counselor?" It was a polite inquiry, posed in a level voice, as if to a point of academic interest.

Gordon hesitated. He watched Nico's still face and understood completely what he was seeing. This was the commander at the moment before he signaled to the firing squad. The Spanish grandee about to call for his head-choppers. The judge, affronted in his dignity, mentally drafting a contempt citation for an unruly attorney.

Back away, Gordon warned himself. This is the time for you to walk warily. You won't do Pike much good if Nico throws you into a cell for the rest of the day.

"I'm sorry," he said hastily. "I lost my temper." He thrust both hands deep in his pockets and stood hunch-shouldered, head down as though in a storm. "I apologize to the judge," he said earnestly. "I ask an old friend for a few minutes of his time."

Nico was silent. Nothing changed in his expression. But suddenly the stiffness was gone, and Gordon knew it would be all right. Nico reached forward and pulled down the key of a communications box on the forward edge of his desk.

"Another cup for Mr. Guthrie, please." He gestured for Gordon to bring up a chair.

He said nothing while they waited for Gordon's cup. When it arrived, he stood again and busied himself with coffee pot and sugar tongs. He carried Gordon's cup to him around the desk and sat near him in a big wing chair.

Gordon scalded his tongue on the coffee, muttered under his breath, and put the cup on a corner of the desk. "I can't get through to Pike," he said heavily. "He's put his ears flat back like a jackass about to jump off the top of a mountain. He just doesn't understand what's involved here, and he won't listen. But you know, Nico. You know he'll be destroyed if he takes your deal and makes a full confession in open court."

Nico held his cup high, letting the steam drift under his high-bridged nose. "I think Pike understood me. He is an exceptionally intelligent man." He eyed Gordon thoughtfully. "Or so he has been presented in the press."

Gordon waved an impatient hand. "There's nothing wrong with his intelligence. Okay, a lot of that early stuff was pretty much a con-game to build public sympathy and get a little support for my client. But he has outgrown that long ago, and he's done it all on his own. That's very important for you to keep in mind, Nico. This man has completely remade himself. He isn't the same half-educated sociopath who went to prison all those years ago. The Jonathan Pike you are dealing with today is a totally different person."

Nico nodded gently. He sipped cautiously at his coffee and waited for Gordon to continue.

"Everybody talks about rehabilitation," Gordon said, shifting forward urgently. "And there is a lot to be said for it. As far as our penitentiary system is concerned, rehabilitation is the only target and the only justification. If it was just a matter of keeping these people safe and out of the way, we could find plenty of cheaper ways. So rehabilitation is what we're after. And that's just the point I want to emphasize here, Nico."

Gordon made himself sit back. He took out his tobacco and slowly made a cigarette and did not speak again until he had it lit. "The people who run the prisons feel that a man is rehabilitated if he leaves prison with a reasonable chance of making his way in the outside world without doing harm to anyone else. In fact, they are happy if they can say that the man has a reasonable chance. But look at Pike, Nico. Have you ever seen a better example of a rehabilitated man? In his case it isn't just a matter of a reasonable chance. Pike has already made a place for himself in one of the most competitive areas in our world. He has been offered several good jobs in his field. And he has made quite a lot of money so that he has a good backlog to help him through any emergency. What more could you ask for, Nico? Pike is ready to walk out of your courtroom today and lead an honest, useful life as a decent citizen this very minute. And you know that's true, Nico."

He got rid of his cigarette before it burned his fingers. He picked up his coffee cup and drained it with a quick pull. "But you will wreck all that, Nico, if you force him to make a full public confession."

"Why do you say that, Gordon? I'm not touching upon his future life. It's his past that concerns us here."

"You're wiping out any chance of a future," Gordon said bluntly.

Nico considered the possibility and then shook his head. "No, I think not, Gordon. His future is still in his own hands. His probation officer will allow him to live wherever he likes and report by mail. He merely has to announce any move before he makes it. He can change his name if he likes, as long as he notifies the probation officer. We aren't hampering his future, Gordon."

"You are eliminating his future." Gordon let his voice rise angrily and promptly checked himself. He said more quietly. "He has made a name for himself writing as Jonathan Pike. A respected name. If you go ahead, that name will be destroyed. And if he takes another name, that means starting all over again from the very beginning."

He could see no reaction. Nico was listening attentively and nodding at the appropriate moments, but nothing Gordon said was touching him.

"I was against this deal from the very beginning," Gordon went on, refusing to quit. "I tried to persuade Pike to take his chances with a new trial. I let him talk me out of it because I could see that waiting even a few more months in that cell was more than he could take. He has had a glimpse of the blue sky, Nico. He can't face going back into the dark again. He is willing to do anything, anything at all, to cut his time short by even one day. That's why I finally went along with the initial deal. *Non vult.* No defense. Okay. But not a detailed confession. That's too much. I can't allow him to accept. I'll have to persuade him to turn you down unless you are willing to go back to the original agreement."

Nico shook his head. "I'm sorry, Gordon. I can't do that."

"Nobody is forcing you to take a hard line, Nico. There aren't any rules for this sort of proceeding. It's perfectly okay to deal gently with Pike. No one could possibly criticize you for that. We aren't living in the old days you wrote about in your book, *Rough Justice.* That's the way it was then and probably those hanging judges were necessary in that lawless time. But not now, Nico. We aren't the same people, and these days we don't admire that ruthless, eye-for-an-eye vengeance in our judges. Maybe we've gone soft, but there isn't any doubt that we admire a decently merciful attitude and respect the men who are strong and gentle enough to show it to us."

No response. Nico's face was pale with restraint, but he said nothing. Gordon stared down at the floor, scrubbing a hand roughly across his forehead as if to force a better, more persuasive argument into his mind.

"You are talking to a fairly sophisticated audience today, Nico," he said softly, trying to pose a clear threat in inoffensive terms. "Those newspaper people expect Pike to come out of this without much damage. They have accepted the idea of the *non vult* plea as a device that Pike is using to get himself out of prison without any more delay. I don't think they'll understand why you can't just accept the plea and let it go at that. Maybe they will follow your reasoning and agree that a detailed confession is necessary. Maybe they will. Some of them. But some of the others will see it as needless cruelty, the vengeful destruction of a totally rehabilitated young man who was prepared to enter upon a useful, productive life. Until you made it impossible."

Gordon waited, hoping for some expression of self-justification that would give him an opening. Nothing. Not a word.

"I know you aren't looking for any popularity awards, Nico," he said after a time. "I know you aren't likely to change your mind because of public opinion. But this is a different matter entirely. Pike has earned better treatment. And that is a fact you should think about very seriously, Nico."

"I have thought about it, Gordon. And I am not going to be greatly concerned about the public reaction. But I am grateful for your warning. It may be that I have not made my reasons clear. I suppose we should always remember that the Founders urged us toward a decent respect for the opinions of mankind."

Gordon looked up quickly then with a surge of hope that died completely when he saw Nico's expression.

"I have required nothing from Pike that I do not consider necessary, Gordon." He stood up very straight and moved to put his cup and saucer on the desk. "But possibly I haven't explained myself clearly enough, and I should. I will do that in open court. Are you ready to return now?"

Gordon sighed heavily. Looking at Nico, he could see that there was nothing more he could do here. But he couldn't give up yet. "Let me have a few more minutes, please. I'll have to give Pike another chance."

Gordon went stiff-legged and fast along the corridor to the door an armed guard was holding open for him. He stopped just inside it.

Pike looked up with a small smile. He had placed himself in a faintly theatrical pose against the barred window, one foot on the seat of a chair, one arm propped on his knee, an empty Coke bottle swinging easily in his hand. "No luck?" he asked, as if he wasn't greatly interested in the answer.

"He won't give an inch." Gordon sat in one of the straight chairs, tipped it back against the wall, and took out his tobacco. He watched his fingers shaping a thin cigarette.

"What do you think of me as a lawyer?" he asked abruptly.

"The Great Guthrie?" Pike waggled his empty bottle. "The best. Mr. Unbeatable."

"I could do without the bullshit." Gordon lit his cigarette, staring coldly at Pike.

"Sorry," Pike said. "I didn't realize you were being serious. I think you are the best lawyer I know if that's the answer you want."

"I *am* good," Gordon said confidently. "I don't have to suck around for compliments. My winning record is over seventy-five percent. On homicide cases, I've never lost a client to the chair. So when I give you my professional assurance that I can get you off if we go for a new trial, why won't you accept that and go along with me?"

Pike blinked. His prison-pale face took on a note of color. "You yourself always say that nobody can guarantee anything when a case goes to the jury."

"Odd things do happen with juries," Gordon conceded. "But they don't happen to me. I don't let them happen."

"Your assistant, David Simon, gave me an estimate when I asked him what a new trial would cost. He said it would probably run to fifty thousand dollars."

Gordon considered the figure while he finished his cigarette and put it out. "I'd say that was too high. But what of it? You've got plenty of money."

Pike smiled thinly. "After I've paid my taxes I won't have plenty. Fifty thousand dollars would be more than half what I'd have left."

"That's not good enough," Gordon said flatly. "Money isn't that important."

"Perhaps it isn't to Gordon Guthrie," Pike said. He balanced the empty bottle on the windowsill. "But not everybody is a big money-spinner like you, Gordon. I've got some money in the bank, sure. But I don't expect I will ever see that much in a lump again for the rest of my life. I'm going to have to make it stretch for a good long time."

Gordon leveled his eyes hard at Pike. "You'd be better off free and dead broke than you will be if you take the judge's offer. I don't think you really understand what you're deciding. Let's see if I can make it clear this time. Because the big question here is what kind of a life you can hope for.

"If you went for a new trial—and won—no one could ever close a door you wanted to enter. If the original offer was still open, and you took it, your future would be a little ambiguous. Some doors open, some closed. But, in general, a livable situation. If you accept this final agreement, to go on the stand and answer the kind of questions this judge is going to put to you, the doors will slam. All of them."

"Oh, I don't think it would be that bad, Gordon," Pike said. "Society doesn't cast people into the outer darkness these days." His thin mouth twitched as if he had to struggle against laughter.

Gordon continued to sit impassively, eyes narrowed and thoughtful. "You may be right," he said slowly. "It's a more permissive society now, and in some groups you might even be a celebrity because you've had your picture on the front pages. Maybe that sort of life would suit you fine. But I doubt it. I think you know that you have opened up some very wide possibilities by your own efforts. Those possibilities stay open if you make the right decision. But if you take the judge's offer, you can forget all that. You'll spend the rest of your life on the fringes, hating every minute of it, because you'll know what you could have had. It won't be as bad as prison, but you'll know there are bars all around you, and there won't be any way you can break them."

Pike smiled crookedly, a grimly confident smile.

"The minute you plead no defense," Gordon went on, "you automatically become a convicted felon. You lose most of the rights of citizenship. Felons are not allowed to vote. They can't be employed by any federal, state, or county agency. They can't work in any of the licensed professions. They can't run for public office. They don't get jobs that involve handling money, because they can't make bond. In some states they are required to register with the police and report every change of address. They are the first to be arrested on suspicion and the last to get out on bail. You think about it, Pike. As a convicted felon, your future shrinks down to a very narrow field of action."

Pike shrugged. "I don't plan to run for public office, Gordon. And I'm counting on being able to work for myself."

"You're picking the wrong alternative," Gordon said firmly. "Maybe you will have to spend another couple of months in that cell before we can schedule a new trial. Is that so bad? You've already invested eight years. Why not put in a little more time, now that we are this close to winning everything?"

"You make a good sales' pitch, Gordon," Pike said quietly. "But I'm not buying. I promised myself this morning that this was the last day I was going to spend locked up and guarded by a man with a gun. Sometime before this day is over, I am going to lock myself into a hotel room. And then I'm going to unlock the door and walk out without asking anyone's permission. I may do that several times, in and out, whenever I feel like it. And I'm going to do it today, Gordon. I'm not going to wait one minute more than I have to."

Pike came slowly away from the window. "You want me to trust you to get me off in a new trial. But I can't trust you that much, Gordon." He stood very close to Gordon, staring gravely down at him. "I didn't want to say this, Gordon, but I can't help remembering the time you let me believe that I was going to be executed in a matter of minutes. I thought it was that close. You knew I wasn't going to die. I did not. You knew everything was okay because you were just building up a big dramatic scene to catch headlines."

He paused for a long breath, watching Gordon's face with a look that was half-regretful but wholly determined. "A new trial would give you some great headlines, too, wouldn't it, Gordon? But you can forget that. There won't be any new trial. Whatever that judge wants, I'll give him, in any form he wants it. Now come on, let's get it over with."

Their eyes met in mutual appraisal. Pike held himself confidently, an oddly jaunty expression on his face that one sometimes sees in the faded pictures of those strangely driven men who send themselves over Niagara Falls in flimsy rubber barrels. They too had made their last and firmest decision, and the dread that must have lived in their minds had somehow been transformed into a kind of relaxed, almost amused acceptance.

"You're wrong, Pike," Gordon said with complete sincerity. "You're wrong, and I can't go along with you. If you go, you go alone."

"All right, Gordon," Pike said politely, absently. "Then I go alone."

Gordon caught his arm before Pike could move past him. "One more thing," he said. "One last bit of legal advice. Free." He looked at Pike steadily, forcing his complete attention.

"When this is over, all those newspaper people will crowd in to get a statement from you. Walk away from them. Whatever you do, don't try to sell them on the notion that you answered the judge's questions just as a kind of courtroom ritual to get yourself out of prison, and that you didn't really mean it. Once you confess, you are stuck with it. If you try to say it was nothing more than tricky legal maneuvering, this judge just might throw a perjury charge against you. I'm not sure he could make it stick, but at the very least he could cancel your probation and order you back to prison for another five years. So be careful what you say. For the rest of your life."

"All right. Thanks," Pike said impatiently. "Let's go."

The courtroom was still solidly packed when Gordon followed Pike and his guard through the side entrance. Apparently no one had been willing to risk losing his seat by going out during the recess. The buzz of murmuring rose to a higher note when Pike appeared and subsided quickly the moment the clerk tapped his gavel.

The judge wasted no time with preliminaries. "Let the record show that Mr. Pike is present with his attorney," he said to the court reporter. He looked directly at Gordon.

"Well, Mr. Guthrie, what is your answer?"

Gordon rose slowly, as if he forced his way up against a great weight. "Your honor, I will ask the court's permission to explain why I cannot answer the question the court has put to my client."

Nico stared at him for a moment in bewilderment. Then his expression eased and he nodded his understanding. "Very well, Mr. Guthrie."

"In a proceeding such as this, your honor, an attorney has very little value to his client. Once Jonathan Pike has announced his decision, my protection, my advice, even my physical presence, become useless. All then rests with Mr. Pike and this court. So it may seem, your honor, that

365

I am straining at trifles when I ask the court's permission to withdraw as attorney for Jonathan Pike."

The clerk's gavel stilled the reaction before it could grow loud enough to warrant the judge's official attention.

"During our lengthy recess, your honor, I exercised all the powers of persuasion that I possess in an effort to convince my client that he should reject the court's proposal. I can, your honor, continue to represent a client who refuses my advice in certain areas of small importance. But I cannot in good conscience continue to represent a client who rejects my advice in a matter of such critical meaning. I ask the court for permission to withdraw."

Gordon remained standing, waiting. He could sense Pike shifting to look at him, but he kept his eyes fixed on Nico and, after a moment, saw him nod.

"Very well, Mr. Guthrie. The court appreciates your position. You may withdraw. Let the record so show."

Gordon took his chair away from the table, moved back a short, symbolic few feet to the railing, and sat there, folding his arms, crossing his legs.

It was a small gesture, almost meaningless but not entirely. And in that tiny core of meaning, Gordon could take some comfort. His colleagues would understand what he had done, and he was glad that Nico had not asked for any further explanation. He would probably be roasted by the press for abandoning Pike at the last moment, but he could stand that without twitching. He had, once and for all, made his position clear. He would not acquiesce in any man's destruction, not even his self-destruction.

"Jonathan Pike," the judge said gravely. "Mr. Guthrie was correct in saying that the presence of counsel would be of little value to you once you have announced your decision. However, you have an unquestioned right to counsel at all times, and I ask you now if you wish me to recess for such time as you may need to find another attorney?"

"No," Pike spoke in a clear, resolute voice. "I don't want another lawyer."

"Do you wish this court to appoint an attorney for you?"

"No."

"Then I ask you now whether you have decided to accept the court's requirements."

"Yes," Pike said. "I accept."

"Very well. You will now approach the bench."

Pike kicked his chair away as he rose. He gave Gordon a brief smile. He moved near the clerk's desk and looked up at the judge.

366

"Jonathan Pike, you stand accused in this court of the murder of Angela Morales. How do you plead?"

"No defense."

"Come forward and be sworn."

When Pike had taken the oath and settled himself stiffly on the edge of the witness chair, the judge opened a leather folder, put on a pair of dark-rimmed reading glasses, and glanced down for a short moment.

"To all of my questions," he said, "I want you to answer yes or no. You may then add any explanation you wish. Is that clear?"

"Yes."

The judge pushed his glasses up his nose and swung his chair to face Pike. "Jonathan Pike," he said sternly, "did you, and you alone murder Angela Morales?"

Pike pushed himself back in the chair. He leaned to his left, bracing his hand flat on the arm of the chair. His right hand moved slowly up the side of his face.

And he was right to take a moment here, Gordon thought. Most of us never recognize the turning points in our lives. We slide along from day to day, and it always takes a very long time before the historic moments of decision identify themselves. But for Pike that wasn't true. He could know with absolute surety that the answer he gave now would change the direction and quality of his life. Take all the time you like, Gordon told him silently.

It is a fashionable and comforting myth, he was thinking, that we are poor weak creatures subject to the pressures of forces that are entirely outside our control or influence. And sometimes it is so. But Jonathan Pike was in complete command today. Captain of his soul, Gordon muttered to himself. It doesn't happen often.

Pike looked out from the elevated chair, scanning the room from side to side, not as if seeking assistance or even a known face but merely fixing himself in relation to that time and place.

He nodded to the judge. "Yes," he said in a quiet voice.

The murmurs from the body of the courtroom rose suddenly in a wave of sound. The judge waited until the clerk's gavel had brought it under control.

"This court," he said sharply, "is aware of the unusual public interest in this proceeding. For that reason we have allowed a large number of seats to be set aside for members of the press. But I will remind all of you that you are here on sufferance. You will be quiet or you will be evicted. If necessary, I will clear the courtroom. I will not warn you again."

Pike's pale cold eyes caught Gordon's for a moment, then slid away. That was it, Gordon mused. All that remained were the details, and they could be filled in with little trouble. If Nico had called a brief recess at that moment, Gordon suspected that two-thirds of the press people would have run for telephones. But Nico had another and, to him, more important goal, and he would make sure he held his audience until he was finished. He worked his way, methodically careful, through the long list of questions he had prepared, covering every important aspect of the girl's murder, of Pike's trials and his later appeals. He took his time, and he missed nothing.

It was good careful legal groundwork, and Gordon had to admire it even as he shifted impatiently in his hard chair. Nico was nailing down every solid fact, forcing a clear, unequivocal statement from Pike on every disputed element of the case.

"Mr. Pike, was there anyone else with you at the time you killed Angela Morales?"

"No."

"Did you, and you alone, take her to the groves at El Pinar and kill her there?"

"Yes."

"Did you, and you alone, strike her repeated blows with your fists, your shoes, with a heavy screwdriver, with several heavy stones, so that her head was completely crushed and her brains torn from her skull?"

"Yes."

"Did you also kick her repeatedly before and after her death?"

"Yes."

"Did you tell the sheriff's investigators in the course of their interrogation that you had left Angela Morales alive and well in the company of a young man named Lee Wallis?"

"Yes."

"Did you lie when you said that?"

"Yes."

"Knowing that you, and you alone, were guilty of the murder of Angela Morales, you named your best friend as her murderer. Is that correct?"

"Yes."

Nailed down solidly, Gordon was thinking. And Lee Wallis was finally in the clear. It had been a long time.

Pike was restless on the stand now, shifting often, leaning to one side and then the other, looking only at the court reporter and speaking always in a low, clear voice.

"Knowing that you were guilty of the murder of Angela Morales, you accused your attorney, Mr. James Oliver Delancy, of negligence and incapacity in the conduct of your defense. Did you not?"

"Yes."

"Knowing yourself to be guilty, did you also accuse Mr. David Calder Burrell, the then county attorney, of unfair and discriminatory conduct in the course of the trial?"

"Yes."

"Knowing yourself to be guilty, and knowing that you had repeatedly lied in your several statements to the sheriff's interrogators, did you later accuse them of coercion and inhuman pressure in their efforts to extract a true account from you?"

"Yes."

Pike volunteered no explanations, even though the judge waited after each of his answers to give him time. Pike could obviously see the spectators moving restlessly, eager to get out. He would, Gordon realized, know that none of them was listening with complete attention.

Get it over with, Nico, Gordon groaned silently. It's all good stuff, but you're dragging it out too long. Enough is enough. We really don't need any more of this. You've dropped Pike in the box and nailed down the lid. You don't have to wrap it up in steel bindings.

Nico seemed to agree. Slowly he took off his reading glasses and straightened in his chair. He put aside the paper on which he had written his questions for Pike and took up a second sheet from the folder. He placed both hands flat on the paper and looked out over the bench.

"The law," he said, "is tender of a defendant on trial for his life. It is even more tender of the rights of a man convicted of murder and sentenced to death. It is proper that this should be so. Any society that presumes to take the life of one of its members must always be prepared to assert that it did so with absolute assurance of his guilt.

"For that reason," he went on firmly, "Jonathan Pike was allowed the widest latitude. His every appeal was carefully considered. On twelve different occasions, the date set for his execution was moved forward so that his appeals might be considered without haste.

"I will not again recount the history of those appeals. It is enough to say that they resulted, through the decision of the Supreme Court, in Mr. Pike's presence here today. He himself chose, in defiance of his attorney's advice, to answer my questions rather than stand trial once more for the murder of Angela Morales."

He poured a glass of water and softly cleared his throat. "For more than eight years, Jonathan Pike, from his cell at the state prison at Yucca, has appealed time after time, not only to the courts, but also to the sympathy and human sensitivity of the American public. And toward that second target, he has been remarkably successful. His constantly repeated claims of innocence, which he now admits were lies, were

369

accepted by many well-disposed people. Through his imaginative and reckless lies he smeared the reputations of innocent and honorable law enforcement officers. He has made untrue accusations against honest witnesses, defamed his own attorney and the gentlemen of the county attorney's office."

Deserved or not, could it still be vindication for everyone, Gordon wondered.

Nico shook his head sadly, sternly, very much the judge. "Many people have admired Mr. Pike's talents, which he has demonstrated in a series of excellent fictional tales. Nowhere has that inventive talent been more skillfully exercised than in his recent book which is even now a best seller. Through his eloquence he caught the sympathetic attention of many well-meaning people. More important, he was able to raise serious questions in the minds of many about the very quality of justice in this country.

"Jonathan Pike is before this court today, guilty by his own free admission. He has admitted openly that he alone murdered Angela Morales. He has admitted that he lied time and again. He killed and lied. He betrayed his friend and lied. He repeatedly proclaimed his innocence and lied.

"Presented with this situation, I could not, in clear conscience, allow Jonathan Pike to come into this court and simply plead 'no defense' and walk away. The substance and appearance of justice would not have been served. This court could not allow any element of doubt to remain in any impartial mind about the guilt of Jonathan Pike. For this reason, and not in any spirit of vengeance, the court has required that Jonathan Pike answer the questions that were put to him today."

The judge put away his unread paper, closed his leather folder, and turned again to Pike. "I will ask you once more, Jonathan Pike. Did you, and you alone, murder Angela Morales?"

Pike's pallid face was touched with angry color. Small white knots jumped at the corners of his mouth. He took a moment to make sure he was in control, then said, "Yes."

"Have you anything further to say before this court passes sentence?"

"No."

"Jonathan Pike, for the murder of Angela Morales, you are sentenced to a term of imprisonment of eight years and ninety-three days, and to a further five-year term of probation. You have already served, in the jail of Rincon County and in the state prison at Yucca, a total of eight years and ninety-three days. In accordance with the agreement reached with the county attorney of Rincon County, you have therefore served the entire term to which you are sentenced."

The judge tapped his gavel quickly before any response could be heard. "The sheriff will now escort you from this courtroom to the office of the chief probation officer of Rincon County. There you will be instructed in the provisions that will govern your five-year period of probation.

"After that," he said, his face expressionless, "you will be free to go." He nodded briskly to the clerk. "We will adjourn." He left the stand promptly as he always did, removing his awesome official presence so that human responses need not be held in check any longer.

Gordon could see flashbulbs flaring from the body of the courtroom, but none of the court attendants tried to object. They blocked the gateway in a solid phalanx, waiting until the sheriff's deputy could take Pike away.

Gordon rose stiffly but stayed where he was. He owed that much to Pike, he thought.

Pike moved down slowly from his elevated chair. He studied Gordon for a silent moment, then cocked a quick smile and held out his hand. "Just as bad as you said it would be."

"What did you expect?" Gordon said with a rush of unexpected anger.

Pike laughed. "My old buddy Gordon," he said with real amusement. "Never a sentimental moment. Well, to hell with you, Gordon old buddy. Thanks for everything."

"Good luck, Jon," Gordon said quietly, half-ashamed of himself. "What do you think you'll do now?"

Pike looked at him sharply. "Where will I run? Is that what you mean? I'm not running, Gordon. I'll stay here somewhere in the desert country. I grew up here, remember? You saw it happen."

He swung away quickly before Gordon could answer. He stopped just short of the side door, turned, and brushed the deputy casually aside and stood there, poised, beautifully tailored, a young and vital man with everything to look forward to. He gave the photographers plenty of time before he turned and went out without another backward glance.

No, I don't think you'll stay here in this desert country, Gordon thought. He was feeling heavy and dull and tired. When you are free in it, Brother Jonathan, I think the bright hot light will be a little too much for you. You're a complex, devious man, and devious men don't do very well in light that comes too strong and clearly. Head for the big cities, Brother Jonathan. Maybe we'll meet in one of them someday. And I wonder what your name will be.

Gordon moved quickly along the corridor and through the door to the judge's chambers. He was pleased to find it empty. He was in no mood to

371

talk to anyone. All he wanted now was to retrieve his hat and the two loaded briefcases he had left in Nico's office and then get himself out to the airport as soon as he could. With luck they could be in the air before the dirty weather made it impossible. If he could get to the Los Angeles International Airport, fight his way through the murderous traffic, and get to the courthouse before court adjourned, he could pretend to himself that the day had not been a complete loss.

He found his hat on a rack near the door, smacked it on his head, and hauled the brim down in the angle he liked. He hooked his fingers under the handles of the briefcases, then stopped and looked over his shoulder as Nico came through the washroom door.

He was still in his black robe, drying his hands on a small linen towel, working the cloth carefully between his fingers. Gordon looked at him, narrow-eyed and near to anger. He was very tired in his mind and slipping into bitterness.

"Well, Pontius," he said, an ugliness in his voice that surprised him, "have a good hand wash?"

Nico raised his eyebrows. He studied Gordon silently for a moment, then tossed the towel behind him into the washroom. He pinched at the fasteners of his robe, let the heavy silk slide from his shoulders, and caught it before it fell. He hung the robe on a form beside the door that led to the courtroom and then went around his desk and sat in his tall-backed chair.

"They'll crucify him, you know," Gordon went on, knowing he was being unfair and not caring. "You really gave him hell today."

Nico's eyes were grave and steady, darkly brooding. "I hoped to give him justice."

"Nico-the-judge," Gordon said nastily. "Nico who was born to be a judge. You're always so goddamn sure you're right, aren't you?"

"I try to be," Nico said, holding to a reasonable tone. "I watch the balances very carefully. Sometimes I have to make decisions on less evidence than I need. But that wasn't the case today. I can understand that you are bitter and disappointed, Gordon. But you did everything that could have been done for your client. No one could have done more."

"I could have got him off if he'd been willing to go to trial again."

"No," Nico said flatly. "I don't believe you could have, Gordon. Pike was guilty."

"Thus speaks Nico-the-judge." Gordon's darkly flushed features pulled into heavy scornful lines.

"Goddamn you!" Nico came out of his chair in a quick lithe

movement. He rapped one knuckle against Gordon's chest, pushing him back a step. "I *know* he's guilty. And you know he's guilty. And I know that you know he's guilty."

He watched Gordon's face closely, then drew in a long steadying breath. "Nine days ago." He paused, thinking back to make sure he was right. "Exactly nine days ago, you had a visit from a Mrs. Orlando Linares who came to your office. Do you remember, Gordon?"

Gordon remembered. He remembered clearly. It was the day he was to leave for the start of the Los Angeles trial and he had no time for casual drop-in clients. Mrs. Linares had been waiting patiently for three hours when Gordon came striding through the reception room on his way to the airport and stopped before he reached the hall door.

The name "Linares" meant nothing to him, but when he saw her, he said in his mind "Francisca Guitterez" and knew, without asking, why she had come. Mostly she had been called Paca in the days when she worked as a maid for the woman who had owned the apartment that Pike had rented when he first came to Rincon.

Gordon motioned her into his office and closed the door behind him. He had no time to spare. She accepted his urgency and told her story in a cascading tumble of words.

She began by showing him the half-page torn from *El Informador*, Rincon's Spanish language newspaper. A cousin working in Rincon had sent it to her last week, she said. She had shown it to her husband who knew about her terrible experience with Jonathan Pike. They had agreed on what she must do. She had come to Rincon on the autobus at her own expense because she must make everyone understand why Jonathan Pike must not be freed.

Gordon had listened closely as he studied the newspaper Paca had brought. They had used a picture of Pike that he had never seen before, a murky, smudged scowling face that could frighten children. Gordon's picture was the one most newspapers had on file. The one of Judge Nicanor Davila de Merida Kronstadt showed him severely formal and robed for court.

Gordon could read enough Spanish to get the sense of the story. Mostly it was outrage that the convicted murderer of Angela Morales was to be freed without even bringing him to trial again. The reporter used the word *"ultraje"* a lot, as if outrage were the only word strong enough for him. He hinted at dirty *yanqui* skullduggery and he referred to Gordon in angry resentment. But he was carefully correct when he wrote of the Honorable Nicanor Davila de Merida Kronstadt, president judge of the superior court, who would preside at the *non vult* hearing scheduled for an early date. He always used the full name when he mentioned Nico. That sonorous Spanish name was a valuable asset in Rincon.

Gordon looked up again at Paca's thin, drawn face. He listened with complete attention to her swift harsh voice spilling out her story of a night more than eight years ago.

She had not been asleep when Jonathan Pike came home that night. He had revved his big motorbike in the alleyway and then crashed it through the flimsy wire gate into the garden. When Paca looked out her window she could see him lying in the dust in front of his door. She thought he was hurt and she had gone running to help him. But Pike was only drunk. He was lying there, dazed and still, and when she leaned over to look at him, he had grabbed her and pulled her down beside him, holding her so tightly it frightened her.

"Don't fight me," he whispered in a hoarse voice she could barely hear. "Don't ever fight me. I killed one girl tonight because she was always fighting me. You just lie still. Don't fight me."

She was terrified. He smelled of blood and she had not dared to move. When he knew she was quiet and not struggling he had taken one hand away and pulled a long brilliant silk scarf from the front of his shirt and draped it around her neck.

"Present," he muttered. "Nice girl. Present for nice girl."

He had used both hands to put it around her neck, and then with no warning he had suddenly tightened it so that she flared away in panic, breaking his hold. She darted into the dark garden, hid herself in the bushes, and lay very still, feeling her heart pounding like a wild drum. For a long time she stayed there without moving. She watched Pike struggle to his feet, stagger and fall, and get up again. He called softly several times, but she was too frightened to answer. And then he had lurched into the apartment, tearing the screendoor open, and then she could hear him moving inside. She waited until he was quiet again, and then she crept out from the bushes where she had been hiding.

Pike's motorbike was lying in front of his door and his shoes were there near the front wheel. Paca scooped them up on the run, thinking that if Pike saw her, he could not follow across the rough ground in his bare feet. She ran into the house and up to her room.

And in the morning she had gone to a pay telephone in a twenty-four-hour drugstore and called the sheriff's number.

She saw them come and take Pike away. She was terrified because she still had Pike's shoes hidden in her room, and she was afraid the deputies might find them and say she had been involved with Pike. At night, when she was sure the old woman was asleep and no one was watching, she had crept downstairs and thrown the shoes in a bush where the deputies found them the next day and did not ask her any questions about them.

She still had the scarf. She did not know what to do with it, especially after she had heard that Angela's mother had described it in court and had said that her daughter was wearing it that night. She hid it, knowing she should throw it away but hating the thought that she could not have it for herself.

For days afterward she had lived in fear and prayed for God to help her so she could leave that place and go back to her home in Mexico and never go away from there again. And God heard her prayers and sent help. The fat weighty envelope addressed to Jonathan Pike had seemed to glow with special meaning when she saw it in the mailbox. She had hidden it under her apron and, when she was alone, opened it to find five hundred dollars in twenty-dollar bills.

She waited until it was safe and no one was paying much attention to her. Then she had told the old woman she was leaving, had packed quickly and gone home to Mexico, and tried to forget the terror of that night. Until last week when she had seen the newspaper that said Jonathan Pike was about to be set free.

So now she had come to Rincon because it was not possible for her to remain quiet any longer when she knew that Jonathan Pike had murdered Angela Morales. He must not be allowed to go free from prison. Paca's voice grew harsh. Jonathan Pike was a murderer.

She coughed to ease her throat. She brought up the handbag she had been clutching tightly in both hands, opened the catch and showed Gordon a richly patterned length of silk. In his mind, Gordon said, "Lee Wallis," and remembered that Wallis had bought a spectacularly expensive scarf for Angela Morales. "Forty bucks! I must have been out of my fucking mind!"

Paca wrapped the scarf again in a white cotton cloth and offered it to Gordon. He shook his head quickly. He didn't need it, or want it. He didn't need anything more. He stared down again at the newspaper she had brought, using it as a shield while he tried to assess the degree of danger her story represented to Pike. In the first trial, Paca's testimony could have convicted him. No doubt of that. But now? After all this time?

How many other people has she told her story to, he wondered. It was a fair bet she had already seen the county attorney, but Gordon did not want to ask her. If she hadn't gone to him, there was no point in giving her ideas. But probably she had already seen him, Gordon guessed. And that gentleman would have given her small comfort, for he had been the prime mover in arranging the *non vult* deal in the first place.

Jonathan Pike had been an obsession with David Burrell, but Burrell's successor wanted no part of an eight-year-old murder case which he was by no means sure he could win. He had made his deal. After a brief proceeding before Judge Kronstadt, he would be free of Burrell's obsession and could get on with his own work. No, even with Paca's new evidence, the county attorney would not want to bring Pike to trial again. David Burrell would have jumped at the chance, but the new man wanted no part of it. As far as he was concerned, the Pike affair was a dead issue.

Even if he should decide to break the agreement and take a chance on trying Pike again, he could not be sure that Paca's testimony would win for him. Gordon knew she was telling the exact truth as she had lived it, but he also knew that he could break her into small pieces if he ever got her on the witness stand. No, he wasn't greatly concerned about Paca, or about the new county attorney. But a cold and bitter resentment lay inside him like a stone. Silently he cursed Jonathan Pike, and himself. But there was no more time.

He had told her to wait, summoned his assistant, and given him explicit instructions. "Don't tell her what to do. Don't give her any instructions or suggestions. Thank her for her assistance and tell her I have been called away. Tell her we need nothing more from her. Don't offer her any money, but tell her the state will repay her busfare and allow a little something for food and lodgings. You can offer to advance the money, if she'd like to have it right now. Slip in an extra twenty, at least. Take it out of petty cash and keep the receipt in your pocket. I've got to leave right this minute. Phone me in Los Angeles and tell me what she decides to do."

Mrs. Orlando Linares had decided to return immediately to her seaside village in Mexico. She had been grateful for the small amount of money and was greatly relieved now that she had told someone in authority the whole and true story.

And Gordon was remembering all of this as he stared into Nico's dark measuring eyes.

"I made sure she went to you, Gordon. She came to me first because she saw my picture in her newspaper. Of course I could not allow her to tell me her story. As soon as I understood what she wanted to say, I cut her off and sent her to the county attorney. I also told her to talk to you." He hesitated briefly, then went on. "You know how the courthouse grapevine works, Gordon. Within hours I knew she had valuable eyewitness evidence to offer."

"So that's it. That's why you were sitting up on your throne today, playing God in your courtroom, cutting Pike to pieces just because of some new evidence that probably couldn't even be admitted."

"There was more to it than that, Gordon. If that woman had come to us at any time during the past eight years, I think you can be sure that Pike would have had that new trial he was asking for. David Burrell would have been eager for it. But she waited too long. Of course, she thought Pike was safely in prison and would not have understood that he was edging toward freedom all the time. So when she did come in, we had already agreed to the *non vult* plea. There was no honorable way we could have rescinded the agreement and forced Pike to trial.

"A more interested county attorney might have tried, if he'd had stomach enough for a hard fight. You know what David Burrell's response would have been. But the new man just didn't care to open up that old can of beans, I suppose. He never asked me to reconsider the agreement. I didn't really expect him to. Actually I was much more curious to see what you would do about the woman and her story."

Gordon made a quick angry gesture. "Coming this late, her evidence wouldn't have meant a thing. I could have handled her. Those late-rememberers are never convincing on the stand. Her testimony wouldn't have hurt us. Even after I talked to her, I still wanted Pike to go to trial, you remember. I tried my damnedest to persuade him."

"She would have hurt you, Gordon," Nico said with complete sureness. "She is a sincere, honest woman, worried enough to come all this way to tell her story after she heard Pike was going to be freed. I think a jury would have believed her. But I don't doubt that you were willing to go to trial again. It's just the sort of challenge you enjoy, isn't it? The dramatic almost-hopeless case. I think that Pike would very probably have been convicted because of that woman's testimony, but not until after you had dazzled another courtroom with some of the famous Gordon Guthrie fireworks. Or were you hoping that the woman would never be called to testify? I wondered about that. You didn't know whether or not she had gone to the county attorney with her story, did you? And you weren't going to tell him, were you?"

Gordon stared at him incredulously. "Tell him? Are you out of your *mind?* Me tell the prosecutor how he can hang my client? I'd be disbarred if I did and would damn well deserve to be. What makes you think it is my responsibility to cinch the prosecutor's case for him? I'm working for my side, not his. That's my job. I'm a defender."

He could feel the wild rage building in him, and he fought against it and tried to speak calmly. This was a friend of his boyhood, not an enemy. "In the old days they used to call us champions. They'd give us

377

swords and send us out into the arena with the crowds watching and tell us to win for our side. The adversary was the man on the other side. There wasn't anything personal about the contest. It was trial-by-combat to decide whether the man you were defending was to live or die. The king sat in judgment and maybe you could sway his opinion a little bit by your performance, but what really decided the outcome was whether or not you killed your adversary. Nobody said, 'Don't swing at his head because you might hurt him.' Nobody said, 'Give him first whack at your right arm just to be fair.' Nobody said, 'Be merciful.' Not unless you had your man on the ground with your foot on his neck. What we were told was, 'Get out there and win for your side.' "

Gordon was warming to the idea now and was more sure of himself. "It's not so very different now. But we're less romantic about it. No arenas, no swords, no kings. A courtroom instead of a battlefield. A defender for champion. A prosecutor for adversary. We've added a twelve-man jury and you can sway them more than a little if you know what you're doing, but basically not much has changed. It's still me and the prosecutor slugging it out, no holds barred. The point is to win, Nico, not to help out the other side. We call it the adversary system."

"Adversary," Nico said, almost to himself. "Yes, the analogy of the trial-by-combat champions is very good, Gordon, lively and colorful. But aren't you leaving something out?"

"Am I?"

"I think so. The ultimate aim of the contest, with or without swords, has always been justice. Rough justice then. And now, hopefully, a temperate justice based on the considerations of a jury. In the old days of the champions you were talking about, Gordon, the only aim was to win. That isn't so now. Because we have finally brought the contest out of the arena into the courtroom."

Gordon held himself in with a visible effort.

"When I listen to lawyers contending in my courtroom I sometimes wonder if both sides have not missed the real meaning. They often seem to think that the adversary is justice itself. You have to be absolutely sure, Gordon," Nico said, quietly urgent, "that you have identified the right adversary. I sometimes think that you don't really know who it is."

Gordon looked at him with bleak and angry eyes. "Talk about yourself for a change, Nico. Tell me some more about how God sits next to you on the judgment seat. And then tell me just what was going on in your mind today when you destroyed Pike. Were you really aiming at Pike—or me, because of Claudia?"

He could see the wall come down between them. Transparent, cold.

378

Nico was looking at him through a sheet of ice, seeing him clearly and not wanting to see him.

"I will not talk about my private life with you or anyone else." He was totally Don Nicanor, outraged beyond any hope of apology. "The divorce was agreed between us. You were not an element in the discussion."

"Divorce?" Gordon repeated the word slowly, knowing now that he had gone beyond the last barrier of friendship.

"You didn't know?" Nico almost shrugged. "I assumed you had been told." He looked down at his desk, put out a hand, and absently shifted a dagger-shaped letter opener.

"You are very much alike, you and Claudia." The judgment was regretful but decisive. "You hurt people beyond any enduring and are not even aware of it. I suspect that Jonathan Pike was thinking of that today when he refused to let you take him to trial again. I think that he made a wise decision."

Nico pushed the letter opener away with a flick of his hand and turned back to Gordon. "I wasn't thinking of you, Gordon, when I forced a full confession from Pike. I wasn't even thinking of you when Claudia and I arranged the divorce."

Gordon snorted.

"I will say good-bye now, Gordon," Nico said very quietly.

Gordon bent swiftly, snatched up both his loaded briefcases in one hand, and moved toward the door. Nico looked after him calmly, coldly. The door closed hard and finally.

379

MAINE STATE LIBRARY
BOOKMOBILE A-3
AUBURN, MAINE

S754a copy 3

Spicer, Bart.

The adversary.

S754a copy 3

Spicer, Bart.

The adversary.

NO RENEWALS!

PLEASE RETURN BOOK AND REQUEST
AGAIN.